DEAD DEMON DIE

WHISKEY WITCHES ANCIENTS BOOK 7

F.J. BLOODING

Whistling Book Press

Alaska

Copyright © 2018 Frankie Blooding

All rights reserved.

Per the U.S. Copyright Act of 1976, no part of this publication may be reproduced, scanned, or distributed in any form without written permission from the publisher. Please only purchase authorized editions.

Printed in the United States of America

Published by Whistling Book Press

Whistling Book Press

Alaska

Visit our website at:

www.whistlingbooks.com

ISBN 13:

❀ Created with Vellum

WHISKEY MAGICK & MENTAL HEALTH

Sign up to learn more about our books and receive this free e-zine about Whiskey Magick and Mental Health. https://www.fjblooding.com/books-lp

To Shane,
you are my Dexx

We know that not everyone wants to read all of the books. So, we're not going to force you to do so. Here is a recap of the important stuff you missed in *Double-Double Demon Trouble* and *Mirror, Mirror Demon Rubble*.

Previously on Sven Seven-Tails...

This was an honest to God earthquake.

Alma's door popped open. "This isn't natural."

Natural or not, this was real. Cars swerved. People screamed.

Alma spoke strangely, her hand out, a pillar of solidity as the earth rolled. "Calm."

The earth settled.

Paige touched the barrier, her lips parted to say something.

The dead man raised his head and spoke. "Somewhere I have never traveled, gladly beyond any experience, your eyes have their silence: in your most frail gesture are things which enclose me, or which I cannot touch because they are too near."

"No," Paige breathed.

Dexx stepped in front of Paige, hand slipping over the grip of his pistol, bringing Hattie close to the surface.

The dead man's eyes didn't open. They couldn't with the X cut into his eyelids.

The crowd of FBI agents stopped milling. Many of them drew their guns.

The body raised a hand and lazily pointed to Paige and Dexx. "The time has come. Three to rise, one of three to live. You are mine, and *you* are no longer needed." The man stood tall and straight. With a silent scream of pain, he fell face first to the ground.

***

"This was Sven," Paige found her voice. It didn't sound very strong.

Dexx slashed his hand in front of him. "You don't get to take him on alone. Or at all, if I have anything to say about it."

Paige opened her mouth to protest.

Dexx overrode her. "Sven Seven-Tails. You know, the demon who seared the door to Hell open in your bones? He wants *you* for some twisted reason, and that means that you're going to be the last person he gets to. If the world burns, he doesn't get you."

***

Dexx shook himself and raced for the woman with the blue streak in her hair. Sven seemed to swell with the power he stole from the woman, glowing with a perverted yellow light that wasn't his. Around the yellow light, shadows thickened. The sun's warmth leeched out until only a harsh light touched the ground.

Sven did *something* with the stolen power, turning it cold and foul.

Dexx knew he had to stop Sven and cutting off his power supply was the only way to do it.

One leap. Two. One final leap would take Dexx between Sven and the woman.

Power flared from Sven, from Hattie, and surprisingly, from the woman.

Sven lashed out to kill Dexx. Hattie pushed to protect him. The woman froze in fright.

The three powers converged. The rebound of power should have been enough to kill.

Dexx felt his body disintegrate.

Something pushed back, and they held together. Hattie's power pushed, but it wasn't enough. Golden power from the woman wrapped around the two opposing powers.

Sven speared Dexx with black magick. Dexx glowed and then flared. Purple flecks popped in the air as the powers collided. And then?

Dexx and the woman were gone.

Paige's heart stuck in her chest. She almost forgot to breathe.

Sven turned his attack on Alma.

Paige clenched her hands into fists and ran down the street. Her body reminded her she was still carrying two not-so-small babies in a package not designed for running. She gripped her belly with both hands and continued.

Leslie and Billie ran beside her. Leslie let out a bone-chilling cry.

Alma put up a good fight, jabbing green lightning, wind, and earth at Sven. He returned black spear after black spear, his body nearly twice the size it had been before. At least, it looked like it.

Paige was too far away, and she wasn't gaining much ground. Her body ached and was tired.

One of the spears found Alma.

"No!" Paige didn't know if that was her, Leslie, or both.

But then Alma just reached for her chest, smiled serenely…and her magick exploded.

Paige stopped, raising her witch hands, her magick wrapping wards of protection around anyone she could find.

Leslie and her griffin roared, the griffin's wings flaring in front of Paige, shielding her as she shielded the others.

Billie stood defiantly in front of the protection of the golden and blue wings, her hands out, magick of every color shooting forward, helping to power Paige's personal wards.

And then the fight was over.

The demons were gone, dissolving into shadowy mist.

The white light of Sven was gone, as was he.

Dexx and the woman were nowhere to be seen.

And Alma's body floated to the ground, old and wise again. But spent.

Cyn squinted one eye open to a slit.

Exploding glass. A bear. A magician. A giant freaking porcupine. And most disturbing, a humongous, fanged cat that she was reasonably certain had gone extinct centuries ago coming right at her.

Had all of that been real?

She stared around at the desert she now found herself in and realized…

She wasn't in Kansas anymore.

The cat Cyn had found in the desert, that cute, adorable, dying cat, was now a man.

A tall and very handsome…naked man.

"Where *are* we?" Cyn asked.

Lynx smiled and gestured to the desert around him with pride. "The Vaada Bhoomi. My home."

Lynx went still, his back rigid as he looked at the castle buried deep in the green foliage.

It looked like someone had taken a knife and cut the jungle in next to the desert. They didn't mesh. They didn't blend. One ended. The other began.

This place was so weird. "What is it?"

"That," he said, his voice low, "doesn't belong here."

Cyn stood at the door to the castle and stared at the shield with her family crest in horror. What did this mean? She was a normal person with normal wants and normal issues.

Did this—this coat of arms on a magic castle in a magic world—mean that she was from…this world, too? That she belonged? How…was this possible?

Before she could ask much further, her skin began to glow.

It really did seem as though the castle was a part of her family. Somehow. She still didn't understand how or why. Cyn walked through the hall of mirrors and watched as the scenes flowed on them, scenes from the other world—her world.

She saw her parents, Paige and Leslie Whiskey. A lot of other people, too. If only she could talk to them. Somehow.

When Lynx had decided to go back to Bastet's temple, he hadn't been sure what he would find.

His memories from when he'd been a human hadn't been on that list.

He *had* been a human. In the ancient days of Egypt. He'd been a weaver and had managed to create the flying carpet, something he'd lost almost immediately. But it had gained Bastet's attention.

And that's when she'd taken him and cursed him to serve her as a temple cat.

The mirror flashed, and the location changed. Leslie Whiskey's soap shop. It had to be. But instead of Leslie, Emma stood there, all tall and blonde and gorgeous beside another woman Cyn didn't recognize. But, holy biscuits, that was her best friend. "Emma!"

Emma's eyes shot around the room. "Cyn?"

"Oh my God." Cyn couldn't believe it. "You can hear me?" She pressed her other hand to the mirror, terrified of losing the connection.

"Yes, I can hear you. Where the hell are you?"

The other woman seemed to have tuned in, her gaze still at least in Cyn's general direction. "Who is the man with you?"

Cyn cringed. How was she supposed to explain everything? "His name is Lynx and he's," she hesitated. What *was* he? Hell. "It's a long story, but he's in trouble. That Sven demon guy thing, whatever, is drawing energy from him and the other temple cats on *this* side. Um, Bastet's temple, to be exact."

"Temple cats—" The other woman stopped and blinked. "That's it. Hang on." Billie walked out of view and returned with a mirror. "How are you dialed in?"

"Huh-what?" She looked at Lynx, but he seemed just as lost as she was.

"How are you connecting?" The woman set the mirror on a long counter scattered with bars of soap.

"I just—I don't know. I set my hand on the mirror, and I see you. That's what I know."

"Okay." Billie nodded with understanding as if she dealt with this kind of stuff all the time. "I'm going to charge this mirror. You let go of that one, and when you reconnect, we *should* be able to see one another."

"Or I could *lose* you."

"Just do it."

Cyn waved through the mirror the next time it connected.

Paige frowned. "Have you seen Dexx?"

Well, she went straight to the point, didn't she? Cyn sucked in a breath. "Is he a big extinct cat?"

Paige's entire body relaxed. "Yes."

Right. "He's here. Somewhere." She winced. "I've kind of been hiding from him."

Paige's eyes rounded with indignation.

Cyn held up her free hand. "But, but, but I've been trying to find something you could use in your fight against Sven. So, it's not like I've just been hanging out in a castle playing princess or anything."

When Cyn and Lynx made it back with the stones they'd discovered in the castle, it was to a completely different town, one she didn't recognize.

The safest place in the entire town was the Whiskey house.

That's where they found the spinning wheel and the weaving loom.

And that's where they discovered that Cyn and Lynx were able to weave powerful spells into cloth. They had a chance of defending themselves.

"You're what?" Cyn asked incredulously, staring at her mother.

"I'm the guardian of the library." Her mother smiled like this was every day knowledge. "It's the castle you were in. It's where we store all the important books from all over the world."

"And all the powerful objects," her father said. "Which is why you were able to find the singing stone."

Cyn shook her head. "This is so *Warehouse 13.*"

Her mother looked confused.

But her father grinned. "It really is, but so much cooler. We hide our warehouse in another realm."

Paige rubbed her temples. "We need to set up a ward tree in the center of downtown, and one at Cyn's parent's house to protect the entrance to the library."

Leslie tipped her head to the side in confusion. "You're going to make wards around them?"

"No." Paige stood. "We're going to make one massive ward, using all three ward trees."

"So, including ours."

Paige nodded and glanced over at Cyn. "It's the only way to keep everyone safe and the demons out."

And now on Sven Seven-Tails…

1

What would Alma do?

That question twisted Paige's heart. She didn't know or want to know. She didn't want to push too hard at the question, didn't want to delve too deep. If she did, all the grief she felt would crush her. It was right there, looming over her from the back of her mind. If she let down her internal wall for just one moment, she didn't know if she'd ever come out of the depression.

And she couldn't afford that right now. She was about to give birth to two tiny monsters *and* they were in the middle of a war.

A real, frelling war.

With Sven.

She should have ended him.

When? When she'd had the door to Hell infused in her bones and had no control over her ability to deal with him? Or back in Nederland, when she'd first bonded to Cawli and was still trying to figure out how it all even worked? Or when he'd been stirring up trouble in Portland, but they'd never *actually* located him?

She had to stop being so damned hard on herself. But if she *had* dealt with him earlier, then Alma would still be alive.

What would Alma say?

She'd tell Paige to pull her head out of her ass. And she wouldn't be nice about it.

So…

Paige blinked, took a deep breath, and focused on the coffee maker, swallowing the river of emotions running through her.

She'd pull her head out of her ass.

She stared at her cup as it filled with the dark liquid which claimed it had reduced caffeine. After her coffee. She'd pull her head out of her ass after her coffee. For the moment, she'd be okay with silence.

Someone came into the kitchen behind her, and Leslie's soft voice spoke, "I don't think it's going to get any stronger by staring it."

Paige shook herself mentally, her eyes clouding with tears. She'd been dangerously close to letting those walls down. She picked up her cup and turned to her sister with a smile, sipping. "You're up early."

Leslie humphed and grabbed a mug from the cupboard. "With the town basically closed, I didn't think I'd have to worry about soaps. I've had more business in the past two days than I've had in a single week. I'm going to have to create new spells. Not just soap. But like…other spells. People are getting crazy."

"Well, it's hard to ignore that the paranormal world is right here on their door when demons destroy downtown and then a slew of shifters and witches show up to fight them."

"Yeah. Well, I'm okay with this as long as the mundanes don't turn feral."

Which they would. Paige had already seen the signs of

unease. People were scared. The supplies were down because Sven had the town on lockdown. They could go to Walmart, which was located on the other side of the highway, but it was also outside the wood wards.

They were going to have to think of something. Fast.

And Paige was going to have these kids soon. She didn't want to drop them in the tub. She wanted a hospital and *drugs*. She didn't care if that made her look like a bad mom. She wore that t-shirt enough as it was. She'd own it.

The end.

But the hospital was outside the wards too. She'd visited the hospital in Troutdale and subsequently made the executive decision she wasn't having her kids there. Ever. She'd talked to eight people who worked there and the doctor who would most likely be delivering her kids, and she'd decided she'd rather get stuck in rush hour traffic and go to Portland.

Which really, really, *really* sucked because there was no way to *get* to Portland.

She was going to have to consider the idea she might have to give birth here. Without drugs. And that thought didn't appeal to her at all.

"What are we going to do about Grandma?" Leslie asked, her voice rough, her eyes rimmed red.

It had been a few days. War or not, they would have to put Alma to rest soon. "We find a break and we set up the pyre. Then we..." Paige swallowed hard, "...you know."

Leslie nodded solemnly. "I'm not sure how helpful I'm going to be."

"You always say that." Paige didn't even know what to say. She was just on autopilot, her mouth moving without her. She just felt...numb. The woman who had fought so hard to raise them— good, bad, worse— was dead. She'd died in the blink of an eye, fighting Sven. And Paige hadn't been able to do a damned thing about it.

But after Alma had died and Dexx had disappeared, their world had been thrown into chaos.

Learning that Dexx hadn't died and then figuring out how to get him back had helped her deal with the situation emotionally. Dexx was back, but they had still lost Alma. He was there, but…

She just wanted to sit down and cry.

"We need to figure out how we're going to get supplies into town," Paige heard herself say. "If we don't, we're going to have a riot on our hands.

Leslie nodded. "How?"

Paige shook her head. "Magick? We could really use an elf right about now."

"Elves?" Leslie frowned. "Why elves?"

"Because," Paige said, heading to the fridge. "They travel through Underhill, which is…I don't even know what. It's underground and in an alternate dimension. Freaky weird. That's what it is, but it works."

That *was* an idea. If Kate could figure out how to get to Underhill, they might have a shot at keeping the town alive.

Her phone went off before she had a chance to grab a frozen waffle. Great. It was Tuck. "Whiskey."

"We have a situation."

Even better. "Where?"

She got the address from him and headed out. Dexx was still sleeping. She'd let him.

Leslie headed out with her. "What's going on?"

Paige shrugged and shook her head. "We have a situation."

"That's very informative."

"That's what I thought."

When they got to the station— Tuck's, not Red Star's— they saw what was going on. A crowd had formed on Main Street at the bottom of the hill. Leslie couldn't get her car any further due to the press of people, so she parked at the police station and walked down the hill.

"I'm not making it back up," Paige said. She was really, *really* tired of being pregnant. And the hill back up to where Leslie had parked the car was steep.

"Understood," was all that Leslie said.

The crowd was thick with people, mostly mundanes, but there were a few others Paige had seen around, or in the fight. They all looked in one direction for the most part.

They were all looking at Dolly Gibson.

Paige had had an altercation with her at the local grocery store a few days ago. She'd been an emotional mess, dealing with the loss of her grandmother and the situation with Sven, and she still had no way of knowing how to get Dexx back before their kids were born. She *wasn't* doing that alone.

Dolly had cornered her at the dairy case— which only had skim milk in it— and lit into her.

Paige hadn't responded well. She'd got Dolly out of her face, but not in a great way.

That could be what led to this now. She had to remember even though people knew about them, and their abilities, it didn't mean she was free to use it whenever she wanted. People— humans— were still fragile little snowflakes. Okay. Not all of them. But if the current political atmosphere had shown her anything, it was just there were a lot more ugly snowflakes surrounding her than there were good. It was downright scary.

"We need to get the vermin out of our town," Dolly shouted.

Several people cheered. Or at least it sounded like it. Paige couldn't see anyone who was *actually* cheering. The people *she* saw just looked uncomfortable.

Paige and Leslie pushed their way toward the front of the crowd.

Dolly saw Paige and her face lit with triumph. "They've infected our town long enough. They're in our stores. They eat our food. They're in our hospital and our police department."

That was the downside to all of this. Well, aside from the fact the town was under siege.

They had no way of hiding and humans had proven in a million different ways throughout history, *and* current events, they weren't awesome when dealing with people who were "different." Their situation here, now, wasn't turning out any better.

"Who are these people and what do they want?" Dolly demanded.

A few at the front shouted.

Paige shoved her way to the clearing around Dolly. She stood on one of the few upright benches along the street.

"What kind of troubles do they bring into our town?" Dolly continued, staring right at her. "And what are they willing to do to us to keep us quiet?"

Paige sighed and heaved herself onto the bench beside Dolly.

"This one attacked me," Dolly shouted. "In the grocery store where I was unable to get food for my babies because of the demons she brought into this town."

Time to end this. Paige released her black, witch hands, pick up and gently set Dolly on the ground. Paige had no idea what she was going to say.

Well, might want to tell them what they were up against.

"Hey, guys," she said. Her voice didn't carry.

Cawli pushed forward slightly, and her voice box filled with power.

"You deserve to know what's going on."

This time, her voice carried over the crowd. An eerie

silence filled the street, made only weirder by the fact that there were so many people.

Well, shit. Now what? "There are witches and shapeshifters and other paranormals that live among you. We've been your neighbors and your friends for years."

"Why didn't we know about you before this?" one man shouted.

"There is an organization that keeps a lid on everything we do. We do this because *we* fear *you*."

The few people she could actually make out in the crowd blinked as though they were surprised.

She wasn't really looking at the crowd. Well, no. She wasn't looking at the *people*. There were just too many and her heart was racing. Public speaking. She was speaking...to the public...in public. Give her a demon *any* day. "I'm a witch, and a very powerful one. I've faced off with demons and really mean shifters, djinn and angels. But the scariest of them all were humans. Normal people."

That sounded harsh. Really harsh. But they needed to know their reality.

"Humans— mundanes," she waved at the crowd, "— aren't awesome. When scared, you huddle as a herd and you bleat, and you beat, and hammer, and you drive people away. You beat them down to make yourselves feel better. You're capable of killing millions of people in order to make your- selves feel safe again. Safe so you can go back to hating in private."

"We're not *all* that way," one woman, close to the front, said.

"No. You're not all that way," Paige agreed loudly. "*Most* of you aren't, but you're all pretty easily *led* to hate. You were trained that way by society. You were raised to hate whoever you were told was 'the enemy,' to buy into the propaganda."

"This isn't a soap box," Leslie warned under her breath. "We're here to calm people down, not stir them up."

Too true. "Well, here's a little story for you," Paige said, feeling weary. "Several years ago, I faced off with a demon and lost. That demon is back and is attacking me, my family, and this town."

"And this time?" someone called from the crowd.

Should she lie? "I don't know." She probably should have lied. "He's more powerful now, but so are we. And, thanks to him, we don't have to fight him and hide at the same time. So, that should help us."

"We need food," someone shouted.

"We do," Paige agreed simply. "We need to come together as a society and see what we can do about sharing. If we come together, we will have a stronger chance of winning."

"And what about those that don't work as hard for their share than the rest of us?" Dolly demanded. "You want to force charitable handouts to those who haven't earned them?"

Paige wanted to wring Dolly's neck. What she really wanted to ask was just how hard Dolly had worked for her share. She came off like someone who *demanded* her share more than she actually put forth the effort to earn it. "Do you want to survive?"

"I have enough to take care of my kids."

"Then, you didn't need to sucker punch me in the dairy aisle. You already had enough to feed your 'babies.' Is that what I'm hearing? You attacked me in the grocery store while I was mourning the woman who saved all of your lives—" Paige shouted those last words. "—because you needed extra food for *your* babies and fuck everyone else?"

Dolly's eyes flared, but she didn't respond.

"My grandmother was the strongest witch I knew, and she died protecting *you*." Paige didn't need to tell them that. No one really cared, but the emotions— the grief— was too strong. "That doesn't matter. What matters—"

"She was the old woman that faced off with that… glowing guy?" one woman asked.

Paige swallowed the knot of tears in her throat and nodded. "What matters is that we come together and share our resources so that we *all* can live through this."

"I have a bunch of old cans of soup I can get rid of," one man called out. "My wife bought them 'on sale' and we never ate them."

"My kids *hate* the canned spaghetti they couldn't get enough of last year," another woman yelled. "I could get rid of some of that."

Those voices were joined with several others until the air was filled with people yelling, and from what Paige could hear, they were offering up food they didn't want, or couldn't use.

Paige held up her hand. This was a good start, but it wouldn't be enough. When the din quieted, she continued. "We need volunteers. People who can gather the food and people who can come up with ways to use it best."

"We can use the bakery ovens," Emma shouted.

"Or the senior living center," another woman called. "We have probably the biggest kitchen?"

"I don't know," another man shouted from a distance away. "The high school is pretty big."

Schools. That was a great idea. "We should choose one of the schools, but we also need to keep our kids learning. Just because we're under attack doesn't mean they get off easy."

"Where do *your* kids go to school?" someone shouted. "Are *your* kids safer?"

"They go to school where they're allowed to learn magick along with math," Paige said quickly.

"I'd feel a whole lot safer about *my* kids, if your kids were thrown in with our lot."

That wasn't a *bad* idea. "We teach our kids how to shift. There are occasional bites, or nicks. We play harder. We practice magick."

"But will our kids be hurt?" a woman shouted from the back.

"Probably," Paige said honestly. "My kids come home with bruises and scrapes and black eyes all the time."

"But they're alive," another woman called from the front. "Because you protect them."

"We *do* protect them," Paige said. "But it's a community event. We all take turns as instructors and in watching them."

"Then we will, too!" a man called from somewhere to her left. "We keep our kids safe. We find food. And then *you* kill those demons."

A few people cheered their agreement.

If only it was that easy.

One woman stepped out of the crowd. She was a tall, black woman, her hair pulled back. Her dark eyes lit with a purely mundane fire of determination. "We'll use the high school for food. They have the biggest gymnasium and the largest kitchen. If you have extra food, take it there. We'll start a community kitchen and get it organized."

"Great idea." Paige repeated the information for everyone.

"But," the woman said. "We'll use *your* school for the high school."

That...was going to be interesting. "There's a lot to discuss about the school and we need to get the administrator in on that conversation."

The woman nodded once in agreement.

Things were getting taken care of, which was good. "We're also working on trying to get supplies in."

"Can't you just use magic?" someone asked.

"If it was only that easy, we wouldn't be here now." Paige released a long sigh. "Sven is dangerous, and things are only going to get worse before they get better. We have magickal wards up. Some of you might have noticed that the demons can't get in. That's because of us. The hospital and three grocery stores are located within the protections of the wards, as are all of the schools."

"What about those of us who live outside the protections?"

They could try to add to the ward trees similarly to what they'd done in Alaska. "There might be a way to extend the wards, but it will take all of us."

People looked confused and pleased at the same time.

She didn't know what else to say. "We need to work together if we're going to pull through this."

"Just how bad is he?" a young woman asked. "This Sven."

"He's bad," was all Paige could say. "Real bad."

"So, we're screwed."

"If we fall apart here? If we make it easier for him to win by fighting amongst ourselves?" Paige nodded. "Yeah. We'll be screwed then. Right now? We're inconvenienced."

"Some of us need medicines and without those we'll be more than inconvenienced," a woman shouted. "We'll be dead."

"Yeah. Like our insulin," another man shouted.

She hadn't even thought about that. "I need someone to take lead in gathering a list of medications they need. Don't get stupid. Don't ask for shit you don't need. We'll be endangering *our* lives to get *you* this medicine, so make sure it's something you *really* need."

There were a few grumbles.

"There's something you need to know about me," she said in a cold growl. "I'm a witch. I don't wait for karma. I issue it." With that, she stepped down as gracefully as she could.

Rainbow took her place, along with another man. The town began to coordinate ways to survive.

Well, at least there was that.

2

As the crowd dispersed— well, it didn't, not really. Most people just started making smaller groups and coordinating different things. Paige didn't know what all was going on, but she did know she didn't need to be in the middle of every single thing.

Leslie and Tuck completely disappeared. Paige wasn't even sure where Tuck had been the entire time.

She went to the ward tree located in the— *she* didn't even know what it was. There was this tiny park-like area next to the building with the awesome mural. A few red benches were sprinkled through, and a statue of a man took up the center stage.

That was, until their tree overtook the green space.

The ward trees had gone up just the day before. Cyn's parents had actually *become* the ward tree at their home so they could better protect the library. Paige didn't have all the particulars, but she did know they were both just fine. They would never be humans in this realm again, or until the wards came down. She didn't know if taking down the wards would bring back their physical, human forms or not. But the library existed over on the other side, too, where all the spirit animals did. Dexx and Hattie called it the Land Before, or some-such, which made Paige think of animated dinosaurs. Dexx assured her there were *no* singing dinosaurs.

Which was good.

She'd even been over there a time or two, but she hadn't seen a whole lot.

Somewhere over there— with spirit animals and who knew what else— was a castle, and inside that castle was a library. That library contained as much information on the occult and the strange as Paige could ever have hoped to get her hands on.

But that wasn't going to help her right then and there. She needed to figure out a way to extend the ward.

Something wiggled in her jacket pocket.

It felt a little like having a mouse in her pocket or something. She reached in, her magick at the ready…

And pulled out some of the string Cyn and Lynx had made. It pulsed with power and seemed to…well, it seemed to want to be out. The original strand had been used as the grounding base for one of the ward trees. Cyn and Lynx had made this one last night.

The end reached for the tree like a kid with his arms out.

Well, there wasn't anything for it. Paige walked to the tree and let the thread do its thing. It flipped up and latched onto the nearest branch, slithering out of her hand like the tiniest snake she'd ever seen.

The tree flashed with a golden light and the wards rang like a bell.

The people on the street hushed, looking around.

Whoops.

Paige raised her hand and waved at them. "Everything's

okay," she shouted. Then she switched to witch vision and studied the wards.

They were more flexible. She didn't know how strong they'd be, but they moved with the magickal energies on the other side now. She could tell where there were groups of demons just by looking at the wards. It was like looking at a hot air balloon as it was filling up.

"Is there something special about this tree?" a man asked, coming up to her.

He didn't look angry or upset. Just curious and a little scared.

Safe enough. Right? She was a big, bad witch. She couldn't be afraid of *people*. Paige nodded.

"Can I touch it?"

"Sure." She stepped aside and gestured toward it.

He reached out, touching it with his left palm.

A vine worked its way around the branch nearest him and wrapped itself around his wrist and up his arm.

He let out a startled screech.

Paige moved to help, but nothing in her magick told her there was anything *wrong*.

The expression on his face didn't either. He stared up at the sky as if he could see the wards.

She did, too, and noticed another thread of green energy flow through them.

He turned to her with his eyes filled with amazement as the vine released him. "That's awesome."

It was.

"Did it help?"

She shrugged. "It can't hurt. This is your town, too, and that ward can only help, so...maybe?" It couldn't hurt, maybe. She just didn't know. She didn't know how mundanes could power something magickal. Unless he was a generator.

A little girl came up to him, her dark hair a wild mess that looked like it hadn't been brushed in a week. "Daddy, what are you doing?"

"Hey." He scooped her up in his arms and held her close to the tree.

When she put her hand to the tree, nothing happened.

He looked over at Paige with a quizzical look.

Paige shrugged. "We'll look into it."

He turned back to his daughter and started telling her what the tree did.

That was interesting. Maybe there was a gene or something some people had, and others didn't? Or maybe there were those who had latent magickal abilities and those who didn't? Would that invite more hysteria?

She hoped not. But it was hard to tell.

What would Dolly say? How would *she* react? And would she be able to power the tree? How would Dolly blow up? It wasn't a question of if. It was a question of when.

Turning back to the crowd, Paige raised her voice to see if she could bring anyone else over.

But the wards shifted over them. Hard. As if something had exploded right next it. It was the ward closest to the Walmart on the other side of the highway.

Not trusting herself to fly because she wasn't super graceful on the landing yet, she glanced over at the man and held out her hand. "Don't be scared and don't freak out."

He nodded eagerly, hugging his daughter tighter to him.

She shifted into a cheetah and looked around for Leslie.

Leslie was already in the air in the shape of a hawk.

The little girl in the man's arms shrieked in excitement, hugging her dad close.

Paige turned her head and smiled, though that was probably a bad move because when a cheetah grinned, all she did was bare her teeth. She flipped her tail instead and took off.

As Paige turned the corner, heading for the highway at

full cheetah speed, that ridiculous black car of Leah's sped past her. Dexx.

Well, at least he'd be there, too, though she'd really wanted to give him the chance to sleep. The fear of not having him there still rode her hard, even though she had him back. It was like waking up from the idea of knowing he *could* be taken from her only to realize that he *had* been.

It didn't take her long to get to Walmart. She slowed to a trot, padding toward Leslie, who had already shifted back to human form. Dexx was just getting out of the car, shutting the door slowly as he stared at what had caused the commotion.

Paige couldn't quite believe it either.

On the other side of the ward, eighteen people dressed in black camo defended themselves against a swarm of demons. They defended themselves with magick, but they were barely holding the demons back.

Paige shifted and walked up to Dexx. "DoDO. Willing to bet."

Dexx grunted.

Leslie folded her arms over her chest and narrowed her green eyes. "I don't think I want to help them."

Paige didn't either.

A form began to take shape, even though they were on the backside of the supermarket. The wards didn't extend all the way to Walmart itself. That was something they might need to fix.

Or not. If the store couldn't get supplies, what was the sense in it?

That wasn't what stopped her short, though. DoDO wasn't worth their effort, wasn't worth endangering their lives for. DoDO was the enemy. Maybe not as bad as Sven, but still the enemy.

What would happen if they didn't help DoDO? What

would people say then? Would they even give Paige and them the chance to explain themselves?

Dexx looked over at her with a disgruntled look on his face. "We're helping them, aren't we?"

Paige shrugged. "I think we've got to."

Leslie tipped her head to the side and assessed the situation.

There really weren't that many demons. Well, not when you considered the town was surrounded by an entire mob of them.

Crap.

"Fine," Paige said. "We'll do what we can to get the demons away from them and DoDO in here."

Leslie didn't look any happier than Paige did.

Neither did Dexx.

"But, if more demons show up we're out of there." Paige wasn't going to let *her* people die just because DoDO was a group of fucking morons.

Dexx pointed to the right. "I'll take those out while you and Leslie get those guys through."

Paige didn't like that plan. In order for Dexx to take demons out, he had to shift and get right down into it, so he could bite off their heads. And that meant putting him right in the middle of the horde. She called up her demon summoning gift, her hands extending in their inky, black power. "You leave them to me and you get these guys back here."

Dexx opened his mouth to fight back.

She sent her witch hand out. It pierced the ward, ripped into the chest of the first demon it came across, and dragged it through the gate located in her bones. It wasn't literally located in her body.

It was strange, how these portals worked. But to her

witch eyes, it looked like a hole had opened up at the demon's feet and the thing was sucked down.

Dexx glared at her. "No one likes a show off."

"I disagree." She smiled sweetly at him. "Now, go get our moronic darlings."

Paige focused her attention on the demons, reaching for as many as she could, as fast as she could. Her demon summoning gift sure helped. She'd say that, but with this many demons? Even she was tired.

Power rose in her, power that wasn't hers. But it was wrapped in love.

Love like only unborn children could give.

She took it gladly, bolstering herself to take more of the demons back to Hell, even as more showed up, rallying around those who fell.

She didn't have the attention to give, but it looked like the DoDO jackasses were telling Dexx and Leslie they *weren't* going to retreat.

Paige growled, conjuring another blast of magick to bring them in.

But before she had a chance to do anything, Leslie handled it for her. She moved her hands in two circles in front of her and pushed the people in uniform backward, following them through the wards, the wind whipping her wavy blonde hair.

Dang! Leslie was powerful. It was pretty cool to watch, especially since Paige knew how much Leslie had wished to be stronger than she was.

Dexx walked backward through the wards, flipping the remaining demons off.

Paige took the last two demons she had in her hands back to Hell and recalled her magick. Attacking the demons through the wards had been a good idea, and a bad one at the same time. Those wards had taken power away from her. But she really didn't want to be in the middle of a demon horde if she didn't have to be. She was pregnant, *not* stupid.

Mario Kester took his helmet off and stalked toward her. "That was a rather unnecessary assist," he said in his snide British tone.

"Yeah," Dexx said, turning to walk the rest of the way forward. "It looked like you had everything under control."

Mario turned a churlish glare at Dexx. "You do realize why *we're* here, don't you?"

Did Paige even want to know?

"You've gained worldwide attention with your little situation here," he said dramatically. "The President herself told me to come down here and clean this mess up."

Like this was *their* fault? "You do realize what we're facing here, right?"

Mario daggered her with his blue gaze. "You do realize you had a chance to end this in Louisiana and failed, right?"

"Right." Oh, this guy. She wanted to punch him in the face. "With the door to Hell freshly opened and no way to control it. When I would walk up to a demon and just *be* possessed because they couldn't fight the pull. Even Sven." She nodded. "Yup. Totally could'a done it. You're right. Couldn't have used a little help *then*."

His expression cooled. "And your excuse for Nederland?"

"How is that you *know* about all of that, but you didn't help even a little?" Paige fought to release the magick that balled in her fists. "It's like you enjoy hiding under the bed while everyone fights the bad guys and then blaming them for losing as you're forced to come out and help."

He rested his hand on the butt of the rifle hanging from the strap over his shoulder. "Are you saying you'd like our help now?"

"Sure." Paige advanced on him. "I'd like you to stop whatever you're doing to make my shifters lose control of their shift."

His expression froze in a sneer.

"Because while we're all focused on fighting that—" She pointed forcefully at the demons hurling themselves at the wards. "—we don't need to be worried if our friendly, neighborhood bear is going to eat his not as friendly neighborhood human." She was thinking of Dolly as she said that. Oh, man. If only that *would* happen. It would be karma to a woman in severe need of it.

Mario turned his head and gestured at the person behind him.

She pulled off her helmet to reveal a mess of brown hair. "Yeah," she said in an Australian accent.

What was it with the Aussies invading Troutdale? They couldn't *all* be evil? Could they? Seriously? No. Really. No.

"Turn it off," Mario said.

"Are you sure?"

Mario nodded and then turned back to Paige, visibly pleased with himself.

Was he seriously looking at her like he was the second coming of Christ? She *wasn't* going to thank him. Asshole.

Wow. These babies were making her cranky.

No. The demons surrounding her town were making her cranky. And this asshole threatening her town was making her cranky. And the warning he brought from the freaking *President* was making her cranky.

Shit.

"So," Mario said after a moment. "Does this make us allies?"

Not fucking likely. "Let's talk."

Because as much as she hated the thought, demons and Sven surrounded them, and he was powering himself back up pretty damned fast. They didn't have the luxury to invite *another* enemy to remain an enemy.

She turned to get into Dexx's car and was met with the faces of several dozen humans who looked at her with mixtures of disgust, loathing, and fear.

Yeah. They really couldn't afford it. Not that day.

Shit.

3

Paige got in the car with Dexx behind the wheel.

Dexx laid his hand over the steering wheel. "You okay?" he asked, his expression guarded.

When he didn't crack a joke as soon as they got in the car, Paige knew something was wrong. "I'm fine. What's wrong with you?"

He shook his head and started the car, backing out, and heading for home.

Sometimes that man was so easy to read, and then other times he just shut down and she had no idea how to even get through the front door. But she was the type of person who attacked things head on, and if she'd learned *anything* in the past year, if it wasn't a monster, *he* didn't. Not even close.

She needed another tactic. "They looked like a bunch of fucking idiots out there."

He snorted. "I think Delicate Officer Mario is trying to see how fast he can get his guys killed."

"They're not all guys."

He rolled his eyes and turned the corner, heading toward downtown.

Ah. Paige was pretty sure she saw what was going on. She'd spent a lot of time away from Troutdale in the past two years. One year? However long it'd been. He was used to calling all the shots. And in the past few weeks, she'd not only forced him to take her orders, but she'd forced another boss on him. But how to talk about that with him? If she pushed too hard, he'd just tell her everything was fine, he was fine, the weather was fine, and everything was...fine.

But she *really* didn't know how to deal with a problem any other way. Ever. "Let's just talk about this."

He quirked his lips but didn't say anything for a while. He waited until he turned onto Main Street. "About what?"

Holy crap balls, she hated it when he did that. "You're mad at me."

"Nope."

"Right. Everything is okay. Everything is wonderful."

"Yup."

"Bullshit." Why was it *he* could get *her* to spill her guts every damned time, but she could never get through to him. "Tell me a joke I can use to crack that thick skull of yours."

"What?"

"You only deal with things in jokes, so tell me a joke I can use to get you to talk."

He turned left before getting to downtown because there were still too many people blocking the street. "Your humor is broken. There's no way you'd understand a priest, rabbi, and a demon hunter walking down a street."

"I know. That's why I'm asking for your help." She stared out the windshield. "You're mad about something, but I have no idea what it is. Well, I have a feeling I know, but you'd never admit it out loud."

"And what do you think it is? We can play hot and cold."

Like that? That *tone*? She could *try* to crack a joke. But her humor *was* broken, even when she *wasn't* so very, very pregnant. "You're mad because I took charge of that scene and brought Tony on as your boss."

"Who's doing a humdinger of a job, I might say, with him being locked up in my jail for his own protection and all."

Well, he didn't say cold. "Do you think I picked the wrong guy for the job?"

He crept along the back lot that lined the main buildings and turned on the street that led to the Red Star Division building. "He was the right guy at the time."

"And now?" Warmer, possibly. There wasn't any way to know yet.

Dexx shook his head and shrugged. "I don't know, Pea."

Fuck. "Would you just fucking *talk* to me?"

He waited until he pulled up behind the building and put the car in park. Shutting off the engine, he turned to her, and inhaled deeply.

She could tell there was a bunch of stuff rolling around in that head of his. Getting his thoughts together, or planning to deflect? She just needed him to get it *out,* so she could... do nothing about it, but she'd at least fucking know.

"Before I disappeared, to the Time Before," he said quietly, "I thought I was going to die."

It had been a scary battle. Paige was certain they'd all wondered. But then to have Alma, of all people, di—

She couldn't even bring herself to say it. Her heart twisted inside her so hard, and tears sprang to her eyes as she replayed her grandmother's last moments. She'd gone out fighting. That was certain.

"No. I didn't *think* I was going to die." His words filled the interior of the car like a huge, metal door closing. "That prophecy. I was absolutely...certain."

Oh, for fuck's sake. That stupid, frelling prophecy. Paige was so fucking tired of hearing about it. If it was never brought up again, it would be too soon.

"I thought I was the one to die. That Leslie was the one to leave. And…you were the one to live. You and them." He gestured to her belly.

That *did* make sense. But now that everything was said and done, they knew differently. Alma had been the one to die and Dexx had been the one to leave.

Thank goodness. They'd discovered the castle with the library and had brought back Lynx. And they'd discovered where Sven was getting all his energy from. And Cyn and Lynx discovered they could make powerful thread and fabrics.

Which reminded her. She needed to talk to them about making more.

So many fucking things to do.

"I was scared. And then Alma." He clammed up.

She'd known something was up, leading up to the big fight. Dexx had been acting so weird. And, if she was being honest with herself, she'd recognized that he'd been saying his good-byes in the days leading up to the big fight.

She was scared. Sure. She had to be. But she couldn't focus on that. She was pregnant and about to bring babies into a war with demons she might not win. She didn't know what would be better, to have them now and focus on the fight, or to keep carrying them and have them after this was all done.

If it ever finished.

No. It had to finish.

"And you—" he shrugged. "You don't seem phased by this at all."

"Oh, I am." She stared at the brick building, really not wanting to go inside and deal with DoDO, who were driving to Red Star with the help of a few of the people who'd been standing around. "I'm trying really hard to just… keep it… shut off. I'm afraid that if I…Well, you know me. I'm horrible with emotions. I get stupid. I act irrationally."

"But you want me to explode my emotions all over the inside of Cab?" Dexx made a noise and ran fingers through his hair.

"Not *explode*. But…"

"We're human, I guess."

"Exactly." She rubbed her face with her hand. "I don't think we have the luxury of being human here."

He blinked rapidly and stared at the building. "The alpha in me hates taking orders. Hattie wanted to tear into those demons. She knew we could."

"I knew you could, too, but—" Paige stopped herself as icy fear froze her throat. "I just got you back."

He offered his hand, palm up.

She took it and held it as tightly as she could, trying to force the desperate fear she'd felt and had had to keep pushed into the back of everything for three whole days while they waited to bring him back.

"I'll see what I can do about getting better at taking orders."

She heard the "but" in his voice. "You don't think Tony's the guy."

He shook his head. "Things won't ever be simple here, Pea. And the Eastwoods are right down the street from us."

If he counted Portland as being "right down the street".

"And I'm not sure we won't need their help."

She hadn't *wanted* to think about that. "Ollie seems to be warming up to us."

"I like Ollie well enough. Mostly."

"And he's going to let you keep the money you didn't steal, but just seemed to magically find that I don't know about."

He cracked a smile. "Yeah. That. But the rest of them?" he shook his head. "They're not getting Leah."

He said what she'd been thinking. No. They were *not*

getting Leah. Paige didn't care if Leah's father had been an Eastwood and Leah was the last surviving female who could take over the Eastwood coven. Leah was *her* daughter.

Well, hers and Dexx's.

Damn that man. She wouldn't make it without him. How the hell had he managed that?

"So, to answer your question," Dexx said quietly, "I'm green. I'm emerald green. Super green."

What the hell did that mean?

Dexx must have read something on her face. He cracked a thin smile. "I'm fine."

"No. You're not."

"Okay. I'm fine in the same way you are."

She nodded. That was fair. "Do you think we're actually going to make it through this one?"

"Honestly?"

Goddess bless, yes. "Please."

"I have no idea how, but I'm going down swinging like Alma. I know that for fact."

Because she needed to hear she wasn't the only one thinking *that*.

"But, yeah." He let his head fall back against the headrest. "I think we'll find a way."

And she needed to hear that. She gave his hand one last squeeze. "I love you, jerk."

"Love you, too, you big bully."

She gave him a ghost of a smile and then opened her door, getting out.

Paige could shift into a tiger. She liked moving around as the tiger because she wasn't a physically pregnant woman then. Her human body was displaced in the Time Before, but in a way that made her body super light. If she didn't know how it would affect her babies, she'd remain an animal as much as she could, especially since everyone knew about shifters now and wouldn't freak out or shoot at her. Hopefully.

With Dexx at her back, she walked through the back door. Tony hadn't been on the job for more than a week. No. Crap. Two. Man, time flew. She hated the idea of having to turn him away already, but she wanted her man happy. And the team really *did* follow Dexx better. They hadn't even *thought* of following Tony. And Tuck wasn't helping. Instead of calling Tony, he was calling Dexx.

Shit.

But, if Dexx really *was* going to take the captain's chair, then he was going to *have* to learn the paperwork. And she'd have to be the hard-ass who enforced that.

No. She wouldn't.

Because she was moving on.

Crap. That was if the explosion of this demon mess didn't fuck up her chances at her new position, which didn't really have a title or real description. She was "invited" to sit at the elder's table. Whatever that meant.

Yeah. She had no idea what her life was going to be like, but she did know one thing. She couldn't be worried about the Red Star Division, or Dexx's paperwork, or budgets, or everything else that came with running a department. He was going to have to do that.

Maybe she could talk to Tuck about mentoring Dexx. Paige knew she wouldn't have time. She hadn't yet, and all the elder council had really done was take her away from her work. *And* she was about to give birth to two screaming humans who were going to be super needy. She had no idea how she was going to balance work and kids and...

She hadn't succeeded yet.

Great. She was bringing in two more kids and she *still* sucked at the whole mom part.

Mario sat apart from the rest of his people at the front of

the empty bullpen. Paige knew Rainbow was out in the street, so she assumed those who hadn't locked themselves in the cells in the back were outside.

There were almost as many women in Mario's group as men, a fact that Paige made note of. She realized she shouldn't. The world was changing, putting women on the front lines. Not real fast, though.

She gestured for him to join her in the conference room.

Dexx moved to his desk, a determined look on his face.

She shook her head, knowing she was probably going to regret this, but they needed all the power players on the same page and Dexx was the leader. "Dexx. With me."

He looked up with surprise, and then spun on his heel, following her into the conference room. He closed the door behind Mario and took a chair beside Paige on the other side of the table, facing the door.

That put Mario in the position of having his back to the wall, which in their field was the worst place to be.

Paige would take every advantage she could. "Looks like you got yourself into a real shit storm. Have any idea how you're going to fix this one?"

He gave her a cool look and pulled out his phone. "I have the President on speed dial."

"Congrats. I have demons on speed dial. And angels. And a bunch of other people you probably don't want to think about dealing with."

He tipped his head and folded his hands in front of him. "Are you threatening me? The President?"

It was so hard to take him seriously when he was talking about the American President, in his British accent, after he'd admitted he worked directly for the Queen. "Perhaps you should tell me where your loyalties lie."

He pursed his lips, his dark eyes flat, telling her absolutely nothing.

"What are you doing here?" she asked again.

"Cleaning up your mess."

"And you thought you'd honestly do that with a handful of people."

"A handful of specially trained people." Mario spread his hands in a you-know-this shrug.

"Specially trained to deal with *demons*?" Dexx asked, leaning forward. "Because *we* are."

Mario kept his gaze on Paige for a long moment before sliding it to Dexx. "Only two of you, if we're being honest."

Dexx shook his head. "Four, easy. Five if Rainbow's having a good hair day. Six if Leslie's not trying to eat the local puppies. Oh." Dexx snapped his fingers and glanced at Paige. "Seven. We have seven."

She frowned. "Who's seven?"

"Tyler."

Oh, shit. Right. The kid was only twelve. Twelve? Gods, she couldn't tell time. But the kid was pretty powerful. "But against demons?"

Dexx nodded, his lips pushed out. "He's the only way we survived when the djinn attacked."

"You mean that time when you nearly got me killed in Utah?" She'd been in a trial, proving herself as trustworthy with a pack of shifters down there when Dexx had slammed an angel into the wards so hard, she'd exploded energy, knocking everyone in the game off their feet, seriously wounding two.

And... maybe she shouldn't have said that right in front of Mario. But she was too overwhelmed to care.

Dexx grimaced. "I don't remember nearly killing you."

Funny how he remembered things differently.

Mario eyed the both of them. "So, you have seven."

"Well," Paige added, "there's eight."

Dexx twisted. "Who's eight?"

She widened her eyes. "Leah."

"Oh, right." Dexx groaned. "Zombies." He winced and shook his head. "Yeah. I don't know. Zombies versus demons? I think demons win."

Okay. He might have a point. "All right. We have seven. For now."

Mario dropped his head and shook it before looking up again. "I propose we work together."

"That sounds like a great idea." And it probably was. She really liked the idea of throwing Mario's guys at the demons as fodder, tiring the demon army, but the "karma" of her witchiness said that was probably the kind of idea that would backfire on her. *Real* quick. "But for your own safety, I'm going to have to say no."

He opened his mouth to speak.

She held up a hand to stop him. "So far, the only thing you've proven is that you have no idea how to go up against demons."

Dexx leaned back with a cocky smile. "The learning curve is kinda steep. And these grades are pass-fail. You've failed a bunch."

"Let me spell something out for you," Mario said, his accent thicker. "You're gaining worldwide attention. *Worldwide*. If this isn't handled the right way, things will explode."

"Let me spell this out for *you*—" Dexx leaned in toward Mario, "—if it isn't taken care of the right way, you have no idea."

Mario shook his head. "There are programs in place for an event like this."

"What event?" Paige asked.

Mario looked around as if checking to see if anyone was listening, then leaned forward. "In the case of paranormals making a name for themselves, or making the news."

Paige had a feeling she didn't want to hear the rest of what he had to say.

"They're kind of things you wouldn't like. I can guarantee that."

She got a flash of the *Avengers: Civil War* in her head. Or was that *Captain America*? She couldn't remember. But she knew her government and she knew the views of the current President. That woman really hated paranormals.

"Well," Paige said out loud, keeping the rest behind her lips, "we'll be lucky if the world doesn't split in half. We'll be lucky to keep the demons *here*. We'll be lucky if this doesn't spill out everywhere else."

"And if it does, then I can assure you that the measure the President has in mind *will* be strictly enforced."

Paige didn't doubt that. "So, are you here to make sure we lose? Or to make sure we win?"

He smiled. "I'm here to survive."

About what she thought.

4

The rest of the meeting went about the same. Mario invited Dexx to go see their headquarters, to see what they had to offer. Dexx told him no without a second thought, and Paige had sent Mario back to the bullpen, closing Dexx and herself in the office so their conversation couldn't be seen.

Dexx peered through the blinds, then let them slam closed. "You can't seriously think this is a good idea."

She shrugged and sank onto the couch along the back wall. They always seemed to forget about it, but the thing was comfortable. "Think about it. You'd be able to get in there. See what they have. See if they could help. Figure out who they are and what their agenda is."

He rolled his eyes and sank down next to her. "I can already tell you what they have. Nothing we need."

It was time for her to roll her eyes. That *would* be the Dexx approach.

"Look at it. They're always getting in the way and looking for us to save them, so what could they really have?"

"Thanks for looking at the picture right in front of your face."

He glared at her.

She sighed and leaned back into the couch. "I need eyes in there to see what they're really doing. They're after something. That much I know. And it isn't just Billie."

Oh, shit. She was going to have to warn Billie that DoDO was there.

Because they didn't have enough problems.

Crap.

He narrowed his eyes at her but didn't ask. "I don't care what they're after. Right now, we have a demon army on our ass."

"But what happens after? When we've taken care of the demons. What's DoDO going to do? We have no idea. We have no clue what they're doing or what we're even up against."

"So, you're telling me that you want me to go to their headquarters now. While we're in the middle of all this."

Okay. When he said it like that... "Just to see if maybe they *do* have something in their arsenal that they have no idea how to use." But what was the luck they'd actually managed that? Probably, like slim to none at all.

"And what if they decide I don't need to come back?" He tipped his head to the side and gave her a *very* frank look.

Yeah. She didn't like that idea. At all. "You'll find a way back to me," she said softly. "You always do."

He quirked his lips, visibly upset, and looked away with a nod.

Yeah. He didn't like the idea. She pulled herself off the couch. She wasn't going to save the world sitting down. "Let's at the very least get a few more details."

He growled low as he followed her out of the office.

Mario stood surrounded by his people, their guns slung

over their shoulders. They looked like they were ready to take out zombies, not a mob of demons. The woman beside him saw Paige and Dexx approaching and gestured.

Mario looked up and walked toward them. "You've had a chance to talk," he said with a smile. "All good, I hope."

Paige really just wanted to wipe that smug look off his face. "What do you think Dexx will be able to see that you don't."

Mario shrugged and looked at Dexx. "We've gathered objects from all over the world to a warehouse."

"How far away?" Dexx asked.

"In Montana." Mario's expression wavered a little, but his smile returned quickly. "We could be there in a jiff."

Paige frowned at him, not quite sure he was getting the whole picture. "We're in the middle of a war, and you want to get Dexx out of here, drive or fly to Montana, and then come back? Do you even know how far away that is?"

"It's not too far." Mario actually looked confused.

She was starting to doubt his intelligence. "How are you going to get out of here? You think we haven't tried *every* road? Every pasture and plot of land? They have us surrounded. *No* one comes in or out of Troutdale."

"And yet," Mario said smugly, "we got in."

Yeah. How *had* they done that? "You think you could smuggle in a few supplies?"

"Like what?"

She gave him a well-duh look. She'd got enough of them from Leah and Mandy that she felt she should be well-practiced at them. "Bread, milk, diapers, formula, tampons, insulin."

"Toothpaste." Dexx turned to her. "I'm out of toothpaste."

Great. "Toothpaste. You know, supplies."

"No." Mario closed his eyes and raised his eyebrows

before opening his eyes again and shaking his head. "I don't do supplies."

"Okay." She had to try.

"But," Mario said, "I do have a way and I could have Dexx out and back in less than a day. Longer, if he was keen to stay."

Over her dead and pregnant body. "I have an idea." She didn't like her idea.

"What?"

Dexx turned to her, demanding to know what she had in mind.

He wasn't going to like her idea either. "You can have Dexx in exchange for something."

"I've already stopped interfering with your shifters." Mario folded his hands in front of him. "What more do you want?"

"You lay off Billie Black."

Mario shook his head. "She's a threat."

"She's *my* threat." Wait. That didn't come out right. "She's our ally and we need her in one piece if we're going to survive Sven. Maybe not even then."

He considered it, then finally nodded. "Fine. While he's in my care, Billie Black is safe."

"But when he returns? And presumably *with* you, *while* we're fighting a horde of demons, *she* needs to be worried?"

He looked up and away, thinking, and then returned his gaze to her. "Fine. Until this is over."

Well, that at least bought them a little time. "Fine." She held out her hand.

He pulled out a knife and sliced the palm of his hand. "I swear my oath by blood."

Oh. Shit.

Dexx handed her his knife.

It *might* be a little more sanitary, though she doubted it.

She took Dexx's because he was already upset with her and sliced her palm, knowing she'd heal quickly thanks to her shifter abilities.

Taking Mario's hand, she braced herself as the blood oath washed over them. She hadn't agreed to hand Billie over. She wasn't sure why Mario had offered a blood oath, but if it kept Billie and Dexx safe, she'd take it.

Mario smiled and wiped the blood off his palm with a white handkerchief.

Who still carried those? "Okay. Well, you boys work out the details. Dexx, go if you like. Stay if you like. I've got to go figure out supplies."

Dexx glared.

She couldn't allow herself to care. She gave him a kiss and walked out. As a tiger because fuck that walking as a pregnant human woman thing. For freak's sake.

She left Red Star and strolled into town, and no one really paid her much attention. They still moved out of her way. They weren't stupid, but they were working together and that's what was in important. Paige found Rainbow and shifted back to human.

The woman beside her let out a startled yelp and then laughed, her bright amber eyes lit with an almost paranormal hue. Her brown hair was loose around her round face. "I'll get used to this. I swear, I will."

Paige just smiled and looked at Rainbow. "Do we have a supply list."

"We do," Rainbow said. "And I got in touch with Chuck and the mayor." She gestured to the woman who'd screeched.

She offered her hand to Paige. "I'm Suzanne West."

Oh, right. Paige had seen her name around a bit. "Paige Whiskey."

They shook before Suzanne turned back to Rainbow. "We

have most of the list, and I have the funds to pay for the supplies if you have a way to get those supplies in."

"I might." Paige took in a deep breath. Aside from having really spectacular eyes, Suzanne seemed perfectly normal. "We're going to need help."

"I have a box truck that will be ready and eight people willing to help load and unload it. And they all know to handle guns."

Paige wasn't sure if guns would even work in Underhill.

Well, she didn't even know if they'd be able to *use* Underhill. The elves weren't super useful or open to the idea of humans, witches, shifters—anyone who wasn't an elf. Kate might not be able to help them like Paige had hoped. "I still haven't got the details worked out on my end."

Suzanne nodded, every inch a businesswoman. "I've handled all the rest. So, you go do the hard part."

Paige smiled. She actually liked the woman.

Rainbow handed her the list. "If you can get to the Costco on the eastside, we've got people who will have all of this ready to be picked up."

Wow. The power of people working together. Paige wasn't going to knock it. "And the medicine?"

Rainbow shrugged. "Some of it, we were able to get? But Pip's out there and she's..." Rainbow shrugged again, but this time, it was the shrug that said that her friend *might* be breaking rules. "...working on the rest? Do you know when you're going?"

"I still have to figure out *how*."

"Yeah, okay," Rainbow said with a grin. "Well, when you do, let *me* know and I'll let *her* know and she'll shag her butt. Or break people."

Paige stared at her incredulously.

"Probably, just shag," Rainbow said with a laugh.

Paige blinked. She realized what Rainbow *meant*. She

wasn't always a great communicator. Half of her thoughts were half thoughts and all of them spilled out of her mouth. "Okay. Great." She turned to find her way home. "I'll see what I can do."

She hadn't got very far when she was attacked by Cyn, Lynx not far behind. "Holy biscuits," Cyn said, staring around at all the people. "This is crazy."

That was one word for it. "I actually needed to see you two."

"About the thread," Cyn said, her blue eyes lighting with something that almost looked like anger.

Paige wasn't sure, but she had a suspicion Cyn didn't like her a whole lot. "Yes. I was wondering," Paige said more to Lynx than Cyn, "if you could weave anything else? Like, I don't know. Um, shields that could also send the ammunition back at them or something? I don't know. We need weapons."

Lynx nodded, keeping his hand on Cyn. He looked very uncomfortable in the crowd of people pressed all around him. "I was thinking on that very thing, and I think Cyn and I have a plan."

"We're actually trying to get back to your place to test drive it right now."

Oh. Great. "So am I. I need to talk to Kate. She's down here in all of this, isn't she?"

Cyn shook her head. "The kids *wanted* to come down, but Tru told them to stay."

Which meant the kids were probably in town. "Okay. Thanks. How did you—"

"Paige?" Faith called above the crowd.

Holy balls of crap. "Okay. You guys get back to the house. Start working on that. We're going to need as much of it as we can."

Lynx nodded and turned, seemingly lost in the sea of people.

"Paige," Faith called again.

Paige raised her hand and waved. "Over here." She turned to Cyn. "Hey, if you need supplies, let Rainbow know."

"Rainbow?" Cyn's expression looked almost pained. "There's actually a woman around here named Rainbow?"

Paige chuckled. "Rainbow Blu and she's rusalka."

"Holy— wow. Okay. Uh, she's not going to eat us or anything, is she?"

Paige shook her head as Faith came into sight. They acknowledged each other as Faith made her way through the crowd toward her, another woman in tow. "Okay. Get your list to me and I'll get it to Rainbow."

"Are you kidding?" Cyn spun in a slow circle. "I need to meet this woman. Rainbow!"

Rainbow turned and smiled. "Lost girl!" She hugged Cyn like they were old friends. The two of them were on their own since Paige didn't have any more time for delegating.

She did, however, grab Lynx and tug him back toward Cyn so he didn't get lost before plowing through the crowd to the corner.

Faith and the woman who had been talking about using the schools met her there. "Paige, this is Wendy Green. She's the head of the Board of Education here in our county."

"Oh." That would be the reason she was so knowledge-able about the schools.

Wendy was taller than most of the people there, and she didn't look phased by the press of people. She was calm, cool, collected. She held out her hand. "It's a pleasure to formally meet you."

"You, too. You found Faith."

"She found me."

"You offered our school up to the mundanes," Faith growled, sending an alpha push.

Paige pushed with her own alpha will. She didn't have the luxury of backing down. "It's a good idea."

"And the first time one of their kid gets hurt," Faith said, the scar on her face jumping, "they'll all cry to burn our homes to the ground."

Wendy held up her hands, her mouth open to speak. But she looked tired, as if she'd been trying to tell Faith things would be tough, but they'd weather through.

Yeah. Paige could read it all over Wendy's face. It was time to get Faith in line. She grabbed Faith's arm and pointed down the street where they could *see* demons through the tree line. "Do you see that? That's our death. And the death of every other man, woman, and child who lives here."

The people immediately around them calmed down, quieting to listen.

Faith might be the regional high alpha female, second only to Chuck, but it was up to Paige to somehow save the fucking town, and everyone in it.

Paige quieted her voice, but not her tone. And she kept pushing with her alpha will. "So, think again when you're shaking in fear about how your kid is going to hurt one of theirs and then they'll bring out their pitchforks."

The man from the tree leaned in on his way by and muttered, "We don't even *have* pitchforks anymore."

Paige snorted, but he continued on, knowing he wasn't a part of the argument.

Faith glared after him, but her gaze eventually fell on the demons just outside their wards.

"We're fucked, Faith," Paige said as quietly as she could. "I need you and Wendy to work this shit out. And just tell us what we're supposed to do with our kids and what shifts we have. Work with her."

Wendy made to speak again.

Paige cut her off and offered an apologetic expression. She really was out of time. She needed to get moving. "She's the alpha. Not only that, but she's the regional high alpha. So, you answer to her. Sorry. I know you're top dog in the mundane world, but you're in ours now. And what she says goes. But, Faith?"

Faith refused to meet Paige's gaze for a long moment.

Paige let the silence fill the space between them, her alpha will battling it out with Faith's, until the other alpha finally met her gaze. When it did, Cawli came to the top of her mind, roaring his will. It took effort to keep him back. "You listen, and you work with her." She infused each word with *will*. Not just alpha will, but her witch will as well.

Faith swallowed, the wind blowing a few strands of her long, black hair into her face. She let off the force of her will with a sigh. "Fine."

Paige released her own and turned.

Faith grabbed her arm and leaned in close to whisper, "But if you challenge me like that again, we *will* end this in a fight. And you might win, but do you really want the entire region?"

Paige turned to her and growled so low only Faith would hear her. "I don't want your region, Faith. I don't want your packs. I just want to survive this fucking war."

Faith studied her, and whatever she saw must have been what she was looking for because she let go of Paige's arm.

Well, that was certainly not something Paige had seen coming.

5

Dexx leaned against Paige's car, his arms crossed. "I thought you said you were ready to go."

"We're almost ready now."

Dexx tilted his head to the side. The rest of the DoDO people were milling about, swinging little sensors and gadgets around the area, sweeping them up into the trees and around the front of the station.

"Yup, they *look* ready. Was this a today thing, or engraved invitation thing?"

"Funny, mate."

"Mate? I thought only the Aussie's used that."

"Actually, we Brits use it more."

Dexx nodded. "Interesting. So, the big question is *why?* Why share? Since we *clearly* don't *need* you."

"What if you did? What if I was the only thing keeping you safe?"

"But we already *know* I'm the only reason you're still walking. So, I'm still not sold."

"Cute. I'm talking about the rest of the world. I think

you'll find it hard to do… things. Your purchasing power will be reduced, if I'm not putting too fine a point on it."

Well shit. This wasn't about fighting demons, this was about being able to live. In between fighting demons.

"So, you're working a blackmail angle here."

"See, they said you were thick. I said you weren't. But no, this isn't blackmail, this is life. Your kind isn't pure."

"Pure. How very Aryan of you." He'd bet they all thought he wasn't too bright. Maybe with some things, but he could smell a rat a mile off.

He could usually gauge a bad idea off Hattie's reply. *What do you think?*

He should not be trusted.

Not as far as I can kick him. But that's not what I asked. What do you think about checking out the facilities? We could do some recon, maybe learn something.

You think to lay a trap in the ambush. You think to play dead when you are already in their jaws?

Dexx smiled at Mario.

Good thinking, they'll never see that coming.

Hattie growled at Dexx. *Foolish cub.*

I think you mean sneaky.

"I'm getting bored. Mario. Are we leaving today? What kind of name is that for a Brit, anyway? Shouldn't it be Jeeves or Winston, or something equally British?"

Mario flattened his eyes at Dexx for a moment, then smiled tightly. "We're ready." Mario turned to his team. Excellent. Dexx still had the gift.

He clasped his hands behind his back, and half-skipped. "So, how do you intend to get us outside?"

Mario pulled his two-way radio out. "We need a portal at two-one-three mark seven. My position."

"Portal?" Of course. Gateway magick was pretty rare on

this side of the pond, but who knew what still lived over there. "You can do this anytime you want?"

"Of course. Why do you think I'm not worried about where I am?"

"*Of course.* How *silly* of me." Dexx stopped when Mario did, acting like he knew what was about to happen. Moments stretched into something longer, but then the air... wiggled in front of them. The air wavered and solidified into a hole with a room filled with people and equipment on the other side.

Okay, *that* was pretty impressive. "Neat trick. Remind me again how you keep getting your *asses* handed to you by demons?"

Mario gave him a dry look. "As you said, the learning curve is steep. But we don't make the same mistake twice."

"Can't. Not in this business."

The team filed through the portal until only Dexx and Mario were left.

Mario motioned for Dexx to go through first.

Paige had done something similar with the whole car and both of them inside, but that messed with Cab's electricals. Was this the same?

Banks of monitors with a technician at each lined a large room. Really, the place reminded him of Mission Control whenever a space shuttle went up. Honestly, the place was pretty neat.

They stepped into a golden circle in the middle of the activity.

Runes and symbols were inlayed with white marble inside a five-pointed star, flecked with bits of red and blue stone on a standard concrete floor. Gold and marble? He'd have to ask Paige about that. What was the crushed stone made out of?

"Welcome to our home. Well, home away from home."

Dexx sniffed the air, with help from Hattie. The tension-smell from Mario tapered away to nothing in a few moments. So, he felt fear out there, *whenever* he was out there. Good to know.

"Home isn't real inviting, but whatever blows your skirt up. The whole *E.T.* meets *Supernatural* dipped in Mission Control has a real mad scientist quality to it. Creepy, but I see why you like it."

"Whitty as ever, Dexx." Mario pulled his tactical vest off and hung it on a rack filled with the team's, then plugged it into a USB port on the side. "If you care to follow me, I'll show you where the magick *really* happens."

Mario busied himself stowing his equipment in labeled bins.

Dexx pulled out his phone and shot a text to Paige. *With Mario. Safe.* He pressed send just before Mario turned to face him with a smile.

Mario led them by one bank of monitors, and through a curtain of slatted heavy vinyl, like slaughter houses used.

Dexx eyed the monitors before he ducked through. Several screens showed the confrontation he and Paige just pulled DoDO's asses from. Most of the split screens showed the action from a body cam, and the rest of the screen displayed the vitals of that person. Two screens didn't have footage, but the names at the top were labeled D. Colt and P. Whiskey.

The goons probably didn't think Dexx had enough time to see the screens. With Hattie, he had all the extra sight he could have hoped for.

Dexx pulled Hattie up as he went through the doorway. *They watched the fight. And they have us recorded.*

Hattie nodded. *They lay a trap for you. They do it in your sight, so you know. They will use that to push you.*

That's the stupidest plan of all time. Unless they don't think we're very smart.

That is often a failing in the best predators. They become lazy.

Dexx grinned. *Good thing I watch TV.*

If Dexx hadn't seen the transition between the two rooms, he would have thought they went through another portal. "Now *this* is more what I thought you'd be into."

Mario stepped into what could only be described as the *X-men* mansion. Wide, dark paneled hallways led into rooms with desks and wall-length windows. Those were surely classrooms.

Hall niches held little objects. Maybe not little, but not big. He'd seen pictures of things like those. In Alma's— Paige's journals and grimoires. They looked old. Really, *really* old.

He stayed a couple steps behind Mario, but one of the objects *called* to Dexx. Not with sound, but he almost reached out for it before he stopped himself.

The things in this place just got more interesting by the minute.

An alcove held a suit of armor. Real armor.

Wow, these people.

Dexx shook his head.

Mario turned up a set of steps along the hall and went up.

Oh boy. Now I know how Wolverine felt.

At the top of the stairs, Mario continued to the end of the hall and knocked on a door. After a moment he opened the door and went inside.

Whatever Dexx had expected, it wasn't what he found. The office looked a lot like Oliver Eastwood's, spacious with a monitor on the desk and neat stacks of paper.

The woman behind the desk looked up from a second monitor recessed in a cubby on the desk.

She was pretty, like statues were pretty, and looked as hard. Okay, so not hard, but severe. Like the mean old aunt who always rode down on people. She only spared a glance at Mario, but then studied Dexx. In detail.

"Mario, how nice to see you."

"Mum, I've brought a guest."

"I see. You must be Mr. Colt." She stood from her seat and stepped in front her desk, offering her hand. "Angela Hopkirk. I've been hearing things about you."

They *knew* Dexx would be coming back with Mario. Probably the stupid earpiece they all had. "I hope it's all lies." Dexx took her hand and squeezed. He could play well with others when he had to. He put some pressure on the squeeze. Maybe not *that* well.

Angela's eyes narrowed.

Cub. Hattie warned. *It is not a good idea to step on a snake. The fangs go deep.*

Only if they get you. Dexx released her hand.

She didn't immediately rub her hand, but she did cross her arms.

"Since you're here of your own free will, I'd like you to stay a few days. I think there's a lot we could teach each other."

"A few days." Dexx repeated. "Sure. Teach me something."

Paige finally gave up and shifted into an elephant to get home because, otherwise, there was no way she was making it. She realized she could have chosen any shape, but she'd learned a lot about elephants in Alaska. Odd thing to learns there, but true. There was something rather peaceful about being one, and she could cover a lot of ground with very little effort. The woods had become a little tricky, given her size, so she'd changed into a fox for the rest of the way. Once at the house, though, she shifted back to human.

The kids, for once, were at the house. All of them. They were being good. Well, for kids. But Kate wasn't with them.

Paige shifted to a cheetah again and raced to Nick and Mark's cabin not far from the main house. Most of the shifters in their pack had decided to keep their homes off the ground and in the trees. That had seemed odd since most of the animals in their pack were wolves. But she wasn't going to judge. She skipped the rope ladder leading to her brother's house and climbed the tree with her claws instead.

And there was Kate, sitting in the living room, reading a book.

Paige shifted into a human again as soon as her feet found the floor. Nick didn't really have a front door so much as a wide opening. He said Mark liked the breezes. Their main house *was* on the ground with an entertainment area and theatre located in the basement. They had several rooms located at different levels around the tree that eventually led to the ground floor house, where Nick preferred to stay.

Nick the witch was afraid of heights.

Mark the human was fearless in the face of witches, shifters, and other occult danger.

She really liked him.

But neither of them was anywhere in sight. "Hey, Kate," she said, sitting on the couch. She really was a big fan of couches.

"Hey." Kate blinked balefully and closed her book, turning toward Paige. "You want my help."

"I do." If it was that obvious, then Paige *really* needed to work on her interpersonal skills. "How did you know?"

"You never come to see me."

Oh. Well, the girl had a point. "Sorry about that. We've just... we've been very busy."

Kate nodded. "You want to go to Underhill."

"I do. We need to get to Portland and we need to drive a truck there."

Kate shook her head. "Your truck won't work."

Crap. "Well, we've got a lot of supplies. How do you think we should do it?"

Kate looked down, thinking, her little elf face crumpled on the right side. "You'll just…" she stood and offered her hand. "Let me just take you so you can see."

Paige rose to her feet and took Kate's hand. She was thinking about how she was going to get down when she realized they weren't in Nick and Mark's living room.

She spun in a slow circle, looking around. It was like all the colors were muted. The jungle was thick— and it was a jungle. Not a rainforest jungle, though. She didn't even know what to call most of the plants she saw.

"This is what we call the Wildelands," Kate said. "And you need to be careful here. There are wilde creatures, and the plants will eat you."

"Great." If this didn't work, then… "Can we get to Portland through here?"

Kate nodded and raised a hand as she carefully walked forward.

Paige wasn't certain if she should shift, or if she should remain a human with full control of her magick. As an animal, she had no magick, and without it she felt a little naked. She followed Kate on her tired, human feet. She really should have worn better shoes, but the boots she wanted to wear required her to bend over and tie them. That just wasn't happening.

It was neat there. That was for certain. It was like stepping into a creative mind on cocaine. Maybe. Paige really didn't know her drugs. But maybe?

A flower snapped at her.

She jerked away and decided to keep her mind on the here and now.

Cawli crept forward in Paige's mind, intrigued.

Oh, so you decided to join us. Finally, she said with a laugh. Her animal spirit had been quieter as her pregnancy progressed.

I have never been here, he said with a happy growl. *I've heard stories, but my kind are not allowed.*

Oh, crap. *Is there a reason for that?* Like was he about to lose his mind? Would she lose control of her shift?

She felt Cawli shake his head in the back of her mind. *No. Nothing like that. We merely are not allowed into the land of the elves.*

Paige certainly hoped she wasn't about to get Kate into trouble.

Kate held up her hand and then disappeared.

Concerned, Paige hurried forward.

And stumbled into a parking lot overlooking the Portland docks.

How handy.

"Do you think you could do this for a large group of people, so we can get our supplies?"

Kate shook her head. "It will be dangerous."

"I'll make sure they're prepared to fight."

Kate ducked her head and thought. "No shifters. They're not allowed in Underhill."

"But you took me."

"Because you are a witch and witches are respected and revered."

Something finally flickered through Paige's mind. "You treated Dexx with respect. Why him? He's a shifter."

Kate smiled softly. "He's the first of the greatest," she said simply, then raised her hand and disappeared again.

Paige followed, having a better understanding of what she'd be walking into.

Kate dragged her to the ground as soon as she came through and put a small finger to her lips.

"I felt the tear in here," someone said.

"One of our own?" another asked.

Paige couldn't immediately tell if one was a female or the other male. If she had to guess, she'd have said they were both male.

"Not a wildeling," the first said, and continued with a sneer. "A darkling."

A darkling?

Kate glanced up at her with a faint hint of alarm, but quickly looked back down, her ear tip twitching as she listened.

"A dark elf. Here. Why?"

The first one smacked something nearby, making Paige jump slightly. "Who knows. But darklings, I don't care about."

The two wildelings walked away until their voices disappeared.

Kate stood and walked forward, gesturing for Paige to follow, and motioned her to be quiet.

Paige waited until they stepped into the backyard behind the Whiskey house. She turned around, a little amazed.

Kate flinched, her arm up as if to protect herself.

Now, that reaction didn't make Paige feel amazing. "What is the difference between a dark elf and a light elf?" she should probably start with the basics.

Kate lowered her arm and looked at Paige, gauging her reactions. "It is as it sounds. The dark elves follow the darkness."

Paige realized that could be evil, but everyone had thought *she* was evil because she'd been born the demon summoner. "Well," she said, looking around, searching for the words to say. "You don't look evil."

"I am not," the girl said indignantly.

"And I figure your 'darkness' is probably as misunderstood as the Whiskey's 'dark' gifts."

Kate raised one ebony eyebrow.

That expression was so damned adorable on that damned small face. "I'm a demon summoner. Everyone thought I was evil. My daughter, Leah? She's a necromancer. Lots of people think she's evil. Hell, even Ripley. She's a death-dog."

Kate's eyes widened in intrigue.

Paige nodded. "People thought she was evil. So, maybe we treat you like you're evil a little less and we just give you a chance to show us who you are instead."

Kate let those words sink in and then she nodded slowly.

"Okay. Serious question though." Paige considered throwing a funny question out there, but her humor was *seriously* broken. Like. All the way. It might even be forever. "How do we get all those supplies from Portland to here because if we don't? We're dead before the battle even begins."

6

When they got back, Rainbow was there, along with Leslie and most of the pack. Apparently, the commotion in the town had settled down enough for them to go home. Well, except for Rainbow. She just spent an awful lot of time on their couch. Especially of late.

But Paige was grateful because Rainbow and Leslie were a lot better at details than she was. Okay. She *could* be good with details, but in the past few months, there had been a sharp decline.

She was so ready to have these kids.

She stood there and listened to them, though, showing her support. Kate was hesitant about stepping up, and Paige had to tell them that the wildelings really were a danger, though, Rainbow seemed to think they weren't, for whatever reason.

Before Paige could fall asleep on them— or eat half of the refrigerator— the wards popped, letting her, all the Whiskeys, and the pack know a witch was at their front door.

Leslie stopped, and looked at Paige with a concerned frown.

Paige was hoping it was just Ollie Eastwood, because at least she liked him. She stood and held up a hand. "I'll go check it out. If I need help, I'll call."

Leslie frowned but nodded, settling back into her chair.

Everything seemed to happen around that dining room table.

The hallway from the kitchen to the front door seemed to be getting longer, if that was even possible. Of course, it probably had everything to do with the extra weight she was carrying in the most awkward place of the body possible. Why couldn't women get pregnant in a pouch like kangaroos and then make the men carry them like a sea horse? That sounded like a great idea.

But then she thought of Dexx carrying their children until they were old enough to run on their own and she changed her mind. She loved that man, and he was great with kids, but he was *rough*. Babies, while not super delicate, were still a little fragile. You only wanted to drop them once in their lives. Not repeatedly.

Oh, goddess, she was going to Hell or she'd be reborn as a fly a million times for being the worst mother of all time.

By the time she got to the door, the wagon had come to the front and stopped. A man and a woman were at the front. She immediately recognized the dark hair and eyes and the near Amish dress code as the Blackmans, most specifically Eldora and Derrick. Derrick was Paige's brother in the same way Ollie Eastwood was. They all shared the same father. It made Paige feel more than a little gross.

Oh, that family was just weird. Super weird.

The Blackmans were creepy in the "drink my Kool-aide" kind of way Paige just didn't appreciate. They'd wanted her to join their family when they'd arrived, to send her kids to their school, to join their way of life.

But Paige had politely told them no and had made bonds

with the shifters and other paranormals instead. She didn't regret that. Not one bit.

But she didn't quite know if that made the Blackmans enemies or not. They were led by Eldora, their coven leader, and the mother of Paige's *four* Blackman brothers. Derrick was just the oldest. Paige was the illegitimate child, along with Ollie, that Eldora probably wished she could forget all about.

Derrick jumped off the wagon and came around to help his mother. They didn't drive Amish wagons, but the old western kind with the long bed. But that's what they drove when they were home. Paige knew they had a car and could fit into the real world because the first time she'd met them had been in Texas when they'd hired someone to kidnap Leah in an attempt to see how strong Paige was. After that, they'd had the audacity to try to enlist Paige's help to take down their nemesis, Merry Eastwood. Paige had succeeded in that, of course, but it hadn't been to help her Blackman family members. It'd been to save and protect *her* family, *her* coven, *her* pack.

Eldora walked toward the porch.

Paige wasn't going to wait on formalities. She pointed to the wooden rocking chairs one of the wolf boys had made. She couldn't remember if it'd been Boot, Clem, or Garek. They, for whatever reason, seemed to meld together in her head.

Margo walked around the corner of the house, and stopped, folding her arms over her chest.

Paige held up her hand and felt her alpha will extend toward the woman, telling her without words to stand down, but to be on guard.

Margo nodded.

Since figuring out she could shift, Paige realized she could do a lot with that alpha will. She used it a lot more than she probably should and *had* been probably using it for a while and not even realizing it.

She sank into the chair and leaned back, waiting for Eldora to join her.

Derrick stayed at the top of the stairs, his back to them as he leaned against the post.

So, Derrick was the guard dog today. Good to know.

Eldora sat down and gestured to Paige's belly. "It looks like you're ready to give birth at any moment."

"I am. I think I was ready two weeks ago."

Eldora smiled. She was a handsome, older woman with little signs of aging, but not much. She was plump, which probably helped her look younger. Paige really didn't know just how old Eldora was, but she had to be about the same age as Rachel, which was just hard for Paige to wrap her mind around. Eldora and Rachel were the same age— roughly— because they'd shared the same man and had kids the same age. Roughly. Paige knew the truth, but… It was still just hard to imagine Eldora as…family.

"I remember when I was pregnant with that one." Eldora gestured to Derrick. "I was ten pounds heavier than I needed to be and it was all him. He was a big baby."

Leah had been a rather normal sized baby at seven pounds, so this pregnancy was a lot different. Also, thirteen years apart, which Paige was certain made a huge difference. "Well, I've got twins."

"You don't say." Eldora's eyes almost lit with interest. "Witch twins are a powerful thing."

Power wasn't something the Whiskeys were going to be in short supply of, that was for certain.

"And are they shifter witches, do you know?" Eldora tried not to look interested, and it showed.

Paige wanted to lie so hard, but how the hell was she

going to hide that? Seriously. "I know they're shifters. I've met them. In a spirit cave."

"Oh," Eldora said in real surprise. "You do like to do things differently."

Paige snorted and glanced at Derrick. "What are you here for?"

"Well, a few things." Eldora gestured at Paige's belly again. "Do you know where you're delivering? Here, I hope?"

Paige shook her head. "I'm going to have drugs. There are two of them. There are going to be drugs."

"So, the hospital, then?" Eldora's tone rang with judgement.

"Yup." She could go ahead and judge all she liked, but Paige wasn't crazy. She was about to push *bodies* out of her *vagina*. No. There was going to be *drugs*. There wasn't room for debate.

"Well," Eldora said, disappointed, "there are ceremonies and rituals that should be made when they're born, and it's best to do that when the placenta is still fresh."

Oh, goddess bless. This was just one more reason Paige thought they were completely out of their freakin' minds. That sounded so…cultish. "I had Leah in a hospital and she's just fine."

"And her gift exploded out of her, just like yours did."

Paige frowned. What the heck was this woman talking about?

"That's the reason your momma left you, isn't it? Your gift. Your Blackman gift."

"Look," Paige said as calmly as she could. "The demon summoning gift is a Whiskey gift."

"But not the way you have it," Eldora said patiently. "You also have door magick. That's the reason you're able to summon and banish demons so effectively. You're the strongest demon summoner born to the Whiskey line."

Maybe. "And you're trying to tell me if there'd been a ritual when I was born that my mother would have stayed? You obviously don't know Rachel."

Eldora's expression cooled as she looked away, her eyes unfocused like she was remembering something. "Oh, I knew your mother. I actually talked to her right before you were born."

Oh, shit. Paige hadn't known that.

"Yes." Eldora smiled. "My husband had told me what he'd done. He had a plan, you see, and the only thing I could do was to support him like a good wife. But your mother knew exactly what *she'd* been doing and had thought my husband was going to leave me to support you two. She was so very, very wrong."

Paige didn't know what to say about that.

"I told your mother that you would be born with a very powerful gift and that the rituals would need to be performed as you were born to ensure that your gifts didn't explode into maturity until you were ready."

"Or until you were."

Eldora's eyebrows rose. "You sound just like her. I believe she used the exact same tone on me."

That was something Paige didn't want to hear. She didn't want to be *anything* like her mother. Paige hated that woman with every fiber in her being. "What kind of ritual are you talking about?"

Eldora shrugged and then smiled. "It's rather simple, really. It just binds their abilities to you."

There was something in her tone, or maybe her body language that made Paige just not trust a word that came out of her mouth. Something said, *bind your gift to your children,* though Paige had *no* clue where that voice had even come from. "Well, I'll do things the Whiskey way, thanks. Normal babies. Normal births. We'll be fine."

"But shifter witches, Paige," Eldora said, sitting forward and placing her hand on Paige's knee. "Think about how powerful they're going to be."

Oh, she already knew they were going to be super powerful shifters. There was no way of knowing if they'd become witches, too. They might not. "I really don't care. I will teach them to learn control."

"Like you did?"

Oh, she was nothing like Alma either. "Alma banished my power. She made me promise never to use it."

"But you did anyway."

"Of course, I did. It was a gift inside me. It was like telling me not to use my hands because someone thought they were bad hands." Except they were hands that called demons, but whatever. Potato. *Potah*-to. "But the thing was, I learned. Not through Alma. Through someone else."

"A demon."

Well, at least she hadn't sneered. "I have no idea what Balnore is." But she was starting to suspect he wasn't a demon. Though, what the hell else could he be? One of Bastet's lovers? So... holy crap. That was a road she just couldn't travel just now. "My kids will have me."

"Like your current kids do."

If that bitch was trying to get her goddammed hands on Paige's goddammed kids to take them away from her the way Rachel had, she was in for it. "You want to stop there."

Eldora's eyes ticked, as if she saw the nerve she'd struck. She smiled. "I wouldn't do to you what Rachel did."

"I don't believe you. I think you want in any way you can get in."

"You're my daughter."

"No. I'm really not."

"My husband cared for you and so did I."

"The same way you care about Ollie?"

Eldora's eye twitched.

"Right. So, you only care about me now because I'm here. Because I'm your next-door neighbor. And, I'm guessing, because we're in the middle of a fucking demon battle and you want my protection because the Whiskeys are stronger than the Blackmans."

Eldora went completely rigid and then turned a frigid gaze on Paige. "We're not weak."

"Of course not, or your lands would be overwhelmed with demons right now."

"But our wards are taking a beating," Eldora forced out. "And I don't know how much longer they'll hold."

Well, they'd finally got to the heart of the matter. It'd taken long enough. "You want me to extend my wards."

"I want—" Eldora took in a deep breath and held it for a moment before releasing it. "I want to blend our wards with yours."

That would be a great idea if Paige *trusted* them, but she just didn't. She flat out didn't. She didn't want the Blackman magick tainting her Whiskey and wood magick wards. How would Eldora use that against her? She knew—she just *knew* that that's exactly what Eldora *would* do.

At some point, she was going to find a way to use those wards to... get at Paige? To worm her way into the Whiskey home? Because what had once been a ward around the Whiskey lands was now attached to the wards that enveloped Cyn's parents' house, and the ward over town. And that had taken the combined power of a lot of people. If the enemy got within their wards, then they would have free access to the Whiskey house. Crap. Shit.

Eldora saw the answer on Paige's face. She rose to her feet. "When the demons overtake us— and they will— just know that *you* are the one who brought the demons to *your* wards."

Well, when she put it like that.

Eldora walked back to the wagon and got up onto the bench.

Derrick turned around with a sigh. "You won't even consider it?"

Paige liked Derrick a lot better than she liked Eldora. His mother was always trying to manipulate people and Paige just *loathed* manipulators. Derrick, though? He was a straight shooter. He was still a Blackman and he'd *definitely* drank the Kool-aide, but he shot straight. "I'm afraid of what she'll do once her wards and her magick is combined with my wards and my magick."

Derrick nodded, glancing at his mother. Then he perched on the railing and leaned in a little, as if he was hiding what he was saying, so his mother— with her older hearing— couldn't hear. "What if it wasn't hers? What if it was ours? Just ours?"

"Ours?"

He nodded. "Your brothers."

She still didn't like it. She really should put additional wards around the Whiskey house, replace those. She hadn't even thought about it, but it was something she definitely needed to do. "Fine," she said quietly. "But the second your mother puts her magick into *my* wards, you're cut off. Completely. End of story."

He nodded and glanced at Margo. "How much trouble are we in?"

Paige groaned and leaned back. "A lot."

"So, you might need us as allies, anyway?"

That was a dark thought she didn't want to cross. "I'll be by in the morning."

He smiled and straightened. "Good. We'll be waiting."

She was sure he would.

7

Paige waited until the Blackman wagon was out of sight before she stood up.

Margo joined her on the porch. "I don't like her."

"Neither do I." Paige respected the *hell* out of Margo and her intuition. Margo and her brothers might have come to Dexx because no other pack would have them, but Paige was glad to have them. Well, Margo. She knew Margo a lot more.

"Are you really going to join the wards?"

Paige clamped her lips shut and then shook her head. "It's time to get our wards back up again."

"I was hoping you would say that. I feel better having *our* wards up and not sharing them with everyone else."

Paige grinned. When they'd first arrived, Margo hadn't agreed with joining with witches.

"I'll gather everyone."

"Great. Meet in the backyard." Paige disappeared into the house. If something wasn't happening at the dining table, it happened in their backyard. That was just the way this family worked.

She kicked a box as she moved to close the screen door,

keeping the wooden door open to allow the breeze in. She frowned and looked down at it. It was addressed to her and Roxxie. Frowning, she squatted to pick it up because there was *no* bending over. Oh, she was so looking forward to getting *her* body back! "Hey," she called, "where'd this box come from?"

Ripley popped her head into the hallway, her long, dark, wavy hair cascading down. "Uh, that one? I don't know. It just showed up at the door."

"And you brought it in?" That was another thing. With their wards down, anyone who was already inside the wards could get *in*. So, there was nothing protecting the house.

"It didn't look like death," Ripley offered and then her head disappeared toward the dining area.

It didn't look like death. Well, wasn't that helpful? Ripley was a death-dog. Kind of a shifter? Kind of. Though, it turned out that she was more of a witch whose ancestor had struck a deal with Death. Or had been cursed by it? Paige didn't remember. Either way, her shifter animal was a dog and she saw death. Neat trick, but not super helpful all the time.

Though, the box itself didn't scream uber evil vibes, so maybe Paige was overreacting. It was addressed to her *and Roxxie?* Who would send anything for the angel at the Whiskey house?

Goddess, she hoped Dexx would take her name. She didn't want to think of it as the Whiskey-Mooney-Colt house.

Okay. Random. And unlikely to happen. He was dead set against changing his name.

Well, she might not change hers. So... there.

She took the box into the dining room. The adults were gone, and it was just the kids, getting ready to play a game of UNO. Of course, when she said the kids, what she really meant was the kids and Joe and Ripley because they loved spending time playing games when they weren't running the bar.

Oh. That reminded her. "It's getting late. Don't you have to go to the bar?"

"It's closed," Ripley said. "A lot of people are willing to be nice and open their stores to people without money, but I can't. Liquor costs money." She tapped the deck.

Leah took it and started dealing them out.

Paige shook her head and went to the island to get a knife.

Leslie came out of Alma's room, the door next to the one that led to the garage. She gave Paige a tired look and joined her. "Tell me you got something fun."

"I have no idea what I got. It's addressed to me and *Roxxie*."

Leslie's face screwed up in confusion. "Are you going to slaughter me if I have a glass of wine?"

"Only if you don't pour me one." Paige retrieved the dull knife that everyone knew better than to use on anything other than opening boxes. "Just not a Leslie glass of wine." Because that was almost a bottle.

Leslie snorted and pulled down two glasses.

Paige cut into the box and peered inside. No body parts. Well, then, this was a good day. But the wooden box left her confused. She pulled it out. There were lines all over it and no lid. "It's a puzzle box." Paige hated puzzle boxes.

"That definitely shouldn't have been addressed to you, then." Leslie set a glass of wine next to Paige.

She picked it up and looked at how little there was inside of it. She really looked forward to the day when she could *drink* wine again. Enough to get her light headed and ready for bed. She tried pushing a few spots on the box, but then set it down in favor of the wine. "Maybe Roxxie's meant to figure it out."

Leslie picked it up and tried her hand at it. "That's if she wakes up with her mind intact."

That was a dangerously true statement. Whatever had happened to Roxxie had been bad. Really bad. And Paige was afraid to ask what that had been.

Paige gestured to the door to Alma's room. "Cyn and Lynx busy in there?"

Leslie nodded, then shrugged. "It's weird to watch. That girl, she just zones out. And then there's Lynx. I don't even think he's conscious as he's weaving."

Paige snorted, took her wine, and went to check on them. It was only right. She was tired and just wanted to sit down and play with her kids, to spend a little time with them. But that could wait. She had duties first. Always duties first.

Oh, crap. Wards. Backyard. Shit. Baby brain. Fuck. "We're gathering in the backyard to get our wards up."

"Oh," Leslie said, saluting with her wine glass, the puzzle box already forgotten. "Great idea."

Paige decided that it might be a good idea to use a little bit of Cyn's thread again, if she had some she could spare. She didn't want to overwork the woman, though she hadn't complained at all. Well, that was a lie. She knew *how* to complain. She just chose not to do it when Paige was in the room, which was probably a good idea. Paige had the patience of a hungry hippo.

She opened the door into her grandmother's bedroom. Most of Alma's things had been removed, so it looked like someone else's room now. It still had the spinning wheel and the large loom. Paige hadn't even realized her grandmother had either one of them. Alma had really been a mystery. Still was, really.

Shit. They were going to have to put her to rest.

Soon.

Fuck.

Cyn sat at the spinning wheel, wool or cotton or something going in, glowing, golden thread coming out. And that went to Lynx's loom where he wove it, the gold turning to colors and he created a fabric that—

Paige had no idea what it did. Honestly, they were dealing in a kind of magick that was completely foreign to her. She cleared her throat.

Cyn stopped spinning and turned to her. "Oh, hey, Pea."

It was so weird to hear someone other than family call her by that name, but she didn't have the heart to tell Cyn that was a "cool kids only" pet name. Because…Cyn kind of *was* part of the cool kids. They just didn't *know* each other super well.

Lynx still worked the loom, which was fine. Paige really didn't want to interrupt too much. "I wanted to just check and see how you're doing."

"Great," Cyn said excitedly. There was a very large pile of thread on the other side of her spinning wheel, and she still had a ton of energy.

Paige was a little jealous, but that's what happened when you were a generator, she guessed. "We're going to put up the wards around the house again."

"Ah," Cyn said. "You need thread?"

"Yup." The woman caught on quick, at least. She didn't know what Emma was saying about how Cyn liked to freak out about stuff. All Paige had seen was a perfectly normal woman dealing with a lot of shit rather well. Sort of well.

"You want us to help with the wards?" Cyn asked.

Lynx stopped and turned in his seat.

Paige wasn't sure what to make of Lynx yet. He'd been one of Bastet's temple cats for hundreds of years. Hundreds of years. Like… a servant to a goddess. A real one.

He smiled at her.

It was hard not to like him or to think he was suspicious

at all. She didn't think that man could lie. His face told her everything going on in his head. "Sure," she said, forcing her tone to go up with pleasure.

Lynx tipped his head to the side with a concerned frown. "Are you sure?"

And he could read people really well. "I'm just tired. Seriously. Yes. Please join our wards."

Lynx grinned and looked at Cyn. "I would be honored."

When he said it like that, Paige felt like a complete ass. This man was hundreds of years distant from anything resembling home, and he probably just wanted a place to belong.

Okay. So, he'd been a cat, but he wasn't exactly a stray cat. And, besides, he was *Cyn's* stray cat. Literally.

But that didn't mean Paige wanted to exclude him. In *any* way. She turned to Cyn. "If it's possible, we'll tie our wards to the grounding tree outside your home so both places are double protected."

Cyn's house was the gateway to the castle in the Vaada Bhoomi that housed their library. Hidden in that castle were the last two fragments of the key to Hell and there was no way in any reality Paige was going to allow Sven to have all three parts of the key. Ever.

Paige stepped back into the kitchen to discover the dining room abandoned and the house empty. As soon as she stepped into the backyard, she saw everyone.

It hadn't been so long ago when she'd thought the Whiskey family had been big with Alma, Leslie, Paige, Mandy, Tyler, and Kammy. Then they'd added Bobby and Leah. And Dexx. Then Nick. Then Mark.

Then, they'd come to Oregon and their little family had exploded. Margo, Clem, Garek— the two of those boys looked a lot alike— and Boot— who looked different with the boot imprint on his face— Alex, Ripley, Joe, Rainbow, and Michelle.

Frey stepped out from behind Boot and raised her chin as if to say, "Hey."

And then little Kate stepped out with a sigh.

They were only missing Dexx.

Cyn and Lynx followed her out of the house with a handful of thread.

Billie came around the back of the house and a look of surprise washed over her face at the crowd. Reece followed on her heels.

Paige was glad to see the wood witch, but her grandfather? Not as much. Paige really had issues with father figures in her family. They'd all abandoned her at some point.

Dexx had better not abandon *his* kids, or she was going to kick his *ass*.

Paige took a deep breath but refused to set her wine glass down. It was the only thing grounding her to the here and now. "We're going to put up our wards."

Tyler let out a hoot.

And Griff appeared around another body. That boy— Joe's brother or cousin or something? — was always around. Another one of the Whiskey strays.

Paige shook her head and held her hand out for the thread Cyn offered her.

Billie came to stand in front of her. "You can take the lead this time. You should know it well enough now."

Paige hoped so. She'd helped strengthen the wood wards in Alaska, and then the wards around the town. She'd have to figure this out for the Blackmans, too, and she might not take Billie with her. Not because she didn't trust Billie, but because of Eldora.

Reaching inside herself, she tapped her magick. It rose in inky black waves, threaded with silver from her thunderbird daughter and fiery orange from her rajasi son. She let the magick coalesce around the thread, melting it all together.

Then, she reached into the earth found a seed and began creating roots, wide and deep, healthy and strong. As the roots grew downward, a tree rose from the earth in front of her.

She should have placed the tree further from the house.

It walked backward.

The people who had been standing around shuffled out of the way.

Billie raised her eyebrows in surprise.

Paige was just grateful it had worked.

The tree grew bigger and more beautiful until it felt… right. Paige didn't have another word for it.

She closed her eyes and called on the elements. Earth rose with a nurturing smile at the babies in Paige's womb. Air ran around her, chittering like a school girl. Water rolled in, a little drowsy.

Rainbow reached out and the water came faster, as if awakened.

Paige carefully reached for fire. When *she* called it, it came from the bowels of the Earth. It wasn't the pleasant fire that Mandy called, but hot, rich lava.

With the elements in hand— which was a terrible way of describing it because elements weren't things you could *put* in your hand. Not really anyway— she touched them with her inky magick. Black turned white and blazed with silver, spiraling around the tree like silver veins, and working their way upward. They rose into the sky and then created a dome that came down around *her* family and *their* homes.

Cyn reached out with her golden light and that dome extended in a kind of tunnel almost toward her house. And then when Lynx added his blue light to hers, a dome appeared over it. Paige couldn't *see* it. It was too far away. But she *felt* it.

One by one, each of the people in their odd family added a piece of themselves to the wards, including Reece. He asked permission wordlessly.

She'd granted it. She had to.

When the last person joined their energy to the wards, the tree towered above the house and the surrounding trees, the bark white with the power of Paige's magick. The wards were flexible, strong, and powerful, taking the strengths of each person into them.

Paige touched her breastbone with her right hand, releasing the magick.

A resounding ping registered, sending leaves flying and branches waving from the force.

Paige looked up into the branches of *her* tree, *her* wood magick, protecting *her* family.

It felt good to be *home* again.

8

W hen Paige woke up the next morning, she knew—
she *knew*— it was time to put Alma's body to rest.
She sincerely wasn't looking forward to it, but it needed to be
done. And she wanted to get everything ready before she
went to the Blackman's to help them with their ward.

She really wasn't looking forward to *that*, either.

Getting up was easy that morning, knowing what she
needed to do, what needed to be done. She might be a hard
person to get to know, but she did what needed doing. That's
just the type of person she was.

Leslie was already downstairs working on a pot of coffee.
The one-cup brewer had died. For good this time. They'd
done everything they could to revive it. They just weren't
built to last. Paige often asked herself if they were really
worth the money. And then she'd have to make a pot of
coffee for one cup and the answer was immediately yes.

Leslie leaned against the counter, watching Paige as the
coffee pot gurgled. She was waiting for Paige to let her know
it was safe to talk.

It wasn't that Paige was a mean person. She just didn't

speak first thing in the morning. That was all. Her ability to *understand* what people *said* greatly lessened the earlier it was.

Sighing, Paige leaned against the counter beside her sister. "It's time."

She nodded and looked away. "It is. Backyard?"

That was the other thing Paige appreciated first thing in the morning. Brevity. "Yes."

"Where are you headed today?"

"Blackmans. They want wards up." Paige was tempted to ask Leslie to come, but she wasn't related to the Blackmans at all, so she really didn't want to get her involved.

"I'll take care of Grandma. You get back here before dusk."

That sounded like a good plan. The coffee pot had enough to steal another cup from, and she did so without making too much of a mess. She sipped at the cup as she walked through the back door and into the woods surrounding their rather large backyard.

She spotted Margo's tree house first. There wasn't much to see of it. Margo liked to keep things low-key.

The spare tree house was next. Margo had *insisted* her brothers be kept as far off to the side of the living area as possible.

Paige stopped at the bottom of the tree to the guest house and sent an air current up to rouse Billie.

Her head popped over the top, her black hair cascading down. "Leaving already?"

Paige nodded and saluted with her coffee cup.

"I'll be right down."

The tree houses had everything: plumbing, electricity. They were homes, so it was easy to assume that Billie'd had her coffee already. But Paige wasn't going to chance it. As soon as Billie's booted feet touched the earth, she offered the mug.

Billie grinned and took it, taking a sip before speaking. "So, what do I need to know about the Blackmans?" she asked as they walked at a leisurely pace back to the house.

It was strange to remember Billie didn't know all the families. "They have door magick."

"I've never heard of that."

Well, if she hadn't heard of the Blackmans, then that made sense. "We can open doors to other dimensions."

"Which is the reason you can send demons to Hell so easily."

"One of them." There was also a door to Hell imbedded in her bones, and she was the Whiskey demon summoner.

"Are they the good guys?" Billie asked with a sigh as they came within sight of the house.

Paige wished she knew the answer to that question. "I don't know."

"Fair enough."

They continued the rest of the way in silence. Paige downed the rest of her coffee and set the empty mug on the front step. She had talked to Ripley the night before about borrowing her truck, so she already had the keys. The Blackmans didn't use motorized vehicles often, so their driveaway left a lot to be desired, especially if you wanted to keep the bottom of your car in one piece.

She did, actually, which was another reason she'd asked to borrow the truck. The trail the Blackmans had possibly taken from their house to the Whiskey house was *probably* the game trail that ran off the road. It was a theory, but if worse came to worst, Paige could just shift and head to the Blackmans by herself.

She turned off the road just before the wards ended and headed back toward the river.

Billie grunted. "I haven't thanked you for what you did."

Paige didn't even remember what she'd done. "Huh?"

"Getting DoDO off my back."

"It's only temporary. As soon as this is over, they'll be back."

Billie nodded. "But it's a reprieve. I don't have to worry about them *and* these demons."

"You're welcome."

Paige really wished she was two kids lighter by the time they made it to the Blackman house.

They could visibly see where the wards ended. Demons lined the circumference. The wards extended past the road at the end of the Whiskey driveway and continued toward town. But as she turned away from town, she was quickly met with the end of the wards.

Okay. So, she could understand why the Blackmans would want their wards connected to the town's.

There was a small stretch between the two wards, but the gap was so small luckily the demons couldn't even fit between them. So, they'd been mostly fine.

She was going to see what they could do about extending the wards to the road. Because she wasn't going back that way. At least, not in a truck.

Coming up the backside felt a little like they were invading. They pulled up between fields where people in Amish-style clothes worked. She didn't know if they were all Blackmans or if they were all witches, even. But they all lived there in a sort of commune which gave Paige the heebie-jeebies. Probably because of the reports she'd heard about things gone bad. They couldn't all be bad. Right?

She sure hoped not.

By the time they made it to the house, they had a following. The people from the fields walked beside the truck or around it. They all looked happy enough, so there was that. She didn't *feel* like she was in trouble.

That was until Eldora stepped out of the house, and then

she felt like a dark cloud had crossed over the sun. When she looked up, there wasn't a cloud in the sky.

She pulled the truck to a stop and got out. "Eldora."

"Paige." Eldora smiled, but it didn't look like a complete smile, like she meant it. It looked fake.

Billie got out of the truck and smiled, her hand out. "Billie Black."

Derrick was the first to take her hand with a huge grin. "Nice to meet you."

A few other introductions went around as Paige pulled Eldora aside. "Where do you want your ward tree?"

"I don't understand this ward tree."

"That's because it's not our kind of magick. It's hers. She's a wood witch."

"I've heard about them."

Paige wasn't certain what she'd heard, but by the tone of her voice, it hadn't been awesome. "Well, she's here to help. So, be nice."

With all the Blackman's gathered— well, all the people there gathered— Billie led the creation of the ward tree. They all put their energies to it.

Except for Paige. She just had the sneaky suspicion she shouldn't. It was a gut feeling, and she'd learned to trust those.

But when it was time to connect the Blackman ward to the town ward, Billie turned to her. The tree was wider than it was tall, but it looked sturdy. She didn't say anything. She needed... well, kind of a key. Almost. Except that it was magick. It was the touch of Paige's soul, to tell the other wards it was okay to connect with this one.

With one touch, she gave her wards— the town wards— her approval and a note rang out. This one didn't move many branches, but it was low and toll-like. And it had none of Eldora herself in the warding.

Eldora blinked, looking around with a smile.

The demons who had been around their rather tight wards were gone.

"Just remember," Paige said under her breath. "If Trout-dale falls, your wards will, too."

Eldora gave her a cool expression. "Then don't fall."

That wasn't the response she'd been looking for.

***

Dexx mom-armed Alwyn back against the wall. He let up and gave the signal to stay pressed hard against the wall.

Alwyn tossed a can of magickal smoke in the room.

A fireball scorched through right where he'd been standing and cleared the smoke away almost instantly.

The two shared a look and scooted back the way they'd come.

Three days, and three demons. All in different places. Alwyn said they were in Mexico City. The heat almost confirmed it.

One small demon nest. Just like the others. If there was one thing certain, every "nest" was different except that even *one* demon was enough to kill a bunch of pretend hunters.

Good thing Dexx wasn't a pretend hunter.

He lowered himself to the ground and motioned for Alwyn to do the same. He pressed himself to the wall as tightly as he could, with nothing taking space that shouldn't be.

Alwyn had a hard time, considering he had the bulky tactical vest loaded with unneeded things. Unneeded for *this* case, but nobody would know that until they faced off with whatever it turned out to be.

So far, DoDO turned out to be little more than poseurs. They had a training facility of sorts, with lots of classrooms, history, and things, but real demon hunting and killing didn't look like anything they trained for.

They certainly weren't ready for what they found. Not with Dexx in the lead.

Dexx yanked Alwyn close, and whispered fiercely, "You—" he tapped Alwyn's chest, "—stay here." He pointed at another of the team. He didn't even know his name. "You, I want you to circle back and catch it from behind. If you can't, take up position and blast anything that isn't us that comes through. Clear?"

The DoDO looked ready, all dressed up in his gear, but he smelled thick with fear. DoDO had rotated his crew every day; except for Alwyn.

The new guy would get them all killed, but at least he kept his fear from showing. His buddies might appreciate that until he got them dead... or worse.

Outside lights from the city cast deep shadows in the new construction. Hattie made sure he saw everything almost as well as high noon, but his team had to rely on tech.

He'd had a brief, but adamant talk with his team before they entered the building that under no circumstances were they to lead with those things that dissolved demons.

If he could capture one, they could... Well, something. Sven *had to be* playing a game.

Alwyn nodded.

If nothing else, Dexx had earned their trust. Three days and three demons. Nobody died.

Their body cams had to be getting a lot of useful data, but not from Dexx. He refused to wear the vest.

If DoDO helped with Sven, maybe they could find common ground somewhere. Paige would be happy to hear that.

Hattie's improved ears picked up a sound.

The demon wasn't hiding too well.

Dexx slid forward a few inches. *You think this is a trap? It's not scared, and it knows we're here. No way it couldn't, not with these guys clomping around.*

They are better today than yesterday.

Shut up, fat cat. As much as he hated to admit it, they *did* learn. And stealth was important.

Alwyn leaned close to Dexx's ear. "Why don't you shift? You could kill this thing easy, right?"

And let them record Hattie? No way. "We don't need her. Besides, I like these pants."

Alwyn twisted his head to the side in confusion.

"You ready for this?"

Alwyn nodded once.

Dexx charged around the corner, *ma'a'ashed* in hand.

The demon turned and smiled.

The thing looked like it had been carved from a pile of boulders. Its skin too dark to be grey, bordered on black with deep golden tones, looked like veins of gold peeking through a mine wall.

Large bat-like wings extended, making the beast more than a little intimidating. "Shedim, stop."

Shedim was the demon's name for him. Shedim Patesh. Demon Hammer.

The request worked. Dexx skidded to a halt. "What?" Demonology one-oh-one. Assume everything a demon says is total bullshit.

"Do not send me back. I want to work for you. Tales have a demon working for you."

Tarik. He's the only demon Dexx would ever trust, and he was a djinn. "Yeah, so you want the same deal?"

"I will pledge myself to you. Spare me, and I am yours."

"Mine? Who the hell talks like that? And *why* would I believe you?"

The demon deflated, the wings shrank and disappeared,

until finally the demon looked like a man in a suit. He looked a lot like Ollie Eastwood, really.

"Dexx?" Alwyn called from behind the corner.

"Stay back. I've got this." He held his *ma'a'shed* in front of him.

"I am Furiel. Long I have waited for a chance to turn from my chosen path. I watched and waited."

"For what, someone to lead the way? So again, *why* do I need to believe you?"

"I have information you can use. I have heard Sven Seven-Tails speak."

"Me too, but that doesn't mean I know what he's planning."

Furiel bowed slightly. "What I meant was that I have heard what he has planned and how he will accomplish that. I swear by all that I am that I will not try escape, and I will speak plainly."

"No fuckin' way." But wasn't that what he was just asking for? A demon he could interrogate? "You were there when you tried to fry us all, right? Or was that your way of opening dialogue?"

That was the right word, right?

"The smoke was magickal. Meant to paralyze and not kill. And I had to be sure it was you. You *are* the best."

"Dexx?" Alwyn peeked around the corner. "What are you doing?"

Turning his body so he could see Furiel and Alwyn at the same time. "I said stay back and be ready."

Alwyn retreated.

"So, I've always wanted to know, does it hurt when you go back? Do they punish you for failing?"

Furiel cocked his head to the side.

"Never mind. Okay I want a show of good faith here. You think I can save you. But I know you're full of shit. So, help me out here, what will you do so that I believe you? Oh, and if you try anything, I'll kill you. Send you back, whatever."

Furiel smiled.

Perhaps it was meant to be reassuring, but the smart money said be ready when any demon smiled.

As he reached into his suit coat pocket a door slammed open and his scared little buddy screamed a war cry and fired.

"No!" Dexx tried to stop the shot, but as Dexx moved, the demon moved, and disappeared.

Gone.

"Well fuck. Thanks for barging in here and turning it all into a big lump of bollox." Dexx speared the kid with a stare.

"That was a demon. You said to hit it from behind."

"And you just thought shooting first was a good way to help me? When I was right here?"

Dammit. He sounded like Paige.

"Call for a portal. Let's get back." The portal opened, but no dead demon to account for this time.

Dexx had no more touched a foot to the concrete in the bunker than Mario was at him. "What do you think you're doing *talking* to a demon?"

"Communication. That would be communication." Dexx had a few inches on Mario, and he used the extra to tower. He couldn't really tower, he just wasn't that tall. He brought Hattie up a little but had to restrain from more.

She had pushed since the time they stepped out of the portal. He *really* wanted to keep the clothes he had.

Relax fat cat, we have to play nice.

We should not be here, cub.

Dexx backed down from Mario. "Look. I had the situation under control. He was talking. Might have been a load of crap, but it might have been a crack in their walls. And I was going to get it figured out when trigger-happy-Howdy-Doody started blasting rounds."

"He acted according to his training."

Really? Mario was defending that waste of resources?

"Great. Glad he had the best teachers. I'm going to bed. I'm tired."

"Colt, you *will* learn discipline while you are here."

Dexx's first instinct was to leave back to Troutdale, but Paige wafted through his thoughts. They *had* to know what DoDO was up to.

Dexx inhaled deep and let it out slow. He relaxed his shoulders. "While I'm here, I will learn discipline."

Mario twisted up his expression. "See, not that difficult, is it?"

"Nope." Too flippant. "But I'm still tired, so I'm still going to bed." He pushed by Mario and to the too fine house.

He was awakened in the morning by a text from Leslie.

Dexx blew out his cheeks and let his phone flop to the bed. "Son of a bitch."

He picked it back up and hit Tuck's number.

"Dexx. You aren't about to do something stupid are you?" Tuck had reason to believe Dexx might.

"No. Actually, I want to invite you. Today is the day we, uh, Alma. We're going to… she's—"

"When?"

Tuck went from accusatory to sympathetic faster than Jackie could break tires loose. "Sundown. I would appreciate if you could come pay your respects, too. I want to warn you though, this isn't how people usually do these things."

"You guys never do the usual. I'll be there."

"Thanks Chief. See you tonight." Dexx swiped the phone off and dressed.

Dexx met Mario in the chow hall. They called it something different, but that's what it was, a chow hall. Dexx picked every member of every team he'd been sent out with over his days at DoDO.

Alwyn sat just a few spaces down from Mario.

"I need a trip back home."

"You done already? Didn't take you for a quitter."

Alwyn smirked.

"I'll be back tonight. But I have something I need to do. At home."

"Tonight?"

"Yeah. You have my word. Which I would say is a bit better than yours right now."

"Fine. What's so important you need to go back?"

"I have to see a man about a horse."

They stayed a lot longer than Paige had intended. Billie had to give Eldora instructions on how to maintain the ward, and then they'd invited Paige and Billie for lunch. She'd been floored to realize *that* much time had passed.

Then Paige and Billie drove along the ward's edge to see if there were any weaknesses and to discuss the possibility of enlarging the wards. They'd invested the entire afternoon at the tree downtown working with the locals, the mundanes, to see who could add their power to the ward tree.

Surprisingly, quite a few. The tree refused to take kids, but the adults? The tree accepted all of them. Neither she nor Billie understood that one at all, but Billie said that Paige's trees were different than typical wood witch trees, so there were several possible reasons.

While intriguing, they weren't important. With the sun sinking in the sky, it was time to go home.

Paige and Billie weren't the only ones headed to the Whiskey house. It turned out quite a few people had been told about the burial, including normal people in the community. It was a big gathering, and almost reminded Paige of

Sunday picnics after church, the kind she never went to but always saw in Hallmark movies.

She was a sucker for a good Hallmark movie, though she'd *never* tell Dexx.

There were several folding tables set up around the house with food on most of them. It seemed like people were treating this as a potluck. Most of it was homemade, which was an upside to being cut off. They couldn't buy junk food. They had to make their own.

She didn't know most of the people who were there. She tried to grab Leslie's attention, but she was being assaulted by random people, so she failed. Well, not really assaulted, but she was the one organizing everything, so everyone was looking to her for directions.

"You look like you just stepped into another world," a woman said with a chuckle in her voice.

Paige turned to see Wendy Green.

She wore a pair of jeans and a plain tank top. She held out her hand. "Good to see you again."

"Didn't expect to see you here," Paige said with a chuckle of her own. "What happened?"

Wendy shrugged. "We heard you were—ah, going to, well... your grandmother. A couple of us thought we should show our support. She..." Wendy blinked rapidly and looked away. "We know what she did for us and we have a lot to be thankful for."

Paige felt the tears rushing to the top, but she cut them off at the pass. Well, she tried. They formed a knot in her throat she had to swallow down several times. "Thanks. But, uh, this is a couple of people?"

"Well, a couple of people told a couple of people, who told a couple of people."

Paige could see that.

"I think more than a few of them are here to see if you're real witches."

Several of those people had *seen* her shift into an animal. She'd done it right in the middle of town. "Well, I was kind of going for more of an intimate… thing." The word slipped her mind. Pregnancy brain. But she didn't think Alma would appreciate having a bunch of strangers coming to her funeral, looking for a show.

"If you need us to leave, we will." Wendy gave Paige's arm a squeeze. "We're *really* just here to give our support."

That was nice and a little hard to accept. They'd been forced to live in hiding for so long, it was hard to fathom being "out of the closet" and accepted at the same time.

Wendy tugged her toward one of the tables. "You should see all the tuna casseroles."

Paige's surprised laugh was a little loud.

Wendy laughed with her. "What do you bring to a funeral? Tuna casserole. I don't know why."

Paige finished laughing, her emotions she'd suppressed for the past few days rising up again. "That's a lot of tuna. Maybe you taste less when you're grieving?"

Wendy flattened her still smiling lips, her dark eyes tinged with sorrow. Not a sorrow she felt, but an empathetic sorrow. "Maybe it's that."

Paige took in a deep breath, not pushing Wendy's hand away, and turned to survey the crowd. They really did have a lot of people there. "They're really all here for Alma?" she whispered.

"Yeah," Wendy said, her eyes welling with tears. "We are."

Paige didn't need to see other people cry. Especially people who'd never met Alma. She pinched her lips together and turned away, brushing away the tear that escaped.

"Well." She closed her eyes, sorrow hitting her hard as she attempted to think through what she had to do next.

Wendy didn't ask. She just wrapped Paige in her arms and held her.

Other arms joined hers until Paige felt like she was surrounded by a whole pile of people. But she didn't care. She let her tears silently fall, her body wracked with quiet sobs. She wasn't sure whose shoulder she had buried her face in, or whose shirt was getting soaked. She took the tissue that was offered and wiped ineffectively at her nose.

And when she was strong enough, she stood on her own.

The people gathered around her weren't... *her* people. But they offered supportive smiles and more tissue. Without questions, or judgement or demands.

Maybe, just maybe, things would be *better* after all of this was over. There was hope.

Wendy gave Paige's hand one more squeeze and then let her go.

Paige mouthed "thank you" and headed toward Leslie, who had managed to find a break in the people. "What happened?"

Leslie shrugged. "They just started showing up." She headed toward the backyard.

Paige followed. "I really wasn't intending on putting on a show."

"We're witches. Well, we're the *kind* of witches who *don't* put on a show. But..." Leslie paused once they got to the backyard, her eyes focused ahead. "I think it's happening tonight whether we like it or not."

Paige had to agree. "Where's Grandma?" she asked quietly.

"In the kitchen."

Seemed appropriate.

They stood in silence for a bit longer.

"You ready for this?" Leslie whispered, her lip trembling, but her voice strong.

Paige took in a shaky breath and whispered back, "No."

Taking each other's hands, they walked back to the house to gather their grandmother. The sun was setting. It was time.

Dexx met them in the kitchen, his eyes rimmed with red, standing next to Alma's linen-wrapped body. "You didn't think you were doing this without me, did you?"

Paige went to him and hugged him tight, so glad he was there. She hadn't wanted to pull him away from DoDO. She'd thought she could handle this on her own. "How's DoDO?"

"We can talk about it later."

"Are you staying?"

He shook his head. "I'm going back. There's a few more things to do."

"Okay." But at least he was there for this.

Together, Paige, Dexx, Leslie, Tru, Margo, and Reece carried Alma's cloth wrapped body to the pyre that had been built in the back. People parted to make a path for them, several reaching out, as if offering support.

They laid her on the ground and stepped back. The Whiskeys gathered close.

Reece stood at the pyre a while longer, head bowed. He placed something small on Alma's wrapped body and walked back to them, still with his head bowed, tears falling.

Paige was overwhelmed with emotions, she still had a hard time believing they were sincerely there to offer comfort. In her heart of hearts, she knew at the first sign of trouble, these very same people would be the first ones to cast rocks at them. She wanted to rail at them, to tell them to go away.

But then she saw Wendy's face.

And Ripley's.

And Cyn and Lynx and Garek and Chuck and Faith and Tuck and Joe and Griff and Billie and Michelle and…

And realized she was probably thinking out of grief and not with her head on real straight.

They placed Alma's body on the pyre with a little help from Paige's water, Leslie's wind, and Billie's roots.

Dexx stood beside Paige, silent. On her other side with Leslie, Tru took their hands.

Leslie gestured to the pyre. "Should we say something?"

Paige had no idea. She was all emotion and no thought. "Were we going to say something before?"

Leslie numbly shook her head and just stared at Paige.

She looked up into the sky and saw the moon, full and pure, brightening as the sky darkened. She turned her tear-tired eyes to Leslie. "Help me call down the moon."

Leslie smiled, but her expression folded into tears. She didn't sob. She let them fall quietly and nodded.

Wordlessly, Paige closed her eyes, pushing more tears to fall down her cheeks, and raised her hands to the sky. Alma had always been the one to lead before. Now, it was their turn.

Paige called on the earth. She rose easily, murmuring as she always did to the babies in her womb. The ground rumbled slightly under their feet, but nothing major.

The air came to Leslie's command, running through the crowd, dancing in everyone's hair.

Billie stepped up and raised her hands, the branches of the nearest trees shifting, sprouting more leaves, and then reaching toward them with vine-like grace.

Leah raised her chin and flicked her fingers, water rolling from the river, cartwheeling toward them.

Rainbow squealed with delight.

Mandy stepped forward and called on the fire, both of her hands lighting with it. "Should I, Mom?"

Leslie blinked and nodded. "Yeah, Man-Pan. Do it." Fire wound slowly to the pyre weaving through the wood, catching both the dry and wet easily.

Tyler raised his voice and sang a song without words, filled with all the emotion of a young boy.

Nick joined them and pointed a single finger, glancing at Paige, then Leslie, and the fires that licked at the wood of the pyre turned white with soul energy.

With all the Whiskey elements joined as they'd never been joined before, Paige wove them together, like a braid, and reached up with their combined energies toward the moon itself.

It wasn't like what people thought. She wasn't reaching to the far distance of the actual moon. She reached for the energy of the moon, what the millions of people projected up to it; the longing, the hopes, the dreams, and wishes. She gathered their energy, then pulled. Drawing down the moon.

The moon's energy filled each of the Whiskeys. She saw it in the others first. Tyler, then Mandy, Leah, Nick, Leslie, Billie— who wasn't a Whiskey, but Paige was claiming as theirs— and then finally Paige.

It felt like . . .

It felt like touching Alma.

She could almost hear Alma's voice in the back of her mind, hear her laugh, or how surly she'd get if you refused one of her cookies.

Memories. She was reliving her memories.

The good ones. And there were a lot of those.

Like when Paige had told them she was pregnant with Dexx's kid and the look of joy on Alma's craggy face as she'd briskly said, "Well, it's about damned time."

Or the time Paige had come home after flunking a test in college and they'd made F's-Aren't-So-Bad-Oatmeal cookies.

The bad ones. There were a few of those, too.

Like when Alma had forbidden her to use her gifts and had made her feel horrible for being a demon summoner.

Or when she'd *banished* those gifts after Paige had summoned a demon to kill Rachel, who'd taken Leah.

They all flowed through her, and by the looks of the others, they were relieving *their* memories as well.

Paige couldn't hold onto the light of the moon for much longer. It wasn't theirs to keep, only to borrow. She gave the rope a brief tug to let everyone else know what she intended to do.

One by one, they nodded, letting her know they'd said their good-byes.

Good-byes.

Reece hung on, almost desperately, but finally, he too, let go.

When it was her turn, Paige almost couldn't do it. She didn't want to. Everything inside her cried out to keep Alma there with them for just a little longer. To refuse to let her go.

But then she heard Alma's voice say, *It's time. You can't keep me here forever.*

Paige didn't know if it was the magick, the moon, or her imagination.

Leah looked at her, her big, blue eyes wide.

Had she heard it too?

Paige swallowed, fighting around the tears to do it. *I don't want to.*

You have to, child.

The last time they'd talked, she'd called Paige child. *How do we do this without you?*

The same's you been *doin' it.*

That wasn't the answer Paige wanted to hear.

You lot are a lot stronger than I ever was, and trust me, you got this.

Paige took a deep breath. She hoped so. *I don't want to say goodbye.*

Well, I don't want to haunt your scrawny butt forever.

Someone chuckled in the crowd.

Was everyone hearing this?

Paige licked her lips. *Will you be okay?*

Yeah, Peanut. I'll be fine.

Leslie took Paige's hand and squeezed. Hard.

Paige didn't dare to look at Leslie's face. She was afraid to see all the emotions running there.

You gotta let me go, Peanut.

A sob escaped. One with sound. A whimper, really. "I can't."

You can.

A hand of light and life touched Paige. Teal. Alma's magick. With that came a push, a push to release the magick of the moon, to release Alma.

Dexx squeezed her shoulder. "I've got you, Pea. I will *always* have you."

Paige nodded, struggling to regain control of her emotions with each nod. "I love you, Grandma."

A chorus of I love you's and good-byes and thank you's followed.

And then...

Paige did what she had to.

She released her hold on the moon.

10

The next morning, Paige felt better. She wasn't over her grief, but it wasn't as hard to push it down as it had been. It didn't feel like a fight, even though she wasn't the kind of person to truly focus on that anyway. She was the type of person who said there was nothing wrong and that she'd be okay. She was like that knight at the bridge in *Monty Python* who was trying to keep people off the bridge without his legs and arms and *still* saying he could take them on. Yeah. That was her.

Which was why she was *this* pregnant and still in the frelling fight.

She went into the backyard with her coffee cup in her hand, hoping to the All Mother she wasn't doing damage to her babies. She stopped in surprise at what she saw.

Clean.

Tidy.

Everything put away.

It didn't *look* like half the town had arrived at her home the night before to send her grandmother to the afterlife.

And that thought didn't choke her up.

She closed her eyes and breathed a sigh of relief. She was just glad she was able to get mostly past it.

Dexx had disappeared again after tucking her in, saying it was his turn to be dark and mysterious. She worried about him. Yes, it had been her brainy idea to send him into the lion's den, but they really *did* need answers. She didn't think for one moment DoDO was ever going to be an ally, or even anyone she could trust.

She felt naked without him.

But she was okay. She opened her eyes and whispered, "Bal, I need you. And don't make me summon you. You *will* regret it."

A few seconds later black smoke appeared, and he stepped out of it, looking like he always did. Dress pants, nice shoes, dress shirt, no tie. His shirt sleeves were rolled up. Dark hair brushed back and always well-kept. Dark, beady eyes.

She really should be mad at him, but it felt like her dad had arrived and she really needed him. Lilim or not. Demon or not. Whatever he was, or not. She needed the only man in her life who had been there for her since she was a kid and who had never *truly* turned his back on her. Well, there were a few times, but not really. He'd never *abandoned* her.

His expression folded as he took in her face. He was to her in three strides, taking her coffee so he didn't spill it and wrapping her in his arms.

She missed his smell, the feel of his arms when he held her. *He'd* been the one to keep her together after Mark's death— not Nick's Mark. Leah's father, Mark Eastwood. He'd been there when she'd fallen apart after Leah had been taken by Rachel. He'd been there through her career, in high school, middle school. All the schools. Helping with demons. Going where he was needed, where she couldn't be.

She just held onto him. She didn't have any more tears, thankfully. She was tired of the clogged nose headache.

"I'm sorry, Peanut."

Alma didn't know this, but *she* wasn't the one who's started calling her Peanut. That'd been Balnore. Paige didn't know how it had caught on, but it was one more way of reminding her of him when he wasn't there. Though, now she knew he was a Lilim, whatever that was, it might explain a little.

She pulled away, pecking a kiss on his cheek, something she hadn't done in *years*, and took her coffee. "I have questions."

The last time she'd called him with questions, he'd turned her away. This time, he licked his lips and nodded once.

Okay. She might actually get some answers. "What is a Lilim and don't give the me the Lilith and an angel shit. I need to *know* what you *are*."

He drew himself up and moved to take a step away.

She wasn't letting him off *that* fast. "I just need to know, Bal. Please."

He stared at her for a long moment and then bowed his head. "I'm... kind of a demigod, I guess. Like Bastet."

"She's a full goddess, dear."

"But not like the All Mother, or God."

True. And Paige had always wondered why that was. "So," she flattened her lips and raised her eyebrows, trying to show him she was okay with that, "it makes you pretty badass."

He snorted and rolled his eyes slightly. "Makes me *very* badass."

They laughed for a minute.

But then Paige's humor fled. "We're screwed, Bal. I don't know what to do."

He looked up and rubbed her shoulder.

"You're a *demigod*. Can't you do something?"

"No. Even as powerful as I am, I'm still not as powerful as him. I've been working for the past two years to keep him from getting *any* power. But, it seems I've failed."

"You and me both."

Bal wrapped his arm around her shoulders and guided them toward the picnic table. "I like what you're doing, though. I think it's really going to work."

She hoped so. "The wards are holding."

"But at some point, you're going to need more than wards."

That she knew. "We have Dexx, who's a really powerful shifter."

"He's more than that, love."

"Like?"

"Well, Hattie is the first of the big shape shifters. Not the ancients. They're still greater than she is, I guess. But they're volatile and more than a little unstable. But Hattie? She was the first big shifter who came with a great deal of power and the stability that was needed to make a difference in this world."

"First of the greatest." That was a line from the stupid prophecy. "Well, we've got them, and Leslie and Robin."

"Robin. That's what she's decided to call him?"

Paige chuckled as they got to the bench and she sank onto it. "Yeah. And we've got me and the power of the wee ones. I can feel them. They're sharing their power with me."

"Be careful with that," Bal cautioned. "They're ancients. There's a reason my brethren forced them to remain in the safety of Vaada Bhoomi."

"Okay. So—" Because she *had* to say it out loud. "You're Thor's brother."

Bal shook his head and held up a hand as he sat beside her, draping his arm on the table behind her. "The Norse Gods are nothing like we are. They come from a different planet."

"Another one that God created."

"No. One like him, though. But, no. Thor is not my brother."

"Is he stronger than you?"

He gave her a look intended to kill, she was pretty sure. "Yes. But he's also dumber."

She laughed and shoved his ribcage with her shoulder, careful not to slosh her coffee. But then she sobered. Again.

"Tell me."

He always seemed to be able read her mind. "I need to know you'll be here when we need you."

"Peanut." He took her chin and forced her to look at him. "Now that you've learned what you needed to, I'm not going anywhere."

She didn't want to tell him just how great it felt to know her father-figure— who happened to be a freakin' demigod— was going to be standing by her side in the biggest battle of her fucking life. "Thank you."

He gave her a look that told her she should never have had to ask, then pressed a kiss to her forehead as he stood. "Now, if that's all, then I need to go. There are things I'm working on that need to be watched."

She could get behind that. "Am I doing everything I *could* be? Am I missing anything?"

He shook his head. "I'm sure there's something. We need to figure out how to cut him off from his power first, and then how to take him out. I'm working on trying to cut him off from his power."

That was great news.

"So, you focus on taking him out."

She could handle that. She hoped. "Will do." She gave him a two fingered salute.

He turned to leave, but then turned back as the dark smoke gathered around him. "I will miss Alma."

"Thanks," Paige whispered.

But he was already gone.

11

Leslie had no idea how Paige expected her to just get the supplies coming.

She'd asked it like it was some easy task she could just *do*.

Though, knowing Paige, that was exactly why she'd given the task to Leslie. Because she knew what a hassle the entire thing was.

Dolly stood in front of her, a hand on her wide hips. "Are you trying to tell me I can't get my medicine? Is it because I'm not special enough?"

Dolly had been here for the last thirty minutes trying to get Leslie to risk life and limb over skin cream.

Skin cream. It didn't matter what Leslie said. This woman could not get it through her head they were only risking their lives for the essential stuff.

It was time for a different tactic. "Look, Dolly, I'm sure that your skincare products are incredibly important. Life and death important. So, I'm going to let you join us."

Rainbow's eyes grew three times bigger. She had gone through Underhill with Kate just one time. And when she'd come back, she had a whole new appreciation for the elves and where they lived. And if Dolly had any sense in that big brain of hers, she would have read that all over Rainbow's face.

But Dolly only cared about Dolly. Even in the face of war.

Still, it was good to see something was finally sinking in because the look on Dolly's face said it wasn't worth her life.

"I'll just call Chuck now and let him know she'll be joining the team. Rainbow, can you please get ahold of your contact and tell them they need to pick up this skin cream…" Leslie looked over at Dolly. "What was it called again?"

Dolly held up her hands and took a step back. "It's not that important."

Dolly disappeared through the still shattered window that had once been the front of Leslie's store.

If only that was the last time they would see her.

"You could've made her something better," Rainbow said in a hopeful tone.

Leslie realized hopeful was probably the wrong term to use, but every single time she talked to Rainbow, she always felt as though the woman was trying to bring hope into the situation. It could have been because she was a rusalka and therefore a death-bringer.

Leslie didn't know. And she didn't care. She liked Rainbow and that's all that really mattered. "Well, at least we put an end to that one. Were there any other serious orders that we needed to add?"

Rainbow shook her head and held out a clipboard for Leslie to look at.

A clipboard. They'd actually had to dig around to find that thing. But for the last few hours, they'd been having rolling blackouts, or brownouts. So, technology was one of those things they didn't know if they could rely on anymore. She took a look at the list. "This is a lot of stuff."

Rainbow nodded eagerly. "It really is."

Leslie frowned. Sometimes she wasn't entirely certain Rainbow got the full grasp of any situation. "Does Chuck know how much he's expected to haul?"

Rainbow just shrugged. "He says it's not going to be a problem."

Well, if the regional high alpha wasn't concerned, Leslie wasn't either. She had better things to do than worry about crap that wasn't hers to worry about. She handed the list back to Rainbow. "All right. You make sure you stay close to Chuck. And whatever happens, you protect Kate. Without Kate, we don't have a doorway outside of our wards."

Rainbow took the clipboard solemnly and nodded. Then mock saluted, turned, and left.

It felt really weird not going. Since Leslie had become a shifter, Dexx had sort of started to depend on her, and that felt good. For so long, she had been nothing more than the weakest witch in the Whiskey family. And now? Well, she wasn't weak anymore.

But she was there for something else.

She heard a pop in the back.

Stepping into the back of her shop, she watched Kate step out into the middle of the room, almost appearing out of nowhere. Except behind her, Leslie could see woods. Everything was muted as if the sun wasn't up. It looked like it was dusk on the other side.

Leslie held out her hands and gathered Kate close to her.

The girl was still getting used to the way things were in the Whiskey house. Still getting used to being received warmly. She shied away from contact, physical or verbal. Leslie wasn't sure how elves brought their kids up, and she wasn't one who would protect her babies against *everything*, but she knew how to give a little sugar when it was needed. She certainly believed in doing that.

Several people followed Kate into the back of the shop.

The delegation from Utah. This was the group of shifters Paige had gone to earlier that year. And Leslie was there to greet them because everybody else was busy doing other things. She screwed a smile onto her face and offered her hand. "Leslie Whiskey."

The first woman to make it through had long black hair and dark eyes. She gripped Leslie's hand with a firm handshake and returned the smile. "Dorothy Rains. But everyone calls me Doe."

Doe introduced Leslie to the rest of her pack. The woman with the fantasy colored hair was named Kathy. The Middle Eastern man Mahir. The list went on and on. Leslie was sure there was no way she was going to remember everyone.

But then, Doe laid both her hands on the shoulders of the tall teen. "This is Max. His parents were witches and he was bitten."

Which meant this was the shifter-witch Paige had been talking about. Leslie smiled at him, hoping to put him at ease. "You're a Pegasus?"

He returned the smile and nodded, looking embarrassed.

Leslie chuckled a little. "There's no need to be embarrassed."

Max pressed his lips together for a moment. "Then you must be the griffin. It would've been a lot cooler if I'd been a griffin."

She couldn't disagree with that. Being a griffin was very cool. "Well, if you think that being a Pegasus is too girly, I'll let you meet my son. He can sing people to death."

Max's eyes grew big and his smile became genuine. "Are there real kids here?"

Leslie leaned forward as if to tell him in a conspiratorial whisper. "Well, they're not pretend."

Leslie straightened and looked at Doe. "I need to get Kate

to her next appointment. And then I'll show you where you'll be staying."

Doe smiled appreciatively and gestured for Leslie to lead the way.

Leslie brought them through town and to the Red Star Division, which was located behind most of the shops.

The new shifters gaped at everything. Leslie had to laugh a little. "It's a little different isn't it?"

Doe walked beside her and nodded. "It is. To see so many mundanes accepting us for who we are."

"Well, I'm not sure that it would be going this well if it wasn't for the fact that we're surrounded by killer demons. The mundanes have two choices. They can accept us and let us fight the demons, or they can go fight the demons themselves and die. So, right now we're just the lesser of two evils."

Doe nodded appreciatively, or in acknowledgement. Leslie couldn't quite tell. "You have a point. It would be neat if we could all live together in the open like this someday."

"That's probably coming a lot sooner than you think."

The Red Star Division had been a kind of gathering place for all the shifters coming in from Chuck's region. Kate had been instrumental in bringing those in who couldn't find a way through the demon's barricade. There were still those who had managed to make it through on their own. Mostly they were flocks of bird shifters. Those who were stuck to the land were forced to find other means.

The parking lot in the surrounding woods looked like a hippie convention. There were tents everywhere. And people wandered around aimlessly. Leslie guided Kate toward Chuck. Rainbow was already there.

"You make sure that Kate is safe." Leslie made sure Chuck understood through the tone of her voice she didn't care if he was the regional high alpha or not; if he brought danger to one of her kids he was going to wish he wasn't.

He nodded gravely and then smiled at Doe. "I'm very glad you were able to make it."

"Times are dire," Doe said.

"If you would do me a favor," Chuck said glancing at Leslie. "And help greet the other clans as they come in?"

Doe frowned and glanced at Leslie.

Leslie wasn't for sure why he wanted a babysitter either.

Chuck grimaced and then gestured at Doe again. "You know our traditions. And, there are those who still do not believe that we should have witches with us. It is my hope that the two of you can greet them together and put everyone at ease as they arrive."

Well, that made sense. Though, really, it should be Paige's job.

Doe looked up at Leslie and smiled. "I would love to."

Leslie just hoped she kept thinking that after spending any amount of time together.

She was certainly ready for this war to be over.

Paige had just got back into the house when a strange smell hit her. She looked up and saw Bastet standing in the dining room.

She frowned, not quite sure how she was supposed to take that. "What are you doing here?"

Bastet flounced her way to the dining table.

Paige was sure it was supposed to be sexy and seductive. But really, it just looked like a woman trying entirely too hard to catch the attention of any man. Especially ones who weren't even there.

"There's no one here who actually wants to talk to you, Bastet."

The goddess sat down in a chair and held up a hand as if waiting for something. "Then, I guess you don't want to hear what I have to say."

"What you have to say?" if she was actually going to play ball, as Dexx would put it, then Paige could at least listen. But how much of what Bastet said could they trust?

Bastet sighed and flicked her hand as if to remind Paige she still had an empty hand. "Aren't you going to offer me something to drink? After all, we are playing by the rules of guest."

Paige really had no idea what the "rules of guest" even meant. But, she turned around and pulled a cup out of the dish drainer, filling it with tap water. She brought it over to the goddess and handed it to her with a flourish. "Oh, wonderful and great goddess, what amazing information have you brought to my door today?"

Bastet took the glass and frowned at it holding it between her thumb and forefinger as if the glass were contaminated. She set it on the table and grimaced at Paige. "You mock me."

"I feel as though," Paige said mockingly, "you're beginning to understand human interaction."

Bastet quirked her lips and then folded her hands upon her bare knee peeking out from the slit in her dress. "If I tell you what I know, what will you give me return?"

"I didn't realize that we were in a bid for information."

"Of course, we are. What else would we be doing?"

"I don't know Bastet. The last time I saw you, we were all pretty sure that you would betray us. Matter of fact, some of us actually saw a vision of you doing that very thing."

"Not you surely. You don't seem like a seer."

Paige wasn't even sure what that meant. Was there something wrong with the way she looked?

Her question must've been on her face because Bastet dismissed the idea with her hand and a goddessly graceful eye roll. "You do not act as though you have any clue or hidden information into the future. You're always reacting on what you see at the present."

Paige was fairly certain the goddess was trying to insult her, but it felt more like she was giving her a compliment instead. "Thank you. And no, it wasn't me."

"So, you do have a seer."

Not exactly, but Paige wasn't telling that bitch anything. "Bastet just get to the point. What amazing information do you have and why should I believe you?"

Bastet gave her a withering look. "I admit that when I left the last time, I was little upset. And perhaps I said a few things that I shouldn't have."

So, she had finally figured out Sven wasn't the right horse to bet on. Or she was just betting on both sides while playing both sides, so then whichever side won she'd come out on top. Yeah. That was probably the case.

"But I'm here to mend fences."

"That's probably a hard thing for a goddess to admit."

Bastet flattened her lips. "You say that like you believe I have an ego problem."

She wasn't serious, was she? "Well, since you're the first goddess I've met, I'm gonna go with yes. How about you get to the point of this conversation. I have places to be, people to do." It really felt like she was channeling Dexx.

"I wanted to let you know," Bastet said primly, "that Sven is experiencing what you would call a 'power outage'."

A power outage. Maybe that was the reason for the rolling brownouts. Maybe he was trying to pull from the power grid.

Or, maybe it was just the fact they were in the middle of a mini apocalypse, and that's what happened in the apocalypse.

"Do you know why?"

Bastet gave her a dry look. "I do not."

The look on her face said she did. So, the bitch was playing them. "Look, if all you're going to do is lie to my face, the get the fuck out of my house."

Bastet looked affronted. "I am not lying."

"You most certainly are. I have a teenage daughter, so I can tell when people are lying to my face. You're certainly lying."

Bastet frowned. "Honestly, I have no idea what teenagers have to do with anything."

"Then you should have some." Wait, on second thought… "No. You should definitely not have any. The world wouldn't survive it. Just take my word for it. Teenagers will bring on the end of the world."

Bastet waved that off. "If you must know, it is because the ancients are now on this side of the veil. One of each have come across."

Well, that was certainly information.

"As such, Sven is no longer able to pull energy from any of them."

"And with Lynx on this side," Paige said, "he can't pull from your cats anymore either."

Bastet smiled at her as if she was the prize stupid student. "And here you thought I would side with him. He killed my cats."

Well, they had one good piece of information news. But, how long would they be able to trust Bastet?

Until someone new pissed her off. She was the goddess of cats after all.

Still…

Excellent information. "Thank you."

Bastet smiled serenely. "You are most welcome."

Right.

Yeah.

Now if they could just figure out how to get the upper hand.

C yn needed a few words with her parents. A few *choice* words about what they had done. Of course, she was happy they were still alive, but did they really have to scare her like that?

Maybe they hadn't thought they were going survive.

Cyn stood at the door to her mother's bedroom closet, twisting the ring around her finger. She didn't know why she was so anxious about going back. She had every right to be angry. They'd frightened her more than she'd ever thought possible. She been more scared watching them turn into a *tree* than when she'd found herself in the middle of the desert after watching her best friend turn into a bear.

And yet, the only thing she really wanted was to hear her mother call her by her full name and hug her.

Tightly.

With a deep breath, she touched her hand to a blank space on the wall. The door materialized and swung open to the castle. As she stepped through, a blast of cold air sent goosebumps rushing up her arms. She really should learn to wear more clothes.

Keeping the door open behind her, she turned to the left and headed to the library.

On the inside, the castle looked as much the same as it ever had. Except when she looked out the windows. The storm still raged outside, and it gave the castle a rather gloomy hue. As if the sun had been turned off. She didn't know what that was all about, and she wasn't really sure she wanted to ask. There were still times she wished she could hit the rewind button and go back to being naïve to all of this.

She knew better, though. She didn't want to do that because that meant her best friend would be lying to her again. And her boyfriend would still be a cat. And she would lose that fantastic image of Mason trying to be modest while shifting into a fat porcupine. She definitely wasn't willing to give that one up.

Somehow, she still wanted to know everything. She also wanted to be safe. She wanted Sven to disappear and never come back.

What was the likelihood of that happening?

"Mom?" Cyn called as she walked. She wasn't entirely sure where the secret door to the library was. She'd only seen it once, but she felt like it was close. "Mom!"

A door materialized on the wall behind her. With a relieved sigh she put her hand to the door and it opened on its own.

"Cynthia?" Charlotte's voice cried out. "Is that you?"

Who else would it be? Cyn stepped into the library and was immediately overwhelmed with how many more books there were. This wasn't just a library. This was like... the Atlantis of libraries.

Charlotte appeared between two stacks, her arms out as she descended upon Cyn. She was wearing clothes obviously found in the castle— she'd opted for one of the frilly gowns, which didn't surprise Cyn in the slightest— and she looked entirely at home.

Cyn hugged her mother, wishing, not for the first time, this was the mom she had always known. Pulling back, she gave her mom a hard stare. "What was that back there?"

"Back where?" Charlotte looked genuinely surprised. And confused.

Cyn had forgotten time was different at the castle. It was very possible that a week, possibly even two, could have passed in the castle when only a couple of days had passed in Troutdale. "At the grounding tree?"

A light dawned on Charlotte's face. She threw her hands out in exasperation and slapped them down on her thighs. "I saw only that we had to become the tree. I didn't know we would survive."

So Cyn was right. Her parents had intended to leave her behind. They had genuinely thought they were going to sacrifice themselves to protect her, and everyone else. Okay. She *was* mad now. "And you were just going to leave me like that? Without a real goodbye?"

"I told you that I loved you."

"It was super windy. I couldn't hear anything. If it wasn't for Lynx, I never would've known what you said at all."

Charlotte winced. "That was something I did not take into consideration. Visions are odd. Sometimes they give you all the information you need. Most times, they don't."

"Obviously." Cyn really wanted to yell at her mom a little more, but she was just glad she was still alive. She pressed her eyelids together, trying to focus. After all, they were trying to kill a demon. And a very powerful one. "Tell me you've learned something."

All the anxiety and stress Cyn had seen and experienced throughout her entire childhood evaporated from Charlotte's face as she smiled. "I have no idea how or why, but the moment you stepped foot inside this castle, it was like you brought it to life. There are books in this library that I never knew existed."

Seriously, this woman looked like a kid at Christmas. She was practically bouncing.

"Anything useful?"

Charlotte turned away, her hands gesturing wildly.

Yeah, this? This wasn't the mom she knew.

"The library has given me a wealth of information. A lot of it still has to be sifted through, but I am sure the answer is somewhere in here."

"You do realize we have a demon knocking down doors out in the real world right now. You know, like a real one and stuff. And the real people outside would really like to know how to defeat that very real demon. So, if you could happen to find something that could be helpful?"

Charlotte gave her daughter a grieved expression. "Oh, but I have. I've discovered Sven's weakness."

"Tell me it's something good. Like he has an allergy to cake." She would be all over that.

Charlotte shook her head with a smile. "Almost as good as that. His weakness is his kitsune blade."

That didn't make any sense. "I thought that's what made him so strong."

Charlotte gestured to a table piled dangerously high with books. She tapped one that was currently open. "Apparently, Sven is fourth generation Lilim."

Cyn had no idea how that helped. Aside from the fact that it meant he was very powerful, she knew she didn't know much more than that.

Charlotte kept going as though Cyn were actually keeping up. "This means that he's not nearly as powerful as the rest of his kind."

"We're not talking about demons here."

"We are. Demons and other Lilim. And, the whole reason why he stole the blade in the first place was that he has a life expectancy."

"So, he's mortal."

Charlotte nodded. "He should have died centuries ago. You see, he was born with several others, and during a time we now call the dark ages. And believe me, it was called the dark ages for a reason."

Well, that kind of made sense. "And all the others, his brothers and sisters? They're all dead now?"

Charlotte nodded. "My theory is that if we can break that blade, we will end his life."

Cyn blinked. When she said it like that, it sounded super easy. Except, they were talking about taking a sword away from a very powerful demon. Cyn was fairly certain if she took that information back to Paige, she'd give Cyn another one of those death glares she loved so much. Yeah. Cyn wasn't entirely sure she wanted to have that conversation with Paige. "How confident are you of this?"

Charlotte shrugged, her hands open and wide. "About as sure as I can be. The references are vague. And no one has faced anything like this before."

Cyn plopped into the seat next to her mother, blowing out a long breath. "When are we going to talk about..." she waved her hands around, "all of this?"

Charlotte turned toward her, giving her, her full attention. "All of what?"

Cyn gestured to the library. "All of this. These secrets, the library, the house being connected to a castle? All of this. And, how our family is attached to all of this and I never knew."

"What more is there to discuss? Your father and I have already told you that unless one of you girls showed the talent, we couldn't share any of it with you."

"You know that they're completely freaked out right now, right? I told them you took a spur of the moment trip out of the country. But that isn't going to last."

Charlotte shook her head. "You can't tell them."

"And what am I supposed to tell them then? They are close to filling out a missing person's report. Can you leave the castle?"

Charlotte gave a sigh and folded her hands in her lap. "We can't Cynthia. Our physical bodies are in the tree."

She tried not to give much attention to that idea. "Okay. So, what do we, do *I* tell them?"

Charlotte gave Cyn a worried expression. "They did get out, right?"

Cyn nodded. "I got a text saying they landed safely and they're with Grandma. But they're wondering when they can come back. I'm not good with lies and secrets, Mom."

Charlotte looked pained. "I don't have a good answer."

"Well, I wish somebody did. What happens if this goes on until Christmas? What do I tell them then? Oh, I'm sorry you won't to be able to see Mom and Dad, but don't worry they're not dead. They're librarian ghosts. I can see them, and you can't because I am special." Cyn realized she was babbling at this point, but she really didn't care. This was the kind of family situation she had no idea how to handle. This gift really should have fallen to their older sister. She could at least handle responsibility a little bit better. Well, at the very least she could lie better.

"Cynthia," Charlotte said quietly.

Cyn looked at her mother with a sigh. "Yes?"

"No matter what, you cannot tell your sisters about this."

"Then give me something. Anything, because I can't lie to them and say you are dead. Which is the only solution I see at the moment."

Charlotte's face was filled with sadness as she looked

down. "That is the solution. You tell your sisters that we died. You tell them that it was quick and that we didn't suffer."

She'd really hoped there would be another answer. She didn't want the responsibility that came with all of the secrets.

She wanted the world to be filled with teddy bears and cinnamon rolls, not demons and lies.

She didn't want to be the one to tell her sisters their parents were dead when she knew differently. When Cyn knew she could just take them to the Vaada Bhoomi where they could all talk and be together.

She looked up through the windows at the top of the library. "What's up with the storm? It doesn't look like it's as bad anymore."

Charlotte looked up as well, relief washing over her face at the change of topic. "The storm carried us back to the original location of the castle. We're back in the rainforest. The desert's nowhere near us."

Well, that was something. Still… "Bastet knows about the stronghold."

Charlotte's face immediately filled with anxiety. "What makes you think that?"

"Well, there is the fact that she's a goddess. And then there's the fact she's a cat. And the fact that she's a biscuit eating horrible person." So, that last part it sounded a little bit lame. "Also, I might be getting a little bit better at reading situations. It's just in the way she looks at me, like I'm dinner, or can lead her to a special treasure that she's been after."

Charlotte flicked her eyebrows. "It wouldn't surprise me in the least if she was looking for the stronghold. She wouldn't be the first," she said, her hands on the book in front of her with a grim expression. "And I doubt she'll be the last. And that is the reason we must take this charge seriously. We are the guardians of the stronghold. If we fall, all of this information—" Charlotte leaned back to gesture to the room at large. "—all of the artifacts that we've collected over the years, everything that we have kept safe and out of the hands of those who could use it for evil. Would be let loose into the world."

"Well, the mundanes know about shifters now, and they're doing okay. Maybe it wouldn't be so bad." And then maybe she could get her parents back.

Charlotte shook her head. "No. Some of the things we protect in here are very, very dangerous. And you need to keep in mind the only reason the town is doing so well right now is because they're under threat. If this was any other situation, if they had learned about this on any normal day, I can guarantee you that the people of that town would not be so accepting."

Cyn sighed. Well there went that idea of getting her parents back. "Okay. So, exactly what bad news did you want me to take to Paige?"

Secretly, Cyn decided she was going to tell Leslie and let Leslie deal with Paige. It was enough she was taking all of this in stride. She didn't need to take all of this in stride and deal with that scary woman.

They had a demon to kill. That had to be enough.

13

Lynx enjoyed having a little alone time. For the last two hundred and fifty years, he had been surrounded by hundreds of temple cats. He now knew those cats had been priestesses or prisoners of Bastet.

But he also enjoyed this loom. Weaving had always been one of his simple pleasures. When he had been a human there just hadn't been much call for it. But now? It seemed as though he couldn't spin the weave fast enough.

He became lost in thought as the shuttle moved between the threads. He didn't even realize what he was doing until the project was almost finished and the picture had presented itself.

Why couldn't he have done this in his time as a human before?

"Why is it," Bastet asked behind him, "that you couldn't have done this while you served me?"

Lynx started and turned around. "What are you doing here?" he had thought being in the Whiskey house would have protected him from having to see her.

She just smiled and seductively moved forward to inspect

his work. "Do you know how many times I allowed you to be a human, so you could weave for me?" she looked at him through the corner of her eye.

He had wondered. However, there were so many memories he still didn't have.

She turned back to his work raising her eyebrows. "Hundreds. It didn't matter what I gave you and it didn't matter which loom you used. You always refused to weave for me."

Well, if she had allowed him his memories, he could understand why.

"Oh, you would weave. But nothing like this. Nothing like your flying carpet."

Since they'd got back, Cyn had made a point of teaching him pop culture references. And one of those references was about a magick flying carpet a man named Aladdin apparently had used in order to seduce a woman. He was sure there was more to that story than she said, but after having watched what she called a movie, he had to agree with her.

Lynx wasn't sure what he thought about his magick carpet being used to seduce a princess.

Bastet made a mewling sound and turned to him, pouting. "When am I going to get my carpet?"

Honestly, Lynx didn't know. "Right now, I am making as many products for Paige as I possibly can. I don't know if you've noticed, but right now she is preparing for war. I feel it is my responsibility to assist."

Bastet seemed to ponder that.

Lynx was almost afraid she would take him back to her temple and make him a cat again. "Just tell me what you want, and I will get it as quickly as I can. I have no wish of going back with you."

She flared her fingers dismissively. "Oh, I'm much happier having you here. No. I just needed to know when I could have my treasure."

That was Bastet. The great goddess he knew. All she wanted and cared about was her toys. "Well, if you want it sooner, perhaps you could help us defeat Sven instead of trying to help him win."

Her brow furrowed as she looked at him. "You honestly think that I would be helping him? I admit that I'm a bit disappointed in you. I realize you were never that observant, but I hoped you would be better than that."

Really. She wanted to go that route. He rose to his feet. "What I know about you? You like to trick people so that you can take what you want. You're like a spoiled child."

She made a guttural sound and huffed away. "I really don't know why so many people are trying to tell me that I am childish. Nor do I know why I need to hear that so many times in the course of the week."

"Well, perhaps you should listen."

Bastet turned toward him with a smile. A real one. She looked like a little girl who was quite happy. "Look at how confident you have become, Lynx." She said that name with a great deal more emphasis, but it lacked disdain this time. "This place? It is doing great things for you. It is almost as if I saved you."

He wasn't entirely sure he understood her logic. "Saved me?"

"Of course." Bastet approached him again, her expression eager. "If it wasn't for me, you would never have found this place, it is as if you have found your home. You know," she said, looking down at him, "you really do have me to thank for that."

He was tired of having her there. "Did you want something specific?"

"Well, now that you ask?" she gave him a sly look as she walked away from him. "I believe I do."

He waited, knowing she would tell him in her own time.

"I want another magick carpet. Like the one you made before."

"I thought you would've wanted something new. Where did the old carpet go?"

"Funny that. It disappeared." She nearly growled that last part.

"So, someone stole it before you could."

She tipped her head to the side and put a hand on her hip. "No. It disappeared to another dimension."

He wasn't entirely sure he fully understood what she was saying. As far as he knew, there were only two dimensions—this one and the Vaada Bhoomi. "You're trying to tell me that you were unable to find it?"

She hissed at him. "And there you are again being so shortsighted. There are so many worlds, so many dimensions. They're limitless. If I cannot make a place for myself here, I want a magick carpet that will take me anywhere I want to go."

He was able to read between the lines, as Dexx would say. She wanted to find the world where she could rule, where she could live as a goddess. "I'll do what I can."

She gave him a tight smile.

A sudden thought hit him. "You're not going to help us in this fight against Sven, are you?"

She seemed to ponder his question and then finally sighed. "I haven't decided."

Lynx knew when the day of the battle came she would decide based on a whim which side to choose. She might even flip a coin for it. She might even flip the coin and then decide to go the other route just because she felt like it. She was a very fickle goddess. "If I make this rug for you, will you leave as soon as I get it to you?"

She smiled at him, the expression lighting up her face.

"Oh, you are so bold. You were meant for this world. That is certain."

"Is that a yes?"

She paused, blinked and then finally nodded. "Yes. You bring me my flying rug and I will leave as soon as you present it to me."

He nodded and watched her leave in a cloud of smoke. He knew Dexx wanted to use her in the fight, but he also knew there was no real way of guaranteeing which side of the fight Bastet would eventually choose. The best thing for them would be to get her off the game board entirely. He just hoped when the time came, Dexx would understand.

Paige sank into the recliner with a groan. The day had been long, and she was ready to be off her feet. Her body was ready to rest. She wasn't even quite sure how she was still pregnant. It was as if she was telling her womb the babies had to stay in for as long as possible and her womb was actually listening.

Which was the first time ever. Usually, her uterus was really great to deciding to flow on a vacation day. Or when they decided to go to the swimming pool or anytime she didn't want it to work.

She realized menopause was supposed to be horrible, but she was kind of looking forward to it. She was really over the whole menstrual cycle, which included having babies.

"Paige?" Reece's voice filled the kitchen and dining room, reaching her in the living room.

She closed her eyes and pretended to be really small, hoping her grandfather would just keep going and not even see her.

"Ah, there you are." Reece came into the living room and

sat down on the red and green couch on her right. "I wanted to let you know that both pieces of the key are safely stored away in the stronghold."

Well, that was certainly a good piece of information. "Do we have any idea how to bring Sven down?"

Reece shook his head. "But when I left, Charlotte was still in the library looking."

Paige was a little curious about this whole disappearing and reappearing castle thing. A part of her wanted to go check it out. But she really had too many things on her plate and didn't have time to go sightseeing in a castle. "The sooner we find something out—"

"The sooner you'll be able to get rid of me?"

Paige was on her feet so fast. Sven Seven-Tails was standing inside of her dining room. This was the safest place in all of Troutdale. Or, at least it was supposed to be. "How did you get in here?"

He smiled mischievously. When he did that, he reminded her so much of Spike on *Buffy the Vampire Slayer*. "You really should be careful of who you invite into your house."

Bastet. It had to be. Though, how? She had never heard of anyone being able to slip through a witch's ward. Okay. Some witch's wards. But not hers. Sven continued to smile and turned his attention to Reece. "You must be the grandfather I've heard so much about. Won't you have an interesting conversation when you go to the pearly gates."

Reece sighed as if he was talking to a child. "What do you want Sven?"

Sven looked innocent and widened his hands on either side of himself. "World peace."

"Then take down the barricade." If he was going to be there, they might as well try to bargain with him. "Let supplies in. There are people here who need food, clothes, medicines."

"Well, about that." Sven propped a finger on his chin. "Imagine my surprise when I heard rumors that some of your people had found a way into my city."

No. There was no way he could've found that out. Leslie had promised they were so careful. "You really didn't think that you were going to stop all movement in and out of my town, did you?"

He laughed and dropped his hand. "Oh, Paige, you do surprise me."

"You're not disappointed, are you?"

"On the contrary. I'm quite pleased."

That irritated her. It was like she was his pet student or something. "What the hell do you want, Sven?"

All of these years, all of the toying, the playing, the games, and she still had no idea what he wanted from her.

He tipped his head and studied her. "Now, that would be telling. And I don't want that. I want you to keep guessing."

"Because that's so much fun."

He grinned, his blue eyes wide.

That only irritated her even more. "I don't think you fully understand what it means to piss off a pregnant, hormonal witch."

She didn't even realize what she was doing, but she felt the pull of the power inside her. It was stronger than ever before. Fueled by the grief she was still feeling from losing Alma, and all of the anger, frustration, and the hormones from being pregnant. She had a lot of power.

He took a stumbling step back, appraising her hands appreciatively. "Now, now. Let's play nice."

Why couldn't she just take him right here, right now? She had the power. He was in her house. She should, by rights, have the upper hand. "You came into my home, Sven. You were uninvited. You have been a thorn in my side for years. I want you gone. I want you out of my house, I want you out of my town. I want you off my planet."

He threw back his head and laughed. "You are so feisty when you get upset." He looked over at Reece. "But, I'm not here for you, love."

She didn't care who he was there for. She gathered a ball of energy and shot it at him. It hit and encircled the arm he had raised to deflect. As they both watched, her black and silvery blue magick seemed to wrap around him, like a venomous web.

His eyes widened, this time in alarm. He looked at her in surprise. "Paige, love, what are you doing?"

"What I should have done long time ago." Whatever she had done, it looked as though it was working. All she had to do was more of that, whatever that was. She gathered more energy and threw it again.

He ducked, but she still managed to hit, this time his shoulder. Like the first one, this magick started to circle around him from his shoulder, crawling up his neck.

Sven pulled away as if trying to get away from the magick crawling up him. "Paige, love, there is no need to do this. You know me. I'm just playing.

"This? This is not playing. You are endangering the lives of everyone in my town. You are endangering the lives of my children, my family." The energy that gathered in both of her hands was a large ball of boiling rage. "You killed my grandmother." And with that, she launched the ball of energy at him.

He blipped out of existence, and it looked as though the energy she had thrown at him had missed. But as soon as he reappeared, standing next to Reece, the energy found him again. This time, it hit him squarely in the back.

He cried out and grabbed hold of Reece. He no longer

wore a smile. His face was twisted in pain. With his hands gripping Reece's shirt, he howled, "You're coming with me."

And then he and her grandfather disappeared.

For a few brief moments she thought she had won.

Until she realized Reece knew where the library stronghold was.

And where the other two pieces of the key resided.

Aw, shit.

14

Paige had to figure out how in the hell Sven had got inside her wards. What had he said? She needed to be careful of who she'd invited in?

Bastet.

Where had that bitch of a goddess roamed inside of her house?

Paige didn't even know who was in the house with her. She reared her head back and roared, more tiger than human, but she felt that alpha will push out of her.

Footsteps thundered down the stairs. People came in from both the front and back doors.

"Bastet left something here," Paige growled, her eyes scanning everything. "Whatever it is, Sven was able to get in." She went still and turned to look at each person individually, so they would understand the full implications of that statement. "Sven was in our house."

Leslie was on high alert. "What happened? Are you okay?"

A chill rippled down Paige's spine. "He took Reece."

Leslie frowned, but didn't look extremely upset.

Was this the type of people they were becoming? One of their own was in the hands of Sven and they were just like, "Okay." No. That was wrong. Paige and Leslie might not agree with how Reece handled the whole fathering of Rachel situation. But he was still their grandfather. And a really horrible demon had him.

"Sven knows that Reece knows where the two parts of the key are."

Leslie's eyes widened, and her lips formed an "O" of surprise.

The kids were already searching. Frankly, they really didn't need much of an excuse to tear apart the house. They probably didn't even know what they were looking for.

For that matter neither did Paige. Who would? She had an idea. "Balnore, I need you."

Leslie shook her head and continued her visual search. Tru had Kammy in his arms as they came down the stairs. "Do we have any idea where she was inside the house?"

Paige shook her head. "I don't remember. So much happened."

Lynx stepped into the room from the back.

Paige had almost forgotten he was still in the house and had been spending quite a bit of time there. He just hid in Alma's old room and worked on that loom. A part of her was angry about that. An irrational stupid part of her. Yes, he was using her grandmother's loom. But he was doing so to help them. And that was something she needed to keep in mind.

"Lynx, you know Bastet the best. Where would she hide something that would allow Sven inside the wards?"

He shook his head. "I may be the one who accompanied her the most, but I can assure you I know her the least. I have no idea what she would use to gain entrance into your wards. I don't understand magick."

Well, that was certainly unhelpful.

Balnore walked through the wide entrance that separated the dining room and the living room. He looked around at everyone in confusion. "Peanut, did I miss something? Disaster?"

She really didn't have a sense of humor at the moment. "Sven was in our house. He took Reece. He's trying to get to… the pieces of the key." Paige had hesitated on that last part. She had almost said the stronghold. But how much did he know?

And how much did they know about him? He was like Bastet. And, it turned out he was a lot more like Sven than any of them had thought. Yes, she had learned to trust him over the years, but how much of that was because he had designed it that way, and how much was because he'd actually earned it? Yes, he had helped her a great deal when she needed it. But what was his ulterior motive? She had to guess he had one. So, what was it?

The answer was she just didn't know.

Balnore frowned. "Do you know where the keys are?"

Paige nodded. "But I can't get to them." And that was all she really wanted to tell him. "But Reece knows where and he can get there."

Balnore grunted. "That is certainly a problem."

Bal always knew how to under emphasize the situation. "I need to know how Bastet let Sven in."

Balnore turned in a small circle, scanning the immediate area. "That's not the only thing you need to be doing. You need to protect the stronghold."

He *did* know more than he let on. "How long have you known about the library?"

He looked at her in surprise. "I'm the one who helped them build the protections. I'm the one who bound that keep to the family line. Peanut, I am not your enemy here."

It was certainly easy for him to say. She had no idea who

her enemies were anymore. Though, she really did feel like an idiot for doubting him. "Can you tell me what she hid or not?"

By this time, Tyler, Mandy, Leah, and Kate had all managed to destroy the living room. Although, in Kate's defense, she was picking up just as much she was destroying. But the other kids? They were tearing things up with abandon. Most of the adults had disappeared and were searching other parts of the house.

Balnore held up his hand and, for whatever reason, all of the kids stopped moving. He walked over to Leah who had something in her hand. Raising one dark brow Bal took it from her. "I believe this is what you're looking for."

Paige went to inspect it. It was a small wooden figure of a cat. A black cat with a golden collar, just like the figures of the cats at Bastet's temple. If it wouldn't have been for Sven showing up at her door, it was quite possible that that trinket would have remained in the house indefinitely. That sneaky little bitch. "What does it do?"

Bal quirked his lips and then crushed the trinket in the palm of his hand as though it were made out of nothing more than sand. "The rules of the gods and goddesses are intricate and unique. They were put down upon us by the elves."

Kate's ears perked up.

Bal nodded in her direction. "The elves and the Fae are terribly good with rules and how to get around them. So, naturally, they were the best ones to use to bind a goddess's power, to limit her, and to limit her influences on the world."

Paige had a feeling he wasn't just talking about Bastet with that one. "I feel as though there's a whole lot more that we need to learn. So far, I've got one god, one goddess, and one that wants to *be* God." And if Dexx were there he would probably have something smart ass to say about how it was the war of the gods. And it was probably in some reference to some movie that she had never watched before.

She really missed Dexx.

"The good news is," Bal said, "that neither Bastet nor Sven should be able to simply enter your wards anymore."

"Really? Because so far I haven't been able to keep that goddess outside of my wards since day one."

Balnore gave her a steady look and then asked one simple question. "Do you trust me?"

Paige should say no. She had learned more about him in the last two days than she had in the last twenty years. That didn't mean anything. Every ounce of her will said yes. So, she merely nodded.

He turned on his heel and headed toward the back.

She was quick to follow.

He walked out the back door and into the yard, heading straight for the ward tree.

Okay. There was trust and then there was allowing him into her ward. And she didn't quite know if she was ready for that. There were so many things he would have access to.

How many times had she fought to allow Bal inside of their house? For how many years? And now she was doubting?

And why? Because she had discovered that he was a Lilim? That he was a demigod?

She stopped at the tree and looked up at him. "You want me to trust you."

Balnore nodded solemnly "That is all I have ever wanted."

"Then tell me what you were the god of."

He licked his lips and bowed his head. He thought about it for a long moment and then finally raised his eyes to meet hers. "I was the god of death."

That didn't make any sense. "You were Hades?"

He shook his head and waited.

Yeah. She really wasn't going to figure this one out any time soon. "So, you're the Grim Reaper."

He shook his head again.

Paige ran through all of the information she had over gods and goddesses, which wasn't a lot. She'd never really been interested, not remotely ever. But she could honestly say she had never once heard of the god of death. But in her defense, there was a lot she didn't know.

"So? What did you do?"

"I was more of a judge."

"You judged people after they died?"

He nodded.

"So, if you're not doing that anymore, then who is?"

He licked his lips and thought about what to say next. "Let's just say that a few of my brothers and sisters were smarter about how to manipulate mankind than we were. Now, you have an army of angels and demons to look after the dead and to judge them after they've lived."

This was rich. She was standing in front of the person who very well could be judging her after she died. And he had just basically informed her that the whole judging thing, the whole Heaven and Hell thing, was all a scam. "Well, Mr. Death. What's your plan here?"

He took in a deep breath and looked up at her tree. "This is most impressive. I have not seen wards like this in a very long time. At least since the gods walked the Earth. It's not because you are one-of-a-kind. It is because you understand that you are not. And that is how your wards are so supreme."

Well, her ego had needed a boost. "*But?* I'm hearing a 'but' in there."

"But," he said with a nod, "Bastet knows wards like these very well. And she knows how to get through them. You allowed her into your backyard. In so doing, you invited her inside of your wards. Once she was inside your wards, she was able to walk freely around your place. And, she left an invitation locket so that in case you changed your wards, she and any who she gave access to would be able to enter your home."

That was very sneaky of her. "You gods and goddesses should really come with the rulebook."

"There used to be rulebooks. However, when the Church changed the world and all the rules, most of those books were destroyed."

The way he said that made it sound as if there was a reason. And if what he was saying, or rather implying was true, then the Church had been created by Balnore's kind. By Bastet's kind. So, if that was the case, then sure. They wouldn't want anyone to be able to lock them out. They wouldn't want anyone to understand how to deal with them.

"Originally," Balnore said, "that was the reason the stronghold was created. To ensure that those texts were safe and that is what Bastet is looking to destroy. That's what she's always been looking to destroy."

That was all very interesting and good, but it wasn't helping them solve the mystery of how to keep Bastet out of her wards. "So, what are we doing outside of the house and at my ward tree, Bal?"

Balnore looked at her and sighed. "I thought it was obvious, Peanut. I need you to let me add my essence to your wards."

A part of her thought, *Wow. What a great idea. Let's let a powerful god add his essence to the ward. That should keep Sven out.*

The other part of her was freaking out just little bit. Balnore, the guy she always thought was a demon, was now a demigod. Not only that, but he was the god of death. He judged people when they died. And if she bit the dust now, she might end up coming back as a fly. Repeatedly. Many times.

But she really needed to go back and listen to her instincts. And they said she could trust him.

So, she held out her hand to him, extending her magick with her other.

He smiled at her, it was almost like old times, back when he was teaching her how to use her abilities.

When his magick touched her tree, with its silvery shining, the tree flared.

The magic swelled, and grew, towering even higher, the branches widening even further. And the wards? She could feel them growing as well. They extended further, encircling more of the town, and the surrounding areas.

But the wards were different too. They spoke to her in a different way. It was so hard to describe what it was like. Before it felt like she had a few voices talking to her, and now she had dozens. Hundreds even. And it was as if they were speaking to her not just in this timeline, but in multiple.

She released her magick and looked up at him. "You really are a god."

He chuckled and let go of her hand. "Only on this world."

As much fun as this was, they still had another problem. Reece. "What's the possibility that our house god could go pay Bastet and Sven a visit and retrieve our priest?"

It was going to take her more than a minute to fully wrap her head around that particular visual. It was one thing to make light of it. It was a whole nother thing to see it in person. She couldn't take her eyes off her ward tree. It was the most amazing thing ever. And the voices, her wards, they were telling her so many things she barely comprehended. But somewhere in the back of her head, the center of her soul, she seemed to understand everything it told her.

Balnore nodded and then disappeared.

Paige wasn't entirely certain what she was supposed to do. Was she supposed to go inside? Worry? Should she be preparing for an assault?

Cyn stepped out of the back door. She looked awkward and out of place. And more than a little intimidated.

Paige had to consider everything the woman had gone through. And if she really thought hard about it, Paige would understand she hadn't been entirely super when it came to Cyn. Unfortunately for the little generator, she'd entered into this whole mess on a really bad day. "Hey Cyn," she called and approached. "Are you looking for Lynx?"

Cyn played with her hands, but she didn't back away. "No. I'm here to talk to you."

After all this was done, Paige was going to sit down and have a glass of wine with that girl and see if she could get her to unwind just a little bit. Of course, they would have to survive the fiasco first. "All right. Spill it. I've got goddesses invading my home and stealing people."

She really meant that to come out sounding like a joke. However, the truth just wasn't that funny once said out loud.

Cyn's eyes grew wide. "My mom was able to find something in the library."

"Reece was just there, he didn't say anything about that."

Cyn shrugged. "He wasn't in the library when I was there." She looked around uncertainly. "Have I mentioned how weird that place is? With all the time differences and stuff?"

Paige took in a deep breath and held it for a moment. She wasn't making Cyn feel any better. "You may have mentioned it. What did you find?"

Cyn nodded and swallowed. "So, we found Sven's weakness." Paige would've jumped with excitement if it wasn't for the expression on Cyn's face. "Why do I get the feeling that I'm not going to like this?"

Cyn grimaced. "It's his sword."

His sword? "He has a sword? I've never even seen him with a sword."

Cyn shrugged and took a step back ready to retreat inside the house. "You asked for the information, we found the information, and I bring the information. I didn't say it was going to be good." And then she disappeared inside the house.

Paige turned around, wondering when Balnore was going to make it back, or if he would. How would she know if he needed assistance, would there be some kind of godly flare in the sky?

Before she could take that thought further, Bal appeared in her backyard with Reece at his side.

That was honestly the easiest save ever. "Is there anything we should be worried about?"

Balnore said nothing.

And that got her worrying. "What happened?"

"Nothing. Your grandfather's back. I suggest you keep better track of him next time." And then Balnore was gone again.

Leaving her alone with her grandfather.

Right. Her grandfather. "Does Sven know how to get to the stronghold?"

Reece shook his head. He looked like he was waiting for something.

Something she just couldn't give him. So, she turned around and went into the house. It was long past time for bed.

15

The next morning, Paige rose bright and early. She didn't know why. She just couldn't sleep.

No.

She knew exactly why. Dexx wasn't there. She missed him. He really needed to get back home.

That, and the fact Sven had invaded her home the night before, stolen her grandfather, and nearly unraveled where and how to get his hands on the two halves of the key he didn't have, and that they'd magickally barricaded their wards against gods.

The night before had been terribly busy. And to think she had done all of that without the man in her life.

When she talked to him last night, he had mentioned the possibility he might be coming home soon. She realized she had sent him out there for a very good reason. That didn't mean that she didn't want him there though.

Leslie greeted her at the coffee pot again.

"This is becoming a habit." Though, one Paige wasn't going to complain about. If they were going to make a habit of something, waking up under the same roof and sharing coffee was one she was happy to have. "Do we have any new information on *anything?*"

Leslie nodded and took her cup of coffee to the dining table. "The supplies went well. They're being distributed this morning, and everyone seems to be a little happier."

Well, that was certainly good. Paige poured herself a cup and joined her sister at the table. "How's the school going?"

"I wish I could say things were going well on that department." Leslie wrinkled her nose. "There are surprisingly a lot of parents on both sides of the fence who would rather keep their kids in the home rather than allow them to go to school with different people."

Now that was more along the lines of what Paige had originally expected. "And Faith? How's she dealing with this?"

Leslie leaned back in her chair. "Faith is part of the problem. She says she never agreed to any of this, and so she's not allowing any of her kids to go to school with the mundanes. And because the school is located on her land, she's not allowing class to be held."

Now, that was a problem. "And Chuck?"

"Chuck's been a little busy."

That was truer than Paige would've liked. She took another sip of her coffee and rose to her feet. "I'm going to go have a conversation with Faith."

Leslie eyes widened and she nodded. "Good luck with that."

Paige paused before she entered the hallway leading to the front door. "I assume you've got enough to keep you busy for the day."

Leslie snorted. "Don't even get me started."

That was good enough for Paige. She turned and exited the front door. She decided she wasn't going to drive. Now that everybody knew about witches and shifters, it was just easier to shift.

She really needed to get better at flying. It wasn't that she didn't like it. It was just that landing was so difficult. She had considered landing on her bird feet and then shifting, but for some reason that just wasn't working for her either. After a moment of debate, she decided she would work on her flying abilities on another day, preferably when they weren't in the middle of war. For now, she would continue in her favorite form, a snow tiger.

On four feet and not carrying two children, covering the distance between their home and the land Faith had the school on was much easier. The school was located well within the wards that now covered most of the town, so she didn't have to worry about walking into unprotected space. However, what she ended up walking into was not what she had expected.

A school bus was stopped at the driveway that led onto the property. The school bus was filled with kids and another one was coming up right behind it.

Blocking their path were four shifters, all four of them being in Chuck and Faith's pack.

The school bus driver of the first bus was visibly shaken. She didn't want to get out at all. And her hand was firmly on the handle keeping the door closed. Paige really couldn't blame her. She remembered being a human and coming face-to-face with her very first shifter. She hadn't handled herself with extreme dignity. She really couldn't lie about that.

Faith came from behind her shifters and stood in front of them, crossing her arms over her chest and staring up at the big yellow bus.

This wasn't going to work. Paige walked up to Faith and shifted into human form. "I thought we talked about this. This is what we need."

Faith gave her a dirty look and shook her head. "This is what you said we needed. I never said I was going to do this. I never agreed to it."

What Faith wasn't saying was she was still a little upset with Paige for the Alpha will battle.

Okay. So, she probably had gone a little too far. However, if Faith wanted to — that was it. Faith wanted to be the alpha. She was the regional high alpha. So, basically, she was Chuck's partner. In all things. Okay. Perfect.

Faith must've seen something on Paige's face because she unfurled her arms and glared.

Paige grinned. "You know what? I've been taking all of this on thinking I needed to be the one to solve all of this. And I yelled at you because you were a roadblock and I didn't have time for roadblock. So? Guess what? You get to deal with all of this. You're the high alpha. I'm not. The decisions I've made needed to be made. So, if you don't like my way, you figure out a better way. Meanwhile, can you see what... *you* can do about stopping that demon trying to destroy our town? Or, would you not like to go home sometime this year? Or ever?"

Faith and Chuck's house was outside the protection of the wards. Paige wasn't going to put another ward just around their place.

Faith frowned at her.

Paige didn't know why she hadn't thought of this sooner. She was just so used to everybody looking up to her and expecting her to come up with answers and solutions to these ridiculous problems that just kept coming up. She totally forgot her best resource was the alpha. And as much as it hurt Dexx's pride, he wasn't the alpha she needed to hand stuff over to. It was Chuck. And his mate, Faith.

Faith looked at the buses over Paige's shoulder. And then she looked at Paige again. "The schools have always been mine. That was something that Chuck and I agreed on from the beginning."

Paige seriously didn't have time for this. Of all of the egos in town, she never once thought Faith was going to be a problem. She leaned in and got in Faith's face. "Then deal with the school. But understand, little wolf, that the world just got a whole lot bigger. And you need to be thinking of the entire community, not just your small pack."

Paige understood Faith's pack was one of the biggest. And she wasn't even talking about the entire regional pack. She was talking about Chuck and Faith's pack alone. They had over fifty shifters.

That was a heck of a lot more than Dexx and Paige's head-count. Eight? No. There were more than that. Oh crap. Paige was a really bad alpha mate. She couldn't even remember how many people she had in the pack.

Paige felt the wards shiver. She turned around looked up into the sky just in time to see the dome of her wards ripple.

The demons were attacking the wards in force. And it appeared as though they were doing so close to the Whiskey wards. At least it didn't feel like she was the only person keeping them up. They were stronger now, more rigid and flexible at the same time

Paige wasn't entirely sure what they were trying to do. Though, Sven could just be throwing a tantrum. She should probably check it out. So, she turned to Faith to give her an option. "You can go fix that, or you can stay here, and figure out how to instruct children no matter who or what they are. The choice is yours."

Faith narrowed her eyes.

Wendy joined the two.

Paige nodded at her. "You two figure this out. I'm gonna go see if I can keep us all alive for one more day. You know, so that this real argument will seem trivial now and tomorrow and the next day."

Paige didn't wait for a response. She realized it was a pretty low blow, but she just didn't care anymore. She shifted into a cheetah and ran toward the part of the ward under attack.

By the time she made it there, she wasn't alone. Leah was getting off the back of a massive black horse. That horse shifted into the little body of Ashley, Leah's best friend.

It was still really weird for Paige to see a teenaged girl standing in the nude and not caring about it one bit.

However, that teenage girl was being raised in a society where her body wasn't seen as a tool for sex. She was seen as a person. Mostly because she could also turn into a horse that could kill a person with her hooves. That probably had a lot to do with the respect that teenage girls received in this society versus any other.

"What are you two doing here?"

Leah barely glanced at her mom as she handed Ashley a backpack. "School was canceled today. So, we decided it was time for us to do a little something to help."

"And you honestly thought I was going to let you help me fight demons?"

Leah turned a somber gaze to her mother. "Yes. Of all of us, I think you and I are the two who have the best chance of doing anything with these guys."

Paige frowned. "What do you mean, us?"

Leah screwed up her face in thought and then turned back toward the demons throwing themselves repeatedly against the ward.

Sven hung back, not attacking the wards himself. And he looked pissed.

Yep. He was totally throwing a tantrum right now.

"I have a theory." Leah gestured to the demons and then

she gestured at Paige. "I think that if you and I were to open a door, we could send them all away."

Paige wasn't entirely sure how her door magick even worked. Sure. She was capable of opening a door to Hell. And that was before the door to Hell had been seared inside her bones. And Leah was capable of opening a door to Heaven and Hell. But she wasn't entirely sure how that was going to help them unless of course Leah opened the door to Heaven, then shoved the demons through, and then the demons could be an angel problem.

That was actually a pretty good solution. Well, for them. Maybe not for Heaven. Or the angels. But Paige didn't really care about them. Fuck 'em. But she couldn't do that.

"Okay. What did you have in mind?"

One of the things Paige was supposed to have been working on with Leah was how to work her door magick. She really didn't want to have to go to the Blackman's in order to get a few lessons. But as fate would have it, she hadn't had much time to spend with her daughter.

Leah raised her chin. "We open a door right over there." She pointed to a spot by some trees, "And then? Hopefully the door just kind of sucks them in."

Paige wasn't certain how the door was going to suck them in. "Because of the vacuum?"

Leah shrugged. "Kind of? I saw it in a movie?"

Paige really didn't know what the worst thing that could happen would be. So, she shrugged. "Let's give it a try."

Paige hadn't had many opportunities to work magick with Leah before. But, it was surprisingly easy to get their magick to sync together. She hadn't really noticed until that particular moment when working with Leslie or even Alma it felt as though her magick had been resisting the other a little. But with Leah, it was as if they were made out of the same stuff.

Leah was the only other witch she had cast with who had door magick. And it felt really good. Natural.

Together, they reached out, with Paige's inky black hands and Leah's black smoke, and drew a circle in the air on the other side of the ward. Sven turned toward it, looking curious. It was then that Paige noticed that the places where her magick had touched him before were healed, but not perfectly. They were scarred.

Interesting.

Not knowing what the hell they were doing Paige and Leah pushed their magick through the circle.

At first the circle was filled with black. And that made sense to Paige but then, the black disappeared and became a landscape unlike anything she'd seen before. Well, not quite. It kind of looked like the landscape of Mars.

But instead of the door sucking the demons through, it just kind of sat there.

Paige and Leah exchanged a look.

"What if we try to move the circle toward them?" Paige asked.

Leah nodded and frowned, her hands working as if dragging it.

Paige really couldn't say anything. She probably looked just as ridiculous.

But together, they moved the door toward the demons. Sven watched, his eyes growing wider and wider as one by one, his demons slipped through the opening Paige and Leah had made and disappeared.

Holy crap! It was working.

Paige and Leah continued pulling it as fast as they could, but Sven was on to them. He called his demons back.

They scrambled as fast as they could away from the portal.

Then once they were safely behind Sven, he saluted, and they all disappeared.

Blinking, Paige retracted her magick.

Leah did as well. "I'm a little disappointed the vacuum didn't work."

"Me too. It would've been so handy."

Leah giggled. "A little bit. But we actually did it." Her voice was filled with so much excitement.

"We did." Paige wasn't going to get too excited about it. That was one very small battle in a very big war. She wasn't entirely certain what she and Leah had just done. But hopefully they could do more of it.

Paige needed to talk to the Blackman's. It was probably time to make them allies.

Paige walked into the house and right into chaos.

Mandy ran down the stairs as though her tail was on fire, and Tyler ran up the stairs.

Leslie shouted to Tru to hurry his ass up.

Tru, meanwhile, was in the kitchen, with the water running.

Paige stopped Mandy. "What's going on?"

Mandy's eyes widened as if surprised to see Paige there. She blinked and then shook herself. "Roxxie's awake and she's completely freaking out."

This was absolutely enough. Paige pulled out her phone and dialed Dexx.

"Hey, babe." He sounded unstressed.

She needed to change that. "How quickly can you get home?"

"Are the babies coming? For real?"

"No. Roxxie's awake and I need you to come here and help me deal with her."

He paused, then said, "Give me a few minutes. I'm on my way."

She certainly hoped so. She walked up the stairs feeling a lot lighter than she had just an hour or so ago. She wasn't entirely sure why, but she wasn't going to look a gift horse in the mouth either.

Leah was close on her heels. "What can I do?"

"Until I see what's going on? I have no idea how to answer that." She stepped onto the landing and headed straight for the guest room.

Roxxie was convulsing on the bed, and Leslie was doing her best to hold her down.

"When did we move her back to the guest room?" because the last thing she remembered, Roxxie had been in Margo's cabin.

"Since about thirty minutes ago," Leslie said gruffly. She grunted as Roxxie bucked again. "Margo went to work on the perimeter and got hurt. So, we needed Roxxie out of the cabin."

She was going to be so his debtor when Dexx got back. She was doing a really crappy job of watching out for the pack. What had happened at the perimeter? "And when did this start?"

Leslie shook her head. "About three minutes ago?"

"Why?" Paige was trying to think of anything that might help them determine what was even going on with her.

"I was downstairs in the kitchen. I wasn't the one who noticed it. Mandy did."

Paige just looked at Roxxie. She tried to remember what a person was supposed to do if someone went into an epileptic seizure. "Let her go, and just make sure she doesn't fall off the bed."

Leslie gave Paige a look that said she hoped Paige knew what she was talking about. She got off the bed and guarded the edge.

Tyler entered the room. Paige wasn't entirely sure how

she'd beat Tyler to Roxxie's room. But he elbowed his way in and set something on the bed next to the angel.

Leslie frowned at him. "What are you doing?"

"Well, when I talked to her, she said she really liked this."

"This" turned out to be one of his model airplanes. Paige wasn't entirely sure how that was supposed to help, but couldn't hurt either.

A moment later, Roxxie settled.

The bedroom was crowded, but quiet. Tyler sat next to Roxxie with his model, keeping her calm.

"What did I miss?" Dexx asked quietly wrapping a robe around himself. His few minutes were closer to ten.

Paige turned to him, grateful he was back. "I have a lot of questions." She turned back to the angel on the bed.

"So do I." Dexx stood close to Paige and rested one hand on her shoulder.

Roxxie's eyes shot open.

Dexx went to her side, almost touching her hand, but held back a bit. "Roxxie? You with us?"

She seemed to be taking everyone in. "Dexx? Paige? How did I get here?"

Paige took a step forward. "We were really hoping that you could tell *us* what happened. We nearly ran over you in the road."

"For your information," Dexx said holding up a finger. "I was nowhere near and in no way was I about to hit her. I still had a good foot and half."

Paige ignored him. She wanted to know what was going on with the angel. Roxxie's gaze went unfocused and then she shook her head. "I really don't remember."

"Well," Paige said, "whatever happened, the wards allowed you in. And I had closed those off to you after the last time."

Roxxie frowned at her confused. "After the last time? I don't understand. Why would you do that?"

How much her memories had she lost? "The last time you took me to Heaven and I disappeared up there for three weeks?"

"Why would you have been there for three weeks?"

This couldn't be good. "That's what I was trying to get you to tell me."

Roxxie shook her head and tried to sit up. She winced and then fell back to the bed. "Something is wrong with me."

Dexx looked up at Paige with concern in his eyes. "What could affect an angel like this?"

Leslie narrowed her eyes. "Another angel?"

That was possible. "If Roxxie really did break me out of Heaven against the will of the other angels last time? It's possible."

"I broke you out of Heaven?" Roxxie sounded really confused.

Leslie touched Roxxie's hand. "How do you feel?"

Roxxie's brow furrowed. "I think I'm hungry."

Now that was odd. In all of her time in the Whiskey house, Paige never seen Roxxie eat once. "And what else?"

"Tired? And my entire body hurts. I feel like…" She looked up at Paige. "I feel like I was run over by a truck."

Paige was unaware angels could ever feel that way. "Do you have enough energy to get yourself downstairs? Or do you need help? Because the food's down there."

With a little help, Roxxie wiggled herself to the edge of the bed.

Paige saw two bloodstains along her white shirt in the back. She placed her fingers along the bloody fabric. "Roxxie? What happened to your wings?"

"My wings?" Roxxie twisted around and touched her

back. She swallowed hard. "They're still there," she said quietly. "But I can't get them out."

"Well, at least they're not gone." Small favors. But Paige had no idea how to help an angel. "Let's get you downstairs and some food in your belly."

Roxxie nodded but she did not look certain.

"Tyler," Leslie said. "You get to take care of Roxxie. Make sure she gets enough to eat."

Tru and Mandy appeared at the doorway and helped Roxxie out of the room and down the stairs.

Paige waited until they were all out of earshot. Leah hadn't moved, and Paige wasn't going to tell her to leave. She'd earned a stripe or two. That idea with the door magick? That had been brilliant. At least she hoped so.

Leslie looked over at Paige, then glanced at Leah.

Paige shook her head.

Leslie shrugged. "Okay. What the hell was that?"

Dexx shook his head. "Whatever happened to her, it had to be pretty bad. That little angel can kick a lot of serious ass."

Paige wasn't going to disagree. Roxxie had grown considerably over the years. And, truth be told, Paige wasn't really miffed at her anymore. Yes, she had been upset when Roxxie had taken her to Heaven and she'd been abducted, for lack of a better term, for several weeks.

Paige honestly believed Roxxie when she said that she hadn't known what was going to happen. She was certain if Roxxie had known what the angels had intended, she never would have brought Paige to Heaven.

So, what if that's what this was? "Maybe this is the angels."

Leah looked at her with a question on her face.

"Think about it. Angels are not supposed to make decisions on their own. That was the whole reason why Lucifer was kicked out of Heaven. He wanted the freedom of to make his own choices."

Dexx frowned. "I'm pretty sure he was kicked out because he didn't like humans."

"That is a hair we could split. But the bottom line is, he chose not to follow the marching orders he was given. So, what if the same thing happened to Roxxie? What if we inadvertently put her into a position where she had to choose between following the orders and doing what she thought was right?"

Dexx seemed to think on that for a moment. "So, you're saying this is our fault?"

Their fault? That seemed a little odd. As if giving someone a choice was something to be blamed for. But in the case of the angels? Where they could be punished for thinking on their own?

They just had to admit she really didn't like angels, the whole concept of them.

Leah leaned against the doorframe, crossing her arms over her chest, almost mimicking the stance Paige was certain she'd seen in the adults. "So, what does that mean for us? Do we care right now?"

That direction took Paige a little by surprise. That was an approach *she* would have taken. "I have to agree with her. Is this something that we have to deal with right away?"

Dexx shook his head, smirking. "I'd really rather have her at full strength and in this battle with us. But if she's not, then she's not. We have other fighters."

Leslie nodded. "I agree."

Well, if they were all in agreement. "Okay, we've had a few things happen in the last few hours I should probably get you all up to speed with."

As quickly as she could, Paige filled Leslie and Dexx in on the information Cyn had been able to provide for them. And the effect Paige's magick had had on Sven, as well as what she and Leah had been able to do.

"Is it too early to hope we might have a solution?" Leslie asked.

Dexx took a breath and crossed his arms over his chest. "I can tell you that DoDO isn't going to be a lot of help. They've got a few things that're actually pretty cool, but not for this. I told them they needed to stay out of this fight and let us deal with it."

That would be neat if any of them thought Mario would actually listen to them. "And do you think they're going to stay out?"

Dexx shook his head. "Not a chance. But it will mean they'll be fewer of them to deal with later."

While grim, that was a very realistic viewpoint. "All right." She looked at Leah. "I think you and I need to go talk to the Blackman's and make nice. If this door magick really is going to be helpful, then it would be beneficial if we could get more witches with this ability together."

Leah nodded.

Leslie held up her hand to stop them. "Do you really think that we can trust them?"

"I really don't think that we are in a position to ignore them. We need all of the allies we can get."

That was just an unfortunate reality.

Dexx nodded. "I don't like it."

"I don't either. But that's the reason she and I are going to go together."

Paige's phone rang. She dug it from her pocket and read the caller ID.

Tuck.

She pressed the green call button and put the phone up to her ear. "Whiskey."

"I have another body for you." Tuck's voice sounded tired.

"Where?"

"I'll text you the address." And then he hung up.

"What did he want?" Dexx asked.

Paige waited for the message with the address to pop up. "We have another body."

"But I thought you said you fixed the wards." Leslie looked confused. "Did we fix the wards or not?"

Paige shook her head, but as soon as the address came up, she was just confused again. She didn't answer Leslie. She just dialed Tuck's number again.

Talk answered gruffly. "Yeah."

"Where are you?"

"At the crime scene."

"But it's in Portland." She didn't *want* to point out the obvious. However, she felt as though she might have to. Troutdale had been cut off. All of the demons had been keeping people in *and* out of Troutdale. There was no way out.

"You'll see for yourself. Get your ass over here."

Paige shoved her phone in her pocket again and frowned up at Dexx. "Our body is in Portland."

Dexx shook his head. "How are we supposed to get there?"

17

Paige couldn't believe what she was seeing. The highways were open. And, when Paige checked her scry globe, she didn't see any demons anywhere close.

Was it too much to ask that this be done?

Probably.

"This is too easy." Dexx wrung the steering wheel.

Paige agreed. "We've had a few wins. But I didn't think they were big enough for him to just quit."

"I wouldn't have taken him for a sore loser. Not like this anyway."

Neither did Paige. Which meant Sven was planning something else. And they probably weren't going to like it.

They rode the rest of the way in silence. Sometimes, being able to just sit with another person was enough. It also didn't help the interior of the car was noisy. Paige really wanted Dexx to drive a quieter vehicle. But she also knew that was unlikely to ever happen.

The crime scene was located at the Portland docks. Again.

Paige got out and walked to the crime scene tape. There were several police cars, lights flashing. And there were police scattered randomly. They were actually doing a rather good job of keeping the reporters away.

And with good reason.

The body was strung up between two power poles. A large pool of blood had already formed underneath him, but his eyes were open, and his mouth was moving.

Tuck and Special Agent Jack Scott met Dexx and Paige.

"What's he saying?" Paige asked

Jack shoved his hands in his pockets. "Only that he has a message for Paige."

Paige didn't like this. What if this body was Sven's way of getting Paige out of Troutdale? And if that was the case, what was Sven planning?

As far as she knew, Sven had no way of getting inside her wards.

But that didn't mean someone else couldn't. He could have another shifter he was trying to secret in. Or a human. Or another paranormal. Her wards kept demons out, and now gods as well. Or demigods. Whatever. But everybody else? They were still pretty open.

Paige just had to have confidence in the people of Troutdale to keep an eye on the place. Like her sister. Or Tony. Or the rest of the Red Star Division. Chuck. There were a lot of people who were capable of looking after Troutdale in her absence.

Paige moved past Jack. "Okay. Let's see what this guy has to say."

Dexx stayed by her side. "The body still has a temperature."

She knew what he meant was he still had a heat signature. "So, this is like the last two love bodies he dropped."

Dexx nodded. "We weren't able to get a lot off those two."

"We don't need to. We know exactly who this is. The only thing we need to know is where he is and how to stop them."

Dexx glowered.

"This isn't a murder mystery." Why Paige was even saying that was beyond her. She was nervous. Anxious. She wanted to get this over with and to get Sven as far away from her town as possible. "I think I'm just talking to talk."

Dexx stopped and then turned to face her, putting his back toward the body.

Paige could hear the man mumbling now. She couldn't quite make out words. But she could hear his voice. It was unnerving to say the least.

Dexx lowered his voice. "If we already know who this is, then why are we even here? We need to be figuring out where Sven is. This is a waste of time."

Paige really couldn't argue. "What is he planning? He's always one step ahead of us."

"What if," Dexx said getting even closer to Paige, "we actually have the advantage here? What if we are actually gaining ground? What if he's scared and running?"

That would certainly be a first. "While I enjoy that thought, we still have no idea where he is."

Dexx shook his head. "I seriously hate this guy."

So did Paige. "Maybe, this guy has some clue. Let's do what we do best. Let's take the evidence and process it. And hope like hell that Sven messed up somehow and is giving us a location."

They walked up to the body.

The eyes of the victim found her almost immediately. "Hello, Paige."

At some point, Paige was going to have to get over hearing Sven's voice coming out of other people's bodies. "Hey, Sven. Couldn't just pick up a phone and call like a normal person?"

The body laughed. "You've put me in quite a position."

"I'm so terribly sorry I didn't just take it laying down."

"Oh, no. I'm quite pleased that you're able to step up so well. It means that you're ready for the next part."

That didn't sound good. "The next part? Any chance you're going to give me a clue as to what that is?"

"Where would the fun be in that?"

Paige opened her hands and then let them fall to her sides. "Oh, I don't know. We might have been able to get to the bottom of this sooner." She put her hands on her belly. "I don't know if you've noticed, but I'm about ready to give birth. And I'd kinda like to get this all done and over with *before* that happens. Any way we could speed is up?"

The victim's eyes fell to her belly. "I will say, that is one thing I did not take into consideration."

"I'm not entirely sure how to take that."

"Neither am I."

Paige was really done with the games. "Are you going to tell me why I'm here? Or are you stalling for time?"

The body drooped, as if the connection was being lost.

Paige gestured toward it. "I think your body is about to expire. Did you want to maybe hurry this up a bit?"

"I want you to meet me somewhere."

"You think that's a good idea?"

Dexx leaned in and muttered, "We could end this now."

Paige nodded. "Maybe. Maybe not."

The body spoke to the ground, not quite mumbling. "A white flag."

Paige shook her head. "You killed a man and are using his corpse as a way of offering of peace talk? Sven, have you lost your damn mind? Do you have any idea how this really works? If you were really serious about peace, you would've chosen a live body."

"But, what would be the fun in that? This is our thing. A *live* love body? That's just not the same."

"You're right. I might actually appreciate that a little bit more." Paige gestured around her. "There'd be a lot less media coverage, a lot less people."

"A lot less paperwork," Dexx said. He looked over at Paige. "What? Now that Tony is in control, he wants me to do my own paperwork. I'm not really down with that."

Paige shook her head. There were times when she just couldn't get enough of Dexx. And then moments where she had no idea what to do with him. The thought crossed her mind that if she did tell Tony to step down and told Dexx to step up, there was no way she'd be able to fill that role of paperwork maker. Dexx would have to actually do that. On his own. And she just wasn't sure if he was capable of that.

But that was a conversation for later. There was no way in hell she was having that conversation with Sven right there.

"What do you want?"

"Meet me at the address on this body, and you'll know."

Sven really was a sick fucker. "You do realize that if this is your form of flirting you really missed the mark with me. Right?"

The corpse's lips widened to a smile. "I look forward to talking to you. Alone."

Paige just took in a deep breath and released it. "And if I choose not to?"

"Ask Bal about the laws of treaty. Parlay." And then? The body drooped further. Sven had disconnected the call.

Paige didn't like this. Not one bit. "Bal, I need you."

Dexx gestured to the body. "Do you want me to go get the address?"

Paige really wanted to be that woman who had the iron stomach and could take just about anything. But she was at the end of her rope. She didn't want to look at another corpse. Not while she had two babies using her stomach as a kickboard. Which reminded her. She'd forgotten to eat. She should probably do that. She nodded at him and then turned around. "Thanks, babe."

Dexx didn't say anything as he approached the body. Bal appeared out of air a few feet away. Paige scanned the cops around them, but no one seemed to be looking in their general direction.

Bal glanced at the body and then frowned at Paige. "Sven?"

Paige nodded. "I need to know about the rules of parlay."

Bal grimaced. "It's really quite simple. While both parties are at parlay, neither side can inflict harm on the other."

That didn't sound bad. "So, his guys won't be attacking us."

Bal nodded. "But you will need to keep your people in line as well. If you inadvertently break parlay, then the other side is free to do whatever they want to your side and there will be no repercussions. No consequences."

She didn't like the sound of that. "Like what?"

"Like, he would be able to break through your wards. They would no longer hold against him."

That was certainly something she couldn't risk. "Well, pretty sure we can make that happen."

"Are you sure about that?"

What the hell did he know that she didn't? "If you have something to tell me, now is the time."

Dexx walked up to them. "Bal."

"Dexx." Bal gestured in return. "You have two loose cannons who are out of control right now."

Paige looked over at Dexx with a confused look on her face. "Who?"

Dexx appeared to be just is perplexed as she was.

Bal raised an eyebrow. "Frey and Tarik."

Dexx narrowed his eyes. "What about them?"

"They are attacking demons as we speak."

Wait. "You know where they are?"

Balnore shrugged. "Some of them. But not Sven. The only reason I know where some of the demons are is because Frey and Tarik led me there. They're currently pinned down. They could use a little help."

Paige shook her head, not sure what to do. "Okay, well go get them."

"There is no way for me to bring a Valkyrie anywhere against her will."

"You're a demigod." Paige wanted to make that point perfectly clear just in case he didn't get that. "So, go figure it out."

Bal gave her a look that told her it wasn't that simple, but then he disappeared.

Paige turned to Dexx. "Do you think that we could actually get a cease-fire out of this?"

Dexx shook his head. "It sounds another trap."

"What do you mean?"

"He's probably trying to get us to bring Frey and Tarik in. He probably knows that the two of them will do whatever they want, and that they're not great with obeying rules."

"Kind of like their boss?"

Dexx just grinned.

Paige really couldn't risk the consequences for breaking parlay. She had just gotten her wards to the point where nobody could get in. She wasn't going to lose that just because two members of their team decided they were going to do whatever the hell *they* wanted. "I don't care what you have to do. You get those two in line."

The expression on Dexx's face said he understood what she was saying, and he was pissed off she felt she needed to tell him that.

There were times when working with the man she loved was great. And then there were times like this where it wasn't. "If you break my wards Dexx, and if you endanger the lives of my children —"

"Our children."

She nodded once. "Then, understand that death will be too easy for you."

His eyes understood the danger, even though his lips curled in a grin. "You should probably marry me before you threatened to kill me. That way you get the insurance."

"Good call. But, if you and your team risk the lives of my children I won't care."

Dexx nodded. "I read you loud and clear."

"Good." Because if she was going to make it to that address on time, she needed to leave now. "I love you."

"Love you, too."

She didn't wait. She turned and shifted into a hawk. It was probably a good idea not to run through Portland as a tiger or a cheetah.

Dexx had better not screw this up.

But she knew he could.

18

Paige found the appointed place and landed on her bird feed before shifting. It turned out, that was a solid approach. It was so much easier to balance when she wasn't trying to shift and land on human feet at the same time.

Was it possible she was one of the most uncoordinated shifters ever? Looking around, Paige understood why he had chosen this location. It was reminiscent of Louisiana.

For whatever reason, Sven seemed to want to re-create that. Though, why? That was the million-dollar question. Dexx believed he was courting her in a weird way.

If that was the case, then Sven seriously needed to rethink his game.

An eagle cried overhead. Paige looked up in time to see Leslie shift as she landed.

Paige was more than a little jealous of the fact Leslie was able to make it look so incredibly easy. "What are you doing here?"

"Good to see you too." Leslie closed the distance, looking around. "He hasn't shown up yet?"

"I'm a little early. I wanted to make sure I wasn't about to be ambushed."

Leslie looked around, scoping the area. "I didn't see anybody on the way in."

"Neither did I." Though, that really didn't make Paige feel any better about any of this. "I really need you at home."

"I needed to fill you in on what's going on."

If this was an attack, Paige needed to know. "What?"

Leslie held up two hands. "It's nothing like that. We just have a whole bunch of people leaving Troutdale. They found out the roads were open and most of them didn't even wait to pack their things. They got their families in the car and they're fleeing the situation, evacuating the area."

That wasn't necessarily a bad thing. "What about people getting in? I'm kind of afraid that Sven is going to try and sneak someone in who is already able to get through the wards. He might even have another device or something like what Bastet had."

"Already on that one. We've got people stationed along each of the roads leading in. We're searching cars and people. Mostly, it's reporters and other shifters who are answering Chuck's call."

That couldn't necessarily be a bad thing. "I need everyone to refrain from fighting any demons until I give the order."

Leslie narrowed her eyes. "I don't understand."

"This might be the trap. According to Bal, under the laws of parlay, if I, or any of my team attacks a demon, then we have broken the laws of parlay and he can come right through our wards."

The look on Leslie's face was damn near priceless. "Do you have any idea how hard it's going to be to make that happen?"

Paige wasn't stupid. "Something tells me that that is exactly what he's looking for right now. And it would make sense. With so many of us scattered? With so many people leaving and so many people coming? It would be really easy for the demons to just show up and wait for someone to strike out at them. And they would probably think they're doing exactly what they're supposed to."

Leslie swore. "I fucking hate this guy."

"So do I. But that doesn't change anything. I need you to go home and make sure that no one, and I mean *no one* makes a move against those demons until I give the all clear."

Leslie shook her head. "Way to give me the easy tasks." But she didn't say anything else. She simply spun and leapt into the air, shifting into an eagle on her way up.

Paige knew if anyone could make that happen, it would be Leslie.

Dexx?

Probably not. He had many strengths. Following orders and meeting the minimum requirements of the situation were not one of them.

He would probably break the rules, break parlay, and then find some other way to win the battle.

And while Paige appreciated the fact he always seemed to win, the reality was there was more than one time he had barely won. She didn't want this to be the time he lost instead.

Once Leslie left, Paige didn't have much longer to wait for Sven to show up. He flew in on his demon wings, landing several feet away in the empty parking lot.

He walked toward her, scanning the area as he approached. "I can't tell if I'm disappointed that you showed up alone or if I'm proud."

Paige shrugged. "There was no sense in bringing anyone with me if were under the flag of parlay. You can't hurt me, and I can't hurt you."

"Until the parlay talks are done."

That was true, and she hadn't missed that. She'd watched *Pirates of the Caribbean*. "Why don't you just tell me why we're here?"

"Straight to the point then?"

Paige gestured wide with her hands. "You know me."

Sven smiled. "Indeed, I do." He walked forward, approaching her on the side as though he intended to circle her. Which he probably did. "I do so miss Louisiana."

"What exactly would you miss from Louisiana? It wasn't as if we shared anything special there."

"You don't think so?" he came around in front of her and stopped within arm's reach. He reached out as if to touch her chest.

She batted his hand away. "No."

His smile said he had forgotten the basic rules of human propriety. "My apologies."

"Are you going to tell me why we are here or not?"

"We can't just have a moment?"

Paige didn't have time for this. "As if we were lovers? That might be a highly interesting conversation. But we're not. Never have been. Not even a little."

"Pity that."

That wasn't something she was going to regret. "Besides, you and I both know that you're just trying to stall me while my people do something stupid and heroic and break the parlay."

Sven threw back his head and laughed. "And here I feared you wouldn't see the trap for what it was."

Paige was really too tired to play that game. "You and I both know the longer we stay here talking the greater the likelihood my people will fuck this up. So, I would take it as a personal kindness if you just went along with the parlay in good faith and told me what the fuck you wanted."

She had a suspicion after having dealt with the elves, if *he* broke the parlay, there would be just as much consequence on his side. So, for the sake of that, it was just best to call him out on his own shit.

Sven smirked, raising his chin. "My, my, look at how far you've come in such a short amount of time."

"Please. You don't get to take all the credit for this." If only Dexx were here. He would've had something funny to say. But, unfortunately, he was off trying to make sure they didn't lose this for the next five minutes.

And he damn well better be succeeding too.

"So, how about we get to the heart of the matter? What do you want?"

Bal took Dexx to the place where Frey and Tarik were holed up. Just like Bal had said, the two were buried in demons. They'd somehow found themselves in a great big huge nest of them.

Dexx crouched behind the rock the two had hidden behind and hissed, "What the hell are you doing?"

Frey looked at him, startled to see him. "What the hell are you doing here?"

Bal set his hand on Tarik's shoulder. "We really should get out of here."

Frey shook her head. "We're about to bring these demons down."

Oh, if only this was any other day. Dexx leaned in so that both Frey and Tarik could hear him, even though he knew they both had excellent hearing. "Paige is in the middle of a parlay with Sven at this very moment."

Frey's expression folded into a look of "Why the fuck should I care?".

But understanding dawned on Tarik's expression. He nodded sagely. "Frey, we should leave."

Frey shook her head "Not a chance. This is the biggest nest we've found. We can take them out right now. And he wouldn't even know what hit 'em." She gestured at Dexx. "And now that Dexx is here? And this guy? We can take them *all* out right now."

Dexx could get behind the Valkyrie's position on getting the job done. However, this was one of those times where Paige needed him to toe the line. He *really* needed Frey to just shut up and do what he told her to do. "Frey, if you fight these demons, even *swing* at one, you'll break the parlay, and then all of them will be able to get through Paige's wards. I don't like it either, but this is bigger than one nest."

She frowned, glancing to the side, as if she could see the demons. But she couldn't. They were on the other side of the massive hidey-hole boulder.

"Now, I realize that you can take on a whole bunch of demons and not even break a sweat." And, honestly, that's one of the many things Dexx liked most about her. "But, if you endanger my kids Paige will kill me. Slowly. So, do me a favor and don't ruin us."

Fray narrowed her eyes. "Fine. But we'll stay right here until the parlay is done."

Dexx shook his head. "Trust me. You're the trap that's been set. He knows you're here. And he knows that I can't control you. He *wants* you to kill these things. So, if you want to play right into his hands, you do that." He really, really hoped she wouldn't. "But just know, that I will do everything in my power to stop you."

Frey glared at him.

Well, at least she wasn't attacking the demons right away. "Bal get us out of here."

Balnore shook his head. "I can do nothing with these two. They are beyond me. I can only take you."

Frey smirked at him. "It's not going to be that easy."

It was time to get her to understand. He got in her face. "You do anything stupid or irrational, or if you allow them to trick you into doing something stupid and irrational, and if you endanger the lives of my family, or my children, understand that Paige won't have to get to you." Dexx leaned in even further so that she would get the full weight of his words, his alpha will slipping to the front. "I will end you myself."

"Many have tried," Frey said, "and all have failed."

"Well, a god may not be able to touch you. But let me assure you. I *will. Don't* fuck this up."

Doubt entered Frey's expression. She turned to Tarik and took hold of his arm. "Let's get out of here."

That was all Dexx needed to hear. He turned to Bal and nodded.

Their mission here was done. At least Dexx hoped it was.

Sven looked at her and smiled. "I want the key. All of the pieces of the key. And I happen to know that you can get it."

Oh. That was all? "What do you want with the key?"

"Isn't it obvious?"

"With you? Nothing's obvious."

Sven laughed. "I plan to bring Hell to Earth."

Somehow, she doubted that. "You know I'm not going to give you the key to Hell. So, what is this really about?"

"I had to give you the opportunity. A lot more lives are going to be lost if you don't just hand over the key."

Paige shook her head. "I'm pretty confident that we're a

lot closer to gaining the upper hand than you think. Or at least than you're willing to admit."

Was that doubt that crossed over his expression?

She liked it.

"You don't even realize how perfectly you are playing right into my game."

"Really? Because that's not the impression I got when I sent your demons away. How are they doing? Did we really just send them to Mars? Because it really looked like we sent them to Mars."

Sven's expression darkened. "I will admit that you surprised me. You and your daughter are a great deal more powerful than I had originally anticipated."

"See? I've got the upper hand."

His smile was tight. "Go ahead and think that, little bird."

So, the real point of this entire parlay was to try and see if he could get her side to break the rules. It was time to end this. "If the only thing you want is the key, and you know that I'm not going to give that to you, then we're done here."

Alarm crashed over his expression. "No. Wait."

Yep. That's exactly what he was trying to do. "I'm officially calling an end to this parlay."

Bal and Dexx appeared not far away.

Dexx had damn well better have been able to fix his Valkyrie problem. "Is there something formal that we need to say? I don't want there to be any misconception."

Sven gave her a cold stare. "I really had expected more from you."

"Trying to goad me into attacking? That's something a twelve-year-old would do." She smiled. "You're talking to a mother. I may not be a great mother. But, I've had my experience with the twelve-year-old beating me into an argument. So, Bal? How do we close this?"

Bal smiled. "You have done so."

"Great." She took a step back. "Now, unless you want us to just finish this right here and now?"

She really should. He was alone. Or at the very least, it appeared as though he was alone. She knew her magick had power over him. She also had door magick she could call on and send him someplace else. All she had to do was one of those things and the Sven problem was gone.

Bal put his hand on her arm, stopping her. He shook his head.

Great.

"You both are safe until you have left the area. Parlay ensures that both parties will be able to leave in safety."

"Of course."

She bowed slightly and gestured for Sven to leave. "After you, douchebag."

He snorted and left.

They'd won? Well, that was a first.

19

When Paige and Dexx drove back into town, it was to find everything in total chaos. Leslie hadn't been kidding when she said it was a mass evacuation.

The entrance ramps to the highway on either side of town, heading in either direction, were clogged. People were trying to get out of Dodge.

And Paige really couldn't blame them. While it had been nice everyone had played well together for as long as they had, she wasn't stupid. It wouldn't have lasted much longer.

Tensions were already fraying, and it would just take one fuse to set off the powder keg.

She just hoped the demons would stay away long enough for the town to be evacuated.

However, now that the terms of parlay had been lifted, it was a free-for-all.

On the way over, Dexx had been making phone calls to everyone, letting them know if any demons appeared, they were to take them out. Well, take them out and not get dead. That was key.

Paige couldn't release the sense of unease plaguing her,

though. Whatever had just happened, she was certain she had only seen half of it. Sven was too tricky.

Yes. She had absolutely no doubt whatsoever he had intended for one of her people to break the parlay. She was really surprised no one had.

But, she didn't think for one moment this was the only thing he had planned.

Before they made it to the Red Star Division, Paige's phone rang. Well, it vibrated in her pocket. Whatever. She pulled it out and frowned. The number didn't make any sense. The elder prison. She hit the green button and put the phone to her ear "This had better be a joke."

"I assure you," Merry Eastwood's silky voice said over the line. "This is no joke."

Paige pulled the phone away from her ear and stared at the screen for a moment before putting it back. Merry Eastwood should not be able to make any phone calls from prison. "How did you get a phone?"

"Let's just say that a few of the powers that be aren't nearly as stupid as you would hope."

Weren't nearly as stupid as Paige hoped? "What do you want?"

"Come see me. I have information you need."

Whatever this information was it damn well better be pretty damned good. Important, too. "I have things on my docket already today. I'm full up."

"Make an opening. You're going to want to hear what I have to say." And the line went dead.

Paige put her phone in her lap, trying to figure out what the fuck she was supposed to do with that.

"Who was that?"

"Merry fucking Eastwood." What kind of trap was Paige about to step into this time? She'd just got out of one. "She wants me to meet her at the prison."

"Are you going?"

"I think so?" Though, did she really need to? She had what she needed. She had a way to defeat Sven. They had succeeded in cutting him off from his energy sources. And for *whatever* reason her magick had an effect on him. And if that wasn't enough, they had the door magick. If anything, she needed to be dropping everything and going to talk to the Blackmans.

Though, if she really wanted to be smart about this, she would divide and conquer.

She really didn't like the thought. In order to do that, she would have to send Leah to either Merry or Eldora. And she didn't like either of those choices.

"Talk to me, babe. What's going on in your head?"

"Remember when you said that we might have to make a few alliances that we didn't want?"

Dexx nodded.

"I need to go talk to Merry Eastwood. And we also need to go talk to the Blackmans and see if we can get them on board."

"And you are thinking of delegating one of those."

The reality was Paige was spread out ridiculously thin. It was time, past time, for her to start delegating a few things. But could she really delegate something like that to her teenage daughter? Wasn't that just kind of a dumb idea?

"Let Leah take the Blackmans." Instead of turning left at the light, Dexx went straight through, heading home. "They're the lesser of the two evils, and I'll be there with her."

Paige had to admit she felt a lot better thinking Leah would have someone with her. "Do you think that's a good idea?"

"What I think?" Dexx glanced at her out of the corner of his eye. "Is that everyone needs to do what they can if we're going to survive. And it's probably high time that the three which families figured out how to play nice together. At least for now."

Paige was a little surprised. That was very grown-up. "Okay. Let me out here and I will fly over to the prison. But…"

Dexx pulled over midway up the hill.

Paige speared him with her gaze. "You don't let anything happen to my daughter."

"I will *not* let anything happen to *our* daughter."

That was the thing she loved most about her man. She doubted he'd ever thought he would be a father. But he had certainly stepped into the role and done a pretty damned good job. She leaned over and gave him a kiss. "I love you."

"I love you, too. Now get out of here."

She did, and as she stood there on the sidewalk, staring around her nearly empty town, she hoped she wasn't about to do something incredibly stupid.

Dexx really had no idea what he was supposed to do. Was this a negotiation or a demand?

As he and Leah pulled into the driveway leading to the Blackman house, he was overwhelmed with doubt. He was about to have a conversation with a bunch of witches. And not the nice, cuddly Whiskey kind.

"If you feel, at any time," he said to Leah as he found a parking space between two wagons, "that you need to leave, we leave. *However* we need to do it."

She looked terrified, but nodded. "Okay."

"Now, they're probably going to try and get you kids to go to their school. Your mom is not going to allow that. Frankly, neither am I."

Leah swallowed hard and nodded.

"You have an idea on how to defeat Sven. So, just stick with that. You think they could play an important part. They take you off course, steer them back. But they need to know that you do *not* have the authorization to make any big decisions." He stopped the car and put it in park, cutting the engine.

Eldora and Derrick came out of the main house.

"I'll follow your lead. You're the one who understands what you're trying to accomplish here. I don't. I'll just make sure that you don't do anything too stupid."

Leah nodded. "Nothing too stupid. Right."

The poor kid looked terrified. "You've got this."

The look she gave him said she didn't have this, but she opened the door and got out anyway.

Eldora held out her hands to Leah. "It is so good to see you again."

Leah refrained from taking her hands. "And while you're not trying to kill me, even."

A shadow passed over Eldora's face.

Derrick just grinned. Leah turned to him. "Remember when you said that you could help me?"

He nodded. "I also remember you and your mom turning me down."

"Well, you scare me."

Derrick shrugged apologetically. "I really don't mean to. You're my niece. I just want to make sure that you're okay."

"Well." Leah took in a big breath. "I have an idea that might work. But I think I'm going to need your help."

Derrick frowned, the corners of his lips falling. "I'm listening."

Dexx would give Derrick one thing. He knew how to talk to kids where Eldora didn't.

It visibly bolstered her courage.

Like she had put on lipstick. It was the closest thing Dexx could compare it to. And he only knew this because he had seen two teenage girls apply lipstick so many times it was scary.

"Mom and I did something amazing and we think that with your help we could do even better."

"Go on."

By this time, two other young men who looked remarkably like Derrick and Eldora had come to join them. However, they remained quiet.

Leah barely glanced at them. "So, Mom and I made a door and then we sent the demons through."

Eldora narrowed her eyes. "What door did you open? And where did you send them?"

Leah narrowed her eyes. "I'm not really sure where we sent them?"

At least Dexx knew about this part. "Paige said it looked like Mars." Though could it really have been Mars? Dexx didn't know. But anything was possible with Paige these days.

Eldora gave him a measuring look. "Are you certain of this?"

"Certain that she said that? Yes. Because I clarified. Certain that she actually sent demons to Mars? She's certain of that. Because I clarified that, too."

Eldora frowned at him as though he was being impertinent.

Let her frown. Impertinence was his middle name.

Derrick seemed to find him funny anyway.

Eldora glanced at her sons. "It is possible that we can help."

The way she hedged, though, Dexx knew she was looking for something in return. "Just understand that the only person who can really negotiate this is Paige. Leah is here just to see if you'd be willing to help us win a war against a demon who is trying to destroy our town. So, if you need some form of payment for your heroics you're just going to have to talk to Paige. But you can't do that right now because she's on another mission. Again, trying to save our town."

Eldora glared at him. "Well then, I guess we will just have to see how we can save this little town and then remind Paige afterwards of what we did."

"Yes. Please do that. Remind her how you helped save us after we gave you the idea of how to do it. Because up until this point, you've brought nothing to the table on your own."

Eldora didn't have anything to say to that.

Derrick's grin sure did.

It was time to get out of there. "So, would you like to come over sometime tomorrow to discuss particulars?"

Eldora seemed to be fuming. But, she nodded. "We will be by after breakfast."

"Perfect. We'll see you then." He gathered Leah and guided them both back to the car. "That could have gone a lot worse."

"Yeah. Nobody died." Leah's voice was hopeful. "Including my car."

Oh, that girl was learning. At least she was learning.

***

Paige shifted as soon as her feet touched the ground. The elder prison was out in the middle of nowhere. Quite literally. It was unlikely anyone would ever find themselves at the location accidentally. It was also surrounded by so many wards and other protections, she was sure she had tripped about a dozen just flying in.

The place kind of looked like a medieval castle. Almost? More like a castle made out of dark concrete.

It didn't look like any prison she'd ever seen before.

It also lacked the chain link fence with the barbed wire rolled on top. Probably because there were so many other defenses that breaking out and running away was clearly not a good idea.

Paige walked in and was greeted by… no one? That was a little concerning. Because every other time she'd been there she'd been greeted by dozens of guards. Where were they?

Everywhere she went on her way to Merry Eastwood's wing— because Merry Eastwood had an entire wing— she saw no one.

What the hell was going on here?

When she made it to Merry Eastwood's wing, the doors were all open. There was literally nothing that would have kept anyone inside. However, there was Merry Eastwood, sitting at a hexagonal table, playing solitaire.

Was this a trap? If it was, it was the strangest damned snare ever. And after having just survived Sven's little attempt, she wasn't really looking forward to another one.

She just wanted one day, *one day*, where she could sit down in front of the TV and veg out, maybe catch up on a little bit of *Once Upon a Time*.

Remaining on high alert, and bringing Cawli forward, Paige took a seat across from Merry.

She wasn't looking really great. She was starting to show her age. This witch was over two hundred years old and had been using a spell of some sort in order to maintain her beauty. Or retain it. It was painfully evident Merry hadn't been able to perform her spell in quite some time. She didn't look ancient exactly. But she certainly didn't look young either. "Why am I here, Merry?"

Merry flicked another two cards on a stack, then set the deck down folded her hands, smiling up at Paige. "You're here to break me out of prison."

"Like hell I am."

"Trust me. You want to win this war against Sven. You're going to need me, and the power of my coven in order to do it. I've made it easy for you. All you've got to do is walk me out."

Yep. Trap.

And Paige had fallen for it.

"How did you get everyone to clear out?" Paige asked.

Merry gestured wide with her hands, calmly looking around. "With what you have going on down there, do you really think it was a hard sell for my assistance?"

With as badly as the elders had wanted her in that prison? Yeah. It was pretty hard for her to believe.

Merry shook her head as if trying to get her head wrapped around the fact Paige was struggling to understand this. "The elders may not appreciate my methods, but they all understand that of all the witches out there currently, I am the strongest, the most powerful."

Well, prison certainly hadn't changed her ego. "I'm certainly glad you think so."

"You need my help. I'm simply offering it."

"Well, I'm not going to just walk out of here with you. I don't know if you noticed, but I worked kind of hard to put you in here. I'm not going to just let you out of here scot-free. You murdered a lot of people."

"Which, oddly, is exactly the reason why you need me. I can do the things that you can't. Or won't."

The way she'd said that last part, made it seem as though Paige was a weaker person for not sacrificing the lives of others to suit her own personal gain. Paige stood. "I thought you had information. But apparently all you want is freedom. I'm not giving you that."

A metal door opened and closed behind Paige.

She turned around and saw Elder Yad walk through the door. He still reminded her of the old wizard from *Legend of the Seeker*. The TV version. He was tall and gangly and more than a little old. He was not what Paige would call handsome.

She held out her hand for a handshake. "Elder Yad."

He took her hand in greeting and then gestured toward Merry. "She has told you of our arrangement?"

Paige was aghast. "You actually agreed to this?"

The elder sighed and folded his hands in front of him. "You will find, Ms. Whiskey, that the longer you do this job, the more you discover just how grey every situation is. We feel that it is in everyone's best interest to allow Merry out of prison."

Paige couldn't believe what she was hearing. "And when we're done with her? Does she just come back?"

Elder Yad shook his head. "No. something like time served. In exchange, she is to return to her coven and bring it under control."

Paige read between the lines. What he was really saying was that she was to bring the Eastwood coven under *elder* control. Now that was something she believed. Because the one thing the elders seem to appreciate the most was to be the ones with the power. "And are there any ramifications on me if she slips your net?" because Paige really didn't want to have to bear the consequences of anything else going wrong. She had her hands full enough already.

Elder Yad gave Merry a long, hard look. "She knows exactly what will happen if she doesn't play by the rules."

Well, as long she knew. "And what are those rules?"

Merry turned a cool gaze to Elder Yad. "That's between me and him. But leave it to say that I am honor bound to assist you in any way I can." She turned that cool gaze to Paige. "And, *you're welcome.*"

Well. Thanks. "I didn't bring a car."

"I did." Merry smiled sweetly. "But I will need you to walk me out the doors. Otherwise, I can't leave."

That didn't sound like a trap. At all. Paige speared Elder Yad with her gaze, her alpha will pushing forward just a little. "Tell me again that the consequences of this isn't going to fall back on me."

"It will not."

"Then, why do *I* have to be the one to walk her out?"

He sighed darkly. "Because there are protections set up against any of the elders doing so. It's so we do not abuse the power."

Something in the way he said that made her think someone *had* abused that power. Possibly long ago.

Or *not* so long ago.

Whatever. It didn't matter. "And what help do you think you're going to be against Sven?"

Merry's smile was damned near frigid. "I'm a blood witch, and moreover, I'm the most powerful blood witch in existence."

"And you're going to need blood in order to do whatever magick you intend to use?"

She nodded. "But I promise not to spill the blood of the innocent. Does that make you feel better?"

It did and didn't at the same time.

Paige ground her teeth together. "Fine. Let's get out of here. I've got a lot of things to do."

She didn't wait for either Merry or Elder Yad to say

anything further. She just walked out. There had to be something more to this, something she wasn't seeing.

Just like that "parlay" with Sven. What had he *really* been after? It felt too easy. It wasn't like her and her team to actually guess what he was after and then be right.

Or maybe they were finally getting good at this?

Right.

Probably not.

Paige stopped outside and turned to Merry. "You got it from here?"

Merry tipped her head to the side. "What did you come in on? A broom?"

If only Paige could shift into a broom, that would be funny. But as far as she could tell, a broom didn't have a shifter spirit.

Cawli snorted in the back of her mind.

She was apparently right. "I'll see you at my house. Don't dawdle. I don't know how long the demons are going to stay away. And if you don't get back to Troutdale before they make it back, there won't be a way in and then whatever deal you cooked up with Elder Yad will be toast."

She had a few more things she had to take care of first.

Like getting Tony the hell out of Troutdale for one.

She turned and leapt into the air, shifting into an owl. They were surprisingly fast *and* super quiet.

But she still wasn't super graceful on her take-off. She needed to get better at that.

She flew from the prison, watching as Merry stepped into a shiny, black car that had been parked out front.

Paige should probably give Ollie a call to give him the heads up, but she couldn't do that while she was flying, and Tony was the priority. She needed to get him out of Oregon before the Eastwoods descended on Troutdale, making it absolutely unsafe for him to stay.

She scanned the surroundings on her way in. There was no sign of demons. Whatsoever. It was like they'd never existed.

But the TV crews? They were everywhere.

The steady stream of cars headed out of the little town had finally trickled, and by the time she made it through the wards and into town, it was like no one was there. Few cars were parked along any of the streets. She didn't see a single pedestrian.

It was sad to see, especially after how they'd all managed to come together to get supplies, work on the school, share meals, and everything.

She did, however, see a lot of shifters. They were out in force in every variety of animal she could imagine, including a Pegasus.

So, Doe had made it from Utah. That was good.

Paige winged into the Red Star Division parking lot, which was full of people. She *tried* to shift and land at the same time but stumbled on her own two feet and nearly fell.

A tall, dark man from Doe's pack caught her. He chuckled. "Still learning to stick the landing?"

Oh, God, if he only knew. "Yeah."

He let her go and reached for her belly without touching it. "Well, I can see why. You just wait for them to come out of the oven, and you'll be just fine."

She doubted she'd ever be a super graceful flier. Not like Leslie was, anyway. "Thanks."

Scanning the parking lot on her way into the precinct, she looked for faces she knew and came up blank. The parking lot was full of a bunch of people she'd never met in her entire life. Well, her entire "knowing the paranormal" life, which hadn't been that long, if truth be told.

Wow. Chuck's regional pack *was* big.

She disappeared into the building and the noise from

outside died. She hadn't even realized how loud it had been until it was gone.

Walking to the back, she listened for the sounds of anyone, but it was a ghost town in there too. When she made it to the cells, the only person was Tony.

He stood and went to the cell door. "I don't like that face."

He'd been her partner for five years in Denver, so, yeah, he probably knew her face pretty well. "We're getting you out of here."

He shook his head. "As soon as the Eastwoods are gone—"

"They're coming here. The entire coven." He needed to grasp the *entire* situation. "And they might not leave again."

The color drained from his face. "You can't be serious."

Oh, she really was. "Things are changing here, Tony, and I have no idea where we're going to tomorrow, much less next week."

"Are you firing me?"

Yes. "You could be a bigger liability than we can afford."

"So, you're firing me."

She was quiet as she studied him. She didn't know the words to say. "What do you think I should do?"

He flattened his lips, taking a deep breath and raising his head, looking away. "The team didn't like me much anyway."

Her eyes widened as she recalled the stories of some of his blood craze. "Do you blame them?"

His dark eyes met hers and then he shook his head. "No."

She gave him a curt nod. "Merry's on her way into town as we speak. You get in your car and head south as fast as you can. We'll mail you anything you leave."

He clenched his hand into a fist and then released it forcibly. "I could have done good here."

"I agree, but you could do good in Dallas, too. There are

no blood witches there. And they could use a person like you. That job is probably still open."

He glared at her and then looked away in defeat. "I'll give him a call."

"Great." She knew her old boss would be glad to hear from Tony. She'd played him up quite a bit. "Just be honest with Henry. He can't help you if you hide from him."

"Fine." He gripped the bars of the door. "You gonna open this up and let me out?"

She did and walked with him to his desk— her desk? — Dexx's desk. He grabbed his keys and a few things. Then, she escorted him to his car. "I'll fly with you out of town to make sure you don't get into any trouble. Merry's coming from the east."

Technically, she was coming from the north and the east and she'd probably cross the Columbia river just south of there. But Paige didn't want to take any chances.

Tony nodded grimly and slammed his car door shut behind him. He tore out of the parking lot, letting his anger out on his tires.

The shifters in the lot hurried to get out of his way.

Paige shook her head and then took flight. It was a crappy thing to do.

But it was the right thing. For Tony. For her team.

For Dexx who would never admit it out loud, but he *really* wanted the Red Star Division to be *his*. Now, all she had to do was make him realize how hard he was willing to fight for it.

And then make him do his own damned paperwork.

Yeah. That was all.

Paige waited with Leslie at the empty Red Star. They were alone and waiting for the other coven leaders to arrive.

Tony was gone, and safely headed south, hopefully not hating her too much.

After a short conversation with Leslie, Paige decided the convention of witches wasn't going to happen inside the Whiskey wards. Inside Troutdale? Sure. But she wasn't inviting the Blackmans, or the Eastwoods, outside of Ollie because she genuinely liked him, inside her wards.

And she decided it was time to invite Leah and Mandy into the talks.

"You're not to speak," Paige said solemnly as they sat around the bullpen of Red Star.

"Unless," Leslie modified, holding up a finger, "someone asks you a question. *Then* you can speak."

Leah nodded eagerly.

Mandy narrowed her eyes, showing she intended to butt into the conversation the first chance she got.

"You haven't earned your voice in this meeting," Paige

said, pushing a little with her alpha will. "You're still learning. You're here to see what the big kids do and how the big kids handle things so when Leslie and I want to retire— like, when you're both sixteen and know everything— we can hand it off to you, knowing that you'll be able to do everything *we* can."

Mandy rolled her eyes, but she kept her lips shut.

Leah just quietly chuckled and shook her head, but she too, kept her lips shut.

Paige and Leslie had made a solemn vow— as only sisters could— their children wouldn't be kept in the dark in the same way they had been. When they died— and they would — they wanted their kids to be better prepared to pick up the pieces. So that meant taking the girls into a type of apprenticeship. Of sorts.

That was going to be interesting in Paige's new role with the elders.

She hadn't informed Dexx she'd escorted Tony out of town yet. She was sure he knew. He seemed to always know what was going on in this town, which made her believe he might be ready for this.

Oh, crap. She was going to have to talk to Tuck about this. She'd made the decision without consulting him first. But, since Tuck hadn't even bothered to call Tony once, she was fairly certain he'd be fine with it.

Eldora Blackman was the first to arrive, with her sons — Derrick, William, Ian, and Steven. Paige still had a hard time placing a name to all the faces. She was almost certain the one she thought was William was actually Ian. She wasn't sure which one was Steven. She felt lucky she remembered her half-brother's names at all.

Derrick was easy. He was the only one who smiled, the only one who seemed half-way human. She hoped when Eldora stepped down, he would be the one to take over the coven. But like the Eastwoods, she had a suspicion the coven leadership would have to go to a female.

But who? They were in the same boat as the Eastwoods, as far as Paige knew. They didn't *have* a female heir. Except for Leah. *She* was the heir for both—

Shit. No. Leah was the heir for the Eastwood coven.

Paige was the heir for the Blackman coven.

Fucking Christ. She shook herself.

Sorry. Blessed Mother.

They had a *seriously* fucked up family tree.

But Paige and Leah were going to remain in the Whiskey coven. The end. That was the magick they knew the best and it was what they were going to keep to.

Right?

Right.

They exchanged pleasantries and then waited for Merry Eastwood to show up. Which she did several minutes later.

Paige went still. All the years Merry had gained while in prison were gone, erased. "You performed the spell?"

Merry Eastwood's youth spell had been how Paige had caught her in the first place. It involved a lot of kids dying, along with their parents. So, if she was back to her old tricks, Paige was going to have more than a few words with Elder Yad about his practices and what he allowed to happen in his back yard.

Ollie rolled his eyes as he perched on Michelle's desk. "No. This is something different. And trust me, I haven't heard the end of how unjust everything is."

Paige had barely got the call into Ollie to warn him about what she'd done before Merry had shown up on his doorstep to greet him. She'd actually still been on the phone with him when Merry'd arrived. To say that Ollie wasn't pleased would be putting it mildly.

Merry gave them all a serene smile, appearing no older

than thirty. The woman looked damned good. Hell, Paige wished *she* looked that good, but she wasn't going to kill a bunch of people just to look pretty. Well, unless they were *her* kids and they'd made her *really* angry.

Eldora glared, turning in Rainbow's chair, putting her back to Merry.

Merry pranced further into the room and took a seat where Eldora couldn't ignore her. "Eldora."

The other woman still ignored her.

Time to get this party started. "We're here because it's time we come together and start acting like the founding witches of this area, protecting the lands, instead of our own best interests."

Eldora sniffed. "Says you. You're the one who put the entire town under your own wards."

"I didn't keep you out." Even though Paige had wanted to.

Derrick smiled grimly. "She really wants your kids in our school. Better for witches."

"That's not going to happen." Paige wanted to make that clear. "They're welcome to join our school, but we won't be joining yours."

"What makes yours so special?" Merry asked way too innocently.

Paige kept her gaze on Eldora to ensure the woman got the point. "*Everyone* is welcome in *our* school."

Merry chuckled. "Well, that's perfect then. Where do we sign up?"

Paige turned to Merry. "Our kids go to school with all the paranormals in this town." Though that might be changing if the covens and packs keep growing.

Merry made a noise.

Ollie smiled appreciatively, his gaze distant. "That is certainly unique."

It was, and it hadn't been easy. "We need to discuss what we're going to do about Sven."

"I'm serious," Merry said, "about getting our kids into your school."

What?

Content she had everyone's attention, Merry smiled primly. "We're retaking our ancestral land."

Wait. What? No. That hit like a freight train.

"The Eastwoods are returning to Troutdale." Merry raised her hands wide, palms up.

It was a good thing Paige had already made Tony leave. But what could she do? Tell Merry they weren't able to return to the lands they owned? That was a tactic Merry would employ. It wasn't one that Paige would. "You will have to obey the same laws as everyone else."

"I will only spill blood that is volunteered."

Because that would happen? "And no murder."

"Unless it's necessary and only if they've deserved it." Merry tipped her head to the side, her gaze lowering. "Doing my part for a society that can't do it on their own."

Paige didn't even know what that meant. "We don't kill, Merry. Anyone."

"*You* don't."

"No one plays judge and jury." Paige needed Merry to understand this loud and clear. "Not in my backyard."

Merry smiled warmly. "Then, I'll do it in your *front* yard."

Paige was going to bitch slap that woman.

Ollie raised a hand, keeping it low, trying to calm Paige. "She's playing with you. Don't take the bait."

Paige loathed that woman. And had a weird respect for her at the same time.

But she was right. She might be exactly what Troutdale needed. But that wasn't what Paige wanted to hear or to think about.

But it was the honest to goddess truth.

"Excuse me," a male voice with a British accent called from the front as the door closed. "Is this a private meeting?"

"Yes," Paige shouted back. "Get out!"

Merry raised both her eyebrows, peering around Derrick to see the front desk.

Mario cleared the front and entered the bullpen with a smile. He wore dark jeans and a dark t-shirt today, which was dressed down from what she'd seen him in before. "I thought this was a meeting of the local witches."

"*Local* being the key part," Paige said stiffly.

"I don't think I've had the pleasure," Merry said, rising to her feet.

Mario looked equally intrigued. "Mario Kester, Director of Delicate Operations."

"He's DoDO," Paige said firmly.

Merry gave Paige a frown, but took Mario's hand in hers. "Merry Eastwood."

"In the flesh," he said in his light British accent.

Paige hated him a little more just then. "She's a killer."

"Of course, she is," Mario said with a smile as he kissed the back of Merry's hand. "She's a blood witch. It would be a terrible waste to be a blood witch and not murder those when needed."

Eldora rose to her feet and offered her hand. "Eldora Blackman."

Mario turned to Eldora and took her hand as well. "A pleasure."

Paige sighed loudly.

Mario pulled back and found a place to perch. "The four most powerful witches in the territory in one room."

The back door opened, and Billie Black stepped into the room, her dark gaze on Mario.

His eyes twitched, and his hands went for his belt. Then his gaze landed on Paige.

She hoped she was making it clear what he *wouldn't* do in her presence. "Remember that you're in the room with the four most powerful witches in the area, and you're not one of them."

He held up his hands in surrender. "Billie, what an honor to have you join us."

Merry sniffed. "The Blacks ran to Alaska to hide in the filth."

"You might see it that way, but *I* don't kill for looks," Billie said, sinking into a chair beside Paige. "I saw him come in and decided I needed to stick close. Just in case."

"Good call. Okay. If we're all done kissing everyone else's asses?"

Leslie snorted and then licked her lips.

Eldora's lips twitched in a sneer.

Merry huffed slightly.

Leah and Mandy quietly waited, their eyes wide, mouths closed.

Yeah. It was time.

"We're here— if DoDO would allow me to continue this time? You gonna remain quiet? Oh, good. Because Sven's here and he's about to take this town apart."

"Do we know what he wants?" Eldora asked.

"Yeah." Paige wasn't going to tell everyone the whole truth. She didn't trust most of them. "He wants the other two parts of the key to the gates of Heaven and Hell."

"Why would he want that?" Merry scoffed.

"He's a demon." Billie said as if the answer was obvious.

Derrick raised his eyebrows and nodded, gesturing to Billie as if seconding her.

Paige rested her hands on her belly where the kids kicked. "He wants to bring Hell to Earth."

Merry rolled her eyes. "It's all very dramatic, the angels and demons always duking it out. Leave us out of it, I say."

"Except that *we* are the guardians of this Earth." Or to the entrance of the library stronghold. And the Vaada Bhoomi. Or whatever. "You are free to leave if this is too crazy for you."

Eldora waved Paige off. "I've fought angels before."

That was good to know. "We'll be fighting demons too."

"And that's why we have you," Merry said. "The mightiest demon summoner in history."

Mario's eyes lit up as if finally seeing Paige as a prize mare.

That didn't make her feel creeped out. At all. "And yet, I think the Blackmans might have the better weapon."

That got everyone's attention, especially Merry's. "I am the most powerful witch here."

Mario made a "whoops" face and pointed at Paige. "She's got you beat, love."

Merry daggered Paige with her gaze. "How?"

Paige wasn't about to tell her. "The door magick," Paige said instead, looking at Derrick. Fuck Eldora. She really didn't like that woman.

"Leah mentioned something about how you two sent a bunch of demons to Mars," Derrick said with a smile.

At least he had a sense of humor. "Well, it looked like Mars. It could have been Utah for all I know. But the point is that they disappeared, and I don't think they made it back."

"Do you really think that we can send these demons to a different planet?" Eldora demanded.

"I think," Paige said, pointedly looking at the woman, "that you have the ability to open doors to other realms, dimensions. Planets? Sure. I think that if you tried hard enough you could open a door to an asteroid and dump their fucking asses in the Kuiper Belt."

Mario's expression widened in surprise. "The Kuiper Belt?"

"Tyler is studying astrology."

"Astronomy," Billie corrected.

"Yes. That." Whatever. "What I'm saying is that your door magick might only be limited by your imagination."

"And that's where you're wrong," Eldora said, "which you would know if you had decided to learn how to *use* your door magick. But instead you make a mockery of it. *You* need to be in our school."

"So, you can force me to buy into your thinking, too? Sorry, sweetie, but that shit ain't happenin'. And before you get it into your goddamned mind one *more* time, you're not getting your goddamned grubby mitts on my babies!"

The air grew excessively hot and wind whipped papers from the surrounding desks.

"Mom!" Leah shouted.

Paige swallowed and forced herself to calm down.

Merry's eyes were large as she took in Paige. She sat back in her chair, staring at her bulging belly. And then she pointedly met Paige's gaze.

Whoops. "Plans. That's what we need. And we need to figure out how to work together."

"As long as we're following your lead," Eldora sneered.

Paige had *had* it. "No. You want to take lead? You want to make all the decisions? Great. Let's arm wrestle for it. Let's see who's the strongest? The most powerful? Maybe we should test to see who's the smartest?"

Merry frowned.

"Or maybe," Paige shouted, her alpha will in full force, "we just realize that the place at the top isn't super awesome and you settle your shit."

Mario whistled low and held up his hands. "She has my vote."

Merry assessed her quietly for a long moment.

Ollie raised his hand and nodded, as if silently giving her his vote.

Eldora didn't seem moved.

"What type of experience do you have in this situation?" Paige asked. "When was the last time any of your family *fought* against anything? When was the last time you were up against demons? Or angels?" She gestured toward Merry. "When was the last time you fought *beside* a shifter? Can you even get the other paranormals to come together under *your* flag? What about the mundanes?"

Mario gave Eldora a long look and then tipped his head to the side, raising one shoulder in a shrug.

Eldora glared, but backed down. "Fine. We follow your lead."

The rest of the meeting went much smoother.

But as everyone got up to leave with their homework assignments, Merry pulled Paige aside.

Paige wasn't in the mood. She really wasn't. "You're not getting your hands on my kids, either."

Merry nodded. "They're shifter witches, aren't they?"

Paige wasn't going to confirm or deny.

Merry glanced around. "You better hope that you're still pregnant when you go to face off with Sven."

"Really?" because Paige was sincerely hoping she wasn't.

"Yes." Merry speared her with her gaze, closing the distance so her low voice could be heard by only Paige. "Because after they're born, you'll lose power."

That was something Paige hadn't thought of.

"And without all this amazing power?" Merry pulled back. "You won't be able to fight against him. Those babies? They're the weapon we need. But only while they remain in your womb."

Crap.

"And don't let Eldora get her hands on them. If she does, they will belong to her, not you."

"That isn't going to happen."

"You say that now," Merry said, stepping back to head toward the front. "But you aren't the only one who's said that, and you won't be the last."

But she was going to be the one who meant it.

Neither Paige nor Leslie were particularly thrilled with the idea of the Eastwood witches coming back. But what else could they do?

However, the fact Merry Eastwood seemed to be looking out for Leah *and* for Paige's unborn children did give her a little bit of hope. Not a lot. She was fairly certain Merry was only looking out for Merry. She only wanted Sven dealt with.

That led to another scary thought.

Paige was going to have to fight this battle pregnant. If she didn't, they would likely lose. She was just now getting used to having all this power. To understand it would leave as soon as she gave birth? That was only terrifying because they were faced with such a huge problem at the moment.

Paige wasn't power crazy. She wasn't like Merry Eastwood in that she always felt the need to find more. To *get* more.

She just really hoped once Sven was dealt with, there wouldn't be any more Sven's that would require her to have this power.

Leslie had decided to fly home. Paige decided she was going to walk in the form of a four-legged beast. She wasn't stupid. She still preferred the big cats, but she was having a hard time figuring out which one she enjoyed most. Frankly, she loved them all.

As she shifted back to human, walking up the stairs to the front door, a thought hit her. What if she lost the ability to shift after she gave birth?

Now that? That would hurt. She'd really come to enjoy being able to shift.

She reached inside of herself, trying to get Cawli's attention.

But he was ignoring her, which was their new norm.

If she lost her ability to shift, she would survive. She had only been shifting for a few weeks. She had survived how long before that without the ability to shift? She'd function like she had before.

But she would mourn the loss. Especially now that she could shift whenever she wanted in her town.

She stopped to gather Bobby and made her way to the kitchen. She was greeted by Roxxie who appeared to have her strength back. A lot of her color had returned. She didn't look like her full self yet, but she did appear to be a lot stronger than she had a few hours before.

Roxxie stood up from the dining room table. "I remember what happened."

That had to be a good sign. Paige went to the cupboard and pulled down a glass, filling it with water. "Okay. Were you attacked?"

Bobby jumped up at down at her feet. "Dwink. Dwink."

"Yes," Roxxie said. "By Sven."

"Watew gwose."

"Water good." Paige really wished that Roxxie's answer would have been a surprise. But it just wasn't. "Do you need a sippy cup?"

"I a big id now."

Oh, she wished, but he'd really been pushing the whole big boy thing for the past couple of weeks, and if that's what he wanted, she wasn't going to hold him back. Though she *knew* what a mess there'd be, so she reached over and grabbed a towel, handing it to him as they walked toward the table. "He attacked you in the open?" she asked Roxxie.

Roxxie shook her head and sank back into her chair. "He attacked several angels just outside of your wards. My squad and I came to stop them. He —" Roxxie shivered. "It was as if he was taking our energy. He was...draining us."

Paige had wondered where he was going to continue to get energy from. She doubted seriously that Bastet was going to allow him to drain her cats. The ancients had been looking for the thing that had been trying to kill them for a few years now. She hoped they'd managed to end the siphon.

Bobby pushed the glass onto the table and looked up at Paige. "I eat now."

"Don't eat dirt." The last time, he had. She eyed her glass of water and all the floaties that were now in it. Toddlers were awesome.

He frowned at her like only an almost two-year-old could. "Not dewt. Ceweal."

"Try something healthy." She really needed to try and get her kids to eat better so when they became adults, they'd make better food choices than she did. She didn't even want to *think* about how hard it was going to be to get her baby fat off.

"Hewfy is gwose."

"I don't care. You want a snack before dinner, so you're going to eat something healthy. What about an apple?"

He made a face, but he thought about it. "Kay. Apple. But not puckwy kind." He held up his hand and shook his head. "Dose gwose."

They were the only ones she bought because if Bobby and

the kids didn't eat them, she had to, and she didn't like the others. "What if we put peanut butter on them?"

"Jelly! Jelly!" Bobby bounced up and down for a second and ran to the refrigerator.

Roxxie got up to help him cut it up.

Well, at least Paige had got him to choose something other than cereal or chips. Score one for Mom.

But that left her with the current situation. Damn it. Where was Cawli?

I am here. I am always here.

Great. *And you've been ignoring me?*

You haven't needed me, he said, his voice soft.

Whatever. *Have you figured out what's been targeting the ancients?*

He was quiet for a moment before he answered. *That is what I've been focusing much of my energy on. After you learned about the temple cats, we looked again. Each of the ancients who is in your world is no longer being targeted.*

I don't understand.

He growled. *There are many of us and there are many of each type, aside for a few, like the griffin. What we've learned is that those species who have already sent one of their kind into your world are no longer being targeted.*

The way he was phrased it made her mind twist, which might be baby brain. Paige just didn't know. *So, the griffins aren't being targeted because Robin's with Leslie.*

Cawli didn't agree with the name Leslie had given the griffin, but he affirmed her thought nonverbally. *Along with the other ancients. So, we have been sending as many of our ancients into your world as we can to ensure that all the species are protected.*

Wait. That was good…and lethal. *You're creating how many powerful shifter witches?*

The witches are being chosen rather carefully.

But how many?

He was silent. *At least a hundred. Probably more.*

Oh, awesome. *Any that we know?*

You aren't the only witches in the world.

I know that. I want to know if you've decided that the Blackmans or Eastwoods are worthy.

He didn't answer immediately, and she felt he was gauging his response. *There are witches all over the world who have received an ancient. What you need to know is that Sven is nearly cut off from siphoning energy from our realm. We have a handful of beings left.*

Is he still pulling from you?

It appears that he's slowed. For now. I would say that he's found a new source.

Great. *Any ideas on what that could be?*

Do you know of any other realms with powerful beings?

Angels. Great. It was unlikely that he'd choose to pull from the demons. They were his allies in this. At least, for now. *Thanks.*

You are welcome. Now, if you're done with me, I have other things to attend to.

Yeah. Sure. That was the way it always was with Paige and Cawli. They were both on missions and rarely on point together. Not like Dexx and Hattie or Leslie and Robin. She was a little jealous of them both.

Cawli sent her something close to a hug, but it felt more like a fatherly pat on the head.

Well, there was at least that. But siphoning energy from angels? Paige didn't even realize that was a thing. She met Roxxie's gaze from across the kitchen. "Sorry, I was talking to Cawli."

The angel finished slicing the apple, handing Bobby a blue plastic plate. "What did he say?"

Paige was still upset with Roxxie about what had happened in Heaven, but she had always been a trusted ally.

Roxxie had trusted in the wrong people, that was all. Paige had certainly done that in the past. "He said that he's the reason the angels are being siphoned now. He cut Sven off from the ancients. And with Sven unable to siphon the temple cats thanks to Bastet cozying up to him? Yeah. You're next in the food chain."

Bobby plopped down on the floor with a jar of jelly and his plate of apples.

Roxxie groaned. "I've been trying to get a message to Heaven all day."

"No luck?"

Roxxie shook her head, staying close to Bobby.

Paige was sure she didn't want to know the reason. "Are you okay?"

Roxxie shook her head in amazement. "Yeah? I think? I don't know how, but I somehow managed to get away. If I hadn't, I would be dead right now. I watched him drain four angels. And they just disappeared."

That wasn't concerning at all.

Bobby was actually managing not to make too big a mess, and what mess there was, he kept to the plate. Except a tiny bit of jelly that fell on the floor. But he licked it up. Literally.

Kids were gwose.

Dexx walked in the back door, wearing a robe. He looked surprised as he took in Roxxie. "Is everything okay here?"

Paige leaned back in her chair, her legs open to give the twins more room. "Sven is now siphoning angels."

"I wish I could feel sorry for them." Dexx shrugged and headed to the garage. "I just can't."

Paige was about to ask a few more questions when a knock sounded on her wards.

A knock. Someone had gone up to her wards and had rapped on them three times.

Paige got to her feet and headed to the back door.

Dexx turned to her. "Something going on?"

Paige shrugged. "I'm about to find out."

"Want me to go with you?"

"I think I should be fine. You do what you need to do. You've got Bobby. I'll let you know if I need help." She was really glad to have him back. "Maybe check on the school. We probably have a lot less kids now, but I need to make sure that Faith is working with Wendy. We kind of had a fight of the alpha will, and I don't think that went over well."

Dexx just frowned, but he nodded and glanced at Roxxie. "I'll be right back." Then he disappeared into the garage.

Roxxie shifted on her feet, leaning against the counter and staying protectively close to Bobby. "What do you need me to do?"

Paige had no idea. "Are you back to your old self again?"

Roxxie shook her head confused. "I can't connect to Heaven. It's hard to explain. But..."

Paige had no idea what she was walking into or who would be *knocking* on her wards, but she knew she didn't need an angel who was only half-powered to be by her side. "You stay here. Hold down the fort. Regain your strength. I should be fine."

Because whoever had knocked on her wards probably couldn't get in. That meant as long as Paige stayed on her side of the wards, she would be fine.

However, as she shifted into a tiger and headed toward the ward perimeter, she started making a mental checklist of everyone. Where was Leah?

She and Mandy had decided to walk home on their feet. They'd wanted to stop by a friend's house on the way.

Where was Tyler? He was supposed to be at the school with Griff.

Bobby was here with Roxxie and Dexx. Kammy was probably with Leslie or Tru.

What about Kate? She had no idea where Kate was. But she certainly hoped Nick and Mark knew where she was. They might be new parents, but they did seem to be taking to it fairly well.

She shouldn't have too many surprises when she got to wherever she was supposed to be.

And where was this person knocking? Probably the highway? Maybe?

Paige trotted over to the closest section of the ward.

The knock sounded again, but this time she saw the ripple. Whoever it was, was pretty close to the Whiskey house. She turned left and trotted toward the origins of the ripple. She slowed as soon as she saw who stood on the other side of her ward.

Oriel. She recognized his demon signature even though he was wearing a different body.

What in the glorious fuck was he doing here?

She slowed her trot to a walk and approached carefully, scanning the area as best she could.

He stood in a vineyard. On one side behind him was the house, and behind him on the other side was a forest of cottonwoods.

But she didn't see anybody else around.

Was he alone?

Oriel had always been strong, so it was safe to assume he thought he was perfectly okay coming to her without any backup.

The question was, was *she* strong enough to face off with *him* alone?

Well, she had the wards. And it appeared as though he couldn't cross them.

Thank goodness for small favors.

But she really wasn't going to play this one loose and fast. She was going to be smart about it. So, while she was still a few feet away, she shifted into human form and thought of calling Bal.

She had no idea how long it would take for him to get there if she did. Now that she realized he wasn't just a demon, that he was a demigod, she didn't expect him to just come running whenever she called. She appreciated the fact he did, though.

She'd call him if she needed him. But for now, she'd hold off.

She stopped at the ward's edge and assessed Oriel. He was wearing a tall, good looking black man and a nice suit. Whoever the man was, he was probably important. Oriel didn't go for low-hanging fruit. "I really didn't expect to see you here."

"I didn't really expect to be here." He smiled. "That's life. I knew you would need me. I just didn't realize it was going to be in Oregon. I thought for sure this fight would take place in Texas."

"Had to keep you on your toes somehow." Paige really didn't care what he thought. She wanted to know why he was there.

No. Wait. Why had he thought there was going to be a war anyway? What did he know that she didn't?

He smiled. "I'm glad to see you're starting to think."

It unnerved her more than just a little he could read her face so well. "Are you here to annoy me, or are you actually here to give me some information that I can use? Because I have other things I could be doing right now."

"I'm sure you do." He gazed at her belly and a light entered his eyes. The sparks were intrigue and a little maliciousness at the same time. He lifted his gaze. "Have you been able to determine what Sven is up to yet?"

She really didn't want to admit how dumb she was to him. "I know he wants to do something with the gates to

Heaven and Hell. But exactly? No. I have no idea how I would even know. It's not like he tells me stuff."

Oriel nodded. "Well, at least you figured that much out." He folded his hands behind his back and hopped up on his toes momentarily. "Sven managed to shift power a little and in a very concerning way."

She was all over that. "We're canceling his power sources almost as fast as he can find them."

"You are doing remarkably well on that front, I will say. But that isn't what I'm talking about. He's…shifted things around."

"I don't understand. Speak a language I understand."

He studied her for a long moment. "He has begun to sever the ties between Heaven, Hell, and Earth."

The thing with Roxxie made a little bit more sense now. That was the reason why she was unable to recharge. "What kind of progress has he been able to make so far?"

Oriel raised his eyebrows in surprise and smiled. "This does not shock you."

"I've surprisingly had my hands full of a lot of stuff. So, this puzzle piece just makes a lot of sense. Now then, how much progress has he been able to make? And what is his full intent? Or are you just going to sit around and wait for me to figure this out on my own?"

He studied her for a long moment. "He intends to fully disengage Heaven from Earth. And then, he intends to open the gates between Hell and Earth, keeping them open so that demons have free rein."

Paige wasn't entirely sure how he was going to manage that last part. But she did have to admit the idea of having a little bit more separation between Heaven's angels didn't make her sad. Bobby would be that much safer. "I feel as though I could probably keep the gate to Hell closed."

"And what makes you think that?"

"It's embedded in my bones." If that wasn't enough to help her, she had no idea what would.

"Is it?" he frowned and studied her body before raising his gaze again. "Do you ever wonder why he put that gate in your bones?"

The question had crossed her mind more than once. "He has this weird flirtation with me. So, I guess he's trying to create a life with me? I don't know. He's sick and demented and I have no idea what goes through his head."

Oriel nodded sagely. "It is my guess that he intended to create a partnership with you. But he may have miscalculated that particular partnership."

"In that, we agree. How bad are things going to get if we don't fix the gate to Heaven?"

He looked surprised again.

Paige didn't want to think about how stupid he assumed she was.

"Imagine Heaven and Hell, and the other dimensions are connected to this Earth like a tree. Now, imagine cutting the roots of that tree. What would happen to the branches? What would happen to the tree?"

Paige knew enough dryads and she'd worked with enough trees in the past few months to know the answer to that question. The branches would fall and the tree itself would become ill. "So, you're trying to tell me that Heaven and Hell are Earth's roots?"

"They are, in a sense. Sven, I think, is intending to separate Earth so that no other creatures like him can come in and rule in his stead. No one would be able to challenge him."

"You mean people like Bastet?"

Oriel nodded. "Like Bastet, yes. But there are so many more of us."

She was starting to get that impression. "How bad could things get if this isn't fixed?"

He didn't answer her immediately. "It all depends on what your definition of bad is."

"What would the survivability rate be?" It felt like she was negotiating the apocalypse.

He clicked his tongue appreciatively as if telling her she had asked the right question. "It would be low. Demons, angels, humans, paranormals, and even shifter spirits, would all die. At high rates."

So, the idea of keeping the gates of Heaven separate was a bad one because he'd just said her entire family would go up in smoke, pretty much. "I'm a little confused. If he intends to separate Earth from the other dimensions, then why would he keep the gate to Hell open? Are there none of your kind —" she was assuming he was like Bastet and Bal, "—in Hell?"

"You are catching on much faster than I thought you would." He shook his head with a grin. "He would only leave it open for so long. Long enough for those who are loyal to him to come through. But then after that, he would close that door."

"Close the door and then sever the ties between Earth and..." Hell. That connection resided inside of Paige's bones. With her alive, that door would always be open and available. That connection would always be made.

It suddenly made sense on why he had created a door to Hell inside of her *bones*.

But that brought up a very interesting question. "Where is the other one grounded?"

Oriel chuckled in pleasure. "I am not disappointed in you, Paige. However, in this, I'm going to make you guess. You're doing so well already. This should be fairly simple."

Well, she really wasn't a betting woman, but if Paige had

the demon door inside her soul, inside her bones, then she bet someone who had a connection to angels would be the conduit for the gate to Heaven. The only one she knew of that fit that bill was… "Rachel."

Oriel didn't say a thing.

But his expression did. It said she was right.

Seriously? "Does that mean that in order to keep the door open, I've got to keep that bitch alive?"

"I do not have the answer to that. I will only say that she is currently not doing well."

So, he knew where she was. "Are you gonna give me a location?"

He studied her for a moment. "Understand that I, and many of those like me, are not opposed to having Heaven separated from Earth. There are many of us who do not appreciate having Heaven forced upon us in the first place."

Paige realized that was an insight that might have been interesting a few years ago. Now, she just didn't care.

"However, I would much rather that the person pulling everyone's strings not be Sven. I would rather it be someone who actually cared about this place."

"Because you care about it so much."

He shrugged. "I do. But likely not for the same reasons you would think."

The more Paige delved into this world of demons and angels and demigods, the more she realized she had no idea what she actually knew. "Just tell me were Rachel is."

He paused for a moment and then nodded. "You will find her at Alma's house in Texas."

And then, he disappeared.

Great. The end of the world was coming, and she needed to go save her mother.

That was certainly not something she'd expected.

23

———————————

Leslie stared at Paige as though she'd lost her damn mind. "You want us to what?"

Paige shook her head. It didn't matter how many times she repeated it out loud. It still sounded just as stupid as when Oriel had said it. Paige watched Leah and Mandy going through the obstacle course.

The Whiskey kids weren't the only kids on that course.

It looked as though the remaining children in town were there. Their parents were as well. The driveway in front of the Whiskey house was filled with cars, and the surrounding area was filled with people from town.

At least people were getting along. But she was wasn't sure how the Whiskey house had become the new place to hang out, though.

No one came empty-handed, so there wasn't a lack of food or drinks. Someone had even brought in an extra refrigerator that was installed under the overhang out back. How was she was supposed to keep it dry, since it probably wasn't supposed to be used outdoors, still needed some thought. But, there it was.

Several adults stood on the sidelines, cheering their kids on.

Bobby, Kammy, and several of the other little kids were running around screaming and having fun.

All the parents— it didn't matter if they were shifters, paranormals, or mundanes— helped keep the kids in line.

That was one of the awesomest things Paige had seen in a long time, and if nothing else good came of this, she was glad *this* had.

Leslie snapped her fingers, bringing Paige back

"We're supposed to go save Rachel?" Leslie asked.

Paige didn't respond. She knew Leslie was just trying to get used to the idea of it.

It was preposterous.

Never in a million years did Paige ever think she was going to have to save her mother in order to save the world.

However, that would be about the only time she'd be willing to save that woman.

After what Rachel had done?

Leslie pressed her hands flat on the picnic table and leaned over. Her sun-bleached brown hair fell over her face, hiding her expression. "How are we supposed to do that? If she's in Texas, and we're here?"

Paige had no idea. She and Leslie could shift and fly to Texas. She didn't know how long it would take for that to happen or how many times they would have to stop. She also didn't know how much energy that would take. Or if she would have the energy to fight whatever it was that might be attacking Rachel. The only thing she knew was if they wanted to save the planet, they were going to have to save the one woman who hated Paige the most.

She looked around. How bad could it really get? If they had already separated Earth from Heaven in whatever way, and if it really was that bad, wouldn't they start feeling the effects?

There were just too many things that didn't make any sense. She wasn't smart enough for this one.

"I have a plane."

Surprised, Paige turned to see Ollie Eastwood approaching from the house. "What are you doing here?"

He gave her a genuine smile that looked pained around the edges. "I came here to see if we could get our wards incorporated into yours. Mother and I are working to rebuild the ancestral home now, but our wards would be a lot stronger if we could incorporate them into yours."

Paige's initial response was "No." But she kept that one to herself. They were trying to build relations here, and it was hard to do that if she wasn't trusting them. "What did you have in mind?"

He gestured toward her ward tree. "You created some-thing very similar to that for the Blackman's. I was hoping you could do the same for us."

Paige wasn't entirely sure how that would work. How the Whiskey magick would work with the Eastwood blood magick. But then she remembered Leah was a Whiskey and an Eastwood. It should work just fine.

She nodded. "That's going to have to wait though."

He tipped his head to the side, not taking offense. "For what?"

Just one more reason Paige was starting to genuinely like Ollie. Tiny moments like that. "Apparently, I need to go save my mother."

Ollie's expression lost all emotion. "You can't be serious."

"Apparently, it's an end of the world kind of thing."

Ollie didn't even hesitate. "Take my plane. For that matter, I'll go with you."

"You don't have to." That was a much easier solution than she had even thought possible.

Leslie straightened, frowning at him. "What do you get out of all this?"

Ollie shook his head. "I'm really just trying to build a relationship with my sister."

And this is where the Whiskey bloodline looked a little redneck because Ollie was her brother and her brother-in-law. He and Leah's father, Mark, had two different sperm donors. Ollie and Paige shared the same sperm donor but had different mothers. She could almost hear the banjos playing in the background.

Paige gave Leslie an expression that said she believed it. Ollie wasn't like Merry. He was a lot more like Mark. And there had been a reason why she'd loved Mark as much she had. She was certain if Mark hadn't died before Leah had been born, they would still be married and she would have had a much different life. She never would've found Dexx. He may never have even made it back to Oregon. She wouldn't have lost Leah.

And they may not be in this war.

Which made her think yet again that Mark hadn't died by accident. Someone had killed him. The more she thought about it, the more she realized Mark's death had led to this moment.

But all of that didn't help her. "How quickly can we leave?"

He shrugged and pulled out his phone. "When will you be ready?"

They made a few arrangements and Paige went to Leah. Well, she went to the edge of the obstacle course and flagged her daughter down.

For once, Dexx wasn't in the middle of all of this. He was

busy patrolling the borders of the town, making sure everyone was safe, and they were trying to do their best to keep as many reporters out of town as they possibly could. It was one thing to make the headlines with demons destroying things. It was a whole different thing to make headlines because people were seeing the strange and paranormal first-hand. One she could sell to the Shadow Sisterhood. The other, she was fairly certain the Shadow Sisterhood would still come down hard on her for.

Leah jogged over and gave Paige a hug. "Where you going to now?"

This seemed to be their relationship. Paige had fought so hard to get Leah back and now it seemed as though she was spending more of her time away from her daughter than with. "I've been called to Texas."

Leah frowned. "In the middle of all this?"

Paige sighed. "I have to go save Rachel."

Leah blinked, a mix of horror and anger crashing over her features. "Then I'm going with you."

Paige started to tell her no, but she was beginning to understand her immediate answers weren't always the right ones. She'd just said earlier Leah was her apprentice, for lack of a better word. Wouldn't going along with this be part of Leah's apprenticeship? "What do you think you'll be able to do?"

Leah acknowledged Paige hadn't immediately said "No" by raising her chin. "I have magick. I've been studying defensive magick with Billie, so I can be useful. I will follow the rules. And if you tell me to do something, I will do it. If you tell me not to do something, I won't do it. But..." Leah breathed heavily, "Rachel raised me. And I have a lot of questions for her. And if you're going to face her, then you're not doing it without me."

Part of Paige wanted to keep Leah safe from all of this.

However, the other part of her realized they were facing a war. "You've been paying attention to Billie in class?"

Leah nodded solemnly.

The best thing Paige could do for her daughter was to prepare her for the eventuality of war. Protecting her child and keeping her safe and secluded in a box wasn't going to help her in the least.

But getting her out there? In situations where Paige was there to protect her? Where her Aunt Leslie was also going to be there to help protect her? Well, and her Uncle Ollie. To put her into situations where she could get her magickal feet wet and still remain alive? That would help her a lot more.

That's what a good parent would do. Prepare her child to become an adult. Dexx had been right. Damn the man.

Paige nodded. "Gather your things. We're not planning on staying overnight. We intend to collect her and get back out."

Leah's face exploded with surprise. "Really?"

"If you're coming, you'd better move your ass."

Leah let out a whoop and leapt into the air. Then, without another word, she ran toward the house and disappeared.

Leslie stepped out of the house glancing at Leah as they crossed paths. She had a bag slung over her shoulder, probably filled with things for her to do. Leslie did not do well with idle hands. And her to-do bag, even on short trips, was usually bigger than her suitcase. She met Paige in the lawn. "I take it she's coming with us?"

Paige nodded. "You don't think I'm being a bad parent on this one, do you?"

"I don't really think I'm qualified to judge anymore."

Paige and Leslie both did the best they could. That didn't mean they were parents of the year.

It just meant they did the best they could.

Dexx followed the last of the assassins. What else could they be with tactical gear and rifles sweeping in aggressive arcs in front of them, always moving forward.

Of course, the shots they were ready to fire were a clue.

Six of them.

Government assassins. Had to be. Or DoDO. Whoever it was had bad intel.

Dexx had told Mario straight up he and the Whiskeys were off limits, and if they were regular mercs hired by the government, they still should have known to leave them alone. Whichever they were, this was not the time to be going after the only people who stood a chance at keeping them alive long enough to grab for power.

Stupid humans, doing the same thing as the stupid demons. Why did they always want more than they had? No matter who it hurt.

In this case, it could cost the team. If they crossed the wards.

That sucked too, because now they were likely to try to spin it as "dangerous beings attacked decorated military persons".

Well, his family was safe. His kids were safe.

As he turned to leave, Hattie felt the prey. Not a large deer, not like she was used to, but enough.

Silently, she leapt on the small animal and pierced though the throat and suffocated it.

The team of assassins stopped at the wards. They pushed, but the invisible wards stopped them.

What the hells? Demon possessed humans? Could they get through the wards all the way to the house?

What the hell is that about? he asked Hattie.

The demons are testing us. Always testing.

Do they have something to help them through the wards?

You and yours are a prize beyond your imaginings. They would do anything to put you in front of Paige to stop her.

Hattie was right. None of them were safe until Sven was put down. Like a rabid dog. With mange. And bad breath. Really bad breath.

The team, every single one fell over.

Demons separated themselves from the men. And took off to the west.

Well, fuck. Another plan inside a plan, wrapped in a plan joining another plan.

The deer stopped moving.

Dexx turned himself around so he didn't have to see Hattie eat.

Paige was glad to see Hattie appear at the edge of the woods by the picnic table, her saber teeth still showing blood. He must've got into some kind fight at the border.

She met him halfway as he shifted, standing in front of her gloriously naked.

Griff ran over with a robe, threw it at Dexx, and then ran back to the obstacle course.

Dexx shouted a thank you after the retreating boy and frowned at what seemed like a party going on in their yard. "Was there an invite I missed?"

Paige shrugged. "Anything of interest out there?"

He shook his head and slipped the robe on. "Nothing too unusual. Kind of par for the course." Then, he focused his attention on Paige. "Why do I get the feeling you're leaving?"

"Because I—" she rose on her tiptoes and gave him a kiss, "—have to go save Rachel. I'm taking Leslie and Leah with me."

He frowned at her. "And how are you getting there?"

"Oliver's plane."

"I thought you weren't allowed to fly anymore."

Paige wasn't entirely for sure how flying affected pregnancy, but she was pretty certain the whole reason why women over eight and a half months pregnant weren't allowed on commercial flights was because none of the flight attendants wanted to have to deliver the baby mid-flight.

"Trust me. I'll be fine." Not that she had a whole lot of control over the whole baby situation. But she was going to do everything she could to keep those buns in the oven.

"I don't like it."

"Neither do I. But this is the world we live in. What do you want me to do?"

"Let the bitch die." He kept his words succinct.

"Normally I would agree. However, apparently she's the key to keeping the gate of Heaven tied to the Earth." She quickly filled him in on what Oriel had told her.

Dexx took a step back and cursed. "So, that's what this whole thing has been about? He put the damned gate in your bones so he could kill you when it was convenient for him?"

"Seems like it."

Dexx was furious.

It was best to keep him focused on other things though. "My guess is that she has a gate to Heaven in her bones. Or something similar. Anyway. What are you going to be doing while I'm gone?"

He snarled before he looked up. "I have to call Mario about something I saw."

"Really?" she didn't trust anything to do with DoDO. "And do you think they'll give you good information?"

"Well, that's what we're going to find out. Just waiting for you to get back. Thought you'd want to go." He ground his teeth and formed two fists. "I love you, vixen. So damn much."

His body language said he didn't, but she read between the lines. He was frustrated he couldn't go with her, that she didn't need him. And he was needed here more than with her.

Oh! Crap! He was needed here, and she hadn't told him why yet! "I sent Tony away. Permanently."

Dexx's eyes met hers. "Then, you're not retiring?"

"Oh, I am." She took a step toward him and put her hands on his chest, opening his robes a little so she could find bare skin. It wasn't erotic. It just felt nice to touch him. Not his clothing. Him. And they hadn't had a moment like this in a very long time. She missed the connection. She missed bonding with him. "You're going to step up into that position. I still have to talk to Tuck about it. However, based on the fact he never once called Tony and always called you, I would have to say that he'll probably be okay with it."

A light touched Dexx's eyes. And she could tell in that moment he really had wanted the captain position. "I'm going to have to do my own paperwork, aren't I?"

"You're damn straight you are." She smiled up at his face. "But I know you can do it. You've grown a lot since we've been here. You've got what it takes."

"I hope I do."

So did she. Because if the world really was changing, and it felt as though it really was, then she wouldn't be able to help him the way she had before.

And the town of Troutdale and the surrounding areas were going to need Dexx. She just had that feeling.

But, it was time to go save her mother.

Shit.

2 4

Dexx swiped the call icon for Mario.

"Mr. Colt. I did not expect a call from you."

"Just makin' sure that those things I saw weren't employed by you. Because if they were, you're missing six. And if they *were* yours—"

"I assure you, I have no idea what you're talking about. Are you saying you killed six humans?"

"No, I said things. Didn't touch 'em, but they dressed exactly like you. And according to our agreement you said you'd leave us alone."

"That wasn't my team."

"How'd you know it was a team if it wasn't you?"

"You might think I'm daft, but I'm not. You said there were six and they were dressed like us. Only highly trained people use our kind of gear."

Oh. Dexx was really stressed if he gave them the answer before accusing them. Well, fuck.

"Fine. But if I find you've been hiring out wetwork to demons, I'm coming for you. *You.*"

"Do you ever tire of the macho American routine?"

"Does it sound like I'm tired? I remember knockin' all your guys' dicks in the dirt."

"So barbaric. Actually, it's a good thing you rang me up. We have some new intelligence that you might be interested in."

"What might that be? You decided you're in over your head and going back to back to your island?"

"When we have you I swear—"

When they what?

"No, we have a lead on a possible nest. Since you have the best track record with these, I'm offering you the lead on the disposal."

"If you want an advisor, you're going to pay a whole boat-load of money, because all this talent ain't cheap."

"You shall be compensated, if that is all there is to you."

Ew. Did he really just quote Star Wars?

"You guys seem to lean on me a lot on me to do the heavy stuff."

Mario sighed into the phone. Good. That guy was an asshole, and he deserved all he got. And what was that about "having him"?

"Are you with us or not Mr. Colt?"

Dexx's turn to sigh. "I'm in. Where do I meet you?"

"We'll have a car meet you."

Thirty minutes later Dexx walked out to the wards to meet Mario and the rest of DoDO.

They left a spot open for Dexx in the front of the lead Suburban.

They headed east along the Columbia for a while, then turned off headed to the Dalles.

"What's off this way?"

"A nest. We've been tracking a strange blip on our radar, so to speak, and we have it narrowed to a place out here."

A water bottle tapped Dexx on his shoulder. He looked

behind him to Alwyn offering a drink. Dexx took it with a smile. "Thanks. Glad to see you aren't demon food, or housing?"

Alwyn flattened his look.

Dexx shrugged. "Hey one more day is a good thing. Remember what I showed you guys."

Alwyn sat back a little harder than he could have.

Dexx held the bottle up "Thanks." *Is it safe to drink?*

If these are hunters pretending to be grazers, it could be a trap.

No, would have done fine.

Hattie rode in silence watching for prey in the thick forests along the road.

Dexx closed his eyes for a moment. Time to give the kid some credit. He turned as far as the seat would allow.

Alwyn looked like someone pissed in his Wheaties.

"Sorry about that. You did pretty good out there. Out of everyone I saw, if you keep doing what I say, you'll do well. There's no such thing as an old hunter, but you may make to middle-aged."

"Isn't that what you are now?"

Point for the kid. "Yup. That's why you're on deck junior. When we get where we're going, stay with me."

Alwyn inclined his head slightly.

All Dexx needed to do now was give him a sucker. Alwyn looked like he'd already given him one. Dexx turned back to the front.

Another little bit brought them to a gravel road and the line of Suburbans turned. At the foot of a hill, a trail led into the woods.

Dexx peered into the brush, looking for evidence of demons. His enhances senses didn't pick anything up. No activity.

Mario threw Dexx one of the Vests the rest of the team wore.

He looked down at the vest with an "are you fucking kidding me" look.

Mario raised chin. "Remember. Professional attitude when you're with us."

Dexx ground his teeth. Shit. Of course he'd agreed to it. "Okay, boss, lead the way."

He fumbled with the vest or pretended to. The vest read vital signs, and transmitted data back to their base. He'd never trust that DoDO would just erase *his* vitals. He found a wire in the lining and pulled. The wire snapped, and he slipped into the vest.

The climb was easy, if steep. The other team members were huffing and puffing, but with Hattie Dexx didn't feel it. A plus to having a spirit.

Mario motioned with an upraised closed fist for the team to freeze.

The entire team stopped moving as though they suddenly turned to statues. Dexx did the same. He'd follow orders if they made sense, and he had no desire to kill the team. Not today.

Mario gave the signal to take cover in the brush, and he crouched. Dexx followed suit.

At another motion, he met Mario at the crest of the hill and looked to where he pointed.

It looked like every enemy drug lord camp in any movie.

Demons wandered around everywhere, but they wandered with purpose. Like they had things to do. What in the hells?

Neglected buildings randomly dotted a clearing with dirt roads. In the center of the whole thing, another house-size building had two demons standing in front. Like guards. *As* guards.

They stood like soldiers straight and menacing. With all the

This wasn't a nest, it was a fortress.

Mario cast a quick grin to his team. "Looks like we've hit the jackpot as the yanks say."

"No, you hit crossbones. We have to leave right now."

"I don't think so, mate. This is what we've been training for."

That was enough for Dexx. "No, *mate*. If you want everyone to die today, be my guest. *I* couldn't go down there and survive that."

He might be able to, after all, he'd charged right into the demon lines in town and survived, but they'd been packed together, and they couldn't maneuver. He'd had an advantage then. Not so much this time. They were spread out, and on guard.

"If you want to play coward, certainly feel free." Mario gave Dexx a patronizing smile.

"I'm a lot of things, but what I'm *not* is a coward or stupid. You go down there and the last thing you said to your boyfriend is how he'll remember you."

Mario's eyes darkened at Dexx, but he had to keep them to away from the demons.

"They won't like us coming back without engaging the enemy."

"You do what you have to do, and I'll take the smart ones home." Dexx looked around at the rest of the team. Ten of them. "Anyone who wants to stick back with me can. We'll record what happens down there. But you better say bye now. They aren't coming back."

Nobody moved.

"Mario, you going to show them who's boss?" Dexx flicked a thumb to the encampment.

Mario raised his hand to his earpiece and waited.

"No." The word felt like it had to be pulled out with a crane. We observe, and report."

"Good call. But without going into the buildings, we can't really see what they're up to."

"Then we have nothing to report." Mario twisted his mouth.

"That's not exactly true. I'll take Alwyn, and the rest can get in two-man teams. We'll see if we can get a pattern to movements and determine what causes the patterns."

They wouldn't get much of course, but they had to feel better about themselves. And of course they might actually find something worth reporting.

"Alwyn you're with me." The two of them trailed away from Mario and the rest of the team.

Dexx found and Alwyn found a vantage overlooking the demon camp and Dexx settled in.

Alwyn wasn't as relaxed. "I thought we were going to kill some demons today? Isn't this what you wanted us to do?"

Dexx never took his eyes off the camp. "Didn't I drive the point home enough? A *single* demon is a problem. Two demons are enough to run away from and retain dignity. At the end of the day, you want to be able to X another day off the calendar. Can't do that if you're busy pushing daisies."

"Then what are we doi—"

Dexx flung up his hand in the signal to freeze. Good thing their training made them obey instantly. "Sh."

Dexx motioned Alwyn forward, but to remain silent.

When Alwyn was in position next to Dexx, he carefully pulled a gun. The bullets were specially prepared, but they hadn't yet been properly tested.

Dexx whispered so low Alwyn might not even hear him. "Sven. He's the bad guy." Dexx slipped backward slowly. And very carefully. He pulled Awlyn back with him.

Oh Shit. Sven's camp was *here*.

"Surveillance complete. We leave *now*."

Paige had one thing to say about flying in Ollie's jet. She was never flying coach again, and somehow she and Ollie were going to have to be the bestest of best friends. Because… seriously.

It was still a long trip down to Texas. It didn't matter which way you traveled. However, there was a lot to say about the conveniences of owning your own plane.

They almost weren't able to land because of the all of the earthquakes in Dallas, however.

Earthquakes like the ones they just had a couple of weeks ago in Troutdale.

That couldn't be good. Of course not. If this was Rachel, then…

She didn't want to think about it. It was too big a mind-bridge to gap.

The good news was that Paige knew exactly where Rachel would be. She just didn't know what she would say when they met.

Ollie got them a car, and they rode to their old home in style as the earth rolled under them. It was one aftershock after another. The streets were clear of cars, but people were out in force.

Paige put in a call into Henry, her old boss. "Paige," his gruff voice said.

"How long have the earthquakes been going on for?" she asked, holding onto the side of the limo. She stared out the window as another hard quake rumbled the area.

"A few hours. Where are you?"

"Headed to the old house."

"Is there something I need to know about?"

"There's something going on, yes, but I don't think there's anything your team can handle."

"Fine. Keep me updated."

He probably had other things to do. "Will do. Oh, hey!" Before she forgot…again. "Tony's on his way down. I was kind of hoping you might have an opening for him."

Henry grunted. "After he stood me up the last time?"

There was that. Henry had been rejected by her and *then* Tony in quick succession. "He's a good guy, Henry. And he really knows what he's doing."

"Okay. Well, I'll think about it. Okay?"

That was the best she could ask for. "Thanks."

"You gonna stop these damned earthquakes?"

"Hopin' to."

"Good. Get it done. I'm ready for an off night."

Paige understood that. "Gotta go." She hung up.

"He okay?" Leah asked.

Paige didn't think Leah even remembered Henry much, but she looked like a kid trying to keep from being afraid and Paige could get behind that. "He's fine."

Ollie met her gaze for a moment, then turned his attention out the side window. Even he gripped the door handle a little tightly.

Seeing the old neighborhood brought back a lot of memories. Memories of growing up there. Memories of fighting off Heaven hounds. Memories of fighting her mother for custody of Leah.

There wasn't a whole lot she missed.

When they got to Alma's old place, they saw a car in the front. If Dexx had been there, he would have something to say about the engine. He'd probably even have an opinion about the car. However, he wasn't. So, the only thing she had to say about it was, it was there. It had Colorado plates, which made her believe it was probably a rental.

With Leslie beside her and Leah and Ollie behind her, Paige walked up to the front door.

She didn't feel any wards. It was as if the house had no protections whatsoever. Why would Rachel stay there and not put anything in place?

Leslie took out her key and opened the front door.

Paige was the first one in. No lights, and the switches didn't work. "Rachel?" Paige called. "Are you here?"

No one answered.

Leah stepped into the entrance and peered around, a flashlight in hand. "Maybe she's not here."

That was a possibility.

Another rumble passed. Dust filtered down from the ceiling. "Find a doorway," Paige told Leah.

Leah didn't question. She just stood in the doorway to what had once been Alma's magick room.

Paige stood in the front doorway and cupped her hands in front of her. It was time to use the globe and see what it had to tell her.

Calling up the elements, she brought her scry globe into existence. It flared into a bubble and then seemed to relax. Inside of the globe was a footprint of the house.

The scry globe showed Paige and Leah, Leslie and Ollie. Ollie was walking around back.

It also showed three faint, golden lights around the perimeter.

Angels.

But why were they so faint? Did it have anything to do with the siphon? If that was the case, how was he siphoning angels all the way over here? It made sense he'd been siphoning angels in the Portland area, angels like Roxxie. But angels in Texas? That didn't make any sense whatsoever.

Unless this was something similar to the Vaada Bhoomi, which made Paige's head hurt to think about. Paige wasn't entirely sure *how* Sven had connected to that other plane, but he had, and he'd been draining ancients and temple cats from across the veil. And as near as she could tell, he had been draining them from multiple locations. But if he was draining the angels in a similar method, then it might make sense.

Unless, he was using his connection to Rachel as a kind of…short cut.

That idea made entirely too much sense.

The last dot she saw was Rachel. She showed up in Paige's scry globe as a blue spec. But judging from the power and the strength of her color, she was weak and *surrounded* in power.

"She's up in the attic."

Stairs. Paige wasn't looking forward to climbing to the attic. Especially not with all of the earthquakes rolling through. Aftershocks. Whatever. She didn't like it when the earth freaking *moved* under her feet.

If Sven was really trying to pull Heaven away from Earth, and if he was somehow succeeding, then this might be the way they were feeling the effects. She wasn't a physicist. She didn't understand the science of it all. But she'd watched enough sci-fi shows to know that everything was connected.

Though, that was about all she understood.

"Rachel?" Paige called again.

Leslie pushed her way to the stairs, her phone out, its flashlight on.

Ollie came in through the back door and walked through the hallway coming toward them. "It's clear out back."

Paige shook her head. "There are a few angels out there. Though, judging by what I saw, they may not be doing so well."

Ollie frowned. "How would you know?"

There were times Paige forgot not everyone knew all of her abilities. "Scry globe. It helps me see who and what is around."

"You could've told me about that."

She probably could have. "Leah, are you coming up? Or you staying down here?"

Leah settled her shoulders. "I'm staying down here with Ollie. Just in case something comes into the house."

"Good plan. And you've got your magick at the ready to protect Ollie?"

Ollie gave Leah a look that said how funny he thought they were.

Leah chuckled in the flare of her flashlight. "Yeah, Mom. I'll keep him safe."

"Good because I don't want to lose the plane." Paige gave Ollie a look that told him he'd better not let anything happen to her daughter.

He raised both hands up as if in surrender and shook his head.

He might make a pretty decent brother. Time would tell.

Paige was pretty proud of her daughter. Two years ago, in this very house, that girl had been a mess of emotions. She'd practically been scared of her own shadow. But the woman standing in front of her— the young woman standing in front of her — had the potential to be absolutely amazing. She had come a long way. Just like Dexx had.

This house was a reminder of how far they'd come in such a short amount of time. So many things had changed. Their entire world. It was a little awe inspiring.

But, that wasn't saving their mother, whether she deserved it or not, and it wasn't getting the situation handled. So, Paige shifted into a tiger and headed up the stairs.

The attic was the third story, and the stairs up were tight. She shifted into a fox in order to fit better. As she cleared the hole in the ceiling where the stairwell pierced the floor, she shifted back into a human and then stopped, staring in abject horror at what she saw.

Rachel wasn't just dying. That didn't even halfway describe what was going on there. A mark, very similar to the one Paige had on her chest, glowed in silver-blue. Rachel floated above the floor, her legs and arms splayed as if being pulled in four different directions.

As Paige got closer, she realized Rachel really was being pulled in four different directions.

How in the hell was she supposed to help her like this? She didn't even know what to do.

Leslie turned to Paige, her expression filled with horror. She was just as speechless.

Maybe that should have made Paige feel better, but it really didn't.

Okay. If anyone would know what to do here, hopefully it would be Bal?

With Alma's wards no longer in place, Paige should be free to call him right into the house. "Bal, I need you."

She really hoped this wasn't one of the times he decided to ignore her.

He appeared in a cloud of smoke beside Leslie.

Balnore didn't even glance at Paige. He only had eyes for Rachel. "I was going to say how odd it felt to be allowed inside this house. But I feel as though that would be inappropriate to say now."

Paige had to agree. "What is this?"

Balnore crept closer to Rachel.

The woman didn't make a sound. Her mouth was open as if screaming silently. Light seemed to pour from her, but there was no sound.

Bal turned to Paige. "This is very similar to your symbol."

She touched her chest, and her own scar. "I noticed." Paige stood beside him. She had thought of a million different ways to get her revenge on this woman. But this? She had never once thought of this. This was disgusting.

Bal glanced at Paige while the world trembled again. "How did you know to come here?"

"Oriel gave me the heads up I needed to come check on my mother."

"Did he give you any indication as to what was going on here?"

"Sven's trying to sever the connection between Heaven and Earth." But standing here looking at her mother and the agony she must be going through right now? Was this what Sven intended to do with her as well? What he'd intended this entire time?

It seemed likely. Paige wasn't sure what scared her more, the thought she could deal with him, or that she *had* negotiated with him. Dexx was alive because she'd given in to Sven's demands and given him part of the key to Hell. Well, the gate between Earth and Heaven and Hell. A three-way key.

Was that the reason the key had been split into three?

It made sense. The more she learned, the more things made sense. But, as with anything she learned, she wished she had put the pieces together a lot sooner.

Bal didn't say anything. It was as if he could tell she was making the connections as well.

"We need to get her out of here."

"How?" Leslie asked. "How do we know that if we move her we won't make this worse?"

Paige nodded toward Rachel. "I am willing to wager that this is the reason Sven was able to drain Roxxie. And, I'm also willing to bet that this is how he's able to drain other angels. Just like with Bastet's cats. We find the source, and then we figure out a way to keep him from it."

Leslie gestured toward Rachel. "But in this case, how do we do that?"

Paige had no idea. She was really hoping Bal had some

idea. "That's the reason why I called the demigod. What kind of great ideas did you bring?"

Balnore looked at Paige for a long moment and then he sighed. "I have an idea, but I can't guarantee she'll survive."

Rachel was the physical tie between Heaven and Earth. "And if she dies? Will Heaven and Earth be severed?"

Bal nodded. "I can tell you that she's not doing well. She will not live much longer."

Paige got a terrible, terrible idea. She reached inside herself and called for Cawli. *Hey. I need you to actually listen. Please don't ignore me, not this time.*

Cawli came forward. *I am here.*

Judging from the tone of his voice, it was almost as if he knew what she was thinking. *I'm an alpha.*

You are.

If I bite her, what's the likelihood that she'll be chosen?

Cawli didn't immediately respond.

I know what I'm asking here. She's not a great person. She has questionable morals. But right now, she's the physical connection between two dimensions. Just look at the tremors.

They are occurring in the Vaada Bhoomi as well.

Which just strengthened her resolve. *All of these dimensions are connected. Who's to say that if Heaven is separated, that the other dimensions don't fall?*

Theoretically, it is possible.

So, let me ask again. If I bite her, what's the likelihood of her being chosen?

Cawli paused for a moment and then finally admitted, *Not good. Whichever animal spirit chooses her would be bound to her.*

A housefly, she hoped. But a snake would suit her personality more.

Bound to her? Paige was certain Cawli wasn't seeing the full picture here. *She would be bound to it. Just look at Leslie. The griffin has almost as much control as she does.*

So, you're saying that I should search for a strong animal spirit?

A strong animal spirit like a griffin would give Rachel more power, but it would be strong enough to resist her. If they didn't risk it, they might lose Earth. *You tell me. Can you think of a better solution?*

Cawli growled. *No. I cannot.*

Paige took in a deep breath and then glanced at Leslie and Bal. "I have a really bad idea."

Leslie just looked at her. "What kind of a bad idea?"

Balnore seemed to catch on. He shook his head. "You can't be serious."

Except, Paige really was.

aige approached Rachel carefully. "Bal, do you have any idea what kind of energy that is? Like, what this glow is?"

"I have no idea. Just be careful."

"Just be careful," Paige muttered to herself. "Very helpful."

"I heard that."

Leslie moved forward with Paige. "Are you sure this is the right idea?"

No. Paige really wasn't. "Sure. This is a great idea."

"Giving the one woman we both hate the same power we have?" Leslie gave Paige a sidelong glance. "It seems a little stupid to me."

Paige crept forward, allowing the light to touch her hand. It didn't burn. So at least there was that. "I'm all for someone else coming up with a better idea. And as soon as that happens, I am all about following it. But, I really need someone to come up with a better idea before I bite this woman. So...what kind of great idea do you have?"

"Well, when you put it like that." Leslie gestured toward their mother. "Bite away, alpha."

With her tentative tests on the light coming back negative, meaning it didn't seem as though she was going to be fried, struck by lightning, or given a smite by God. She paused for one more moment, giving her the chance to think about this one more time. She looked over at her sister. "Give me a better choice."

Leslie just shrugged hopelessly. "I don't have one."

Crap.

Neither did Paige.

Bolstering her courage, Paige took another step forward, the light was all around her now. This energy was something she remembered…vaguely.

With that thought, memories came back of the last time she'd been in Heaven.

She remembered being interrogated.

She remembered why they were interrogating her.

They had known this moment was coming.

And they had thought *she* would be the one who was going to bring an end to Heaven because of her unborn children.

They knew her son was a rajasi and that the last time that spirit animal had roamed the Earth, he had nearly brought the end to Heaven.

They hadn't once considered it wasn't her. That it would be Rachel, their favorite pet.

Well, she was about to change their pet. That was for certain.

Calling up her alpha will, Paige stepped closer. She took a hold of Rachel's arm, allowed her teeth to shift into that of a big cat, and bit.

Rachel's entire body convulsed.

And with it, the entire house. Paige wasn't sure if it was

just the house, or if the quake was bigger.

Leah screamed from downstairs.

Paige shouted down, "Is everything okay down there?"

"Sure!" Ollie shouted back up. "Unless you wanted to save this house at all."

Paige wasn't sure what would happen if the house fell down around them. "Ollie, get Leah out."

Paige didn't hear anything further. She assumed that meant Ollie pulled her daughter to safety. She could hope anyway.

The light around Rachel pulsed. Once. Twice. And then all of the lights — the electric ones — pulsed in time to what Paige assumed was a heartbeat.

It looked as though the power that had been pulling Rachel apart was letting up. Paige hoped the gamble had paid off.

Paige shifted her vision from normal to witch to shifter. She wanted to see when or if Rachel was chosen.

The spirits of the aura above Rachel's head morphed, flitting from one animal to the next. First, a bear. Then a wolf. To a snake. Before a rhinoceros. The visions of spirits showed up and dissipated so fast Paige had trouble following.

Nothing wanted to bond. Satisfaction warred with sorrow. They had to save her mother.

They had to save the Earth.

Finally, the visions stopped on a mammoth.

The mammoth head seemed to solidify. And as it did, the energy that had Rachel bound in place evaporated, freeing her. She fell to the floor with a thud.

Paige rushed forward to see if she was okay. "Mammoth, can you hear me?"

In Paige's shifter vision, the mammoth raised his rose-colored head. "I can," he said through Rachel's mouth.

Leslie knelt on Rachel's other side and glanced at Paige.

"Can you keep her stabilized?"

"I can."

"We're going to take you on an airplane. Do you know what that means?"

The mammoth nodded gravely. "I do."

"You cannot shift while we are in the air."

"I will *not* shift while in this body." His voice was resolute.

"I thank you for helping us."

"I did not do it for you, I did it for *all* of us."

"Understood." Paige looked up at Bal. "I think it worked. But we should get her out of here as quickly as possible."

Balnore nodded his agreement. "Seeing this, I do not think we should risk having her in a plane."

Paige couldn't agree more. "Can you take her home?"

"If that is where you want me to take her."

Paige couldn't think of any better place. Rachel needed to be guarded. Because now, the person she hated the most was someone she had to keep alive. At all costs. "Yes, take her home. Get her under of our wards. And if at all possible?"

Balnore met her gaze, waiting.

"Keep her knocked out."

Bal smiled sickly. "With pleasure." He touched Rachel's hand and the both of them disappeared.

Leslie sighed. "If only he would come back for us."

Paige agreed, but she also had a feeling there was only so much they could do to abuse a god's power. "Think of it this way. We don't have to fly coach."

Leslie smiled like a cat. "This is true."

The tremors had stopped at the same time Rachel had been bitten. Whatever was going on, they had fixed it. At least temporarily.

A win? Could they actually chalk this up in the W column?

Paige really didn't know what they were going to be walking into as they stepped into the house.

Leah was still coming down from her excitement from going with them. But she *had,* and she really wasn't looking forward to the idea that Rachel was going to be in their house.

Paige completely understood. She wasn't looking forward to it either. It really pissed her off that she had to fight to keep that woman alive after everything she had done.

As soon as Paige stepped in the door, however, Michelle yelled at them, "Come see what's on the news."

Paige didn't want to see what was on the news. If Michelle was in her living room and telling her to watch it, it couldn't be good. But she walked in, preparing herself for what she might see. "Has Dexx come back from the hunt with DoDO?"

Michelle waved her off. "It went about as well as everyone thought it would. But he can fill you in later." Michelle turned up the volume.

Their TV screen was filled with a view from a helicopter.

Paige really couldn't make out too much from this angle, but the female reporter was telling them what they should be seeing. "A man calling himself Sven is trying to get a hold of a woman he is calling Paige."

Oh great. Here he goes again. This time on the news.

The camera angle changed, and it was clear the footage they were seeing was from a camera phone. She saw Sven pacing along the sidewalk. He shouted to the people around him. Paige couldn't quite make out what he was saying.

"Witnesses at the scene state that he's demanding she turn his power back on." The shot came back to the reporter. She was pretty, and that was about all Paige could say for her. "We don't know much more than that. Except that he has a person hostage whom he claims is an angel. After all of the strange things that have happened around Troutdale, we have to ask ourselves. Is this the end?"

Paige grabbed the remote and muted the TV. "What we really need to be asking ourselves is what we're going to do about this guy."

Michelle turned to her. "Did you save Rachel?"

Paige frowned. "I told Bal to bring her here."

"She's here," Mandy said as she popped in from the kitchen. "She got here just before everybody else did."

Well that was certainly a blessing. "Where is she?"

Mandy gestured upstairs. "With Roxxie feeling better, I moved her back out to Boot's place and put Rachel up in the guest room."

That guestroom was getting a lot of action these days. "Thank you." Paige moved to head upstairs. "Do we know who he has hostage?"

Michelle shrugged. "I don't know my angels very well."

"Then go get Roxxie." Paige made it to the bottom of the stairs. "And find Dexx. I need to know what happened while we were gone."

She didn't wait to see if anyone was going to follow her orders. She just went up the stairs to check on the mother she hated more than anything.

When she got there, she was surprised to see Rainbow sitting on the edge of the bed.

"What are you doing here?"

Rainbow looked up and smiled at her, getting to her feet. "No one else wanted to sit with her. And I figured that someone should check and make sure that she wasn't going to die on us."

Paige really hoped they all survived this. She really wanted to sit down and have a little bit of Rainbow time. She hadn't had any for quite a while. "Has there been any change in her condition?"

Rainbow shook her head. "Bal came through, dropped her off, and then just left. We didn't know what was going on."

Next time, Paige was going to give him orders to at least talk to someone. Right. Give a *god,* well, *demigod* orders? Their lives had changed so much. Crap. "We have to keep her alive. Apparently, she's the gate between Heaven and Earth."

Rainbow's expression exploded with surprise. However, she didn't say anything further.

Leah crept into the room and stared at Rachel's face. "I can't believe she's here."

"Me either." Not even a little bit.

"I feel like this is my fault."

How in the world could this be her fault? "I can assure you, it is not."

Leah didn't seem convinced. "I wished she would fight for custody for me again." Leah's voice quivered a little as she said that.

That certainly got Paige's full and undivided attention. "Why?"

Leah released a shaky breath. "I can't seem to get your attention."

"*I* can't seem to get my attention. I am being pulled in so many directions. You have no idea how much I want to spend time with you. This apprenticeship idea? It's a last-ditch effort to keep you with me a little bit more."

Leah nodded, but tears still studded her blue eyes. "I know all of that. But... It was a selfish wish. Do you think that I've made this happen?"

Leave it to a kid to think wishing would make something come true.

However, Paige had to remind herself Leah was growing up in a house where magick was real, and she knew a real life djinni. So maybe she should cut the kid a little slack. "No. This wasn't you."

Leah released a shuddering sigh.

Paige gathered her daughter in her arm and pressed a kiss to the top of her head. "This has been in motion for an awfully long time. Probably since before you were even born." Before Paige was born though? How much of the Whiskey bloodline had been about battle preparations for this moment? That was something she really didn't want to think about.

Dexx came through the door and stared at Rachel on the bed. "Tell me I'm not seeing what I'm seeing."

Paige knew he felt the same way about Rachel as she did. "Have you seen the news?"

He nodded, wrapping his arm around Leah's shoulder, and snuggling close to both of them. "I have. Does that have something to do with... this?"

Paige nodded. "Pretty sure it does." She licked her lips. "If I'm right, he somehow got the doorway between Heaven and Earth seared into her bones the way he seared the gate of Hell into mine."

Dexx stared at her in disbelief. "So, we finally learned what he's after?"

She nodded. "It would seem so." And it still didn't make her feel any better. Because if he had been planning this the entire time, then he had been planning on killing her this entire time. "When he had control of her and her door, he was able to siphon angels. And it looked as though he was trying to kill her."

Dexx frowned, not following. "Wouldn't he need her alive, so he could continue to siphon the energies?"

Paige shook her head. "I think that was just a temporary solution to the energy problem that we gave him. We took away the cats and the ancients."

"The ancients?"

"Cawli told me. They were looking for who was attacking them."

"I thought it'd been Cooper."

"I think that Cooper's witch saw what Sven was doing and just decided to do the same thing."

"So, you think Cooper was a copycat."

"Yup. Anyway, Cawli said that he's got the attacks stopped now."

"Then, let me ask you a question. If we took away his power source this time, how is he going to react to that?"

She was pretty sure that's exactly what they were seeing on the television. "He's getting national attention. He's making it to where the paranormals can't hide anymore. He's waking everyone up."

"To what end?"

She didn't know. Except, she did know humans. Humans worked really well together when they had something in common to fear.

"What if," she said quietly as the chill of fear rolled over her, "he intends to send humans after us?"

Dexx just stared at her. "It's one thing to kill a witch who's destroying people with his magick. It's another thing to take down an angel who's attacking your family. But if we fight back against humans?"

Leah blinked from where she had her head against Dexx's chest. "It's what you said. If someone tries to kill you, you try to kill them right back. The only difference is that we've had more practice."

Out of the mouth of babes, but it was weird hearing Captain Mal's words coming out of her daughter's lips. Paige wasn't even aware Leah had seen *Firefly*. "We would have to defend ourselves in human court."

And that wasn't even the half of it. If there was a shootout or fight with other humans, then the media would have a field day. The President would be able to tell the world about paranormals.

And then?

How much longer would it take for the paranormals to be forced to live in concentration camps? All she had to do was look at their own history to see that that's exactly what would happen.

Humans were good at another thing. Repeating their own history.

Michelle called to them from downstairs. "Paige! You might want to get down here."

Paige, Leah, and Dexx all moved toward the stairs.

Leah clung to Paige like wasn't going to let her mother out of her sight.

Frankly, Paige didn't want to let Leah out of hers either. The world was going to Hell in a hand basket. There was no way of shielding her daughter from this. The only thing she could do was prepare her.

"What if we let Rachel die?" Dexx asked as they walked down the stairs. He glanced at Leah apologetically.

Leah shook her head to tell him that it was okay.

Paige gripped the banister firmly. She and stairs weren't a great mix right now. Her body was so unbalanced it wasn't even funny. "The entire area— Dallas— was heaving. It was like that earthquake when Sven released all those demons here. Except, it was everywhere. We almost couldn't land because of it."

"And you're sure that was Rachel?"

Paige got to the bottom of the stairs and headed toward the living room. "I'm positive. She was being pulled in four different directions as she was dying. It felt as though the tremors were getting worse. I don't know what it'll look like if Heaven is severed from Earth. We may not survive it."

"How did you save her?" Dexx asked.

"I bit her."

"No."

"Yeah." She stopped in front of the TV and stared.

Sven stood in front of a man he'd trussed up like the other victims he had left for Paige and Dexx. He was strung up between two buildings. And as the world watched, Sven shoved a long sword into the man's belly, but it wasn't a *mavet ma'a'shed*. She'd never seen one like it before.

The reporters reacted. The person holding the cell phone jerked.

The angel exploded in a bright white light and his wings shone brightly against the building behind him. His head raised to the sky as he screamed a blaze of light.

And when the light faded, his body drooped, spent.

But Sven? He just turned around and smiled. He pointed to the man with the camera. "This is between me and Paige. If any of you want to save your world, you will bring her to me."

Taking the fight to him? It wasn't necessarily a horrible idea. It meant taking the fight away from their home turf.

Leah looked up at her and shook her head. "Away from here, you have no one. You'd be without any allies."

Well, listen to her daughter. She sounded just like a tactician.

Paige's phone rang. She pulled it out of her pocket and looked at the number. "That's a very valid argument. But it also means that we can take the damage out of our own backyard."

Dexx shook his head. "I'm with the chiclet on this one. Taking the fight to him is a bad idea. We have the Eastwoods here. The Blackmans. We have all of the packs here. If we take this to him, we might as well just hand him the keys to destroying our world."

Paige nodded in agreement and answered her phone. "This had better be good."

Elder Yad's voice was solemn. "I'm sure you've seen the news."

"I have."

"And how are you handling this?"

"The way I always do. Which, by the way, is the reason *why* you wanted me. So just let me do my job. Unless, you have *more* good news for me?"

The elder was quiet for a long moment and then the phone went silent.

Paige stared at her phone. "I need to talk to Sven."

Paige didn't even have time to make it to the front door before someone was pounding on it. "Who the hell could that be?"

Leslie kind of glared in her direction and headed for the door. When she opened it, she let out a note of surprise. "Paige, Spock is at the door."

Spock. Leslie could only mean the elves. If the elves were here, maybe they were here to help.

She screwed on her smile and stepped into the hallway behind Leslie. "How can we help you?"

There were two elves on their doorstep, and neither one of them looked pleased to be there. The lead elf was male and had black hair. He was the reason Leslie had called him Spock. He looked at her as though she was a disease and turned up his nose. "We have a report that you have one of our children."

Paige jerked back a little. She had completely forgotten Kate didn't belong to them. She didn't know what was wrong with her. Kate belonged to them. To the elves. Not to the

Whiskeys. "We were trying to figure out where she came from."

"Before or after you used us?"

Used them? "We haven't used you."

"Are you trying to tell me that you have not trespassed upon our lands?"

She had actually forgotten about that. "Right. We did do that. But we're fine now and we didn't disturb anything."

At least, she hoped so.

Spock didn't seem impressed. "You shall return what belongs to us."

The tone of his voice had Paige wondering exactly what they intended to do with Kate. "Does she have family?"

The other elf raised his chin. Paige was going to call him Legolas. He gave her a look filled with just as much disdain as Spock had. "She has no family. However, the elves take care of our own."

That was all well and good, but Paige wanted to know what they wanted with Kate. These two pompous assholes just brought out the mama bear in her. "She is out at the moment."

Spock tipped his head to the side with what she assumed was meant as a polite smile. "We will wait."

Of course they would. She took a step back, moved Leslie out of the way, then shut the door on both their faces.

Leslie stared at her incredulously. "We can't honestly be thinking about sending Kate back to those guys."

Paige put her finger to her lips and moved toward the back.

Leslie followed.

Paige had no idea where the girl would be. So, she snagged one of the kids and asked.

Mandy's eyes grew the size of golf balls. "She's over at Uncle Nick's."

Paige nodded before she glanced over at Leslie.

Leslie nodded, a look of death on her face.

If Paige had gone momma bear, she was nothing compared to Leslie. Leslie *was* the mamma bear of the Whiskey house. They stepped out of the door before shifting into their respective animals.

Leslie beat her to Nick and Mark's place, and because she had flown she was already inside. Paige shifted back into her normal form as soon as she made it into the treehouse.

Nick came out and greeted her, his face filled with concern. "What's going on?"

"There are a couple of elves on our front door." Paige looked around to see if she could find Kate. "But before I send Kate off to them, I want to make sure that she's going to be okay."

Nick looked like a nervous parent. "Do you think they would treat her badly?"

"I think they're elves." And what she knew about elves wasn't a great deal, but it didn't make her like them either.

Leslie and Mark walked into the room, followed by Kate.

She looked anxious. "My family has come for me?"

Paige knew if Dexx was there, he would kneel down in front of her, meet her at her own eye level. However, kneeling was just out of the question for her. She was way too pregnant. "The only thing I can say is that there are two elves here. And they also said that you have no surviving family."

The look on Kate's face said what the elves said was true.

Paige took in as deep breath as she possibly could with the two kids smooshing everything inside of her. "I know that when you came here, you didn't want to be here. You said that we would taint everything. But," Paige spoke carefully, going ahead and kneeling in front of the girl. This moment was worth the effort. And it *was* a lot of effort. "I need to know if you think you'll be safe."

What Paige had seen and experienced in the elf's lands didn't make her think Kate *would* be safe. She didn't care what the law said. She wasn't going to put any kid back into an unsafe environment.

Kate swallowed hard and then met Paige's gaze. "I think," Kate said carefully, "that if I can stay, I would like to."

Paige pulled herself to her feet.

Mark thankfully came over to assist.

Paige wasn't saying she was getting super fat, but her legs were starting to complain more than usual. "I've got a call to make. I'm going to see what I can do, but I'm not making any promises. Okay?" She met Mark's gaze.

He just closed his grey eyes.

"Just understand, we might have a fight on our hands. These are elves. They don't play by the same rules as everybody else."

Nick nodded solemnly and came over to take Kate's shoulders in his hands. "Do what you can. We'll be here."

Paige frowned and then thought about it for a moment. She might be able to forego the phone call and just get this handled right now. "Actually, I could probably use your help in the negotiations."

Nick's eyes brightened as he came around to stand beside Paige. "Are you thinking what I'm thinking?"

Paige still didn't know her brother well enough to be able to tell if they were thinking along the same thought path. But she could guess. No. She could hope. "If you're thinking about pissing off some elves and making them not feel like they're being pissed off, then the answer is yes."

Nick grinned. "That is exactly what I was thinking, but with less pissing."

Excellent. Paige turned toward the door. "I'm still not making any promises." She turned back to Kate. "I may lose this battle."

Kate nodded solemnly. "Thank you for trying."

Paige wasn't going to ask what kind of life the girl had lived before, but she was going to do what she could to help the kid now. She turned around and shifted into a bird, launching off the treehouse and into the air almost gracefully.

Nick shouted back at her. "Don't start until I get there."

Not a chance. There was no way they could win this battle without him. But she also wasn't going to walk all the way back to the house on her pregnant, human feet.

By the time Nick made it to the house, Paige had had an opportunity to make a cup tea. It had already steeped and everything. She threw her teabag in the trash. "Slowpoke."

Nick stuck his tongue out at her and shook his head. "Are we talking about the two people at the door?"

She nodded. She wasn't entirely sure how he was able to know things, but he had never asked how her magick worked. It was only fair she returned the favor. "You do your thing." She headed to the door at the front of the house. "I'll do mine."

Nick nodded and headed for the living room through the dining room.

Paige stopped at the door, hearing Leslie land in the rafters on the other side. She opened the door and plastered on a smile. "I hope I didn't keep you guys waiting too long."

Spock turned to her and glared. "Where is the girl?"

"See, that's the thing."

Paige waited to see if Nick's empathic magic would have any effect.

Within moments, the stiff lines on Spock's neck loosened. His expression lightened minutely.

Legolas, however was just as upset as when they'd started this conversation.

That certainly wasn't helpful. If only she had a telepathic toddler to tell her brother to step up his A-game.

She almost heard Kammy gasp in the background. And then, a moment later, Legolas started relaxing as well.

That was more like it. Paige took a sip of her tea and then looked at both of them with a smile. "Kate has decided she wants to stay here. And I need to see how to do that legally. So, for now, you're going to leave her in our care. We promise not to get her hurt, or to put her in danger."

Spock frowned. "War is coming to your door."

At least the man was observant. "You could help. You know, if you really cared about her."

Legolas sighed and shook his head. "We will not involve ourselves in the matters of man."

She had to try. "In that case, we promise to keep her as safe as we can."

"And keep her out of Underhill. She has already allowed too many people inside our domain. She will have to answer for that eventually."

Paige was going to have to find a way to make that right. Because Kate had done that for her. "How about when this is all said and done, we have a little powwow? Between me and your king?"

Spock narrowed his eyes and then shook his head. "You would be meeting with the queen."

Paige just shrugged and smiled. Even better. "With your queen. Because we need to discuss that."

Spock shook his head as if not quite certain what had just happened. But he took a step backward and motioned for Legolas to join him. "This is not over."

"Oh, I'm sure it isn't."

She waited until both men disappeared, Spock opened a door in the middle of nowhere and they just walked through it, disappearing from sight.

How were they supposed to create wards to keep elves out? She had no idea if that was possible.

"Well, that was interesting." Leslie jumped off the rafter in bird form and landed as a human. She made it look so damn easy. "Now, we should probably deal with this Sven problem."

Life in the Whiskey house was always interesting. It was always one thing or another. But the question was, what *was* she going to do about the Sven thing?

The question was less about *what* they were going to do about Sven and more about *when*. Paige had all the power players she could possibly get on the board. And, it seemed as though they had succeeded in breaking Sven away from most of his power. He was cut off. Finally. So, all they really had to do was draw him out and end this once and for all.

Which sounded great. It was a little terrifying to think about though.

Paige had shifted, choosing to fly to the Portland docks. That had upset Dexx quite a bit because there was no way he could shift and run there. While she could hide as a hawk, he couldn't hide is a sabertooth cat. So, that left him at home.

Nobody put Dexx in a corner. Or at home as the babysitter. Though, he was no longer the babysitter. He really had grown into the daddy.

Yes, she said that in a little girl voice. She didn't care. She loved that man, but he sure knew how to pout.

As she flew over the docks, Leslie beside her, they took it in. It was a circus. There were cameras, news vans, and people everywhere. And the police were doing their best to get Sven to stand down.

Unfortunately, they weren't doing a fantastic job of it. Mostly because Sven was a demon. And they were just humans with guns.

Just humans with guns. They could still ruin her day. She had to make sure not to surprise them. She didn't want to have any stray bullets accidentally finding their way into her. That would be a very bad day.

She landed in a place where nobody could see her. She hoped it would be far enough away from the cameras she wouldn't be picked up shifting. As soon as she landed, she shifted into human form, looking around one more time.

Her eyes said no one else was near.

That didn't mean much. Especially with today's technology. There could be a camera somewhere she didn't know about. She just had to hope for the best.

Paige looked around at everyone. At all of the reporters and the police officers. None of them knew how to handle a situation like this. Even the elders in all of their wisdom had no idea how to handle a situation like this.

She knew she would be granted some leniency when the smoke cleared, and everyone was faced with dealing with the consequences of today's actions. She also knew she wouldn't be given as much leniency as she needed. She couldn't openly defend herself with magick. There were too many cameras in place. She wouldn't be able to openly shift to defend herself. If Sven did something, she didn't know how she would defend herself. Her best bet was to get him back to Troutdale where she could deal with him the way she knew she needed to.

Like Leah and Dexx had said.

She stepped away from the building and raised her voice.

"Sven!" His sword was gone. No surprise, but she'd have to watch for it.

He turned toward her with a smile, his arms wide. "Paige, love. What took you so long?"

Paige had a really hard time taking her eyes off the people surrounding them. So many innocent people. Okay, so they weren't all innocent. There were probably more than a couple jackasses among them. But, she was about to pull the wool off all their eyes. She had no idea how the elders were going to sell this one. The only thing she knew was that the President of the United States was going to use this to her benefit. Not to the benefit of anybody else. And it was not going to end well for the paranormals.

Paige widened her hands and took a step toward him. It wasn't that she wanted to get closer to him. She just wanted to get to the point where they weren't shouting at each other. She wanted to make it a little harder for the TV crews to be able to hear and understand what they were saying. "This is a little public, don't you think?"

Sven talked toward her like he hadn't heard her. "Why did you do it?"

It took her a moment to think about what it was that he might be referencing. And then it hit her. Why had she saved her mother? She held up her hand to tell him he had come far enough.

He stopped and stared at her in confusion. "I did that for you."

Did that for her? She took another step toward him so she could speak a little quieter, "And are you planning to do that to me? Because the same damn door is in my bones."

The smile on his face was innocent, full of joy. "I won't have to with you. I secured another door here."

Paige wasn't sure she wanted to know. "A person?"

He shrugged. "She was brought back from the dead."

Paige frowned. She had no idea who he was talking about.

"The Blackman witch who died two years ago. She was perfect." His accent made it sound perfectly okay. Which it wasn't. He stepped even closer to her. "I put the gate in her bones. You should have felt the difference."

"The difference?"

"That there isn't as much of a pull now?" He gestured to her chest. "And the scars? They should be fading."

She *had* noticed that, but she'd thought it had been a shifter thing. Or, maybe she just thought she was handling things better. She had better control. "How long ago did you do this?"

He smiled triumphantly. "About six months ago."

"Six months ago?" she'd been traveling from one place to the next on missions with the elders. She hadn't had time to even think about this.

But maybe this was the reason why she was able to shift now. Cawli wasn't concentrating solely on keeping the door inside of her bones closed.

It didn't matter. She had to stop him before he was able to break the door to either realm.

"So, why did you do it?" he asked again.

Paige didn't even know if he was capable of rational thought. In Louisiana, he had been. He had been the one sane person on the entire team she'd been hunting. Maybe he didn't even know what he was doing to the world. "There were earthquakes."

He shrugged. "There will be a lot more than just earth-quakes, love. When I'm done, the world will be a different place. This is the end times."

He said that like it was a good thing. Now, Paige wasn't going to claim the world was the most fabulous place ever, but she didn't think it needed to be razed to the ground and rebuilt all over again. "Do you know how many innocent lives would be lost?"

He shook his head. He was so close to her now they didn't have to raise their voices anymore.

Oops. Too close. She took a step or two back and held out her hand telling him to stop.

He did with a frown of confusion on his face. "I was going to kill her for you."

"And take all of the energy from the angels that you possibly could at the same time?"

"What is it that you are always saying? Win-win?" The look he gave her was almost sexy. "Honestly, Paige, I thought you would've been a bit more grateful."

"Honestly, if you were doing it any other way, I would've been. But killing my mother so that you can bring an end to the world? I think that's going little over the top. Don't you?"

Sven spun in a circle, his head thrown back. "You and I could rule this entire world together. You have any idea what that would be like?"

"Do you have any idea what my life is like? And regardless, I like it the way it is."

He looked genuinely confused by that. "But it's so mundane."

She shook her head. "We can't all live the life of gods, Sven. Some of us need to spend time with our hands in the dirt. And some of us like it that way."

He shook his head.

This wasn't getting him away from cameras. "How about we take this away from here?"

Sven went still and raised an eyebrow. "Back to Troutdale? I can't get in."

There was that.

Paige shrugged.

"Where you have all your power?"

Well, it wasn't as though she thought he would fall for her trap. "And you were trying to tell me that a *god* is scared of little old me?"

He chuckled. "Somebody has been doin' her homework."

Paige shrugged. "Someone had to."

Sven turned to the crowd which was actually trying to get closer.

Okay, so some of these people may not be jackasses, but they also weren't *real* bright either.

Yes, people, step right up to the danger. That's a great idea.

Sven looked at her with a smile. "I could take you right here."

"I'm pretty sure that if I defended myself in front of everyone, I could build a pretty good case for myself."

He turned to her. "Imagine a life where you wouldn't have to worry about what you had to explain to others. Imagine a life where you could create the rules. You and me. We could rule this."

Paige had to admit, the idea of not having to live by the Shadow Sisterhood's rules was appealing. And the idea of not having to live by the rules the President of the United States was probably going to inflict on all of them was also appealing.

But not appealing enough.

"Sven don't do this."

He lowered his gaze to the ground as if in disappointment. "I can't get to Rachel. Which means, I know exactly where she is."

Well, if that was how she was going to get him to come back to Troutdale... "Well, I guess I'll see you there."

He stared at her as if seeing her for the first time. "What did I do wrong?"

She wasn't entirely certain he'd asked a real question until he'd moved. It looked as though he was looking for a real answer. So, she was going to give him one. "What did you do *right*? Did you honestly think that sending me bodies with poetry and butterflies exploding out of them was *romantic*? Whatever did I do to give you the indication that that was acceptable?"

He stared at her like a wounded boy.

She didn't care.

"Look, I get that you like me. And I also get that in your weird way, you thought you were being nice to me. But where you missed the mark was in not figuring out what I wanted."

"I was preparing to give you the world."

She took a step toward him and leaned forward. "No. You were preparing to take the world, then you saw me, and decided you wanted to share it with me. You never once asked yourself what *I* would want."

He frowned and took a step back. It looked as though maybe he'd actually heard her, probably for the first time ever. "I was going to kill your mother for you."

"And I am more grateful for that, than I ever want to have to admit out loud again. However, I don't accept it. The cost comes at too high a price. I cannot destroy the world in order to get my own revenge."

He shook his head again, this time as if to clear it. He met her gaze and smiled, a sad, sick smile. "I'm going to let you go home now, Paige. And I'm going to let you have time with your family. And I'm going to let you wait and wonder what I'm doing. When you least expect it, I will strike."

As long as he was striking in Troutdale, she was sure they'd be fine. "And we will be waiting. Now get out of here."

He took three steps back, shaking his head the entire

time. He stopped, spread his arms and bowed, and then left in a cloud of smoke.

That certainly could have gone better.

It certainly could have gone a lot worse, too.

What were they going to do about all of these people and all of their videos?

She had no idea.

She walked behind the building, turned to make sure nobody was watching, and shifted, turning into an owl and flew away.

She was going to do one thing he had recommended. She was going to go spend a little time with her family. While she still could.

And draw up the battle plans to take him out once and for all.

As soon as her feet— her human, booted feet— touched her front porch, she pulled out her phone and dialed Chuck.

He answered on the second ring. "What's going on?"

Paige remained outside for a while. She didn't want little kids to hear this conversation. "I had a few elves stop by."

He cleared his throat. "I take it the conversation didn't go well."

"Kate has no family. And she doesn't want to go with them. I need to know what kind of stance we can make in order to keep her here."

He paused for a moment. "If they really want to make a stand?"

She read between the silence after that statement. "That's what I needed to know. What would get them to change their mind?"

"The thing about the Fae is that they're all about what they can get in return."

Paige wasn't sure what she had to offer them in return. It wasn't as though they were resource poor. They had a lot to offer. But was it something the Fae would want? "I might try that tactic then."

"Just be careful when dealing with them. None of us have a lot of experience in that area. But, I do know that they can be quite shifty."

That wasn't news. It was something she had heard quite a bit as well. "I'll do what I can." So...what resource did she have the elves would be interested in enough to let her family adopt one of theirs? That was the question.

She didn't have an answer.

When she stepped into the Whiskey house, she was met with silence. That wasn't something she enjoyed much. It usually meant people were off getting into trouble. She pulled her head back and yelled, "Is anyone here?"

It didn't take long for people to appear. Mandy and Leah were first, surprisingly, since they had come from the attic.

Tyler showed up shortly afterwards, followed closely by Kate.

Leslie, Tru, and Kammy all came from the dining room. Then Dexx and Bobby came in from the garage.

That was almost everybody.

Nick and Mark came in through the back door, talking to one another in hushed tones.

Now everyone was there. "We have no idea what's coming to us in the next couple of days, or even in the next couple of hours." She clapped her hands and looked at everyone. "So, I vote for game night."

Everybody kind of looked at each other as if they were confused by what they had just heard.

Leslie was the first to speak up. "We're about to head into battle, and you want to play *UNO*?"

She had no idea how badly. "You're damn straight. I'll play *UNO*, Go Fish, Poker, *Munchkin*, *Monopoly*—"

Leslie pulled a face.

Paige had to agree. *Monopoly* really wasn't the game to play on the possibly their last night on this Earth.

"I could be down for *Munchkin*," Leslie said.

"Runch-in!" Bobby exclaimed, jumping up and down.

He didn't get to play ever, but he did like to help Dexx and Paige choose who to pick on. He was…a monster.

But Paige was a little surprised because Leslie didn't like playing games. Leslie was a sore loser.

Paige wasn't the only one to take notice. Dexx grinned. "I vote we combine every *Munchkin* deck we have."

Paige didn't remember how many *Munchkin* decks they had. She did know, however, there were a lot.

The kids all scrambled to get the cards while the adults went into the dining room to make sure there were enough chairs and table space. Even though they had the largest dining table Paige had ever seen, it still wasn't quite big enough to hold everybody. So, they had to extend it in a really awkward way with two folding tables on either end. The table was kind of a U-shaped.

This game was going to be interesting to say the least.

They all grabbed drinks and snacks and took their seats. Leah decided she was going to sit next to Paige, which she was perfectly okay with.

Bobby was all over the place, but mostly with Dexx because he'd go all out on other people. He didn't care.

The game was ridiculous. They had somehow managed to mix six decks of cards together. They had *Steampunk* mixed with *Space, the Wizard of Oz, the Nightmare Before Christmas,* and something else. Paige didn't know what it was, but there were zombies.

The kids were up and down, looking at everybody's monsters and everybody's munchkins. Everyone was slinging spells and curses across the table. *And* the conversation remained light. The sunlight faded and the only thing illuminating the dining room table was the overhead lamp.

Paige wasn't even for sure how to keep track of who was winning or losing. And she was almost certain Leslie had won about a dozen times and hadn't told anybody.

Everyone needed this. And it showed. They hooted and hollered. They discovered Kate was screamer. She would scream when she was excited, and then when she was upset. She was a girl with deep emotions. Or, at least very powerful ones.

Around midnight, however, she sent everybody to bed.

Everybody, that was, except for the adults.

And Bobby. He had fallen asleep in Paige's arms, and she just didn't feel like getting up and putting him down yet. He was so much bigger now. He was able to run around with ease, so getting snuggle time with the boy was difficult. She soaked in his heat and just held him while the girls and Tyler got ready for bed.

Dexx stayed close to her and didn't bother getting up until Leah requested he tuck her in. When he came down, he had a smile on his face. He sat down next to Paige and ruffled Bobby's blonde hair.

Paige needed more of *this*. "What are you going to do when she's big enough that she doesn't want to be tucked in anymore?"

Dexx shook his head. "No clue. I honestly have no idea how that girl even wiggled her way into my life."

That was something Paige had thought more than once as well. "Can you imagine what your life would be like if you had never met me?"

He raised his eyebrows but said nothing.

It was something she just couldn't shake. This thought. That someone had put her on this course, that someone had put them all on this path. She wanted to get it out of her head. She wanted to accept her life was just life, that she was just living it because she was just a person like everybody else.

But it was starting to feel like it wasn't.

Dexx could see something was going on. He touched her hand and snuggled close to her. Well, as close as he could. They were on the couch and she was full of baby and covered in toddler, so it was a little difficult.

"What's going on with you?"

She shook her head. "It's just something I've been thinking about. With all of these prophecies and everything that's been going on."

He nodded. "It's been something I've been thinking about, too."

She was glad to know she wasn't alone. "I really don't want to talk about the prophecies. Just thinking about them pisses me off."

He snapped his fingers and pointed at her. "I did get that memo."

She grinned. "Oh good. I was hoping I wasn't being too subtle."

"You? Subtle?" He shook his head. "Never."

She glanced up at the ceiling, as if she could see her mother laying in the bed. "What if..." Paige gathered her thoughts for a moment. "What if Rachel didn't pick our fathers."

Dexx frowned at her. "I don't think I'm keeping up."

"Think about it. Us three kids have different fathers. And it's not because... Okay. Maybe it is because she couldn't get anybody to stay with her. Maybe she really did have some daddy issues, what with Reece abandoning her and everything. But it feels like maybe someone was looking at the breeding. It — it's like we were bred for this."

Dexx winced. "Is it a little too early for mare jokes?"

Paige frowned at him. "Not where I'm going with this." She licked her lips. "But think about it. I was born as a Whiskey, as the demon summoner, and with Blackman magic."

He nodded. "Door magic."

"Exactly. And who knows about Leslie's father? There's just so much we don't know about him. Who is he? What's his magic? None of us ever asked this before. But now I'm beginning to wonder if we should have. Because... I think there's a plan."

Dexx narrowed his eyes and snuggled a little closer. "So, you think, that someone saw this a long time ago and said, 'I'm going to bake a cake.' But instead of a real cake, he wanted to build a baby cake."

She realized he was trying to be funny. But when he said the words aloud, it just made it seem more real. She patted her belly with one hand and raised her eyebrows. "Do you know what had Merry Eastwood surprised?"

Dexx snorted and shook his head. "I have stopped trying to guess what would surprise her."

Paige pointed to her belly. "She was surprised to learn that she wasn't the most powerful witch in the room the other day."

Dexx looked at her appreciatively. "Well, she just learned something that the rest of us have known for quite a while."

"You don't understand. What if the only reason why I'm this powerful right now is because of all of the puzzle pieces clicking into place? What if there's somebody upstairs putting this all together?"

Dexx leaned back and looked at her. "If you're trying to tell me that you're coming up with a perfectly good reason why we shouldn't fight Sven, because it's been preordained that we're going to win, I'm all for that. I'm the person who likes to take the easy way out. However, I will also be the first one to point out that even when you pick all the best players on your team, that doesn't mean that you're going to win the Superbowl."

Paige laughed and frowned at him. "Did you just give me a football reference?"

He shrugged. "It was all I had at the time. I could have given you a car reference, but I know you wouldn't get it. You'd at least understand the football reference a little."

Paige chuckled, then gave him a long, hard stare. "I'm scared."

With one hand on Bobby's arm and his other hand on Paige's, Dexx situated himself to where he could see her more clearly. "I'm not. I nearly lost all of you just a few days ago. I know what that feels like. And I never want to experience that again."

Paige sucked in a deep breath and let it go. "I don't either."

Sven was the biggest baddie they'd ever faced. If they had been preparing for this all their lives, if someone up high had been stacking the deck in their favor, she hoped it would be enough. But there was a part of her that doubted it. A part of her that remembered Sven was always three steps ahead. There was a voice, and it wasn't Cawli's, that warned her that there was something they were missing.

But did she have the ability to find it?

Before it was too late?

When Paige got up the next morning, she knew what she had to do first.

She needed to go to the Eastwood's and help them get their wards in line with the rest of the town. However, while she was doing that, she was going to see about enlisting Merry Eastwood's assistance in dealing with Eldora Blackman. Paige needed to know why Sheila Blackman was alive. She was the only person who could have been risen from the dead and was now the doorway to Hell.

But how? As far as Paige knew, Leah was the only necromancer, but she didn't know the Blackman coven. She didn't know their strengths or powers.

She gave Bobby a goodbye kiss and leaned in to give Dexx his.

He caught her and held her for a much longer moment.

Paige laughed. "I won't be gone that long."

He looked at her appreciatively. "I've missed a little me time."

When he said it that way, she knew exactly what he was talking about. "You time? I've missed *me* time."

He snickered. "Who are you kidding? Me time *is* you time."

Sometimes. Okay. A lot of times, but she could really just use a night where she sat in front of the TV and vegged or read a book. When was the last time she'd *read* a freakin' book? But as much fun as this was, it wasn't getting the crap she had to deal with done. She pushed away from him. "I'll be home as soon as I can."

He walked her to the front door. "Show those witches what they wish they could be."

She opened the door and walked out. "Don't burn down the house."

"Don't burn down the world." He paused. "Before Sven gets a chance to. He'd be really upset."

She chuckled, and then launched herself off the front porch in tiger form.

She walked toward the Eastwood lands at a leisurely pace. They really weren't that far away, so it didn't take long to get there. She found it more than a little unsettling all three witch families had decided to live so incredibly close together. What had it been like before? Two hundred years before? Had they really worked together? Had they provided a united front?

Paige realized she had the grimoires. She could look into them, but the grimoires frustrated her more than anything. And she really didn't look forward to looking into them again anytime soon.

She crossed the road, and then kept walking past the Whiskey wards. Shortly after that she crossed through the Eastwood wards. Their wards felt like walking through a freezer, almost. They made her feel uncomfortable, like she was in the wrong place.

What did it feel like for Ollie whenever he came by? Because she had spelled the Whiskey wards specifically against the Eastwoods. In her defense, she had a very good reason for it. But, there was no way she could keep the wards against the Eastwood witches up any longer. She had spelled the entire town against them. For obvious reasons. Number one being they were blood witches and they'd had a vampire in residence. Well, okay. It was just because they were blood witches and she didn't...like them.

But now? With them being neighbors? She was going to have to be a little bit more creative and accepting.

It took her longer than she expected to get to the East-wood house. She didn't know what she thought she would see. She had never once come to this area. But the Eastwood home was large and extravagant. It looked more like a mansion than it did a house.

Tall columns stretched to a third story, and arched windows set into wide expanses of bone-white exterior walls.

As she got closer, witches came out of the woodwork.

She waited until she'd got at least a little closer to the house before she shifted to human form. She walked the remaining few feet toward the raised deck and stopped.

She was surrounded by at least two dozen witches. She wasn't sure, but it seemed as though the Eastwood coven was the largest of the three. The Whiskeys might be a tight coven, but they were certainly the smallest. The Blackmans were at least double their number. Though, Paige wasn't entirely sure how many of them were legitimately Blackman witches.

Oh, the roads her mind traveled when she was about to walk into a situation that could go ten kinds of bad.

A minute later Merry Eastwood made her entrance. She wore the kind of clothes she had before she'd gone to jail. They were expensive, and her heels didn't belong anywhere in the country.

And they were certainly in the country. Right up to the

edge of their estate. And then it was all sedate courtyards and paved driveways. It wasn't until she got here Paige realized just how redneck they were in comparison. Like, was that even a thing?

Merry smiled down at her from the top of the stairs. "I honestly didn't expect you."

"You said you needed your wards to connect with ours. So, I'm here to make that happen."

Merry nodded, her expression guarded. "And you came alone?"

"Trust me. I'm enough."

Ollie stepped onto the porch. He greeted Paige with a smile.

She smiled back, but she wasn't feeling comfortable. "How about we get to this as quickly as possible and then I have something else that I'd like to discuss with you."

Merry narrowed her eyes and tipped her head to the side. "Should I be intrigued?"

"I'm not entirely sure what would intrigue you, Merry." Paige was getting tired of this conversation. "But I'll say I'm intrigued." She wanted to roll her eyes but refrained.

Merry smiled. "Well, this will certainly be a look into the life of Paige Whiskey. What would intrigue her?"

Paige shrugged. "I'm a pretty easy mark. Sometimes I'm intrigued by a peanut butter sandwich. It really just depends on my day."

Merry met Paige on the ground level. "What's the topic of interest this time? I hope it's not peanut butter."

Paige took a breath and held it for a moment. She had to remember she was trying to pave new paths. Why was that so hard to remember?

Though, there was a part of her that respected Merry Eastwood a little. Paige would never admit that out loud. But Merry had a certain power. She made it look easy. And that was something that Paige could learn. "I had a conversation with Sven yesterday and he said something that opened my eyes."

Merry tipped her head to the side. "Oh. That *is* interesting." She gestured around her. "I have brought most of my coven. What is it that we need?"

Paige looked around, taking the opportunity to gauge the people around her. They looked cold, hard, and calculating. "First, we're going to need something to ground your tree with."

Merry narrowed her eyes. "Ground my tree?"

Paige shook her head and gestured with both hands. "It's a method we learned from the wood witches up in Alaska. And, trust me when I say, these are the strongest damn wards I've ever come across."

Merry sniffed in agreement. "That is something I had remarked on as soon as we got into town." She gestured at Paige. "And I'm assuming that once we've completed this, it will no longer feel as though my skin is on fire every time I need to go to the grocery store."

So, that's what Paige's wards felt like to an outsider. "We will have to draw up a few base rules. Like, don't kill people in our town."

"And that is what your wards were supposed to prevent?"

"I feel as though they did a pretty good job."

Merry nodded. "I suppose they did. I'm assuming that your vampire is no longer in town. I'm sure he told you what will happen if he's still in town and our magic is combined with yours."

Paige nodded. "I escorted him out of town as soon as I broke you out of jail."

"Very good. Then let's get to this."

Paige was so ready to be done with grounding trees and wards. It just didn't get any different.

She called up her power and sent it out as she'd done several times now.

Ollie gave her a really big rock to ground the tree with.

Paige pushed her magick into it, and then set it down, following the practices she'd mastered, creating the tree before inviting the Eastwood's to join their magick to hers.

She was expecting it to feel gross. But, when her magick touched Merry's, it felt as if her world had become almost complete. It didn't make any sense to her. Her magick was life. Of course, the Blackman magick she'd inherited from her father was door magick, but she'd thought the Eastwoods blood magick would feel like a disease.

In truth, it felt like anything but, and she didn't know if that made her feel better or worse about having them so close.

When their wards were ready, everyone present added their magic to it. Paige widened the wards and connected them to the ones surrounding the town. She still wasn't going to let them anywhere near the Whiskey wards. The Blackman's and the Eastwood's would have to learn how to play nice in her backyard first.

The Eastwood wards met the Troutdale wards with a resounding pop, the repercussion hitting them like a tidal wave.

Merry touched her hair, putting it back in place. She looked up at her tree with a frown. "My magic feels… different somehow."

Paige frowned. Now was not the time to have weakness in any of their lines. "A good different or a bad different?"

Ollie frowned as well but shook his head. "It's really hard to say."

One of the other witches, a blonde, turned around, looking bewildered. "I've lost it."

Paige looked over at Merry, hoping that this was just

some kind of quirk of the Eastwood's.

But Merry seemed to be as confused as Paige. "What did you lose?"

"My magick. I lost my magick."

Paige groaned. It would be just her luck she would go to "help" the Eastwood's and they would then claim she was hurting them in some weird, bizarre way. She held up her hands in surrender. "All I did was what we did with the rest of the wards. The Blackmans did this too. They didn't lose any of their magick. You can ask Eldora when we go talk to her."

Merry frowned at her but kept most of her attention focused on the blonde. "This is actually something I had wondered about." She turned her full attention to Paige. "Not all of my witches got their powers naturally."

What? "What do you mean not naturally?"

Merry gestured around her with one hand. Paige assumed she was gesturing toward the people. "Sometimes, people will come to me and give me things in exchange for power."

Paige had a feeling she knew where this was going. "So, what you're saying is that you would steal power from other people."

Merry nodded. "It was a very simple blood transference. I wondered if it would hold under your wards. Appears as though it doesn't"

"And you weren't going to warn them first?"

Merry shook her head. "I saw no reason to. I got what I needed from them. And they got what they needed from me. As far as I'm concerned, we're square."

Paige made a mental note to herself never to get into a bargain with her. If this was how Merry Eastwood handled her debt, Paige didn't need any part of it. "Well, I guess if we're done here?"

Merry nodded and gestured for Paige to continue.

Paige gestured at all of the remaining witches around them. It wasn't that she didn't trust them. No. Wait. She *didn't* trust them. "I'd appreciate it if we could have a conversation in private."

Merry gestured for the other witches to leave.

More than just the blonde had lost their magick. Looking around, it appeared as though there were at least eight others who were now mundanes again, though they were being a lot quieter about it. And those who were born with magick? Weren't giving them any sympathy whatsoever.

The Eastwoods were a cold bunch of witches.

When the immediate area had cleared, Paige took a step closer to Merry out of pure habit. "I believe Sheila Blackman is alive."

Merry studied her as if she'd lost her mind. "That is a very bizarre accusation to make. If this is true, then there is no case against me. I believe you put me in jail for killing her."

Paige remembered exactly how it was that she had got Merry into jail. "I believe that someone raised her from the dead. And I'm pretty sure that person is Eldora Blackman."

Merry shook her head. "There's no way Eldora Blackman would allow something like that to happen. You don't know the woman like I do."

"I realize that. Which is the reason why I want you to join me. I need to go talk to her and I thought it would be best to bring someone who actually knows her."

Merry waved her hand. "Well, I can tell you that I'm not going to shift into anything and travel there on foot."

"I also knew that you weren't going to ride in any of my vehicles. Because they're all too old for you." Even though Leslie's vehicle was only two years old. Merry had "superior" tastes.

Merry nodded in agreement. "I assume you're the only

Whiskey who will be going?"

"I don't feel as though we needed to bring any more. Do you?"

Merry appraised her for a moment and then agreed. She snapped her fingers and keys appeared in her hand. It wasn't by magick, however. Someone brought them to her, as if able to read her mind.

Now *that* was a handy trick.

Merry led them to a new car. It was shiny and black. That was all Paige could tell. Also, it was very expensive. It had leather seats and a mahogany dashboard.

Paige knew when she got home, Dexx was going to want to know the information about the car, but she would just have to disappoint him on this one. Because there was no way she was asking.

They drove to the Blackman house in relative quiet.

Merry made a little small talk, but it wasn't anything noteworthy. Paige warned her the ruts in the Blackman driveway were ridiculously deep. And Merry complained like Paige did the first time she had driven down that driveway. When they parked and got out, they were greeted by the Blackman witches.

Eldora lead the throng. "I wish I could say this was a pleasant surprise."

Merry stared up at their tree. "It really is almost exactly the same."

Paige frowned at her. "Did you think I was lying to you?"

"The thought had crossed my mind." Merry turned to Eldora. "We actually came to talk to you."

Eldora smiled, though it held no warmth. She gestured toward the house. "We weren't expecting company."

Paige waited until they were in the house, and the door was shut. The only two Blackman's in there were Eldora and Derrick.

Merry glanced over at Derrick with a raised eyebrow. "You don't feel safe in our presence?"

Eldora sighed and then gestured for Derrick to leave. "Now, perhaps you could explain to me what you're doing in my house?"

Merry looked pointedly at Paige.

Paige had no idea how this conversation was supposed to go. Or how she thought she *wanted* it to go. So, it was best to just get it over with. "Is Sheila back from the dead?"

Eldora didn't even blink. "How did you find out?"

Not the confirmation she wanted, but at least she knew for sure. "Sven told me."

Eldora looked surprised.

"Then, he told me that he'd placed the gate between Earth and Hell in her bones."

Eldora and Merry both glanced at Paige's chest.

Paige opened her shirt, so they could both see where the scars had once been. "I can't even begin to tell you how bad this is." She buttoned her shirt. "He intends on killing her, again. Slowly. Over a course of time. And he's probably draining demons for their power right now."

Eldora looked over at Merry with wide-eyed concerned. "Is this possible?"

Merry shrugged. "How am I supposed to know? Ever since this one came into our world, everything changed."

"Well, let me shed a little bit of light in our situation." It was time for them to understand the full repercussions. "Sven is a Lilim. What that means is he's very powerful. However, he's mortal. And right now, he's fighting very hard to find a way to become immortal. He stole a kitsune blade which gave him extra lives, and he is powering his soul using anything he can get his hands on. It used to be the spirit animals in another realm. And then he put a gate between

Heaven and Earth in Rachel's chest, so he could siphon energy from angels."

"Please tell me he's at least killing *that* one," Merry said quietly."

"I wish." Paige really didn't want to have to confess to anybody else, especially Merry Eastwood and Eldora Blackman. "I had to save her."

"Tell me you're joking."

Paige shook her head. "He's planning on severing the ties between our world and Heaven and Hell. And when he was doing that with Rachel down in Texas, there were earthquakes. It felt as if things were coming to an end."

Merry looked over at Eldora. "When this one walks into our lives, she creates a lot of chaos."

Like this was Paige's fault. "I need to know how you brought her back from the dead."

Eldora met her gaze solidly. "I used Leah."

That was what Paige had been afraid of. Because Leah was the only necromancer she knew of in the area. "How."

Merry smiled and leaned back in her chair. Her expression said, "Pass me the popcorn."

Eldora looked uncomfortable and then shook her head. "I simply waited for training to begin on your property, and then, when she opened the door, I pulled my daughter through."

Peace was one thing. But... "You used my daughter."

Eldora closed her eyes for a long moment before opening them again.

Paige didn't see a hint of remorse in the woman. "You're not welcome on my land ever again."

Merry made tsking sound. "That is a very long time."

"And that's *my* daughter." Nobody messed with her daughter, especially when they broke the world with her daughter's abilities.

Paige knew Sven had found a new power source. And now she had confirmation of who it was. What she didn't know was what she could do to stop it.

"Do either of you ladies have any idea how to get him to stop siphoning the power of the demons? Because while he has your daughter," she said gesturing toward Eldora, "he has all of Hell at his disposal. Do you know what that means?"

"I might know more than you would imagine," Eldora said snidely.

"I hope so. Because what we really need is a way to beat Sven. To kill him." Paige gestured to the other two women. "We are the strongest witches I know of. So, if we can't figure out how to win this, I don't know who else can."

Merry looked at Eldora. "All those years, you warned *me* to be careful of *my* magick, and you did this?"

As much fun as this was, Paige knew they didn't have the time. "We need a plan, ladies. Not a cat fight."

Merry looked away.

Eldora looked mildly ashamed. "I just wanted my daughter back. And your daughter was able to give me that."

Paige's daughter, because Merry had killed all of hers. "So then, how was it that Sven got his hands on her? Did you drive her away again? You didn't learn the last time?"

Eldora flinched but remained resolute. "I did what I thought was best for my coven. Both of you would have done the same."

Paige waved that away. "I really don't care. But what I do care about is that I thought I *had* the upper hand with him. I cut him off from feeding on the temple cats. Then, we cut him off from the spirit animals. And *then* I managed to cut him off from the angels by saving my goddamned mother." Paige finished near a shout.

Eldora winced and shied away from Paige.

That wasn't helping. "Only to find out that he still has an open chow line to all of Hell!" Paige really wanted to throttle someone. "So, let me ask you one more time. Do *either* of you two powerful bitches have *any* idea how to stop him?"

Merry raised her eyebrows and smiled. "I can now see what both of my sons see in you."

Paige really didn't want to think about that too hard. Because technically, Merry was her stepmom and her mother-in-law. If Paige didn't have mommy issues before, she really did now.

Her mother hated her guts.

And her *two* stepmothers were sitting in the same room with her, trying to save the world, and neither of *them* liked her much either. "Solutions."

However, after an hour, they weren't any closer to finding a solution than they had been when they started.

Paige finally gave up. "If either of you two come up with any solutions, please call me. Eldora, you're not welcome on my land without a specific invitation. Merry please do me the honor of at least calling in advance. I would like a heads up."

Both women looked at her as though appraising her for dinner.

Let them. Paige was tired, cranky, and ready to stop being the one who had to come up with all the freaking answers.

She didn't even wait to get out the door before she shifted. The woman on the other side of the door screeched, which made Paige feel at least a little better. She was *really* cranky. Which probably meant she was hungry. She should fix that.

She headed home. She wasn't entirely sure what she was going to find there. She hoped she would find something to eat. But what she really hoped for was that someone had managed to come up with an answer to their problems.

What frustrated her the most was it seemed as though they had a legitimate chance. They had all the right pieces. They had all the right players. Everybody was in position.

So, how was it that Sven was still ahead of them? It just didn't make any goddamn sense.

She went in through the back door. Mostly because she didn't want to have to walk all the way through the house on her tired, human feet. What she walked into, kind of surprised her.

Ripley, Cyn, Lynx, and a few others sat around her kitchen table. And it looked as though they were trying to come up with a game plan.

Blessed goddess, could she be hopeful?

Paige went to the refrigerator and pulled out the leftover spaghetti from the night before. She was a little over spaghetti by now. It had become their go to meal ever since Alma had passed away. She hadn't realized just how much Alma had cooked for them until she was no longer there.

She put her plate in the microwave before she turned

toward them. "Tell me something good."

Cyn looked hesitant.

Oh, for crying out loud. "You can't be scared of me. I'm just grouchy and pregnant and have a lot on my plate right now so, please forgive me if I'm not always sweet, kind, or considerate."

Cyn bristled. "I understand all that, but occasionally you could be halfway decent."

She had a point. Maybe. If Paige had an extra fuck to give. "Do we have a possible solution or not?"

Ripley turned to her with a sigh. "It depends. It's at least a solution. But I wouldn't necessarily say that it's a great one."

Paige could take that. "Even a bad strategy is better than what we currently have, which is none at all. I just spent the better part of the morning with two very powerful witches who had absolutely nothing to bring to the table. So, understand, that whatever you guys have, will be welcome." She said pointedly, mainly at Cyn.

Lynx stood and cleared his throat. "We are developing a plan to overpower Sven."

"Overpower?" she didn't want to get her hopes up. "He has a lot of power. I don't know if you guys noticed this or not."

Cyn frowned. "I thought that we cut him off from all of his power."

With so many players, it was hard to remember who she told what to who. "He found a way to plug in to Hell. The only problem is, I have no idea how to unplug him from that."

Dexx walked in, Bobby trailing after him. "A path to Hell?" he gestured toward Paige. "Is this something I should be concerned about?"

Paige opened her shirt yet again. She kind of felt like

flasher. "For those of you who don't know, Sven burned the gate to Hell inside of my bones. It resided right here as a scar. And for those of you who are wondering why this color is fading, that's a very good question. It's disappearing because he moved to the door to someone else."

Dexx looked excited and then he calmed himself in confusion. "I really don't understand why this is a bad thing."

Paige really wished it could be a good thing. "He put the gate into the resurrected body of Sheila Blackman."

Dexx and Ripley both blinked in surprise.

Everybody else just looked clueless.

"She was dead two years ago."

"How?" Dexx asked. "Last I heard, we were in possession of the only necromancer around."

"And as far as I know, she still is. But, Eldora was somehow able to pull her through while you guys were training out in our backyard. I don't know exactly how. All I know is that while Leah was practicing, Eldora pulled her through. And then chased her off into the arms of Sven."

Dexx shook his head in bewilderment.

The microwave dinged, letting Paige know she could feed her attitude. "Sven is very excited he doesn't have to kill me now. He wants me to stick around and help him run this brave new world he's building."

Dexx nodded and frowned and nodded some more. "I'm not sure how I feel about that."

"If you're anything like me, you'd feel creeped out by it."

Ripley folded her arms over her chest. "If Sheila is already dead, then Death is going to want her back. That's just the way it works. So, this must be a temporary thing."

Paige nodded. "It is. His intention is to break the doors between Heaven, Earth, and Hell."

Dexx snorted. "That's a good thing in my book."

And a couple of days ago, she'd thought so, too. "I'm not

so sure."

Dexx narrowed his eyes. "Why not?"

"Do you remember the earthquake that happened here not too long ago?"

Dexx snorted. "Of course. I was there."

"Well, those earthquakes were happening in Dallas when Leslie and I went to go save Rachel."

"So, what do you think that was?"

Paige met Dexx's gaze. "My gut instinct tells me that what we were feeling were the aftershocks of Sven pulling the worlds apart."

Ripley nodded and straightened. "That would make sense with everything I've seen. The death I see is changing. When the earthquakes are going, I can see more. But then, when the earthquakes stop, it's as if the death stops too. It's like… It's as if death is in motion. As if it's still being decided."

Well, that could be a good thing. It could mean they were doing something right for a change. Paige sat down at the table and cut up her spaghetti, dousing it with cheese. "It looked as though you guys were coming up with a plan. Care to tell me what that is?"

Lynx nodded and took the lead. "As I said before, were planning on overloading him. Cyn and I are going to create a material that should overpower his system."

Dexx snapped his fingers and pointed Lynx. "Like a warp core overload or self-destruct mechanism."

Lynx just blinked like he had no idea what Dexx said.

He probably didn't. "Would this overwhelm anyone?"

Cyn shook her head. "For anyone else, we think it would just power them up."

"Much like," Ripley continued gesturing toward Cyn, "when Cyn powers us up."

Paige paused in her eating. "Cyn has powered other people? And she hasn't powered me?"

Leslie joined them at the table. "For one, you haven't sat still long enough for anybody to be able to power you up. And for another, we were testing theories out."

That was fair. However, Paige still felt as though if anybody was going to get powered up, it should've been her. After all she was carrying a lot of people. "What are the downsides to this?" because with any of their plans, there was always a downside.

Ripley gave her a face that was immediately apologetic. "If we power him up with this while he's still on our plane, he'll destroy Earth. It'll be like smashing another planet against us."

"Well." Paige set her fork down. "Way to bury the lead."

Ripley gestured toward the group. "Our thought was that someone could make a door to another realm. Like, Kate could open a door to the elf world. And then, we stab this cloth into Sven, causing the overload."

Paige wasn't sure this was a good idea. "What kind of blowback would hit Underhill? The elves are already upset with us. We don't need to win this war only to have open war with the elves."

Ripley frowned. "The only thing I can say for sure is that the door is open, and we push him halfway through, and stab him with it, the blowback would be shared among the two realms. Neither realm would be destroyed."

That brought a whole host of other questions to bear. "How are we going to manage that? Last I heard, none of us were the Flash. We can't move that fast. What's going to keep him locked between two realms while we go up and stab him in the chest with a piece of cloth?" she wasn't trying to poke holes in their idea. She just wanted to see if it was a full and complete one.

Leslie gave Paige a hopeful two thumbs up. "I still have the demon tears."

Paige had no idea what she was even talking about. "The what?"

Leslie frowned at her as if she lost her mind. "The demon tears? The things that are so powerful that they're melting the cup they're in? I can't even tell you how many times I've had to keep my shop from being melted to the ground because they were almost accidentally spilled."

Paige still had no idea what they were even talking about. However, she was going to let it go. At some point, she had to. So many things happened and there was no way to get them all on the same page. Ever. "Okay. So, with these demon tears, we think that we can hold him in place?"

Dexx paused chewing on a squealing Bobby's belly. "I doubt it. He's a demon too. Probably be like throwing good wishes at him." Dexx began to chew again.

Everybody kind of looked at each other and shrugged.

Finally, Leslie spoke up. "I'm not seeing anybody else coming up with any better ideas."

She wasn't wrong. Paige thought about it for a while. "Before we do this, I want to see if we can do a test run."

Leslie looked at her like Paige had no idea what she was even talking about.

Paige held up her hand. "Look, I know that everybody here is trying to do their best. But we're in a situation where our best may not be good enough. We might be heading into a situation where thinking on our feet could get us dead. So, I would like us to do a test run and make sure that we're not going to blow ourselves or the entire world to kingdom come. I'm going to let you guys figure out how to do that. Meanwhile," Paige rose to her feet, taking her plate with her, "I am going to go play with my son. And maybe my daughter if I can find her." She walked out of the room and into the living room. And then muttered under her breath, "Because God knows if I'll survive any of this."

3 2

The next day, Paige left Leslie and everyone else to figure things out. They were more than capable. She decided to see if she could find Sheila's location. The best thing she could do for the team was to locate the next door to Hell. They really needed to get that closed off before it was too late.

Though, she had reason to believe things weren't too dire yet. Unlike in Dallas, there weren't a ton of earthquakes.

But there had been an earthquake here right before Sven had opened the rift bringing all of those demons to Earth. That had to mean something. But what?

Roxxie stepped in through the back door, smiling at Paige. "I feel better. Like some of my angel powers are coming back."

Normally, Paige would think that was bad thing. But in this situation? It probably wasn't. "But not all of them?" Because that was a fine distinction to make.

Roxxie shook her head. "It's as if I'm sort of cut off from Heaven. Or like it's really far away?"

That made sense. With what she knew of Sven's plans, if

303

Roxxie felt as though Heaven was distant, it probably meant it was. "Let's go check on Rachel."

Roxxie frowned as she followed Paige through the house and up the stairs. "I didn't realize Rachel was here."

Paige nodded. "We had to save her. We think the reason why you're feeling so cut off is because Sven placed the door to Heaven inside Rachel. Now, he is using that to separate the two."

Roxxie shook her head, stunned. "Where would he even think to do that?"

Paige had no idea. "The only thing I know is it was creating havoc in Dallas. It was getting bad."

Roxxie frowned as they stepped into the guest room. "Like biblically bad?"

Paige wasn't going to go that far. "It wasn't good, I can tell you that." She stopped at the edge of the bed and stared at her mother.

Rachel stirred, opening her eyes. "Where am I?"

Even like this, Paige struggled with the festering hate whirling inside of her. She hated this woman with every fiber in her soul. It was hard to see past that. "You're in my home."

Rachel frowned at her as if her eyes were still adjusting. "Don't let Mom hear you say that."

Leslie stepped into the room behind them. "Grandma's gone. She passed away."

"Passed away" really wasn't the right words. "She died saving the town. I need to know when Sven put this door in you."

Rachel blinked furiously and then sat up, gingerly touching her chest. She pulled away her shirt to get a better view of it.

There was the symbol Paige had got so used to having. A little different, of course, but still very familiar.

Rachel stared up at Paige in horror. "I had hoped it was a dream. Just a nightmare."

"It wasn't." Although, Paige could understand her mother's sentiment. Paige often hoped for the same thing. "When did this happen?"

Rachel shook her head. "The last thing I remember, I was going to the grocery store."

Leslie stepped into view, coming further into the room. "What were you doing in Dallas?"

Rachel shook her head, looking up higher. "I wasn't in Dallas. I was in New York."

So, Sven had abducted her from her home, and had taken her to another location? Why would he have taken her to Dallas, of all places? "How long ago was that?"

Rachel looked confused.

Leslie unfolded her arms. "What's the last day you remember?" she asked, her southern drawl getting deeper. To anyone who knew her, that was the indication she was pissed.

Rachel wouldn't know that, though. She'd abandoned them when they were both young. "I was sending in my mortgage payment."

Which meant, it was probably the first of the month. It was almost the end of October now. Paige looked over at Leslie "Have you been able to test drive your theory about the portal and ending Sven?"

Leslie nodded. "They can do it. We just can't test it though."

That was understandable.

"And we don't know if you're going to be powerful enough to get him to the gate they open."

Paige hoped she could. But first, they had to find Sheila.

Dexx came in behind them. "I have a theory on where Sheila is."

Paige was all ears.

"When we went to the Dales, we saw a group of demons stationed around a building. We couldn't figure out what they were guarding. But now that the we know about Sheila?" he shrugged.

That would make sense. And right in the middle of a demon camp. Perfect. "Do you think you can get her back?"

Dexx shrugged. "I think if I can't, then nobody can."

Paige nodded. She just hoped she wasn't sending Dexx to his death.

This was war and that's what war looked like. She had to set a few other people on getting tasks done. It was time to end this once and for all.

Before they all ended up dead.

Dexx crouched at the top of the hill with Leslie. The same hill he'd taken DoDO up.

She'd literally flown up here, but Dexx had Hattie's strength and he wasn't far behind Leslie.

He had a fleeting thought maybe he should have invited Frey and Tarik.

No. They were good, and they'd killed scores of demons, but he needed more stealth than brute force.

Maybe he should have called Mario. He could have run interference and died at the same time. No real downside there, and he seemed eager enough the other day.

No time for second thoughts, though. He and Leslie would just have to do.

He grinned at her. "Ready to give some demons a ration of shit they won't soon forget?"

Leslie looked like she wanted to roll her eyes. "Being a little cavalier about all this, aren't you?"

"I'm the demon hunter extraordinaire, and you're like number one or two most powerful witch-shifter in the northern hemisphere." Not to sound too cocky or anything. "We won't have much of a problem."

Leslie flattened her lips.

"Is Robin ready?"

"He's always ready."

"Okay then. We go down, but we need to be stealthy. Can you do stealth?"

Leslie gave him a smug expression and then shifted into a wasp.

Damn witches. They could shift into anything. He was more than a little jealous. "I guess you can. Scary stealthy. Let's go."

The overgrown foliage helped and hindered him as he crept along. He knew he'd progress faster on four paws instead of two human feet, but he wanted his clothes.

Leslie stayed close, scouting the trail ahead of Dexx and returning every few minutes to check his progress. Every time she flew up to him, he had to suppress the urge to swat at her. As far as stealth went, that was about as good as it got.

At the bottom of the hillside, Dexx found a large tree to hide behind.

Leslie shifted beside him. "You are really slow," she whispered at him.

"Next time, I shift, you creep."

Leslie showed teeth. It *could* have been a smile.

Dexx looked around the area and barely saw anyone. "Something's not right. This place was buzzing with demons the other day. Now there's only the two? They can't be hiding."

Leslie shook her head, but she was looking around as well.

Dexx scanned the camp for more demon signatures. He didn't see demons, but there was something else, something... strange.

"Les, see if you can get to that door. Then come back. If it's not warded, we'll swing behind and take them out." He saw eight demons. The two of them were more than enough to take out eight demons. "See if we can get Sheila out without raising much of an alarm."

Leslie jerked, paused, furrowed her eyebrows, and jerked again. "I... can't shift. Robin's going crazy."

Hattie roared in frustration inside Dexx's head. He felt her push, but like she was collared. She hit a wall somehow.

Oh, crap. Was this a trap designed specifically for them? Not good. Time to retreat.

A spear tip rested on Dexx's shoulder.

Fuck!

"*Shedim,*" a male voice said behind him. "We have heard of you. And this human witch. We have heard of her as well."

Dexx raised his hands. He turned to face...elves. All of them with the wicked hooked spears he'd seen in the Time Before with Hattie. They were well and truly fucked this time.

With Hattie blocked from coming out, he was stuck. Leslie too.

"Really?" Leslie's eyes turned orange and she began to raise her hands.

A spear butt slammed into her head.

She crumpled to the ground.

"The same for you, hunter?" an elf in front asked.

They *all* looked so similar they could all be brothers. At least Dexx didn't see boobs under any of the grey-green tunics.

The lead elf smiled. "We find you guilty."

"Guilty of what, you pointy-eared bastard?" Dexx'd always wanted to say that.

A log of a spear shaft cracked Dexx on the back of his head, but before he lost consciousness, he saw a little girl elf. Dressed in human clothes.

Kate.

Leah couldn't believe her mom had actually given them a task to do. Okay. So, she knew they all had to pull their weight. And that was totally cool.

But Mom had literally looked her in the eye and told her — well, all of them — that if they failed, the world could come to an end.

This was serious.

The only thing she really didn't appreciate was the fact her job was to keep her grandmother alive. It wasn't that Leah wanted to see Rachel dead. She just didn't want to see Rachel at all.

Rachel was trying to make eye contact with her, as if she was trying to make a new connection.

But *they* were focused on other things. Like the other things her Mom had said. Like, how Heaven was being pulled away from Earth. And how Hell was, too. And how that was bad for Earth. Like...none of it really made sense, but...if Leah was supposed to be powerful enough to help bring Sven down, then maybe she was powerful enough to bring Heaven and Hell closer to Earth.

Even though that sounded like a really bad idea. Like, totally.

Leah looked at Ashley and Mandy. "Do you guys have any ideas on how to bring Heaven closer?"

Tyler shrugged really big. His eyes didn't come unglued from Roxxie. "Use an angel?"

Rachel opened her mouth to say something.

But Leah wasn't paying attention. The only thing she heard was Rachel's voice. The rest of it? It was all just noise. She didn't want to hear anything that woman had to say.

Mandy frowned at whatever it was she said. "You can open doors, right?"

Leah nodded. "I can open a door there, but how do I bring Heaven back?"

Tyler finally blinked and looked at Leah and Mandy. "Our job isn't to bring Heaven back. That's what everybody else is doing. What we're doing? Is just keeping Rachel safe. So, if anything comes this way, we just attack back. And that, we've got. We've been training for this."

Roxxie stood up. "I will be assisting. I am not broken."

"Of course, you aren't." Tyler's tone and expression were so dreamy. It was kind of stupid. "But everybody knows that we're really powerful, and we can help you." Tyler shrugged again. "Stay alive."

Leah shook her head. Well, they may be on protection detail for now, but the stomach butterflies were rolling. Leah knew she had a key part to play in the big battle. If she froze, they could all die.

Not could.

Would.

So, she was going to use this time to make sure she was prepared. She couldn't freeze in battle. Her mom, her dad, her everything, was waiting for her to do the right thing.

Ashley looked over at her and gave her two thumbs up. She probably knew exactly what was going on in Leah's head. Leah tried to look positive. She had this. She did.

She just had to make sure Rachel didn't get inside her head. Not even a little bit.

Bal looked around. He hadn't been back to this temple in ages.

Bastet wasn't far away. She leaned over one of her many glowing pools, her black hair cascading around her face, hiding her expression. It was hard to remember the days when he loved her.

It was hard to forget the love he had for her.

But he had learned the hard way Bastet only loved one person, and that was Bastet.

Somehow, he needed to find a way to use that to their advantage. Because in this fight against Sven, even with all of their "wins," they were still likely to lose. They were going to need everything they could get.

"Bastet."

She jerked up and glanced at him. "Very sneaky. Not even my cats warned me."

"I learned to be stealthy long before your cats were even in existence."

"Perhaps *these* cats." She pulled herself away from her scry pool and sashayed toward him, looking every inch the goddess he knew her to be. "What do you want, Balnore?"

Bal let himself admire the goddess. She was a sight to behold. "I need you to see the folly of backing Sven."

Bastet narrowed her eyes and appraised him. "I've already made up my mind. But it will be entertaining to hear your argument."

The thing with Bastet was that even she didn't know what her decision would be. Not until she made it.

"I want to see what arguments you bring to me." She batted her eyes at him seductively. "How you will speak to my morality."

"As if you had morality."

She smiled at him appreciatively. "That's the thing I've always loved about you. You've always seen me for who I truly am."

That wasn't always the case. Otherwise, he never would have fallen in love with her. "I beseech to your selfishness."

She raised an eyebrow, intrigued. "Please continue."

"With Sven in control of the world, there will be very few alive to worship you. And as we both know, that is all you live for, to be worshiped."

She sniffed. "You say that as if it's a terrible thing. However, how many of these people have sought me out recently? They need someone to worship. They want someone who will take their love and abuse them with it."

"They already have one of those. They call him God."

Bastet flicked her eyebrows and looked away. "How garish. But…it worked." She tsked. "Such a primitive thought that turned out so supremely well. It's rather unfortunate that their god is mankind."

That wasn't *entirely* true, and she knew that. But he wasn't going to enter into that debate. Not now. "What did Sven promise you?"

She tipped her head to the side and crossed her arms over her chest, raising her breasts. "That the few who *did* survive would worship me without hesitation."

At least Sven knew who he was talking to. That was something Balnore appreciated about the man. Sven always knew his audience. "You are going to back him, then."

Bastet studied him for a moment and then turned away. "The people of this world worship nothing but themselves. Truly. Even those who claim to worship this 'God.' They've managed to create a world where *they* are the gods they worship. I find the children here to be petulant."

Which was odd to hear coming from her, if she wasn't the

goddess of cats, she would've been the goddess of petulant children. "So, you are siding with Sven."

Bastet turned to him and smiled. "Wouldn't you like to know?"

"I would. Because to defeat him, I could really use your help."

She looked at him disappointed. "I would have thought you would've tried harder to win me over. Instead, you come to me with the same argument he used."

"Perhaps, we both realized that this is the only argument that will work with you."

She raised a regal eyebrow at him in disdain. "I don't think I like your attitude."

Balnore was beyond caring. He had one more tactic to use. "Paige and Dexx have been able to strip him of his power sources. You may think you're on the winning team right now, but you're not. We have all the power players. Look at what he has right now. A bunch of demons? Demons that are being sent back. Or killed outright."

She nodded, listening. "We *are* the winning team."

"You really think that?"

"I do."

"He's killing his team, currently, draining the demons for their energy. Imagine what will happen when he has no demons left. Who will he go after for power next? Who would be the most powerful person then?" he paused, watching her every micro-expression. "You, standing by his side."

The truth of his words was painted all over her face from the slight crinkle around her left eye to the barest tightening of her lips. "I have listened to your arguments and it has not changed my mind."

That was rather disappointing. But not unexpected. Balnore knew how stubborn she could be. "I had to try."

She made a mewing sound. However, she said nothing more.

With nothing left to say himself, he winked out of existence and appeared in Paige's backyard. He had hoped he could have brought Bastet to their side. He knew they had weakened Sven significantly. But would it be enough?

Now, they all had to hope it was. Because they weren't just fighting Sven. They were fighting Sven and Bastet.

Emma walked back to the Red Star Division, not entirely sure how they'd got to this point. She thought when she'd given up being her clan's alpha, she would be beyond all of this.

Apparently not.

Mason came up to her, looking adorably dorky as ever. "So, we're really going to do this."

Emma had tried to get him to leave Troutdale with his parents. But they'd all decided they were going to stay. Emma was a bear. Mason was a porcupine. His parents were rats. She had no idea how any of them were going to survive what was coming. But, there was no sense in rehashing that argument. She'd tried her best to get them to leave. And they decided not to. That was that. "Yep."

The tightening of his eyes said he heard what she didn't say. But when he didn't say anything in return, she knew he was appreciative. He had to be scared as hell.

Emma turned and looked at the woods. They had a sentry stationed along the perimeter of the wards. But so far, no one had seen anything suspicious. "When the demons get here, if you feel overwhelmed, you get out of here."

He nodded, pushing his glasses up his nose. "You'll do the same," he looked at her significantly. "Right?"

Damn him for knowing her so well. She reached up and

gave him a kiss. "Just know that I love you more than anything."

He held her tightly. "Same here. And I'll fight just as hard to stay by your side as anybody can."

Emma just hoped they survived. She knew like everyone else did not everybody would. She wasn't looking forward to seeing who didn't.

But Mason? He damn well better. Or Sven was going to have hell to pay. And she didn't care if that's where he originated from or not.

As Emma turned around, something caught her eye. Movement.

She stepped further into the street and watched in amazement as a semi-steady stream of cars came into town. She pulled out her phone and called Paige.

"Whiskey," Paige answered.

"We've got a new development," Emma said as she watched one car drive by. She knew them. They were her neighbors. Both the husband and the wife were the front seats, but the backseat was empty. They'd dropped off their kids, somewhere safe, probably, and had come back.

"What?"

Emma couldn't believe her eyes. "The mundanes are back."

"What?" Paige asked in surprise.

Emma nodded. Then, she remembered Paige couldn't see that. "Yeah."

"Well, shit." Paige's tone didn't sound as upset as her words proclaimed. "Hope they brought weapons."

Emma did, too.

Paige turned to Merry. "How quickly can your witches turn

regular bullets into demon-killing bullets?"

Merry frowned. "I don't know how."

If Leslie were there, she'd be able to show them. Wait. Mandy and Leah knew how. "You can talk to one of the girls. They should be able to show you."

Merry met Ollie's gaze and raised her eyebrow.

Ollie saluted Paige. "I'm on it." He pointed his thumb behind him. "They're upstairs?"

Paige nodded. She still didn't understand how she'd *invited* Merry Eastwood into her *home,* but there they were. "The mundanes are coming back. So, if they're going to enter the fight—"

"—we need to arm then," Merry finished. She pulled out her phone, then stepped into the other room to complete her phone call.

Billie stepped into the dining room from the backyard. "If we're ready, we'd better move toward town. We need everyone and you're the one who said Eldora wasn't welcome here anymore."

With good reason.

Merry stepped back into the dining room. "I have someone coming over with a small arsenal. That should help. And some of my other witches will be arriving shortly to help prepare the bullets for what needs to be done."

Ollie hopped down the stairs, a grin on his face. He met Paige's gaze and shook his head. "Those kids."

She knew, though she didn't know what *he* was talking about. She didn't have time to ask. "You have what you need?"

He nodded and turned to Merry. "I'm assuming you brought in others. Where are we meeting?"

"At our house, for now."

Paige shook her head. "Have everyone meet at Red Star. It's closer to downtown, and we're not going to bring the fight here, I'm going to bring it to downtown. It has the defenses."

Merry gave her a miffed look, but then gestured at Ollie to follow Paige's direction.

Paige didn't have anything else to say after that. She went upstairs to hug her daughter and to check on her son. Tru was in the boys' room, a sawed-off shot gun near the door.

They exchanged nods, and then Paige was gone. Again.

Once they were in town, Paige looked around the small circle of witches. It consisted of Merry Eastwood, Eldora Blackman, Billie Black, and herself. The four coven leaders of the most powerful witches she knew. And if they couldn't pull this off? She had no idea who could.

"So," Eldora said calmly, "you expect us to somehow keep Heaven from sliding into oblivion?"

"Heaven *and* Hell." It was important to keep that distinction. Everyone seemed to think that one was more important than the other because even those in the pagan community had been led to believe Heaven was good, and Hell was bad.

Was it? She couldn't say one way or the other. The only thing she could say for certain was the two seem to balance each other out.

It *was* nice to see the people of Troutdale coming back, though. The town was starting to get that lived in feeling again, and the wards were strengthening.

And *that* was a relief.

Merry shook her head. "That seems like a bigger task than what we mere mortals should be handling. Just look at us. When was the last time any of us worked together on anything?"

That would've been a fair point a year ago. But who else was there? "We've each laid aside our own personal hate and loathing for one another to save the community, the whole *world*. So, do I think we can do this?"

Merry raised her eyebrows and leaned back, almost touching the brick wall of the building behind her.

Eldora pursed her lips and folded her hands over the picnic table.

Billie just shrugged.

"I think we can do this. And we're about to show that. Now then, how can we use our magicks to keep Heaven and Hell from sliding away from Earth and bringing an end to everything we know?"

If they couldn't figure this out, then Earth was in trouble.

But Paige was going to make sure they did.

33

Dexx swam up through the levels of unconsciousness.

Hattie met him before he was awake. *You take too many risks.*

This time he couldn't blame Hattie for being pissed. She would fight demons, but she couldn't stand being cornered. *They weren't supposed to know we were here.*

Foolish cub. Never go into the hornet's nest and think they won't know.

Dexx hit the last stages of waking up, but he kept his body limp and his breathing slow. He sent his senses out, feeling the room. *Okay. I'm sorry I got you into another mess, but we are the best there is. We had to come here.*

Hattie didn't respond, but she liked the admission of being the best. Cats.

Dexx picked out several scents, one of them being Leslie.

There were more that weren't human but weren't demons either. Elves?

And death. The stink of it was strong.

And dirt. A lot of it.

Luckily, there were only faint scents of demons. They were either not there, or there weren't many very close.

His wrists were bound, but not overly tight. Just enough that he couldn't wriggle out.

Next, he focused on the sounds. What he heard sounded hollow, like they were in a massive room. Dirt in a huge open room. Underground?

Can you reach Robin and Leslie? he asked Hattie.

We can go to the Time Before. I cannot shift, but I am not barred from there.

Then let's get moving. Maybe we can come up with a plan there. Dexx sort of turned inward and felt for the place he imagined Hattie took up residence in his mind. This part was easy now and took only a few seconds.

Hattie nuzzled his touch, and the comfort he felt struck him.

He needed to be better to his cat.

Hattie silently agreed.

They entered the Time Before and touched on Leslie and Robin's spirits. He could feel them, but it was as if they were far away. They were fine but were still blocked.

That might make escape harder, not to mention stopping Sven's plans for Earth. He'd really hoped they could have talked in the Time Before, to regroup, and figure out what they were going to do. But...

Dexx and Hattie came back to the real world. They'd just have to wing it. Like normal.

Dexx opened his eye a slit. There was activity around, but he was halfway facing a rock wall. Great. They *were* in a cave, with no way of knowing how big.

Small hands touched his face. "Great Leader?" The whisper was very close to his ear.

Was this a trick or was Kate in danger? Only one way to find out. "Yeah, kid. I'm here."

A tiny whimper answered.

"It's okay, Kate."

She didn't answer.

Oh, fuck it. Dexx opened his eyes and sat up.

As soon as he moved, Kate jumped behind him to saw at the ropes binding his wrists. With movement, brought the headache. He healed quickly, which meant they must have hit him *really* hard.

The ropes finally fell away. "Sorry," Kate muttered.

Dexx had no idea what she was sorry for. He looked around. They were in a large iron cage, with thick bars. The elves obviously didn't feel the need to put a guard on them.

Dexx twisted around to Kate and took her little knife. Huh, it was the little one he'd given her. She learned quick, that tiny elf did.

In one slice, he cut the rope holding Leslie.

The underground cavern was a large thing, lit with bon fires which gave off a flickering light. A steady light shone from somewhere Dexx couldn't see.

Hattie was still blocked, but they were free to move.

The cavern was an exact replica of the encampment on the surface, dirt and all.

Demons wandered at their leisure, and elves did too, but none of them walked alone. The smallest group he saw was five.

The elves didn't look very pleased to be in the demon's den. But they all seemed to get along well enough. He still smelled a hell of a lot of tension in the cave..

So now they were working together? Demons, elves, and Bastet. Sven sure knew how to stay on top.

"Hells." Dexx stood and scooped Kate into a big hug. "They put you in here because of us? Wait, is everyone safe?" If Kate was here then that meant the elves had gone to the house, past the wards.

Kate dropped her head. "No. I went to Underhill to make a safe passage for Chuck. They caught me there and took me with them."

Relief. Kind of. "Are you in trouble?"

She nodded, her eyes wide.

"Is Chuck okay?"

She nodded again but didn't say anything further.

"Can you open the door?" Dexx put Kate down. He knelt beside Leslie and shook her.

"No," Kate said. "They cut me off from my magic."

"They what?" The only person he'd ever known that could do that had been Alma.

Kate shrugged.

Leslie stirred, turning onto her back and blinking up at him.

At least she was conscious. "Les, you still have some power?"

"No." She groaned, massaging her head. "I'm shielded too."

"Okay, so listen." Dexx had an idea. It might not work, but it was an idea. "Alma told me how she cut Pea off from her gift. She ramped up Paige's powers as high as they'd go and then turned it back on itself."

Leslie looked at him like he was high and shook her head, wincing at the movement. "So?"

"Maybe you could reverse engineer that. You know? Like, maybe that's what they did, too?" but now he'd said it out loud, he was doubtful.

Leslie sat up and shook her head. "Okay. Sure. I mean—" Leslie stopped and looked beyond the cage.

A man with dark hair stopped outside their cage. He didn't say anything, but the man smelled...funny.

Several things happened at once.

Several elven guards shuddered where they stood as they were hit with an electric current.

Demons jerked, trying to figure out what was going on.

And Dexx was no longer shielded from Hattie. Whatever magic had been keeping Hattie bound was released.

Great!

The man at the cage door shifted. His body grew, but his clothes disappeared instead of ripping off.

Another shifter-witch? But he looked so…elven.

At almost the same moment, Leslie shifted. Not into a bug, or a fly, or a bird. She went right for the big one. Her griffin.

The cage tore apart like sticks.

The man was now a beast. Like a real beast. It looked like a lion on steroids had mated with a scorpion.

Hattie recoiled in Dexx's mind. *Manticore.* Hattie's fear drove into Dexx.

Well shit. How many things scared *Hattie?* Not a lot. Like…nothing he'd come across yet. So, this…manticore… was big news. Big, bad news.

The cage still clanged to the ground around them as Leslie took off. Not to the ceiling above, but straight at the lion-beast-manticore thing.

Ripley ran past—no, *through* the elves in death-dog form, her silvery-grey hound shape more fog than physical form.

The elves she ran through fell over and didn't get back up.

Ripley shifted into human form, looking around. Her silver, smoky eyes lit on Dexx and she moved toward him.

He was really glad *he'd* been the one to invite the death-dog into his pack and not someone else.

The cavern lit up with activity. Demons ran. Leslie made contact with the manticore. And the elves stumbled around in confusion.

Dexx still had a job to do. He had to retrieve Sheila.

"Rip get Kate out of here."

"My magic is back," Kate said. She held onto Dexx's hand. "I can take us back."

"Through Underhill?" bringing a kid to a battle was one thing. Sending her into battle was another. "They caught you the last time. No. We need to keep you out of there."

"I'll be more careful."

He didn't like it.

Ripley gave him a let's-not-be-stupid look. "How are *you* going to get out of here? *With* Sheila?"

Good question. "Same way we came, I guess."

Kate sighed. "I'm staying if you're staying."

Kids. "Fine. Then stick close."

Ripley ducked as a boot came flying toward her head. "Where next?"

There might have been a foot in it. Dexx didn't know and he wasn't going to look. He tipped his head at Ripley and gathered Kate's hand in his. "The house."

Ripley nodded and spun on her heel, leading the way. Her hands partially shifted, turning smoky. Her hair sizzled and flowed with the dark smoke and ash of brimstone. Anyone she touched fell to the ground, limp. Dead.

Leslie was drawing most of the attention. Well, her and the manticore.

But he didn't remember inviting Ripley onto this mission. "What are you doing anyway?"

"Decima," she said simply.

Decima was Ripley's shifter animal, the death-dog. If Decima saw death, then he'd heed the warning, shut up, and follow. He was an alpha. That didn't mean he always had the friggin' answers to everything.

Together Ripley, Dexx, and Kate slipped out of the cave. The house wasn't far away. They jogged to it without running into another demon or elf. They huddled next to the side door and paused.

Dexx heard nothing on the other side. He shrugged in question at Ripley.

She shrugged back.

Dexx pushed open the door and followed Ripley in, Kate sticking close behind him.

The house was only a house because it had walls and a roof. The inside was nothing but a large open space with a dirt floor, and in the middle of the room, was an altar.

Or a sacrifice table.

The house boomed. Something big had landed. Hard. Two animal roars vibrated the structure, pebbles on the floor shaking in time to the noise.

Leslie.

They needed to leave. Fast.

Dexx brought his attention back to the unconscious blonde woman on the table. She floated a few inches above the surface, each of her limbs pulled in four different directions. It was as if she was being drawn and quartered. The woman was nearly naked, with tatters for clothes. Her skin was too grey, her bones too prominent.

What in the hell? She just didn't fit anything Dexx could name.

Then the stink hit his nose. *Dead. She's dead.* It wasn't a surprise. He'd *known* she was dead. But…seeing was different than hearing about it.

Hattie growled at the woman. *It is foul.*

Ripley's hands and body solidified, but her hair still danced in brimstone winds. "What…" She pointed at the woman in disgust. "…is that?"

"Sheila Blackman." Dexx answered. "What's left of her."

Sheila turned to them and croaked, "Help…me."

Dexx and Ripley stepped back. Dexx tripped over Kate who hurried to get out of the way.

Ripley's eyes glowed faintly silver. "She's...dead. But she's not. That woman is a...zombie."

"Fck!" Dexx forced the not-word through his teeth. What in the hell was he supposed to do with a zombie? They freaked him the fuck out. "Rip, can you get her off the table?"

"I'm not touching that." Ripley backed up.

"Aren't you the death omen? You should be like fast friends and shit."

"I kill things. Reap them. I don't hug animated corpses."

"Then how are we moving her?"

Ripley held up her hands. *"I'm* not."

Kate took a step forward. "I will." She turned to Dexx with big, baleful eyes. "But you're going to have to unbind her. From the magic."

Right. Sure.

Hadn't Paige found Rachel in a similar situation? What had *she* done?

He groaned. Right. She'd *bitten* Rachel.

Oh...*hell* no.

Leslie was trying to fight this damned, powerful beast. She couldn't figure out how to get ahead of it, and Robin was absolutely no fucking help at all. He'd lost his damned mind. He was all emotion and instinct. She was fighting *him* just as much as she was trying to *help* him fight the beast.

Robin, she shouted into her own head. *What is this thing?*

Aaen, he snarled and lashed out with his talon, raking it across the lion's shoulder.

The thing raised its scorpion tail.

Watch out! Being in the backseat sucked. But only because

Leslie wasn't entirely certain Robin was using his big griffin brain. Or any brain at all.

Robin bent to the side and the tail whizzed by their ear.

What is it?

Manticore.

What did Leslie know about manticores? She tried to remember, but Greek Literature had been too many decades ago.

Robin raised his taloned front claw and smashed Aaen's face into the dirt.

If they were fast enough, they could take its tail off. That was the weapon to watch out for.

Robin whipped around, slashing with a wing, but the manticore rolled away, spearing again with its tail. They didn't even have to move from the wild thrust.

Robin backed up and screeched.

Aaen roared back and rose high, unfolding wings. Big bat, demon wings.

Robin stood back. *It's not supposed to have those.*

Leslie had no idea what was going on. *Well, can we shift and get out of here?*

No. We have to fight. We cannot be in the world together.

Why did Robin have to sound like Tyler telling her why he couldn't wear socks that day? *And you never thought to tell me about a mortal enemy? That's like not telling your date you have an STD. That's important stuff.*

They circled the winged lion, both growling their hatred of the other.

It has not come back for a long time.

Do you hear yourself? You haven't come back in a long time. And how many times have you been in the world together?

Four.

And how many times have you won?

This will be the first.

Are you fucking kidding me? You'd better fucking win, or I'll fucking kick your ass. I'll fucking change your name to Pidgeon. I fucking swear I will!

The manticore charged.

Robin rose to meet him.

Aaen reared up with Robin. About the best that could be said was that Robin was the bigger opponent. The manticore was a little smaller than Hattie, and maybe a smidge slower.

The scorpion tail came whipping in, the poisoned tip slicing the air with a whistle.

Robin brought his claws down at the same time he caught the tail in his beak. The claws ripped through Aaen's face and slammed it right into the dirt.

Demon laughter sounded all around.

Robin didn't stop. As soon as he touched the ground he backed up with the manticore's stinger still in his great beak. He heaved and threw the manticore across the cavern.

Wings snapped out to stop his wild flight but Aaen wasn't fast enough. He crashed to the ground.

Unfortunately, the beast wasn't hurt. He snapped back up almost instantly.

We need a plan. How to get a kid to listen. She'd been a mom for over thirteen years, a wife for longer, and she *still* didn't know how to do that. *And just duking it out won't work. We won't win this way. Sooner or later he'll tag us with that tail thingy.*

The manticore looked *really* pissed now. It moved in a slow circle.

The demons just moved out of his way. They weren't joining in the fight and they weren't leaving either. There were about twenty or so of them just watching. Why weren't they attacking, and where were the rest? Wasn't this a stronghold or something?

Robin snarled. *What do you suggest?*

Did you forget I'm a witch? We can use my *abilities against him.* Seriously. She just needed the griffin to use his brain.

I will not allow it. You will be damaged in your human form.

Kids. Seriously. *You better start allowing it. That's how we win. Be more flexible than he is.*

A red light lit in the manticore's eyes. Real anger. He flexed his claws into the dirt and readied to launch himself at Leslie and Robin. His wings stretched out to their full spread, touching trees on either side of him and almost reaching the house Leslie had seen Dexx, Ripley, and Kate disappear into. Aaen roared pure hate at the griffin.

Okay. Seriously. The fight was on.

Robin, Leslie commanded, getting her Wonder Woman game face on. *Let. Me. Out.*

Because Leslie was gonna show this beast he'd picked a fight with the wrong damned witch.

Dexx ran his fingers through his hair and blew his cheeks out.

Energy pulsed in the room. Not *to* the woman, but *from* her. Like she was a conduit. No, not like a conduit, more like a *fuse*. She was the between. Cut her off and the power stopped. this was just like what Paige had said had happened to Rachel. The power of Heaven being pulled through her and delivered to Sven.

A flash of purple lit beside Dexx. He looked over and saw Kate doing...something elfish. He didn't know. "Don't do anything stupid."

She waved her hand at him.

Such a teenager. Dexx took a step away from Sheila, looking over at Ripley, his hands raised. "I'm not biting her."

Ripley just looked at him, her lips pursed in a grimace. "Do you have a better idea?"

The house trembled. An earthquake? No, it felt more like something smashing into the ground.

More bellowing from outside cut through the house.

Ripley stirred herself, a sense of urgency surging through

her and lighting her eyes to a slivery glow again. "Death is coming back."

"Coming back?"

Ripley's gaze was unsettling when she looked at him. It was like staring into death itself.

Okay. So, he was supposed to bite a dead body and somehow infuse it with a living, highly powerful shifter spirit. This was beyond stupid.

What should we do? Dexx had no reference to draw from.

Follow in Paige's footsteps.

That's, like, super gross. Remember the woman who ate her cats? I'd rather be there right now. Twice.

You lack a choice, cub.

Kate grabbed Dexx's arm. "We have to go. They're coming."

"Who?" Ripley asked. "Demons?"

"No." Kate looked wildly around. "My people. They're coming and you're in danger. They want *you,* Dexx."

"Ah, damn it all to hell." Dexx grabbed Sheila's dead and yet still warm arm. He pulled Hattie to him enough for his teeth to grow and bit, keeping his tongue as far from the bite as he could.

The effect was immediate. An electric blue ring of light expanded outward in a small concussive blast.

Sheila dropped to the table and lay still. Like a corpse.

Ripley shifted to the death-dog and ran through the wall.

With one hard swallow, Dexx bent to pick up Sheila. He might have kept his tongue away, but she still tasted gross. The stench of death was too close to his nose. "Okay, Kate, how do we get out of here?"

The door slammed open, and an elf walked in. "*Shedim—*"

Purple light flared around Dexx, so bright it hurt the eyes.

When he could see again, he was... outside. Next to Leah's car.

Kate looked up at Dexx. "Get home. I have to do something."

"Kate, wait."

Too late. The little girl had already disappeared in another flash of violet light.

Now all he needed to do was get Leslie back. And get Sheila to Paige.

Sheila's body convulsed, and a wild roar erupted from her mouth.

He dropped her body into the back of the Ranchero and got into the driver's seat. One thing and *then* the other.

Leslie and Robin managed to dodge another spear-thrust of the scorpion tail. Robin pushed off from Aaen.

The two sped apart like repulsing magnets.

Robin tore into the ground, stopping his slide. Aaen had managed to land a blow and Leslie could fee blood running down her— Robin's— their side.

We're hurt. Leslie didn't want to state the obvious, but she needed to find a way to get Robin to let her in. Up until now, Leslie had almost thought they were unstoppable. But now?

We will survive.

Right. *If you want to win this, you have to listen to me. The next time he comes at us, we shift. I light him up, and then we shift back and get the fuck out of here.*

She didn't smell Dexx anymore. Ripley was making her way through the demons and through the band of elves who had just arrived.

Robin was still reluctant.

Well, Leslie had learned a lot with Billie and now was the time to push her will out on the griffin.

Robin bunched and charged again, but no quicker than Aaen.

Two massive leaps in, and Leslie pushed. The time she helped Dexx push a car was easier than this, but she kept it, imagining that Robin was just another one of her kids. Robin *was* going to wear his damned socks. Okay. Not that exactly, but it was the same thing. She *was* going to win this argument.

Ha! Just like that!

Leslie shifted back to her witch form and gathered her power. Air and fire came to her a lot easier than ever before.

Without Robin to carry them further, she dropped to the ground and slammed her fist to the earth, releasing her power.

Aaen came on like a freight train, unstoppable.

A lightning bolt as big around as a car struck the manticore. The force of the blast blew Leslie backward along with the demons and elves in the immediate area.

The only person unaffected was Ripley.

Chunks of dirt and trees rained down on them.

Leslie stood slowly. "Now, that is what I'm talking about."

Robin was surprisingly quiet.

The manticore lay in a smoking heap thirty feet away.

Demons picked themselves up from the floor, clearly stunned by the lightning.

Leslie stood over Aaen. "Got you, you little bitch."

"No," the manticore rumbled out. "Got you." Rocks tumbling together might make the same sounds.

Shit, now it *talked?*

Aaen stood and shook dirt from its nearly black mane. "Bitch."

Leslie's fists flared with power. "No, asshole. It's *witch.*"

She released a blast of wind that tore at Aaen's wings, and

then shifted back. Before she was done jumping upward, the griffin took flight.

The roar of demons and manticore were too close behind them.

What superhero moves did she have to pull inspiration from? *If you can go supersonic, I suggest now be that time.*

Robin's wings worked, pushing at the air, gaining height as quickly as he could, and Leslie fed him with all the power she could.

Why wouldn't that beast just *die?*

The back door crashed open.

Leah jumped to her feet with a startled screech, her chair flying back, Tyler, Mandy, and Ashley following suit.

Though Tyler's shriek had a bit more power to it. And Mandy had fireballs in her hands ready to throw.

It was just Dexx. He set the body of a woman in the chair Leah had vacated.

This was a zombie. But...Leah hadn't left any laying around anywhere. So... "Has the fighting started?" and why was he leaving zombies with *her?*

"Yeah. Kate been through here?"

"No. Why?"

"Doesn't matter. We need to relocate everybody into town. Can we get some help with that?"

"Who is this?" Leah asked, pointing to the woman.

Tyler disappeared through the back door.

"Sheila Blackman." Dexx slashed his hand, cutting off the rest of her questions. "She's the other door, so she needs to be protected, same as Rachel. Got that?"

Seriously? It was bad enough they had to protect Rachel from dying and keeping the end of the world from coming.

But now, there was another one they had to protect? "We're just kids."

He reached over and ruffled her hair. "Really powerful, capable kids. And, Lee-bear? I really need you guys to do your best. You're literally our best defense right now."

No pressure.

He looked at Ashley and licked his lips. "Can you help move her? We really need to get them all moved to downtown."

Ashley nodded. "If Leah brings my clothes."

Tyler came back with a robe.

Dexx turned to leave.

No. Leah reached out to stop him. "You have the car. Why can't you just drive us?"

"Because…" He turned around and pinned her with a look. "Someone needs my help right now."

"Mom?"

He shook his head and glanced at Tyler and Mandy. "Your Aunt Leslie. So, I'm going to do that. And you're going to get Sheila and Rachel— Hey. Rachel." He turned his attention to Leah's grandmother. "You guys need to get downtown. Keys to cars are there. Can you handle this?"

Rachel nodded.

"Good. Now, Lee-bear, I love you. Be strong. And don't die."

Then Dexx disappeared out the back door again.

Leah knew what that meant. It was almost time for her to see if she could do the impossible. She was going to have to be instrumental in saving the world.

Right. Yeah. She could do this. She looked at her grandmother. "We need to take Aunt Leslie's car. It has more seats."

She was going to do this.

She was *going* to *do* this.

Paige looked up to see Leslie's SUV park in a no-parking zone close to the park the ward tree was under. Rachel stepped out from the driver's seat and she rushed around to the passenger side door with more energy than Paige had seen in her since she'd come back.

Yay? She really didn't know how she felt about that. The part of her that cared more about the world was happy because that meant the world might stand a better chance of *being* saved.

The part of her that hated her mother's guts? Well, that part wasn't doing cartwheels.

Kids poured out of the backseat. Ashley slipped her robe off and shifted into a tall, black horse with a flowing mane and tail. She positioned herself to take the weight of the unconscious woman in the passenger seat.

Paige got up and walked in their direction, but Ashley was already stepping surefooted toward them, her equine head bobbing like she was telling Paige something.

Which she probably was. Paige gestured to the picnic table and stepped aside, assessing Sheila. She didn't look like she was in good condition. "Did Dexx bite her?"

Leah came up to her and shrugged. "Dexx just told us to protect her. Then, he was gone again."

"Gone where?"

Leah shook her head.

Paige didn't want to know. Did she? Really. She just had to trust Dexx knew what he was doing and if he needed help, he'd ask for it because she didn't have time to worry about him or try to read his mind.

Rachel walked past Paige, barely giving her a glance.

Tyler took position at the corner of the building. "Dexx said the fighting had started."

Paige didn't know about that. "Not here. But keep an eye out." She still felt like a complete moron for asking the *kids* for help. She had no idea what kind of horrible parent award she'd win for this one. Or horrible aunt award. Whatever.

Mandy found a place under one of the saplings— a regular sapling, not a magick one— not too far away, her eyes pinned to the street.

Leah took a deep breath and watched the side street that came off Main and headed toward the sheriff's office.

Paige wanted to check on her daughter, to see how she was doing.

They just didn't have time.

She went back to the picnic table and took a seat again. "We've got the doorways here now. Let's see what we can do."

They'd been *trying* to connect to the doorways, to bring Heaven and Hell closer to Earth again, but it had been nearly impossible. The original idea had been to keep the doors under the strongest wards in town— hers. But that just hadn't worked. She'd been about to call someone to see if they could bring Rachel to town anyway. But she'd realized she didn't have anyone *to* call. Everyone was busy trying win this war.

Merry shook out her hands and flexed her fingers. "Let's try this again."

Eldora touched Sheila's arm, her dark eyes filled with concern.

Billy perched on the end of the table and looked at Paige over her shoulder. "This isn't going to work."

"It has to." Paige regained her seat.

The magicks of the four witches seem to collect naturally. Almost like the magicks were meant to be used together. That was something Paige was going to have to keep in mind. Just in case they came across somebody else, some other big bad, it was nice to know that together, the Whiskeys, Blackmans, Eastwoods, and Blacks were pretty damn tough.

But that didn't make their current task any easier. They needed a god.

But not a demigod, apparently. Paige had summoned Balnore to help. He'd been of no help whatsoever.

The four witches were connected on a level so deep Paige had never experienced before. She'd always thought connecting with the All Mother had been incredible when calling down the moon. But this was beyond words.

Paige had a better understanding of her own magick through this. Through her Whiskey bloodline, she had a connection to the magick of life. Now, that wasn't to say she could bring things *to* life. That's not what her magick was about. Life was more than breathing. It was more than existing. Her magick... When she was connected like this... It kind of blew her mind a little. She was the living, the dead, the plants, the animals, the sunlight striking the earth in the air, the storms on the water, the souls, and anything else she could think of. Her magick was more... No. It was far *more* than she was.

Merry's magick wasn't nearly as evil as Paige had expected. How Merry chose to use it, that was a different thing. But blood magick wasn't inherently evil. Paige could touch Merry's magick and she didn't feel tainted or dirty. She just felt a different kind of life. It was baser. It was more body bound. Eating, sleeping, resting, working, maintaining, heartbeats, how the brain worked. Merry was more like a wild animal. She was instinct and primal. She was also rooted to the Earth. Her magick only worked in places were a physical connection to life already existed.

Billie's magick was everything Paige expected and more. Hers was elemental. But all of them. The wood magick connected every single element. Trees touched everything but were different. Because she didn't just touch them. She utilized them, knew how to shape them.

And then, there was Eldora's magick. Doors. Her magick, the magick that also flowed through Paige, was like opening up entire worlds straight into their minds. It wasn't simply about their Earth. It was about their Earth and every single one that touched theirs. Dimension upon dimension upon dimension. Just touching Eldora's magick was like seeing all of those ultimate earths, all of those other dimensions, stacked one on top of another using cellophane paper.

And with all of that, they still had no idea how to bring Heaven and Hell closer to Earth.

The one thing they were able to see, was Sven had succeeded in separating the three realms. Heaven was considerably further away than Hell. And that was the reason the angels were so weak.

Rachel looked at her, her mammoth head rising over her head, quiet and upset. That mammoth was the only reason Rachel lived.

Sheila was a whole nother bucket of worms. She was still being chosen, which wasn't helping them. Each time another spirit animal attempted to bond to her, it shook the magickal workings the witches were *trying* to weave.

Paige hoped whatever spirit chose her, would be strong enough. And that it'd freakin' hurry up.

But she also worried. It was one thing for the Whiskey line to have so many shifter witches. But to give the Blackmans that power? Paige wasn't certain that was a great idea.

But she had to hope the spirit animals would know what they were doing. She had to hope they weren't as clueless as Paige was. Because she had to concentrate. Somehow, she and these other three witches had to reweave the bonds between the three realms and somehow bring them closer.

Because she could see the connections unraveling almost

faster than they could weave. And if they didn't fix this, things could get a whole helluva lot worse.

But then, as they focused their energies inward once again, something wet trickled down Paige's leg.

Her water broke. Oh, fuck. Her babies were coming.

Now.

3 5

F rey stood with her hand halfway toward the hilt of Brynbitr, her sword.

Tarik stood at her back, but the two of them would know where the other was anywhere in the world now. They'd shared their…essences. The two of them were demon killing machines, and nothing felt better than sending one or dozens of those nasty things back to where they'd come from.

Paige had made them stay in town. Frey didn't like taking orders from Paige. Dexx? Sure. He'd earned her respect.

Paige? Not as much.

She'd come in with a good idea, and then she'd left. And that was something Frey couldn't respect.

Frey glared around the street. She hated waiting. She just wanted to *fight*.

Tarik just waited.

As much as she wanted to deny it, he'd been one of the best things to happen to her. Without his demon essence to cover her, she'd never have got so close to so many.

And her protections covered him as well. He wasn't *nearly* as tempted to return to the demons as before. He'd said they sort of repelled him now. Didn't stop him from killing as many as they found, though.

Now this waiting? Waiting. When they could be scouring the country—

"Holy fuck."

A string of demons arced into the horizon to the east. Fireballs seared through the sky in front of the lead demon.

Wait. That wasn't a demon.

That was a griffin. That was Leslie fucking Whiskey running from a small army of demons. And a… Oh no.

Frey stared in disbelief as she took in the beast following Leslie.

A manticore.

Oh…shit.

***

Paige was pulled out of the magick by a horrendous noise.

She turned, thinking the fighting had begun in the town. People started coming out of the woodwork, staring into the sky.

Leslie was in trouble.

Paige rose to her feet or tried to. A contraction hit her, and she stooped in place, one hand holding her belly. Of all the fool times!

Merry shook her head. "She's on her own. We need to finish this."

Goddammit.

Sorry. Blessed Mother.

The picnic table shook under her one hand.

Sheila was going through so many different shifter spirits, and each of them shifted over her head with enough power Paige didn't even need her shifter vision to see it.

Her regular vision told an interesting story as well. Each

of those animals, were trying to connect to her. And when they did, they shifted with her. So, unlike Rachel and her mammoth, Sheila was getting to do more with each of the animals that attempted to bond with her.

Unfortunately, each of them struggled.

Paige reached into herself and touched the place where Cawli existed. *What's happening?*

Cawli stirred. He seemed restless. He also seemed as though he wasn't fully here. It was almost as if he was fighting a battle someplace else, a place without her. *She is undead. They are having a hard time finding someone suitable to match up with her.*

If they can't figure this out, then we've got a problem. Because I can't be fighting her and trying to bring Heaven and Earth closer to us at the same time.

And try to take Sven out?

And give birth? This was taking a decided turn for the worse.

I need you to figure this out. Do whatever it is that you need to but help them figure out who would be compatible with her. We need this to happen. She may be a witch and she may be one that we can't trust, but we can't allow her to die either. So, you find me a spirit that will work, and get it done now.

Cawli growled, but he moved to obey.

Paige went back to her magicks, trying to block out Leslie's battle, Sheila's fight, and her body trying to wreck the fucking world. She needed to focus on trying to find a pathway. They had finally managed to find the connection between Earth and Heaven with Rachel's help.

Shortly after they'd *made* that connection, Rachel had fallen unconscious.

Which…seemed like that was just the theme of the day.

They were struggling to secure a real connection, and she assumed it was because Rachel was knocked out. They didn't know why. They hadn't paused to question it. She had to somehow wake Rachel up. But how was she going to do that?

Pulling herself out of the magick, Paige reached over and touched her mother.

However as soon as she did, another contraction had her and magick flared, pushing through to Rachel with everything Paige had, which was a *lot*.

Rachel sat straight up, her eyes bright as she looked around.

Merry pulled herself out of the magick and shook her head. "We can't do this with you in labor. Your magick is powerful but it's just too unstable. Is there another Whiskey we can use?"

While it stung Paige's pride more than a little, she realized Merry was right. She looked over to the battle, but it didn't look good. Her first instinct was to say Leslie would be the best one to come in.

But Leslie was battling a creature she didn't even know the name of. Leslie and her griffin were doing a pretty good job at keeping the beast at bay, but there was no way Paige could pull her out of that to come over and do this. Her next choice was Nick, but he was nowhere to be seen. And, frankly, she didn't know if his magick would even be strong enough. He had trained with Rachel, and as far as Paige could tell, Rachel liked to keep everyone powerless.

That left the kids. But the kids were needed to protect the four witches and the two doorways. As ridiculous as that sounded, the four coven leaders would be powerless if they were attacked. Mostly because they weren't on this plane. So, she really couldn't take Mandy or Tyler out of this fight.

And Leah? She was the linchpin in the next part of this battle. That left only one. Rachel.

Merry raised her eyebrows as she came to the same conclusion. They both looked at Rachel.

She stared at them in bewilderment.

"It might be a good thing," Paige said. "This might be the connection we need. We might need her magick in this."

Paige really couldn't call it a spell because it wasn't a spell. It was more like a working. But saying that out loud? It felt ridiculous.

Merry nodded. "Rachel are you with us?"

Rachel swallowed and then nodded. "Whatever you're doing, I can feel it."

"You're about to feel it a whole lot more." Paige gritted her teeth and fought against screaming out loud as another contraction hit. She was really pissed she wasn't having these babies in a hospital with an epidural. "I need you to take my place. I've got to join this battle anyway."

Merry nodded. "You need to fight him before these babies come. Even if one baby comes before your face-off with him, your power will decrease. So, end it quickly."

Paige nodded, getting to her feet. "You figure out how to get these realms together. Before everything unwinds. I have a sneaky suspicion part of the reason why Sheila is having such a hard time getting a match is because the connection between Earth and the Vaada Bhoomi is thinning."

Cawli growled in agreement. But then he grunted. *I have found one.*

Paige looked over at Sheila. The spirit animal that rose over Sheila's head confused Paige. It was less of an animal, and not even truly a plant. I was more of a light. No. It was more like several lights.

Cawli sighed. *The willow wisps. It was the best we could do. Technically speaking, a willow wisp is not a spirit animal. But it was the closest thing that we could come up with. She is not among the living. And you are right. The connection between our two planes is growing thinner. If you do not fix what is going on between Heaven and Hell and Earth, we may lose the connection between Earth and the Vaada Bhoomi.*

Paige shook her head. "Sheila has been chosen by the willow wisps. Get her woke up and into the workings and reconnect the three worlds because we could lose connection to the others as well."

Merry nodded sagely.

Billie and Eldora were still inside the weaving. Their expressions were still blank, their bodies still.

Paige turned to Tyler, Mandy, and Ashley. Griff galloped toward them with a loopy grin on his face.

This was just getting worse. If they survived this, she was going to jail. "They are completely unable to defend themselves. Your job is to not let anything get past you. Use your gifts to kill."

The kids nodded solemnly and then returned to watching the scene around them.

Billie had managed to set up a second ward around the park. Paige just prayed it would be enough. She really didn't want to test the kids in a real-life battle. But she was glad to see they had risen to the challenge.

A string of three shiny black SUV's came onto the street and parked. Eastwood witches — a few she recognized — opened up the back and started handing weapons to the mundanes milling around the streets.

Paige stepped gingerly down the hill. She wanted to shift so badly, but she didn't know how *giving birth* was going to affect that, so she opted not to. She was still early in the labor, so she should have time. Time enough, she hoped, to kick Sven's ass and send him home.

Leslie turned in her flight, heading back toward town, the monster and a pack of demons on her tail.

Okay. Where the hell was Sven?

At the Red Star building, the battle was in full sway. Most of the shifters were there and that's where the demons and elves had attacked first. Dexx had intended to go back for Leslie, but he'd heard Chuck's alpha call and come running.

The parking lot was filled with animals of all types, fighting demons and elves. The elves were good.

The demons…not as much. They moved sluggishly, like something was pulling energy from them.

Sven.

That would work. So, they still had the numbers. There were still more demons than fighters, but they were easier to kill.

Chunks of building rained down from the demon Hattie threw as she ripped off another head.

The demons weren't going back to Hell immediately like usual. The hole didn't grow right away to reclaim their demon souls. It was like Hell had fed enough, or just didn't want to take them.

Demons. Everywhere demons.

Chuck and the shifters were doing a helluva job. They'd finally figured out how to take down demons the easiest. They looked like choreographed dancers. One group here, swung by another group, each taking on demons.

Demons fell. And a few shifters, but mostly demons.

Dexx's pack swirled around him, keeping demons back while he finished them off one by one. Margo, Boot, and Clem surged on his left in wolf form, while Alex, his lone hyena, and Garek, another wolf, worked together to poke demons on his right.

Dexx took whatever was closest.

He and the fight moved slowly toward Main Street. They needed more room to fight. But Dexx knew they didn't want to take the fight to the park, which was about halfway down Main Street. That's where the witches were working. And Paige?

Yeah. Her too. So, he did everything he could to keep the fight in the Red Star parking lot.

But, he was losing *that* battle.

Boot was the biggest surprise. He seemed to know which way the demons would go before *they* did. That wolf could *fight*. More than a few times, Boot had a demon pinned for Dexx to take out. Almost no work at all.

Dexx sent out little mental whips of thought to the pack, directing them through the demons.

How many had they killed? Forty? One hundred and forty? Time slipped by amazingly fast and painfully slow.

Where was Sven? He needed to—

Dexx picked himself up slowly, his head ringing. Some sort of explosion had knocked him to the ground.

The rest of the pack had been knocked off their feet as well. The demons, too.

Elves in tight formations trotted through the demon lines.

Oh, shit. *Now we have the elves to fight, too?* Not that this was unexpected. But they'd been *winning*.

Hattie didn't even miss a beat. *We must kill them as we do to the others.*

So neat! We have even more to kill? When will it be enough?

So long as we stand.

What the hell ever. Are we hurt badly?

Hattie only leapt into the elven ranks in reply.

Lightning streaked down into the demon and elven mass, throwing bodies into the air. Mostly elves, since the demons were a tad heavier.

Dexx took on two demons at once, whipping back and forth trying to keep the demons together instead of catching Dexx in a cross fight.

A white wolf with a dark patch over his eye blurred past.

Boot had recovered quicker than the rest.

He streaked in, taking one demon by the throat. Then, as he swung around the demon, he shifted back to human, using it as a shield against another. Once that demon had attacked, and the demon in his mouth was dead, Boot dropped the limp demon, shifted again, and attacked the newcomer holding the blade.

Boot had never been the fastest Ferrari on the street, but besides Dexx, he'd been the only other shifter to go toe to toe with Cooper McCree. He might have won, too if Cooper hadn't cheated.

Dexx had his own problems, but he watched Boot as well as he could. He followed Boot, demon after demon, and soon they were together.

They faced off with three of the largest demons yet. They must be through all the little guys and on to the real powerhouses.

Boot shifted to human. "I think you guys should go home."

Points for bluntness. The demon waved other away from behind Dexx and Boot.

Hattie crouched. Ready to jump.

When I give the signal, we go. Hopefully Boot would get the idea.

Boot twitched a finger. He'd understood.

The demons chuckled. All three of them pulled out a *ma'a'shed* and the demon blade slowly lengthened to a long black sword, blood red on the edges.

"*Shedim Patesh.* We three have waited for you."

We three? Who talked like that?

Hattie pulled her lip up.

Are you smiling?

These three want us. They get us.

Hattie and Dexx hesitated for the barest moment and leapt.

The demons swiped with their long *ma'a'sheds*, but missed as Dexx went low, and Boot shifted, dodging the swords comically easy.

Dexx swiped the leg out from one of the demons, and as he fell, Dexx went for the other one.

Out of nowhere, Alex, in hyena form, leapt from the back of the down demon and launched at Boot's demon.

Dexx continued his spin to take his own demon.

They no longer looked amused.

Boot's demon had caught Alex and held her easily.

Boot jumped at the demon just as it swung its sword. It caught Boot in the side, but not before Boot clamped onto the demon's throat and snapped his jaws shut.

Alex fell free. She scrambled up and retreated.

Boot lay on the ground, and he wasn't moving.

Crap.

This fight was going to end bloody.

Leah stared out onto the street. Her mom was entering the battle. Leah's entire soul clenched. Watching her out there, so strong and powerful, and so pregnant. Leah could see the pain on her face.

Ripley ran up to her in dog form as demons surged through the streets, coming through holes in the air. She shifted human again as she drew near, her hair still moving like it was on fire or something. Ripley turned toward the street. "Tell me we're protected."

"Yeah. Billy set them up."

Mandy crouched, her fists in flames.

Griff got out of his clothes, leaving them all over the grass and shifted into a bear. He stomped the ground, ready.

Ashley tossed her horse head, shaking her mane and reared up, her front hooves striking the air as she prepared.

Tyler bounced on his toes, shaking his hands and rolling his neck like he'd seen Dexx do a thousand times.

They were ready.

Was she?

Leah looked over at Ripley. She was so uncertain. What if she failed? What if she screwed up? What if she got everybody killed?

A purple elf door opened beside them and Kate popped out with a mischievous grin. "Hello. I'm not late, am I?"

Leah shook her head. "What are you grinning about?"

Kate closed the door behind her and giggled. "You will see."

About that time, a shout went up with the elves. A cry of alarm. Purple elf doors opened everywhere, and the elves slipped through them, leaving the battle.

That...was neat. Leah turned to Kate. "What did you do?"

The elf girl grinned. "I turned the Wildelands against them."

Leah had no idea what that even meant, but if it meant there were fewer people trying to kill them, then...great.

Ripley gave Leah a smile meant to bolster her. "You got this, kid. Just trust yourself."

Kate's expression changed, darkening, as she looked up at Ripley. "You are certain that this will not hurt my realm."

Leah realized it probably made her a worse person, but she was glad she wasn't the only kid having to go through this kind of doubt. Though, it didn't look like Kate was doubting herself so much as doubting the outcome.

Ripley nodded and gripped Kate's shoulder. "I'm absolutely sure of it. This has the best outcome of them all. Just trust me and trust yourselves. Both of you have this."

Leah looked out over the street. She certainly hoped so.

The elves left with a shout of alarm, purple doors to Underhill appearing and disappearing quickly.

That left just the demons.

Good for their team. Dexx didn't know what had happened or why, but he was grateful nonetheless.

Before Dexx had a chance to move again, a stream of elves with long three-pointed spears slammed into the demons.

Wait. Those weren't elves. They were lithe like elves, but their skin was mottled. Some were red, others yellow, green, blue, and they had thick webbing between their fingers and toes.

Mermaids? Mermales? Whatever they were, the demons fell to their spears, and then retreated to regroup.

Boot's form lay on the pavement, still and unmoving. His sides didn't heave. Alex nudged him with her muzzle.

And inside of Dexx's alpha heart, he felt the light of one of his own being snuffed out.

Dexx shifted and picked up a *ma'a'shed* that one of the demons had left on the ground. He pushed his anger and power into the blade.

It grew from a dagger into a sword but turned a silver green.

Those fucking demons were going to pay.

More mermen crashed the lines of demons and the few remaining elves. They were especially vicious when they caught an elf alone.

If there was a million of these guys, they might have a chance. Maybe.

Fireballs smashed into the pavement, melting large potholes.

Dexx looked up to see Robin take a direct hit. His wings folded up and he crashed to the ground like a bomb.

Right behind him was the manticore.

Dexx intercepted the lion thing and swung the demon sword, driving it backward. The sword clanged off the darting scorpion stinger.

Rage rushed through him, through Hattie, who curled like a waiting weapon inside his soul, ready to be unleashed. She growled low.

And then green lightening erupted from his fingers, finding three demon victims, their skin boiling and popping with angry black smoke pouring out of them. They ceased to be.

What…in the *hell?*

Demons around the manticore scattered.

Robin's voice pushed through Dexx's anger. *This one is ours. This is my enemy, and he is mine.*

Fine, there were plenty more where that came from. *You just make sure you win because Leslie is* mine.

Robin nodded his massive eagle head.

As Paige stepped onto the street, another contraction hit her. She paused, her entire body tightening with it. These damn kids had the worst damned timing.

The demons had arrived, and the fight was spilling onto the street. Mundanes with guns were taking out the demons they could. They were working together as a pretty good team. In the zombie apocalypse, Paige was fairly certain, her little town would be okay.

The Eastwood witches were doing what they could with

their blood magick, opening up the demon bodies and draining them for energy as they conducted their other spells, fighting side-by-side with the mundanes.

And then the Blackmans rolled into town. Almost literally in their three wagons. They hopped down in their almost Amish looking attire, and entered the fight, using their door magic to send demons away.

What she didn't expect was to see the merfolk enter the battle.

But...she wasn't there for any of them. And she wasn't going to waste her powers on them. She wasn't going to weaken herself for that. Everyone else seemed to be handling their own.

Sven...was hers.

She rose as the contraction released her and stepped into the street. With his army here, it shouldn't be too much longer for him to appear.

"Paige." Sven's voice carried over the street. "I think it's time we end this. Don't you?"

Right on time.

36

Everything, Dexx included, slowed down when Sven spoke.

"Paige, I think it's time we end this. Don't you?" His voice hit the battle like a hammer.

Dread settled on Dexx's shoulders. How in the hell were they going win against that?

Dexx's *ma'a'shed* shrank, becoming a black-bladed dagger again.

Hattie pushed forward, and they shifted back into a demon-ripping, saber-toothed cat.

Rainbow, Frey, Tarik, and Chuck met him in the middle of the street, the only thing standing between Sven and Paige.

Rainbow turned cold, deep-blue eyes on Hattie and dipped her head slightly. "*Shedim,* let us send this thing away."

So, the currents had Rainbow again. A good thing, since their water magick did a number on demons.

Hattie only growled and launched at Sven.

Leslie and Robin landed in the middle of the biggest battle Leslie had ever seen.

The demons swarmed over buildings and shifters. Pockets of shifters held their own but were being pushed back. There were simply too many demons and the shifters were starting to tire.

From her perspective, they were losing.

The flight from the Dalles and the landing, which hadn't been one of their finest, was taking a toll on Leslie. She, like the shifters, were tiring.

But Aaen was still fighting and Robin was more than eager to destroy that beast.

Aaen charged.

Robin was still a little dazed from the impact, and barely missed the sweeping claws.

The pain in Robin's leg let Leslie know the manticore had hit them. Hard.

But that was okay. Blood poured down Aaen's side too.

Both Robin and the manticore went at each other, full of fury. They locked together in a vicious hug, claws tearing at the other. Wounds were opened up on both creatures, and Leslie felt them weakening.

Robin, for God's sake, stop this. We're not winning this way! Leslie kicked them away from the manticore. Both of them showed deep gashes, and blood poured freely.

Aaen charged, his claws extended.

Leslie shifted as the beast flew over, missing them by a good foot and a half.

She called the elements, and stripped the air from around the manticore's face, drowning him in the middle of the street.

He clawed at the air, as if he could somehow unravel what she had done.

But he wouldn't stay down!

Leslie called lightning and blasted the manticore repeatedly. She'd pinned him down, and caused pain, but that was all.

Leslie had power. A lot of it. But as much as she had, she couldn't keep this up until she killed it. That might take forever.

She needed a break.

Paige didn't let Sven chit-chat. These babies were *coming*, and she needed to defeat him before she lost the power that came with them.

She called the elements to her, earth, air, fire, water… wood. Wood was amazing, more powerful and brilliant than she'd ever imagined. She fired a flurry of fireballs at him. They engulfed him, but he simply brushed off the flames and then sent a few of his own back at her.

She answered with a rainstorm, pulling the water from the air and river that ran behind town. Then, she volleyed with an attack of vines, stabbing through him.

She needed to get him to reveal his kitsune blade. That was his weakness. That's what Cyn had told her. They needed to use that weakness to their advantage.

But nothing she threw at him brought out the blade.

Well, if she couldn't get him to reveal his blade, she could send him elsewhere.

She opened a door to Hell, the only place *she* could connect to. It was sluggish and slow to form.

And then it sputtered out as if it had been snuffed.

Sven threw his head back and laughed. "Oh, Paige, my love," his voice carried over the sounds of battle, "I do so love watching you work. But I believe we're out of time, love.

I need my doors back. Now, be a good girl and hand 'em over."

Not likely.

As another contraction hit, she lobbed pure, white energy at him, stabbing him in his heart.

He arched back and let out a guttural roar.

She kept that energy going, waiting, hoping, praying it would be enough to end him.

But the contraction ended and so did the flow of power.

He got control of himself and stared at her, breathing heavily. "This could have gone *so* much easier."

Not on his life.

<hr />

We have to face him, Robin growled. *As animals.*

Leslie couldn't stop seeing Robin as a kid throwing a tantrum. *Fine, but get ready, I'm going to hit him from behind.* She let go of her attack and shifted.

The manticore gulped in air and grunted as they hit.

They rolled him over onto his side and pinned his face to the dirt. Claws came out of nowhere opening new gashes along their underside.

Pain ripped through them.

A bright, searing white light lit up Main Street, just on the other side of the building they fought next to. Leslie had no idea what that was, but she suspected it was Paige and Sven. She had to hope that Paige was holding her own. If anyone could, it would be her.

The scorpion sting sprang forward.

The strike was fast, but Robin was faster. He grabbed the last segment of the tail before the sting. And clamped his beak around it. Then he leapt on the manticore and pulled.

Fresh screams of pain wracked the manticore and claws shredded them from the back.

Leslie and Robin clung to the tail and pulled for all they were worth.

If we are to win, Robin was losing strength, *we have to sever the tail.*

Leslie couldn't argue, but they were losing strength.

A bolt of golden power hit Aaen.

He shrieked once as he was dragged into the air by the golden power lasso.

Robin tore the tail apart, manticore innards tearing and shredding, and spilling out on the ground.

They stumbled a step with the sudden release of the bits.

They hadn't won. Something had taken Aaen away from the battle and it appeared to be—

Sven. Leslie shifted into human and went to stand by Rainbow and Tarik on the edge of Main. She'd thought with the wards up, Sven wouldn't be *able* to power up, to steal any more magick.

And yet? That's exactly he was doing.

Dexx ran toward Sven's feet, trying to gain the demon's attention. Rainbow, Frey, Tarik, Chuck joined him.

Leslie had no idea what she was supposed to do. She watched as Robin's greatest enemy dissolved slowly before their eyes, absorbed into Sven. For one moment, Leslie stood still, afraid, as a memory played back in her mind.

Robin had once been used by a mage, in the last time he'd been on Earth. His life had been slowly siphoned away. Much like this. If she were to enter into the fight, she was afraid she would become Sven's next target.

Tarik and Rainbow threw blasts of magick, while the others went for Sven physically.

Dexx darted in so fast Sven couldn't keep up, but every hit he scored on the demon instantly closed.

Leslie shook herself and entered the fight.

Tyler was so excited to be a part of this, but it wasn't a good excited.

He was terrified.

All those times, he had thought about being a hero like this, he had never realized what it would actually feel like. Watching all those people fighting in the street, watching his aunt fighting with that big glowing guy in the middle of the street? He really just wanted to go home.

He wanted to find his mom, hug her, and have her tell him everything was going to be okay, but his mom was out there fighting a manticore. A *freaking* manticore.

If that thing turned around and started attacking them, there was no way Tyler was going to be able to stop it. The manticore was freaking huge! And Tyler, for all he could do amazing things and stuff, with his voice and stuff, he was just a boy.

He swallowed hard and got a grip.

Griff looked even more scared than before, even in the shape of a bear. He wouldn't do any of them any good if they all freaked out.

But then, Tyler looked over at Sheila and Rachel.

Whatever the witches were doing, it was making both of them worse. Both Sheila and Rachel were becoming invisible. It was as if they were disappearing right before their eyes.

Tyler wasn't sure what he was supposed to do. He tried calling out to the other witches, but the scary blood witch and the creepy witch didn't even twitch. The only one that did was Billie. She was the only one he really liked anyway. He went over to her and touched her arm.

Billie opened her eyes. "Tyler, what's up?"

Tyler pointed at Sheila and Rachel. "Whatever you're doing, I think it's wrong. They're disappearing."

Billie said something that Tyler was never supposed to say. She stirred the other two witches and pointed at Sheila and Rachel. "What are we doing that's causing this?"

The scary which shook her head. "It seemed like it was working."

Griff came to stand by Tyler. He shifted and put on his robe. Ashley and Mandy joined him to.

The creepy witch shook her head. "This might be exactly what's supposed to happen.

"But," the scary witch said, "it could be that we're making things worse."

Billie shook her head. "I don't think so. Didn't it feel right to you, what we were doing? Didn't it feel as though things were coming together?"

The creepy witch and the scary which both nodded.

"Then maybe what we're doing is right."

The creepy witch glared at her.

This was one of the reasons why Tyler didn't like her. She seemed to always be glaring at something. "But if that is the case, then I will lose her again."

The scary which just looked at her. "You lost her years ago when I killed her."

What kind of person just admitted that out loud? The scary kind.

Tyler was really looking forward to the day when they were done with all of this and he never had to step foot in her area. Ever. Again. She scared him.

The creepy witch glared at her, too.

It kind of made Tyler feel a little bit better that he wasn't the only one who felt that way about her.

"I don't want to lose my daughter again. I just got her back."

Billie snorted. "And then you chased her away. If this is how we save the world, then you need to figure out how to let her go."

Creepy Witch closed her eyes.

When she did, it made Tyler feel a little bit better. For whatever reason whenever she was staring, it made him feel awful. It was almost as if she could open doorways and see right into his soul. And that was just creepy. All the kinds of creepy. With the creepy cherry on top of the creepy sundae.

Billie gave Tyler's arm a squeeze "Thank you. Now we need to get back to this. Keep us safe."

"Sure." No problem.

It wasn't every day a bunch of kids had to save a bunch of freaking adults.

Well, it was in their world.

He looked at Griff, Ashley, and Mandy. "We've got this."

A demon had spotted the kids and was stalking their way. Or…

At least, Tyler hoped they did.

Paige used the distraction Dexx and Leslie provided and hit Sven with everything she had. She was done playing around. The elements answered her commands as though they were one and the same. After having spent such intimate time with her magick, and after having touched the magick of the Eastwoods, Blackman's, and Blacks, it was as if she had a better understanding of what the magicks even were.

And the power of her children, the unborn babes still with in her womb— barely— only seemed to fuel her on. They gave her even more power. It was a heady feeling.

However, seeing Sven take out that beast, seeing how he'd drained the beast of its energy, while helpful to their side, worried Paige. Inside of her wards, he should have been unable to siphon energy from anything else. Cyn was protected here. The angels, the demons, the spirit animals, Bastet's temple cats. They were all protected from being siphoned from Sven while inside Paige's wards.

At least she'd thought so. But Sven was always thinking. And he'd found a way to get more power. Just like he always did.

If he got his hands on Leslie? Or Dexx? He could kill them in an instant.

Another contraction hit her and gave her even more power to slam at him.

She hit him again, and again. She pushed Dexx and Leslie out of the way. She lost track of them, only seeing Sven. He knelt on the ground looking spent.

She had him.

But then he stood quickly, a malicious smile on his face. He held out one hand. It wasn't directed at her. "Stop."

Paige wasn't going to. She had him right where she wanted him. As another contraction hit, she balled up more power and launched it at him. It hit him full force.

And as he staggered backward, she saw what he had done. With his other hand, he held Emma, Lynx, Frey, Tarik, Rainbow, Leslie, Margo, Chuck, a dozen others...

And Dexx.

Paige went still.

Sven rose to his feet and smiled. "Perhaps we could talk now."

37

The third demon went down, a lump of smoking char.

Mandy smiled at Tyler.

They might have actually found a good way to destroy the demons.

Tyler captured the demon with his voice, confusing it, and Mandy blasted it with fire. No, not fire. What Mandy was doing was… amazing.

"Whiskeys stick together, little brother." She gave him a pat on the shoulder and went back to scanning for more.

Tyler had seen Leah push a few demons through those doors she created.

Ripley was in the fight, taking demons down, trying to keep them away. She just passed through them, and the demons fell down. She was scary good with that.

Griff prowled around in bear form, looking as scared as Tyler felt.

He wanted Roxxie there to protect them. But he knew that Roxxie was at home, helping his dad protect the babies. And that's where she was supposed to be.

But Tyler was still scared. Super scared.

He nearly leapt out of his skin as Nick touched him on his shoulder. "Uncle Nick!"

"Hey, buddy." Nick smiled at him. "I need your help."

No way he was leaving his sister and his best friend to fight this on their own. Though, they did have Ripley and she was really good. But what happened when Ripley had to go? Because she would. She was part of the final plan. "We've got to stay here, if anything attacks these guys, they can't defend ourselves."

Nick just stared at him. "I know. But you and me? We can do something a little bit better."

Tyler shook his head. "I'm the best fighter out of all of us. If we get attacked, I'm the best one to defend them."

Mandy didn't even say anything different, which…was kinda nice for once.

Nick tipped his head to the side in acknowledgement. "I think you need to give a little credit where it's due. These guys are just as strong as you are. But what you can do and what I can do is something that none of them can. So, let's do that."

Tyler wasn't sold.

Mandy took in a deep breath. "Look, I can throw fireballs. And Griff and Ashley are great physical fighters. They can take care of themselves. But, Uncle Nick is right." She gestured out to the battlefield. "Look at them. We're losing. And it's because they're starting to doubt. Look at Leah. We need her to be strong, and she's about to fold. Look at Kate. She's scared. Look at *all* of them."

Tyler's gaze landed on his mom. She was being held in the clutches of magick. He knew she could break out of it. She was super strong.

But…maybe they were right.

"I'll work on the demons. I'll get them to doubt and want to run away." Nick turned to Tyler. "But you get our guys to believe that they can win. That's what we can do that nobody else can. You do that, and we could win this."

Mandy gave her brother an arm squeeze and nodded. "You go. Besides, Billie's wards are holding. Nobody's gotten in."

Tyler swallowed hard and met Nick's gaze. "Okay. What do we do?"

Nick straightened. "Save the day, kid."

Another contraction hit Paige hard. She couldn't do this. She couldn't fight a battle *and* give birth. What kind of crazy person was she? Okay, so, there was a crazy guy in the middle the street, and he had all of the people she loved. What did she do?

With the power of the contraction, the power of her unborn children, she lashed out at Sven. She wasn't going to let him win. She felt an uplift of spirit hit her. Hard. And with it came the hope, the renewed sense she could do this.

As the power hit Sven, he lost control of the people he held.

Dexx and Leslie and the others got quickly to their feet and rose right back into the battle.

They were rejuvenated.

She just needed her opening.

That, and she needed Cyn to hurry up with that material. She had no idea how she was going to stab it into Sven, especially since it was material, but she wanted to end this before they all became too exhausted.

And before she had these babies.

A cold chill swept over Mandy. She turned in time to see Sheila rise from the table. She still wasn't exactly physical. She was still disappearing. But she rose and started advancing on Merry.

Mandy had no idea what she was supposed to do. She also didn't know if her fire was going to have any effect on a spirit because basically that's what this woman was now. But she had to try.

Griff's eyes widened, and he launched himself at Sheila.

Mandy gathered as much fire as she could into both of her hands.

Mandy needed to get Sheila's attention. If Sheila attacked Merry, Mandy had no idea what would happen. So, Mandy did the only thing she could. She let her fireball go.

It connected with flesh. Mandy didn't even realize that was possible because she looked so see-through. But it hit her, and then it seemed to inflame around her.

It wasn't like she was being set on fire so much as she had *become* the fire.

However, now, Mandy had Sheila's full attention.

Whatever everybody was going to do, Mandy really hoped they did it fast. Because her fire wasn't having the right effect in this battle.

Cyn saw Lynx scramble to his feet and re-enter the battle. She knew there was nothing she could do to help him. But that didn't mean she wasn't going to. She had the spear she and Lynx had worked so hard to make. It had been his idea to turn the material into something harder, something sharper, something Paige could jam into Sven.

Unfortunately, it had taken longer. And she'd had to get a little bit of help.

How had Lynx got himself into so much trouble in such a short amount of time?

Without thinking twice, Cyn ran toward Paige and tossed the spear to her.

Paige caught it in one hand.

Which was good because Cyn didn't have time to go retrieve it for her. She ran right into battle to save the man she loved. She didn't know how, but that certainly wasn't going to stop her. She was a woman with a mission.

Paige took the spear and focused on Sven.

Mandy's startled scream drew her attention toward Merry and the kids.

Sheila was awake, and she was shifting. She was becoming the willow wisp, and it looked as though she was on fire.

Paige turned to go assist.

Merry opened her eyes once, held up one hand, and Sheila stopped in her tracks.

Paige had to allow everyone to fight their own battles. Because she couldn't fight those battles and this one at the same time. Gathering her courage, she turned back toward Sven.

Contractions were coming faster. She couldn't have these babies right this freaking moment. Right in the middle of the freaking battle.

Someone appeared out of a cloud of black smoke.

Balnore.

Thank goodness. He turned toward Sven and advanced.

Bastet appeared right afterward. She no longer wore the long flowing gowns Paige had always seen her in. Instead, she wore something akin to battle a uniform, even though it was ancient.

Crap! Just when Paige thought they were going to get the upper hand, along came the one woman who could take Bal down.

Bastet reached forward.

And grabbed Sven.

She spun him around.

The look on his face lasted only a moment. He lashed his golden magic, blasting her from her feet, but before she was out of arm's reach, Balnore quick-punched Sven with a ball of lightning in his fists.

Those looked like they did damage to Sven, but a razor thin arc of lightning blasted Balnore back, just like Bastet.

These two demigods were the two most powerful people on their team, but it looked like it wasn't enough.

Paige couldn't move. She just couldn't. Her babies were coming, and they wouldn't last the day if she fell.

Singing touched her— Tyler. Her spirit lifted enough to fight her physical exhaustion. Another contraction brought pain, but also a fresh wave of raw magick she could do anything with. She turned it into a spear of white lightning as sharp and as heavy as she could make it.

Somehow, Sven saw and moved.

It blasted right in front of Balnore and blew him backward again.

Bastet had regained her feet, and well, it was nothing short of amazing. Her eyes glowed with a silver light, and her face was decidedly ugly with the growling sneer covering it. She charged Sven and literally crawled all over him, blasting at him.

From nowhere, Dexx leapt, in barely missing Bastet, and raked Hattie's claws against Sven. He was savage, brutal.

Sven backed away, right into another volley of blasts from Balnore.

Sven shook himself and everyone flew away.

Bastet was slow to move.

Dexx shifted back to human.

Why would he do that?

He bent and plucked a *ma'a'ashed* from a demon. It grew into a long green sword, and he attacked again.

Rainbow was down. Tarik and Frey were down. Shit, even Leslie and Lynx were down. Only Hattie remained.

Well, and Dexx. And he wasn't going down without one hell of a fight.

He just wished he had pants.

Two people-looking things advanced on Sven. One was all in black with tendrils of power, and the other glowed with a hard-golden light.

Dexx focused on the figures. They came into focus. One was Balnore, the other was... Bastet?

Bastet struck with power, taking Sven in the side. Balnore followed up with vicious blows himself.

Sven batted them away, but Dexx saw how much effort it took. Maybe Sven had been weakened through constant onslaught. They had to be careful now, because letting up would hand Sven the world.

In Dexx's peripheral vision, he saw more demons. They were pushing back the shifters and mer...people.

Dexx thought it was weird how the blade turned green in his hand. Did that change it somehow? Alma had said once that he had some magick in his nature. Hopefully that was true.

Bastet and Balnore had been thrown aside again, but at least they had Sven's attention.

Dexx snuck up behind him and swung. Not a pretty swing. A full-bodied swing with no finesse, but with everything he had left.

Even still, Sven had seen or felt him coming. He twisted just in time to take the sword in the arm. Dexx had never been into blacksmithing, but he'd swung a hammer before. Those didn't compare to the pounding he felt as the sword hit Sven's arm.

He knew he had flown away from Sven, but he hadn't felt himself stop. His body was numb from head to toe. His vision darkened around the edges, making a tunnel. It got longer, and things went away. But the last thing he saw was people.

Regular people with guns and recovered spears, and knives attacking the demons.

Huh. Regular folk had come back to save their town.

Okay. Okay. If the regular folks could fight...

Then so could he.

Dexx dragged his tired, naked, numb ass off the pavement. He needed a sword.

Paige gripped the spear and advanced, fighting through the growing pain of her contractions. They were coming closer together. These damn kids were coming right now. There was no holding them back. But she needed their power if she was going to get close enough to Sven.

So, fighting through the pain, pushing it to the back of her mind, making it as small a thing as she possibly could, she advanced.

Bastet turned toward her. She seemed to understand what

was going on because she grabbed Sven, pinning him in place, and turned him toward Paige. Balnore joined her and held Sven's arms pinned behind him.

Sven had very little power left to fight against her. He strained against them, trying. But two gods against one was just too much.

Sven roared and bucked against Balnore.

Paige brought the spear up and pointed it at Sven, getting ready to charge through her next contraction.

This entire fight, this entire moment was beyond ridiculous. Whichever god had decided she needed to fight this battle while giving birth needed to have parts of his anatomy ripped off of his body.

Sven pulled away, freeing one of his arms.

And as he did, he revealed his sword. His kitsune blade.

That was exactly what Paige needed. Paige sent a contraction-filled bolt of power toward Sven's kitsune blade.

The sword shattered. Shards of the blade rained down over all of them.

Paige didn't have time to protect herself. It was now or never. She gestured at Leah.

The girl had the door open.

Paige could see the other side. Kate stood in between, her hands out as if she was catching a ball. Almost.

With the next contraction, Paige took three more steps. As soon as she was close enough, she shoved her spear into Sven as hard as she could. And then, with one final blast of energy. She pushed Sven through the door.

Ripley reached out and caught him on one side. Balnore appeared next to Kate on the other and held onto Sven's other arm.

Sven grew brighter and brighter until it was difficult to look at him.

And then, he seemed to grow.

Paige reached out with her witch hands, hoping she would do less damage with a living person than she did on a demon, with one hand, she reached for Kate and with the other, she reached for Ripley. Hopefully, Balnore would be able to take care of himself.

Sven pushed at Balnore freeing himself, the spear swinging ludicrously as he moved. He took a step toward the open doorway.

And then, the world exploded.

Paige sat on her couch surrounded by friends and family as they all celebrated their victory. Paige still felt as though she was hung over. That much power had consequences.

She had given birth to her kids in the middle of the street. In front of everyone. Paige had no dignity left.

However, as people picked themselves up off the ground, regular mundane people who'd come back to save their town, congratulating each other for being alive; they had all worked together as a team to bring Paige's children into this world.

If Paige hadn't been giving birth, she was sure she would have felt how wonderful that moment had been. However, since she *had* been giving birth, it was just one really fantastically painful process without any drugs.

Everyone was more than a little sore. It'd been a big battle.

And it had been a battle with losses.

They lost a few shifters. In Chuck's pack and in their own.

Boot had died saving Alex. He'd taken out two demons alone, and wounded, had still fought. He'd freed Alex and she'd survived but was hurt badly. He'd saved a lot of people. Merfolk, shifters, mundanes.

One of the leaders of the merfolk had told her what he did. They'd never seen anything like that wolf shifter.

And they had lost Rachel and Sheila.

Somehow, Eldora, Merry, and Billie had managed to bring Heaven and Hell closer. Paige knew because her bond with Cawli was as strong as ever.

However, when the battle was over, Sheila and Rachel had winked out of existence.

Eldora blamed Paige. Paige really hadn't paid too much attention at the time. She was a little busy having babies. But even while in labor, she had been adamant Eldora not touch her children.

And Merry, surprisingly, had been her biggest advocate. She had taken Eldora and kept her as far from Paige's kids as she could. However, that didn't stop her from drawing the power of the blood from the birth. Merry was young and beautiful again. She might even look younger than Paige now.

This was the first moment Paige had really had to be a person since the fight had ended. And she was pretty sure that was the case for most everybody else too.

Dexx held Paige close — their little girl in one arm, Paige in the other.

Paige held their little boy.

Yes, they had a little boy and a little girl. And they looked perfect. Two perfect little children with all the right number of toes and fingers and other appendages.

They weren't shifting yet, so, there was that. Though, Paige wasn't looking forward to when they did decide to shift. These two were going to keep her more than busy, that was a fact.

"All in all, babe," Dexx said in a quiet rumble behind her, "we didn't do too bad."

Paige wasn't sure if he was talking about the babies or Sven. But either way, he was right.

Leslie came in and plopped in the chair beside them, letting her head fell back. "I feel like we all deserve a vacation."

"Me too." Paige didn't care what the elders had to say, or what line they took with her. She was going to take some time off and spend some quality time with her new babies. This wasn't going to be like when she had Leah. She wasn't going to go back to work days after having given birth.

The front door opened, and Michelle came through. She barely glanced at any of them and turned on the TV. "You need to see this."

That certainly couldn't be good.

As the TV came on, Paige heard the news reporter mention Troutdale.

Oh no. With all of the ruckus, Paige hadn't even thought about whether or not there were news crews there. Though, she didn't remember seeing any, that didn't mean they weren't there.

Sure enough, playing on the TV was a video of the final moments of the battle. She saw Leah's terrified face as she opened a portal. She saw the look on Kate's face. So many things. So much destruction. Everyone fighting,

She saw Boot die.

She saw Tyler and Nick working their magick. She saw dryads, merfolk, and mundanes fighting against demons and elves.

And then, the video went still on Paige's face and zoomed in.

She looked like hell warmed over. In her defense, she *had* been giving birth at the time.

The news reporter said, "This is what witnesses at the scene claimed is Paige Whiskey. Apparently, this is the person that Sven Seven-Tails was after. Witnesses claim he was a demon. According to the reports we gathered, Paige drew him to Troutdale where people like her were waiting in ambush to deal with him."

The cameras rotated over to Sven. And sped up to show Paige pushing toward him and ramming the spear into his chest.

"No one is certain what she used, but it does appear as though Sven Seven-Tails is no longer a threat to the public."

The cameras then cut over to Leah, Kate, and Ripley. But instead of focusing on the kids, the camera focused on what was shown behind them.

What apparently looked like an alien landscape.

The vegetation was wild and blue, instead of green. Paige didn't remember seeing blue vegetation when she'd gone to Underhill.

Another reporter, a male reporter added his commentary. "Look at the terror on those children's faces. Who would take children into battle?"

The female reporter gave him a hard look. "I don't remember seeing the National Guard there. Or any other assistance. I think you should be asking yourselves what kind of parents are able to train their kids to stand up and battle a demon, and not run away scared."

Michelle turned the volume down. "This is on all of the news channels. We made national news."

Well, the Shadow Sisterhood wasn't going to have much effect on them anymore.

Paige's phone rang. She had no way of getting it though.

Leslie grabbed it off the table, looked at the screen, and then handed it over to her with a look of disdain. "You'd think they'd at least give you one day off."

After what Paige saw on the news, she wasn't sure the world could handle it.

Leslie took the baby and gave Paige her phone.

She swiped the green call button and put the phone to her ear. "Yes, I saw the news."

"Good." Elder Yad's tone was blunt. "You're being heralded as a hero. We need to get you out in front of this right away."

"Can you tell them that I just had a baby? Two babies."

"You must have missed that part of the news. Everyone knows. It was on TV."

Great. Yeah. She had *zero* dignity left.

If her world hadn't sucked before, it certainly did now. "What did you have in mind?"

Half hour later, Paige was dressed, was actually wearing makeup, and had done nothing more to her hair than to pull it back in a ponytail. It had been decided she was going to go and make a statement to the public.

Because that was a fantastic idea. She had just pushed two babies out of her body, fought a powerful demon, had saved the world from shattering, and she needed to address the world.

Yeah. Her life was *grand*.

She had been briefed by the leader of the Shadow Sisterhood and by the elders as to what she was supposed to say. She agreed with most of it. But she knew it was going to be a tough pill for a lot of people to swallow. She was affirming to the world paranormals existed. There really was no way to put this particular genie back in the bottle. And, she was going on record as being one of those paranormals.

Whatever was going to come down from the President, she and her family were going to have to suffer the consequences. There was no way she could hide from that. Especially, not when they had caught her on video doing magick.

Standing in front of a crowd was one thing. Especially when a crowd was a bunch of angry mundanes who were scared and trying to figure out how not to die in battle they hadn't caused.

Standing in front of TV cameras was a wholly different thing. If she blundered on camera? There was no way of editing that. She just didn't have the money or political power to take back what she said. So, it was important she said the right things.

Chief Tuck addressed the news crews first. Paige wasn't even entirely sure where the podium had come from or the microphone. Maybe it had come from the mayor's office?

That was really the wrong thing to be thinking about. She needed to be finalizing the words she would say to the nation.

But while the elders had told her briefly what she should say, they hadn't written a speech for her. And public speaking had never really been her thing, ever. She had no idea what she was doing.

That was like almost every single day of her life.

She was just a woman like everybody else who had no idea what she was doing at any given point in time. And now she had the grand opportunity of screwing it all up on national television.

Awesome.

Tuck handed over the podium to Paige. She hadn't even heard what he'd said she was so nervous.

She stepped up and grabbed hold of both sides of the podium. She was fairly certain the whole point and purpose of the podium was to keep the speaker standing.

Cawli stepped forward and pushed his support to her. *You will be okay. As you would say, you've got this.*

She wordlessly thanked him.

Paige took a deep breath — so much easier now she had

given birth — and looked at those in front of her. She concentrated on the people. If she concentrated on the cameras, she had no idea if she'd be able to keep herself together. "I'm sure that many of you have a lot of questions. I am here to provide a few answers."

That didn't sound too bad.

The clicking of cameras was constant.

But everybody was quiet, waiting for what she had to say.

She swallowed hard. "My name is Paige Whiskey and I am a witch." Shit. That sounded too close to an AA meeting.

Nobody moved. Nobody shouted a million questions at her. They simply waited.

"I'm sure that most of you have seen the video. What you don't know is that for years, we were plagued by a demon, Sven Seven-Tails. He was very powerful. Yesterday, my family and this town came together to take him down."

Everyone was still silent, waiting with bated breath for her to tell them more. She wasn't used to that. She was used to being interrupted every single time she spoke. So, this was new territory for her.

"Sven was trying to gather power to separate us from demons and angels. He was doing so in order to gather power for himself. He wanted to rule our world."

A few of the reporters shifted at that. She could see they wanted to ask questions.

"But, we stopped him. What you need to know, is that Earth is safe. And that we won't have a lot interference from angels *or* demons. This is a good thing. Neither one of them were great."

Three reporters raised their hands shouting questions.

Paige had no idea what she was supposed to do. She looked over at Tuck.

He tipped his head out to the crowd.

She pointed at one of the reporters and nodded.

The woman cleared her throat took a step forward. "How do we know that we're safe? Should we just take your word for it?"

Paige frowned at her like she lost her mind. "If you want to summon a demon and ask him, feel free."

That was probably the wrong response.

Another reporter raised his hand. Several of them did.

Paige pointed to one in the back.

The rest of the reporters quieted to hear his question.

"Is it true that you just recently gave birth?"

Paige tipped her head to the side. "Are you trying to tell me that you're one of the few people who didn't watch the footage? Because I had the pleasure of viewing that private moment on my television this morning. Next question." Paige chose another woman along the right-hand side.

"How many people are there like you?"

This gave Paige pause. Because this was what could change the world forever. However, the elders had given her the green light to tell the world the truth. The truth on their terms, not the President's.

"There are many like us. We live beside you. We're your neighbors, your friends, and we live in fear of you." Paige stared into the group of reporters, expecting them to have something to say.

They all remained quiet.

"We've been forced into an era where you know about us now. However, that brings a sense of fear and trepidation to both sides. You are not the only ones who think this is the scariest day of your lives. We fought against a powerful demon. But standing in front of you and telling you that we exist? That is quite possibly even more terrifying than facing the devastation of our planet."

That same reporter raised her voice again. "But aren't you powerful?"

"Aren't you?" Paige really didn't know what she was supposed to say to these people.

The woman shook her head.

Paige closed her eyes and hoped the right words would come to her. "We're people. Just like you. We like downtime. We like to binge watch TV on Netflix. Some of us are book readers, some of us aren't. We go to the grocery store. Our kids go to school. We have good days, and bad days. It's that sometimes our bad days coincide with…" Paige shrugged. "With losing control of your body and shifting into another animal. And then becoming human in the middle of the grocery store with no clothes on. So, if you think your life sucks, try being a newly turned shifter. And that's just one example."

Another reporter stepped forward, one she recognized. Dan Brown. "For those of us who have been touched by your kind before," he said, "can you guarantee that we'll find closure?"

Dan had lost his sister to a shifter and she was supposed to have helped him find closure, and she'd completely forgotten about him with everything else going on. "You already know we're working toward that, and that it doesn't always happen. Nobody was supposed to know about us. There were organizations among both sides whose job it was to ensure that there was closure for everyone. You've got criminals on your side. We've got criminals on ours. You've got good people on your side, and there's good people on ours. What we both have in common is that we're people. Just trying to do our best, just trying to get through the day the best we can."

The look on Dan's face said he wasn't through with her.

Which was fine. She *had* promised him. And she *had* forgotten.

But she was ready to be done now. "If you would excuse

me, as one of you kindly pointed out, I just had two babies. They're fine, if anybody wanted to know. And now if you'll excuse me."

She stepped away from the podium and away from the public view. She just hoped that what she had said didn't ruin anything. She went up to Elder Yad and stopped. "How bad did I do"

He smiled. "The President is still going to have something to say. I think we can both guarantee that. But it will be a lot harder for her to do anything secretly. The spotlight is on us now. She's not going to be able to make this all disappear."

Well that was certainly a warm thought. "I really didn't think I'd have to save the world, then be forced to fight my own country for the right to exist."

His smile was grim as he moved away. "We will give you as long as we can but understand the world needs you. So, heal fast. The world has changed. We need you to be ahead of it."

Paige shook her head

And then, because she didn't have to be careful about it anymore, she shifted into a bird, and flew above the crowd, heading home.

Home to her man, home to her kids, home to her family.

The brave new world.

The end

This concludes the Sven Seven-Tails Crossover Whiskey Witches Event!
We hope you enjoyed it.

Be sure to join our newsletter for more information on our latest books!

And keep your eyes open for the next series of books, Breaking Midnight, which will include novels from Whiskey Witches, Red Star Division, and a new spin-off series, Whiskey and Wine Mysteries!

A horrendous crash sounded in the living room followed by the screech of a baby owl and the yip of a baby—Paige didn't even know what. But she was learning fast as her two-day-old twins were quite good at shifting into any animal they thought of. And how they were able to think of all these animals was absolutely beyond her.

Paige stepped into the large living room in time to see one of the lamps fall over and smash onto the floor as a downy baby owl launched herself off the side table. A black and grey wolf-pup struggled to walk or run or dance as he yipped at her from the floor.

Dexx, the baby daddy, snored in the chair in the middle of all of it.

Paige pulled in deep and barked with her alpha will.

The twins froze in mid-leap and yip, turning to look up at her with their big eyes. Rai with her big electric blue eyes, and Ember with his big, fiery amber eyes.

Paige was really just looking forward to getting them past this point in their already short little life.

Bobby, her God's prophet toddler son, ran in on his three-year-old legs, a huge grin on his face. "Big noise!" Which was his way of saying trouble was afoot and he wanted to be a part of it.

Paige still had no idea if God was rolling over in his ethereal grave at the idea of his prophet being raised by witches or if he was laughing it up, dreaming of the day when it was revealed to his followers. She was rooting for the latter, though she doubted He was anywhere in the "caring-verse" anyway.

Bobby gravitated to the broken light bulb.

"Dexx," Paige barked again, keeping Bobby away from the broken glass shards.

He startled awake, immediately wiping the drool from his five o'clock shadow and sat up. "What did I miss?"

Paige narrowed her eyes at him.

His green eyes widened as he took in the room.

Two lamps were on the ground. One was salvageable. The other was completely destroyed. The striped couch had a huge gouge in it where one of the twins had obviously been something with claws and had fallen *off* said couch. And the stuff that *had been* on the coffee table was now on the floor.

He looked up at her sheepishly, grabbing Bobby. "They were asleep. I swear."

Paige growled low in her throat and gathered the twins.

Ember was now a kitten, which made it immensely easier to carry him.

Rai had decided to shift back into a human baby. Which, if Paige could just *talk* to her daughter, she'd have asked for a different shape. Humans were shaped poorly for carrying. How had humans taken over the earth when they were so poorly designed?

Leah hopped down the stairs, her straight blonde hair kind of "flat hair" bouncing behind her. She reached up and took Rai, giving her baby sister smooches. "How is the cutest baby girl in the whole wide world?"

Rai chose that moment to squirm out of Leah's arms and shift into a wolf pup.

Leah giggled and set her down before she crashed, then led the way to the back door to let her pup-sister into the backyard. "At least that one does her business outside already." She reached for Ember and goochy-gooochy-gooed his now human nose with hers. "If only Rai could teach this one."

He let out a screech-laugh that was only cute on babies and flailed his arms.

Leah whipped a diaper out of her back pocket and lightly thwapped him in the face with it.

He startled to a freeze position and then latched onto it with all the strength of a baby much older than him.

With Ember well in hand by Leah, Paige went to the kitchen to prepare bottles for them both.

Bobby came bumbling in and pushed one of the kitchen chairs, intent on toppling it.

"Bobby!" Paige didn't know whether to shake her head, scream, or pull out all her hair. "Stop. Breaking time is done."

He pulled a very pouty expression and clapped one hand to his face, his entire body slumping.

This kid was going to be a comedian one day.

Rai scratched at the door to be let in.

"Bobby," Paige pointed to the door.

The almost three-year-old's face lit with joy as he galloped to the door to let his sister in.

Dexx zombie-strolled to the coffee machine and went through the process of making Paige a cup. It wasn't for him. He liked a little coffee with his sugar and milk and preferred just to drink chocolate milk, if given the choice.

Paige didn't *do* words first thing in the morning. She did grunts and growls and barks and bites and glares and hand gestures. But not words. Occasionally, there'd be a name thrown in there so people *understood* which person had drawn her wrath that time, but that was about it.

Her phone rang as she pulled the first bottle out of the boiling pot of water.

As a new mother, she should be breast feeding. She knew that. But her milk jugs weren't working. They were producing. Kind of. They hurt. But there wasn't enough milk in there for one kid, much less two.

Oh, well.

She looked at her phone on the counter. Elder Yad.

"Doesn't he get that you should be on maternity leave?" Dexx asked, handing her the cup of steaming coffee like it was a sacrificial offering, moving the reusable straw toward her so she could sip out of it without dropping the bottles.

She hit ignore on the phone, grabbed the other bottle, and

took a long, hot pull of the coffee cup as she carefully took it from her lover's hands. "Thank you," she whispered gratefully.

Dexx took one of the bottles from her and went to Rai. "Sorry," he whispered back.

Bringing twin shifter witches into the family had been hard on all of them. None of them had really had a chance to sleep. The twins were up at all hours and there was no way to control what they'd even shift into.

Leslie sleep-stomped into the kitchen, her face blurry with the need to wake up. Her light brown, curly hair was a wild array of…well, wild. She went to the coffee machine and grabbed the cup Dexx had managed to make for her as well. "Those kids are from demons."

Paige knew for a fact they weren't. Paige could summon and send demons back to Hell, something her sister knew all too well. But she couldn't *produce* demon children.

But that brought another thought. A Hell gate had been seared into her bones years ago, making it a struggle for her to… well, be the demon summoner-exterminator. But ever since Sven Seven Tails had tried to destroy the world as they knew it and destroy the Hell gate itself, her bones had been quiet. Like, really quiet. The fight to stop him had put them all on international TV, but at least there weren't demons trying to possess her all the time. It was pleasantly quiet.

Her phone went off again.

Leslie grabbed it on her way to the dining table and handed it to her. "Danny Miller."

Crap. That was one phone call she should probably answer. With Ember tucked into her arm guzzling down the bottle, she tucked the phone to her ear. "Hey. What's up?"

"I could ask the same." His tone told her he wasn't in the mood for small talk. "New babies treating you okay?"

She didn't do small talk either. She didn't understand it,

but she did realize that some people needed it to feel like they were relating. "They're destroying my house one parent-nap at a time." Time to get to the point. "What's up, Danny?"

He sighed. "Have you watched the news lately?"

"Who watches the news?" No one had time to vet all the stories and, besides, she had newborns tearing up her house.

He growled a little. Danny Miller prided himself in his news reporting abilities and didn't believe in this new era of news where the corporation who purchased the station or paper controlled the stories. "Just turn on the TV to Local Six."

Paige rose from the table, keeping Ember firmly in hand. The only TV in the house was in the living room and it was rarely on. She fumbled with the remote, unfamiliar with the buttons. She never got much of a chance to watch it.

The President of the United States was addressing the nation.

"… in a state of emergency," she said, her blonde hair barely moving with the breeze. The lapel of her blue suit jacket moved more. "We now know of the paranormal presence and it must be addressed swiftly."

Wait. What?

"How many of them are there?" the President continued. "How great a threat are we facing?"

Dexx stopped beside her. "What's this?"

Paige didn't bother answering. She knew just as much as he did at this moment.

"We need the funding and the manpower to address this situation with the force and might it deserves." The President's normally distinguished face twisted in anger. "We can't allow another Troutdale situation to happen again, or become the norm. How many lives were lost?"

That was a question Paige hadn't even asked, though, to

be fair, she'd had a lot on her hands after that brutal battle. She'd lost her grandmother and had given birth to her twins on Main Street.

Images of the fight flashed across the TV screen. Sven towered over the street as he pulled in the magickal energies from all around him. Demons swarmed the streets. Shifters and witches and all number of other paranormal creatures fought back, including more than a few normal humans.

They'd all united that day in order to fight back against Sven's demon army . Paige led an army of normal people to save the world.

How long had the President waited for something like this to happen? They'd always kind of felt it, ever since she'd won the vote. There was a deeper pressure on the paranormal communities to remain hidden.

"I'm issuing an Executive Order giving these paranormals four days to register with the government. They will be assessed and provided new homes in more secure areas. I'm—"

Dexx took the remote and turned off the TV, his face a boil of rage. "Relocated? Secure areas?"

Hadn't the U.S. tried this already? With the Japanese? And hadn't that ended badly?

Well, not for the government. For the Japanese Americans, it had.

Rai's fingertips buzzed with electricity as she suckled on her bottle, her eyes moving between her parents. Even her eyelashes danced with lightning.

Electricity and phones were a bad mix. Paige stepped away from her daughter. "How far is she going to go?"

Danny was quiet for a long moment. "We've already received word she's got a few areas set up. They're prepped and ready."

"What kind of areas?" Resorts? Reservations? Prisons? "What do you mean?"

"Areas of 'relocation.' I don't know more yet and my source has to be really careful so her cover isn't blown."

Paige understood that, but just hearing him repeat the word 'relocation' sent a chill of fear down her spine. "But no word on what they're planning?"

"No. But... Tell me you're going to do something about this."

She really wanted to say no, that she was on maternity leave, that she was trying to bond with her two little world destroyers. "Yeah." She offered a few more vagaries and hung up.

Dexx made movements to take Ember.

She moved away, the bottle propped up with her chin and dialed Elder Yad. If she was going to save the world, she was going to do so *with* her kids beside her. Because...

Seriously. She couldn't *choose* anymore. She needed to be an adult and a mom and a responsible person in society all at the same time. She'd just have to figure out how to make it work.

Elder Yad answered quickly but said nothing.

She had no idea if he was having an issue with his Blue-tooth headset or if he could even hear her, but she wasn't going to wait forever, either. "Gather those we need. My house. Lunch."

The line disconnected.

Well, that just left cleaning the house and preparing a meal for a small invading army. Both of which she hated.

Coming up with a plan to save the world?

Well, she was getting better at that.

Don't forget to leave reviews! Let us know what you think!

WHISKEY MAGICK & MENTAL HEALTH

Sign up to learn more about our books and receive this free e-zine about Whiskey Magick and Mental Health. https://www.fjblooding.com/books-lp

ABOUT THE AUTHOR

F.J. Blooding lives in hard-as-nails Alaska growing grey hair in the midnight sun with Shane, her writing partner and husband, his two part-time kids, his BrotherTwin, SistaWitch, TeenMan, and SnarkGirl, along with a small menagerie of animals which includes several cats, an army of chickens, a rabbit or two, but only one dog.

She enjoys writing and creating with her wonderful husband and dreaming about sleeping. She's dated vampires, werewolves, sorcerers, weapons smugglers, U.S. Government assassins, and slingshot terrorists. No. She is *not* kidding. She even married one of them.

Sign up for her newsletter, get free books, and join the discussions on the forums when you visit her website at FJBlooding.com